DEVIL ON EARTH

A Fated Alien Mates Romance

Warriors of Elysius
Book 2

ANGELINA AVERY

C.J. ANAYA
PUBLISHING

Cover Design by Natasha Snow: http://natashasnow.com

Published by CJ Anaya Publishing LLC

Vellum layout by CJ Anaya

ISBN Paperback: 978-1-7373366-2-4

ONE

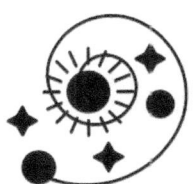

Tarian

I don't envy my brother's position, but I'm not sorry I put him there.

Less than a week since Kyllell took the place of chancellor, and it's been a nonstop shit show with council members pointing the finger at others for Chassak interlopers in our midst. Tarian's mate, Ada, labelled it a witch hunt. I don't understand the reference, but there is certainly plenty of misplaced blame being dispatched.

With his return from exile, and the removal of Derwag, who had subverted my father's authority, Kyllell has found the state of Elysius in utter disarray.

To be expected.

Yet as I watch my brother rein in the council members and get the discussion back on track I have to remember that he was quite literally born for this.

And I'd had to displace him, sending him into exile to save him from himself a few years prior when we had lost our women to those Chassak scum. I still feel guilt over it, but I'm not one to lose sight of logic. Damn Kyllell and his crusade for justice. He'd never been good at backing down, especially when he knew he was right.

And he had been right.

He had also been outnumbered, and I'd had to make the difficult decision to side against him to save his life.

"We're not discussing the issue of Derwag's followers any further," Kyllell says. "It's important to address, but that is not what this meeting is about."

The chamber quiets with all eyes on him. I glance at Ada sitting at Kyllell's side. Her presence here is important. Her relationship with Kyllell is the thing that will save us all.

If these idiots will unwind their tails from their horns to listen.

There's a certain level of peace within Kyllell, even now, while he ponders over the future of Elysius with his mate by his side. They're perfect for one another. I'm almost jealous at how she looks at him, beckons him with that longing gaze. But with the new changes being implemented and treaties already negotiated with Earth—and a crew set to disembark from Elysius—I have little time for such desires.

"So, we all understand what's going to happen moving forward?" Kyllell asks the council. Most grunt their replies with a yes, and only two oppose the motion. A risky move on their end, considering the state of affairs. With a traitor in the mix, hidden in plain sight, there's far too much at stake for those who stand against the orders of the new chancellor. It will simply weaken us if we are not united.

Those who may oppose the new alliance with Earth are giving in to fear. The fact that some of our own council members can't see this as a solution is astonishing.

And unacceptable.

"I don't believe I do," Ordo, a long-standing council member, says. Though one of the two that stood against the progression of this bill, I don't suspect him of being a traitor. He stood beside my father in the battlefields long before becoming a member of the council. With the praises he has received and the titles earned for slaughtering Chassaks, there's no doubt he's on our side, but age cripples the mind and destroys the motivation for change.

Fortunately, the majority vote has passed, and for better or worse, Earth is eager to accept our proposal and assist us in finding bond mates for our people in exchange for our protection.

I consider what we learned in a recent briefing with several of

Earth's world leaders. An alarming increase in missing human females with no ability to locate them, something one president labeled as "cold cases" since it has been going on for decades, according to Earth years.

Based on Ada and Kyllell's recent experience, it is clear the Chassaks have known about Earth, their women, and their desirability in the flesh markets.

The very thought sickens me. How we'll begin to unravel what I'm sure are hundreds of female trafficking operations led by the Chassaks is still unclear, but it's one of many problems we plan to tackle as we work with these humans.

"Then I'll explain it again," Kyllell says.

He has stores of patience, while I'm ready to render Ordo unconscious.

Odd. I'm usually the calm one. He's usually the short-tempered hothead.

"I am living proof that the humans from planet Earth are suitable mates. Ada, at my side, is a perfect example of the women from her home planet, and though there are noticeable differences between our species, we are close enough genetically that if we find our mates, our existence can continue."

Kyllell pauses a moment, looking at Ada and taking her hand in his. Listening to the same sentence again, only wrapped up neatly, has me rubbing my temples in frustration.

How does Kyllell stand the constant need for repetition with these dim-witted council members?

"I've been in discussions with an Earthling named Mark Jameson. The leader of the free world. From my understanding, this title is misleading," he says, turning to Ada.

"Yes, it's an expression. Don't get hung up on that, please. We don't have time for a history lesson."

Kyllell snickers, turning his attention back to the council before him.

"This Mark Jameson, his country, and his government are going to be our initial contact point and base for building a DNA matching center; the first of its kind. He has agreed to allow our visitation and to conduct the multiple tests and studies necessary for matching DNA with females who are willing to participate in the program."

I get drawn into the explanation again, still fascinated by what has been discovered in the last few weeks.

"As you know, the black burning of our horns is something sacred to our species, something we have viewed in highly spiritual terms. Ada reminds me that science is also applicable in cases such as this. Which begs the question, what is it about our DNA that caused this bond? And can we identify what, if any, clues are embedded within our genetic code? And with this information, can we identify other bond mates?"

"To be clear," Ordo says, causing me to grind my teeth in further annoyance. "Your DNA and that of your mate's is now in the hands of human scientists to unlock this secret, and you think it wise? They could use your DNA for nefarious purposes."

"By the Great Goddess Elysarah, it's in the hands of our scientists as well, Ordo," I nearly shout. "We're all working together for the greater good of both species, and considering our superior advancements in genetics and science—no offense Ada—I'm pretty damn sure the human scientists will be scrambling just to keep up with us."

Ada wears a smirk on her face that suggests I'll be regretting my words in the future, but she wisely remains silent.

I continue my tirade. "We've already sent a crew of scientists and builders down with the necessary supplies before we send an administrative team to handle the rest. Thus far, we understand that DNA samples have been collected from multiple volunteers on the planet, and many are expecting our arrival within the next two solar cycles. The crew we send to Earth will help manage and develop further samples, overseeing the scientists—both Elysium and human —and their work in identifying whatever needs to be identified that creates these bonds between the human females and their Elysium counterparts." I point a finger at Ordo and watch his jostling second chin pull up in affront. "No one has time to clone Kyllell. I'm more worried that a Chassak will be on Earth impersonating him. Can we focus on *that* potential problem?"

Everyone in the chamber stares at me in shock, and I realize I'm not only shouting, I'm standing, hovering over the Council.

I clear my throat as the awkward silence continues and abruptly sit. Ada bites her bottom lip in amusement, and Kyllell doesn't even try to hide his glower.

I've just demonstrated high emotion among members of the council after skillfully playing their game for years.

What is wrong with me?

"I admit, it's all very technical," Kyllell says as if my outburst hasn't happened. "I do, however, believe the Elysium people will be able to further their bloodlines with new mates across the galaxy."

"And what if none wish to mate with the Elysiums? Ada excluded, we know nothing about these creatures. Their intentions may be vile," Ordo replies.

"I'm sure they might think the same of us. Ada told me I looked like a devil upon first inspection, an evil creature in their world's lore." Kyllell keeps up a level of diplomacy I've been hoping he would attain for years.

At least one of us is accomplishing that.

It can't be easy for him, being in this position while the entire council sits ready to judge every action and word that leaves his lips.

He holds firm, and that's why he was always destined to sit at the helm of the chancellor's chair.

"The votes are already cast," Ordo starts again, "and I'm humble in my loss. But remember, Kyllell, this is your first act as the new chancellor to the people of Elysius. If it backfires, it's your head on the line for the males that we lose in the process."

I barely restrain an undignified eye roll, something I've learned from Ada.

I understand the need to check all contingencies before moving forward. These are uncertain times, especially considering the probability that more Chassaks are impersonating high members of government within our ranks. There's no telling who may be plotting the downfall of our species.

"I know, and I'd not take the risk if it wasn't in the best interests of our people," Kyllell replies, taking a step back from the podium.

"Remember, the Chassaks intended for us to slowly go extinct. This is a true chance at ruining all their plans and saving our species. We must fight for this. We must take on the risks. The alternative is to simply die out in silence having never fought for the right to continue existing."

I nod, sensing the heavy weight of his words and the impact they have on most of the council members.

Most.

Ordo is clearly the worst kind of imbecile.

"Are there any other concerns that need raising? Or are we free to proceed?" I ask.

"We may proceed," Ordo says, his upright stance turning more slouched as he gets comfortable in the chair. My eyes dart back to Kyllell.

"There is still the threat of Derwag and those who blindly follow him, hiding among our ranks. Each passing day we wait for another mounted attack. Thus, the secrecy of this mission and the crew being sent to oversee everything is only going to be entrusted to the loyal few who I believe can carry it out," Kyllell starts again. His eyes pan the council, moving back and forth between each member. "We tread uncharted waters now, and if we wish to get through this unscathed, we must stand together in everything we face. For this reason, I believe it will be in everyone's best interest if my brother heads the expedition to Earth along with his crew."

My jaw drops at the news.

"You can't be serious!" I say without thinking. "We've already established who will be leading this mission. We vetted the entire group."

"As a diversion. I've no doubt a Chassak or two has already dispatched one or two members and invaded the crew without our knowing. It is how they function. Fortunately, the only people who know you and your crew will be going are the people assembled in this room."

I gaze at my brother and his stoic expression, but I can see the humor radiating from his eyes.

This is payback. I exiled him, and now, in a way, he is exiling me.

I should have seen this coming, but I've been so irritated and distracted, caught up in the planning and political nonsense of the Council, I failed to do what I do best. Remain three steps ahead of everyone, including my brother.

If I stand against him now, I'll show massive disrespect and undermine my own outburst and Kyllell's power.

But dammit, I had planned on staying here and rooting out the traitors on Elysius.

"I'm very serious, Tarian," Kyllell replies. "I didn't make this decision lightly. I know that you and your crew are exceptional warriors. You're a well-rounded set of individuals with different specializations that will be beneficial for overseeing this massive project, and you are the only group I trust to do it."

"My crew knows?" I ask.

"They're boarding your craft as we speak, under the assumption that I am sending you on a peace mission to the other side of Elysius. They won't know what is going on until you board the craft and tell them."

I feel my jaw clench and nod my head. This is not what I want, but I've been effectively boxed in.

The rest of the meeting is dull, with the majority of the conversation dominated by questions that Kyllell artfully answers. All the while, my mind races at the idea of being ripped away from my home and flung across the stars to a planet I know nothing about to spearhead a mission I'm not prepared for.

Well, I'm certainly qualified as an ambassador, and dealing with human officials could be an interesting challenge, but I know nothing about genetics or DNA testing.

On Kyllell's dismissal, the various members get to their feet and disappear through the grand doorway. I stay seated where I am, eyes pinned on Kyllell, glaring daggers at my brother while I consider the various ways I might succeed in assassinating him.

"We've got much to discuss, Brother." The words leaving my lips are clipped. The acrid hiss that accompanies them, completely unplanned.

"Do we now?" Kyllell replies, a broad smile growing on his face.

"When were you planning on telling me that *I'd* be the one venturing off to this primitive *Earth*? Surely you could have trusted me with this information before the meeting."

"Too many leaks. Too many listeners. Even now, I worry that we haven't done enough to cause a diversion. We need to get you on your ship immediately."

"But—"

Kyllell holds up his hands. "You drew up this plan. You've been the face of these negotiations. You've created a relationship with this Mark Jameson, and you can oversee the operations of this facility."

I sigh in defeat, knowing he is absolutely right.

Ada rests a hand on my arm, giving me a sympathetic smile. "You really are the ideal warrior and representative for the job. And it would be in everyone's best interest for you to be there as more females are identified."

"Why is that?" I ask in puzzlement.

"Tarian, your horns have been burning for weeks. You're cranky, irritable, and impossible to be around," Kyllell says.

"What?"

"You need to get laid." Ada pats my arm. "And soon."

My translator chip glitches on the word until an image of what she means pops into my head. I clear my throat and pick at my robes.

"I do not need advice on handling my...er...needs."

"You need to get laid," she repeats. "Although, a mate would be preferable. See if you can swing that while you're there."

A mate! And give up the freedom I have with my crew? Not to mention the many different species of females we encounter on our space excursions? I don't need a mate. And I don't need to endanger one by having her associated with me. I have learned that painful lesson well. It has simply been a while since...

"And what of our plans to rid Elysius of the traitors that roam within? I'm sure that's going to be fun with me across the galaxy." I retract my claws as my fists clench in frustration.

"It's going to be horrible," Kyllell admits. "You are one of the very few I can trust."

"Exactly."

"And that's why you're going. Assigning you and your crew to run this mission is the only way I can trust it's going to go smoothly. The fate of our people relies on the success of this matchmaking program, Tarian. It's got nothing to do with me sending you off, or having you away from the politics of Elysius. I want to see our people flourish again while destroying the corruption from within."

He is right. I hadn't considered the logistics of it all. One wrong move and Kyllell might have put a Chassak puppet in place to oversee the mission, and all these well-laid plans would have been destroyed. Still, I try again, frantic at the thought of being blindsided by a bond mate.

"There are many you can send in my stead, Brother. I have an entire crew of men dedicated to preserving our species."

"Like who?" Kyllell asks, stepping away from the chancellor's chair and taking Ada's hand. I ignore the slight pang of longing in my chest.

"Members of my crew are experts in all things technical. I'm sure they'd be more than willing to find their mates on this new, distant planet," I add emphasis on *distant* once again.

"A crew without a captain? Sounds like a fool's errand, don't you agree? Why, not too long ago, Ada rushed into certain death to save her crew. How would you do the same if you're not present?"

"Is your heart truly set on my going, Brother? Are you not in the slightest concerned for what the future may bring if we're apart?" A pang of fear strikes my chest. Who will protect him if I'm gone?

"I fear everything and nothing all at once, Tarian. Do this, for me. For your new sister."

Ada smiles. "Do this for the sake of our sanity. Being around you when you're like this is like tip-toeing across nails. For God's sake, sleep with as many women as possible while you're there."

I attempt my pull on her just to get back at her, but she shrugs it off with a smirk, like she feels nothing. It was how I knew she was meant for Kyllell, that she could refuse my pull so thoroughly before they had consummated their mate bond. And of course, now that she's mated, it would feel more like a tiny annoyance, barely something to register.

I nod my head. A woeful bobbing up and down. I'm by no means happy with the decision Kyllell has made, nor my own to accept the offer, but what more can I say or do? Fighting Kyllell on this is an effort in futility. He knows what he wants.

"I'll need to pack—"

"Already done. Your possessions and your crew await you on board your ship in the loading dock. We've made arrangements for a T-1 Carrier, all the equipment you're going to need beyond what was already delivered, and more. You're not going to be gone forever, Tarian, that's another thing I want you to understand. You're going to be an ambassador in this new world temporarily, and when everything is running smoothly, you'll be free to pick and choose where you land and leave."

"Oh, little sister, what do you see in this one?" I ask, getting my last digs in.

"I don't know," she replies, slapping his arm. "It's probably just his good looks."

"She finds my horns, and what I can do with them, a turn-on."

"I didn't need to know that." I look at them in disgust.

He gives Ada a lascivious smile before wrapping an arm around her tiny waist.

"We'll escort you to the landing dock."

I let out a grunt of defeat as we head toward a hidden door leading to a tunnel only the Council knows about. As we make our way toward the loading dock, Kyllell continues his instructions as if I'm just now learning the art of subtlety.

"I'd advise caution from here on in. Keep everything under check and only let those on a need-to-know basis aware of what is happening. Apart from those in the council who just learned of your departure, no one will hear of this Earth until it's too late for them to sabotage our plans," Kyllell says.

"Okay. As long as you know what you're doing, I'll follow you to the end." I nod my head. "And you, Ada, don't let this one get out of hand while I'm away."

As we take the various twists and turns that lead to the loading dock, I ponder the assignment and sense the rightness of it. I also feel that ever-familiar sense of panic that comes at the thought of a bond mate.

Just before I leave the tunnel and head for the dock, I give Kyllell one last handshake and Ada one last embrace.

"Thank you for accepting it so gracefully." Kyllell pats my arm before giving it a firm squeeze.

"And bring back a mate so I have another female to speak with," Ada adds.

I head to the ship with that request reverberating in my head.

No bond mate.

I never want to lose another lover again.

"Oh, and Tarian," she calls out.

I turn, assessing the slight smirk on her face.

"Say hi to Bree for me."

"Bree? Who in the Goddess's name is Bree?"

TWO

Bree

I reach my mailbox in front of my house and unlock it, retrieving its contents, pretending I don't see the dark sedan parked halfway down the block.

The same sedan that has sat there for eons. One I don't recognize, unless my reclusive neighbor, Steve, decided to invite family to visit...for the last several months.

Ever since I had that damn meeting...

I'm a geneticist. Not a celebrity. Not the type of individual TMZ would hone in on and follow. I'm a nobody, really, but several months ago, my boss asked me to stay after work for a last-minute meeting. One that turned into a clandestine briefing with the President of the United States.

Yeah.

The gist? Aliens are real. A specific alien species called Chassaks have been kidnapping human women for some time, and a different alien species is willing to help us with that little problem if we figure out who their bond mates are through genetic testing, handing the poor women over to Elysium warriors.

Seems to me we're faced with choosing between the lesser of two evils. And there's that saying…deal with the devil you know. Apparently, we know these Elysiums better in the sense that they're transparent in their desire to take our women from this planet.

Fine. It was a very involved meeting, but at the end of it, I knew we weren't alone in the Universe, and I also knew I would now be working on behalf of the US government to get the first testing center set up, working with some Elysium scientists on cracking the code for bond mates and dooming the fates of countless women.

Micah, my coworker and long-time best friend, keeps referring to our assignment as Project Matchmaker. My other coworker and friend, Remy, actually volunteered her DNA for the project and happily agreed to work on it with us.

They're both mental. Morons. Absolutely reckless in their life choices. It's one thing for me to agree to work on a classified project that will most likely end in my death, but those idiots shouldn't be following in my footsteps.

Project Matchmaker, my ass. It's a dumb name, and Micah says it purely for my reaction, which he gets every time.

Then again, despite my reservations and my open skepticism where Elysiums are concerned, I've battled bouts of excitement to be picked for such a fascinating project and for what it will mean for science, alien and human relations, and space exploration in the future…and then I worry for any woman bonded to an alien and forced to leave Earth.

Remy got an earful from me when I found out she'd volunteered to be tested. I just pray she isn't a viable candidate.

Will they be treated well? Can these warrior aliens be trusted? What if we're being played here and these Chassak dudes are the ones we should trust? The implications on an ethical and moral level have left me dizzy with indecision.

And now I'm constantly being followed, and since I'm fairly certain these folks aren't from the bureau, I'm beginning to get a little nervous.

Just how many players are involved in this shit?

Feeling reckless, I shoot a big smile and a frantic wave in the sedan's direction. The two shadowy occupants sit frozen in their seats.

Disappointing.

Any reaction is better than no reaction.

I turn and walk to the front porch only to stop short at the sight of a dead cat with a knife and note attached to its body. I try not to startle or show any emotion, but I know for a fact that the cat was not there on my way over to my mailbox.

I'm not about to leave myself vulnerable by bending over to retrieve the note, but it's unnecessary since I can read the large red script from here.

Drop the project. Or else.

Not very original as far as death threats go. But it does beg several questions. Who the hell knows I'm involved? Who doesn't want this project moving forward? Why?

And what the hell is with the cat? It's not like it's *my* cat?

Well, I imagine their reasons for not being on board with this alliance mirror my own misgivings. Since the presidential address and an intense worldwide broadcast three weeks ago concerning the discovery of aliens and our need for protection in exchange for the Elysiums' need for women, there have been strong feelings felt.

But we've already seen certain benefits to agreeing to this crazy alliance. Even now, there are Elysium ships orbiting Earth prepared to take on any unknown spacecraft attempting to enter Earth's atmosphere.

But ignorant idiots and fearmongers don't see this as a positive.

White supremacists and other hate groups have made way for opposition against species co-mingling. It doesn't matter that this is purely voluntary on the woman's part...at the moment.

And I suspect that is one of thousands of concerns. How long before it is no longer voluntary and being tested becomes mandatory?

How big is Elysius? Population? How many of us will they need? How many will they demand?

I stare at the dead cat, gore oozing from its wounds.

A perfectly good cat. It pisses me off, actually.

I love cats.

I also think I might be losing it a bit as I stare at the tear in its throat.

I have no idea if there is anyone out there to hear me, though I suspect there are several someone's aside from Mo and Joe sitting in the Sedan.

"Okay," I say, pretending to sound defeated. Fuck these assholes. "I'm not particularly thrilled about this project, either, and I'd like to live. So, I'll resign and quietly walk away from this."

Not allowed to resign, but they don't know that. Once I signed on the dotted line, under duress mind you, there was no going back.

Even to my own ears, the promise sounds lame. I suck at compromise, and I never back down. Doesn't matter that I have major reservations concerning the project I've prepped for and will soon be joining in two days. These fuckers don't get to scare me into submission.

I step over the cat even though I desperately want to cover it in a sheet and give it a proper burial, and then I head for my front door. I open it, swing it wide, step inside, and close it fast.

But I know I'm not safe, and it's time to do something about it.

If these folks know I'm involved then I've no doubt that everything electrical in my house is bugged. So I don't bother with anything that could possibly track me. Quietly slipping into my room, I turn on my TV, hoping the sound will fill any planted mics in the house and cover the noise of me packing a bag. Very small. Because I've no doubt they have a tracking device on my car. Which means I need to get out on foot without being noticed and get to the nearest payphone.

As I go to my closet to grab some clothes, I abruptly stop. What if they planted actual cameras in my house? What if they can see me now?

Shit. I can't pack a bag. I need to play this out and resign. Or pretend to resign. And I know just who to call. I reach for my cell phone on the nightstand and dial a number I know by heart.

"Hey Bree, what's up?" Micah Scott answers with his usual congeniality.

"Micah, I'm calling to resign."

"You —"

"I know you wanted me for this, recommended me for this position," *lies, all lies,* "but you gotta let me off the hook. I have no desire to uncover bond mates for a warrior alien race that may or may not abuse the hell out of these women."

Okay, that has a ring of truth to it.

"Bree, don't you fuck this up," Micah says. "I'm your boss, your superior, and I gave you a leg up in this world. I can take you down and have you testing blood samples for a random, podunk hospital for the rest of your life."

I nearly lose my shit and laugh. Micah never uses the "F" word. He thinks it's unrefined. He never sounds gruff. Which means he's reading me loud and clear.

Also, he isn't, nor has he ever been, my boss.

"I'm not doing it, Micah. Tell the President he needs another head geneticist. I'm out."

"You're sacrificing your future," he says in a stern tone. "A little ungrateful after everything I've done for you."

"I've made my decision."

He gives it just enough of a pause before saying, "Fine. Get to the lab in the next fifteen minutes to sign some documents, not to mention a massive waiver and an NDA."

Thank God. He really does know I'm in trouble.

Bless you, Micah.

Still, I have to play it off. "Micah, it's six in the evening. Can't I come tomorrow —"

"Now."

I let out a put-upon sigh. "I'll leave the house right away."

"You'd better."

The click of the phone signals the end of that conversation. I nonchalantly walk out of my room and enter my kitchen, grabbing my purse from the counter. I place my phone inside and head for the garage door, hoping I'll be able to get in my car and drive away without any problems.

I hit the garage door opener and hurriedly climb inside my car. Then I pray that no bomb has been attached to it. Wouldn't it be just my luck that I explode in a thousand pieces after going to all that trouble to put on a show.

I slowly back out of my garage after letting several relieved breaths loose once the ignition starts.

I'm gonna die. I'm gonna die. But I swear I will take these cat killers down with me.

As I head along the street, I notice the sedan turn on and flip around to follow me.

Fine. Whatever. It isn't like they don't know where I work. They definitely know. I'll just head to the place they expect me to go, and once inside, all bets are off.

I just have to get to the lab in one piece.

I'm two blocks away when I notice that I'm being followed by three black sedans now.

Oh, shit.

Either they bought my little production and are merely being thorough in making sure I get to the lab, or they know Micah isn't my boss and that the entire thing was staged.

I'm thinking they ran a few checks while we were driving.

Figuring we're blown, I hit the gas and make an early left just as a yellow light phases to red. I rejoice in my small victory as the three sedans are stuck at the light, but it only buys me so much time. I pull into the parking lot of Genomic Edge Laboratories a few minutes later—a grand building dedicated to the study of gene therapy and the early diagnosis and prevention of disease—just as Micah throws open the side entrance and ushers me in.

I reach the door right when the first bullet pings above Micah's head and hits the doorframe.

He jerks me in and slams the door, locking it with the security code and then grabbing me and pulling me down the fluorescent lit corridor.

"What the hell, Bree? I could tell you were in trouble, but I had no idea it was right on your ass."

"You just said ass." I laugh, feeling a little shock. Then another giggle escapes me. A giggle. Seriously? "A cat just died on my behalf."

"What?" We round a corner and head toward the lab.

"Is no one else here?" I ask, running to keep up.

His long legs make great time. Thank heavens he is one tough, strong mother fucker to drag my ass behind him when I can't keep up.

"It's Sunday, Bree, and the only other workaholic around here besides me is you, but I've called security, and they're on their way."

I hear a loud crash behind us and Micah curses again.

"Looks like we're not going to have as much time as I thought."

We enter the lab and he quickly grabs a small black radio from his desk. "Mark, we've got no time. Plan B is in order. Over."

"Roger that. Head to the roof. Over."

"Oh, shit no," I say, realizing plan B is not my favorite. "You know I hate flying."

Micah pauses a moment to wrap me in his arms. I don't need the coddling, but I find his six-foot-three-frame extremely comforting.

"Bree, we're getting on that helicopter and heading to the testing center...maybe a few days early...but we were planning on flying there anyway."

"Not under duress, and certainly not without a muscle relaxant," I say in protest. I'm not one to shy away from anything, but even *I'm* willing to embrace my weaknesses, and flying is the bane of my existence.

He kisses my forehead and grabs my hand, pulling me toward the staircase door. Definitely not wise to use the elevator.

"Bree, you are the biggest badass I know, and yet heights drop you more effectively than a tranquilizer. You're fearless until gravity is involved."

I'm trying to catch my breath and respond, but I'm too focused on not tripping up the seven flights of stairs to really be engaged in the conversation.

Plus, he's right. Heights are Beelzebub incarnate.

We hear the stairwell door crack open even though Micah had it thoroughly locked and barricaded. Instead of upping his pace, he suddenly stops and turns to face me. "This is taking too long."

Before I can get out a "What?" he bends down and throws me over his shoulder like I weigh two pounds, something he has never, in the ten years we've worked together, done to me. He's strong, and holy shit, he is fast.

"I need to attend the same gym you do," I say as I stare at his nicely formed ass even though we're being chased by bad guys with guns.

"I keep inviting her, and the lady keeps turning me down," he says, hardly winded.

"I just don't want to show you up."

"Sure. That's it."

He reaches the roof, punches in the code, and barrels through, keeping me over his shoulder while he closes it and locks it, not that locking it will do any good, but the noise of the helicopter is already approaching.

"Set me down," I yell.

"Not on your life," he shouts back. "You'd sooner brave a gunfight than get on that helicopter."

Real panic sets in. The kind that discards logic and opts for ludicrous. I start to fight him, just like I knew I would, which is why the muscle relaxants have been such an important part of my flight plan.

I'm hitting his back as I hear pounding on the door. My hair whips around me, and the pressure and noise of the helicopter as it lands becomes overwhelming.

I fight him like a tigress as we get closer to the bird, but he's damn strong, and I'm not making a dent. I know I don't really want to make a dent, but I also don't want to get in that helicopter sober. I feel a sudden sting in my leg, and a rush of warmth envelops me as my body goes limp. Micah hands me over to one of the crew.

"That is a big-ass gun," I say, pointing to the guy's weapon as Micah gets in and gently assists me into a seated position. I'm struggling to stay awake even though I have no idea why I'm sleepy. All I *do* know is Micah has me in his arms, the panic is blocked by sleepiness, and bullets ping around like so much confetti.

"You drugged me?" I ask him, slurring my words.

He lifts my chin until my weary eyes meet his. "Did you really think I'd make you face this sober?"

"You're the bestest friend…ever." My smile is huge and goofy as I look at his California tanned face and caring blue eyes.

He chuckles. "Well, don't thank me just yet. I'm about to take full advantage of your drugged state and lay a wet one on you."

I screw up my face in confusion. "A cold compress? Do I have a fever?"

His smile goes wide as he looks at me with something bordering on adoration. It's weird. I've never seen him look at me like that before. Then he does something that absolutely shocks me before I lose all coherency.

He dips his head and softly kisses my lips.

I WAKE UP TO A COLD COMPRESS ON MY FOREHEAD AND THE musty scent of slightly damp blankets. It's an annoying smell. I blink my eyes open, grateful for the dim lighting in the room. Micah sits in a chair next to the bed, watching an episode of *The Golden Girls*.

"How dare you enjoy anything Betty White related without me," I croak out.

Micah's eyes shift to mine and lighten before he grabs a glass of water from the nightstand. He hands it to me as I gingerly get into a sitting position. I sip it slowly, grateful for the crisp, cool liquid as it hits the back of my parched throat.

"You're boring company. Reruns have been my only form of entertainment here."

"What the hell happened?" I mutter.

Micah laughs and spreads his arms wide as I take in what looks like a barely acceptable hotel room.

"Temporary digs for the night. How are you feeling?"

"Like a large locomotive decided to hit me. Twice."

He helps me sit up and leans me against the headboard. The cold compress has disappeared, but I'm feeling okay without it.

"What's the last thing you remember?" he asks.

"You telling me to get to the lab to sign an NDA. Quick thinking, by the way. It must not have worked, though, if I'm suffering from a hangover no doubt induced by meds necessary in the advent of a flight. Which means they followed me to the lab."

"And then some." He studies me carefully. "You really don't remember what happened at the lab? The helicopter ride?"

"I don't even remember *getting* to the lab, which is worrisome." Although something else is definitely bothering me. Something I can't really put my finger on.

Micah appears disappointed for a moment, but then he shakes his head. "Well, you missed the showdown of all showdowns, and I pretty much saved your life as well as your sanity."

"Yeah. You drugged me good. How much did you use?"

"The entire syringe."

My jaw drops. "That is meant to be dispersed in two doses on longer flights."

"Yeah, but you were beating me up and refusing to get on the plane while crazy men with guns were shooting at us. I felt it best to knock you out."

"No shit."

"No shit."

"Mission accomplished." I salute him.

"Yep."

"What a good friend you are." That last one may have been stated a bit dryly, but I'm definitely grateful to remember nothing.

Micah shakes his head and stands. "Just wanted to stay with you until you woke up. Had to make sure our head geneticist didn't die of an overdose."

"Asshole," I say, swatting his leg. "Thanks for saving my life."

"Anytime, Bree. I got you." His tender smile warms my heart. I adore this big, hulking softie. Never did have any siblings, so Micah in my life means I have one of the best older brothers a gal could ever ask for.

"What's the plan for tomorrow?"

"The Elysiums have sent a crew to oversee the implementation process. Apparently, a very important ambassador will be here to ensure we don't screw this up."

I roll my eyes. "Delightful. So micromanagement is universal no matter what planet you live on."

"Correct. They're getting here within two days. We'll meet them at the testing center's secret location and then the fun begins."

Great. The last thing I need is alien administration. I hate administration. So much red tape to get through. This has the potential to be a real nightmare. Plus, I'm feeling slightly nervous to work with alien scientists. I'm eager to learn from them, but will they be willing to learn what we already know concerning our own genetics?

It all comes down to markers and sequencing. Which markers within the genetic code of an Elysium male initiate the horns to burn black? What code within the DNA of human females causes this reaction in the male? I'll get my first look at an actual DNA sample of a bonded Elysium/human couple in a few days. Ada and Kyllell's bond, to be specific.

I'm both eager and terrified.

"What do we know about the guys who tried to kill us?"

"Nothing," Micah says. "At least, if the higher ups do know, they aren't saying anything."

I shake my head, furious at the turn of events.

"They shouldn't have found out. No one should have found out."

Micah rubs the back of his neck, his eyes tired and his shoulders a bit droopy.

"My guess is we gotta watch our backs. There's a leak in higher management. A chink in the armor. We play it by ear and look out for each other."

"Okay." Then I remember our duo is actually a trio. "Shit. If they went after us, they'll go after Remy."

"She's already with us. She's in the room next to yours. Right after you called me with that fake resignation speech, I followed protocol, and the rest of the members of our team were located and flown out immediately. You, however, were the only one being chased."

"It's because of my striking good looks and charming disposition. Hitmen find it alluring." I flutter my eyelashes.

"Not interested in feeding that enormous ego of yours, but they have great taste. You're also the brains behind this operation on the human side of things, so methinks they assumed taking you out would shut things down."

"There are other geneticists that can do what I do."

"Humility now? Not a good look for you."

I reach forward, trying to take another swing at him, but he's too far away.

"And do me a favor," he says. "Don't fall in love with any of the warriors. It'll just complicate things, and I'm not losing my best friend to a mate bond. I don't care how big their dicks are."

My laugh is so loud it ends in a snort. "Based on the recent anatomy classes we've taken, it would appear Elysium males are *wonderfully* endowed."

He lets out a bereaved sigh. "Promise me."

"Sure thing."

"Not at all convincing."

"What if I just took one for a test drive?"

"Bree!" Micah says in a stern tone even though he's clearly amused.

"I'm never leaving you, Micah," I say, getting serious for a moment. "It's you and me, best friends forever, fighting the good fight until we die at our lab tables hunched over our poorly funded microscopes. Remember?"

He smiles. "It sounds less appealing when you put it like that, but I'll take it."

"I'm happy to watch you grow old and die in the Bahamas."

"Ha ha."

Micah leans down to kiss my forehead before saying goodnight and leaving the room.

I think about the next few days ahead and worry all over again. Hopefully, once we get to the testing center, a secret government location heavily guarded by trained military, we'll be safe enough to give this project a real shot.

But I've got my reservations.

THREE

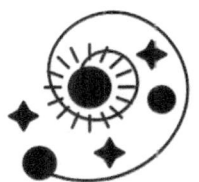

Tarian

My crew and I take to space under the cover of darkness and secrecy, traveling through the distant abyss in hopes of a better future for our world. I'm nervous and anxious, still reeling from this massive departure in my own future plans.

Kyllell is strong, and so is the latest addition to our family, Ada, but strength can only get them so far. I worry about their safety in my absence.

Whoever stands against Kyllell won't do it head-on. They'll send assassins.

"It's not going to be as bad as you're making it out, Tarian," Dywrr attempts to reassure me. Having briefed my crew on the specifics of this new mission, they're far more receptive to it than I am. "Human females. And if they are anything like Ada, I can't wait to get there."

I give Dywrr an amused look. "You do realize if you sleep with anyone before they are tested you could be sleeping with someone's potential bond mate."

Dywrr's excitement doesn't diminish. "Ada told me it isn't official until you put a ring on it."

"What in Elysarah's name is that supposed to mean?"

"I'm still trying to figure that one out, but I'm pretty sure it was permission to enjoy myself."

Dywrr certainly knows how. Although, I'm unclear as to how many females will be on the team assisting our scientists. The male knows better than to get into entanglements at work.

"Just try not to scare the natives. Ada also says we look like monsters to them." I give Dywrr a wink, gesturing to his burning horns. "They're giving you away."

Laoth and Bodeth laugh at the comment, though their horns show the same eagerness. Ready to find a bed partner and enjoy interracial sex with a species they've been salivating over since meeting Ada and failing to distract her from Kyllell.

Yep. Every one of us used our pull on her.

Every one of us failed.

It still rankles some of my crew. Especially Dywrr. He was absolutely crazy about Ada. I sometimes suspect he still is.

"What are we eating tonight, anyway?" Bodeth asks. We sit in the mess hall and wait for one of the cooks to bring out our meal. Our crew makes up the four of us, three crew members in the engine room, one in control of navigation, two cooks, and someone to ensure sanity on the ship by cleaning up when messes are made.

"I have no idea. I don't even know what Kyllell stocked on this craft for the journey," I reply.

"The suspense is killing me," Bodeth grunts. "I'm starving."

Not a single crew member on the ship knew about this voyage until right before we departed. I suspect everyone is still reeling, and I doubt a meal will be dispersed any time soon.

Luckily, I know and trust everyone aboard as they have served in these positions on a consistent basis. I try not to think about one crew member that has been painfully absent for some time.

"It won't be long now, you overgrown *charksis*," Dywrr says.

The name-calling, though childish, is pretty much what I expect from Dywrr. Nothing is ever taken too seriously by him unless we're being attacked.

"I'm just going to say what we're all thinking." Laoth shifts in his seat, his eyes on me. "We're going to be tested—"

"Let me stop you right there," I say.

"This isn't something you can stop, Tarian. As some of the few Elysiums on this new planet, you know the implications. They are going to want every Elysium there to be part of the first round of tests. That means us. That means we find out if there is a female on that planet meant for us."

"I'm aware." I look anywhere but at my crew.

"You don't have to get tested," Dywrr says. "I mean, fuck them, right? Not everyone wants to be matched to a human."

"By the Goddess, Dywrr." Laoth smacks him across the back of his head, further irritating Dywrr's horns.

"He doesn't have to do this. He's the only one of us who lost his —"

"Dywrr, I swear," Bodeth says.

"Lynnak wasn't my bond mate, though," I say, finally uttering her name for the first time since she died as a result of a contract killing.

My crew goes silent for a few moments as I try to push away my feelings of anger and pain, and mostly shame. Shame that I hadn't been able to save her, although I had thought sending her away was saving her. But we've all lost someone now.

I haven't been the only one suffering.

"I'm getting tested. I'm setting the right example. For the good of our race, we're all getting tested whether we want to or not."

"And what if we match with a human female?" Laoth asks. He appears appalled by the idea, although he has different reasons.

It's one thing to fool around. It's another to be bound to a female for the rest of your life. While most males of my species feel it is the greatest gift the Goddess could offer, some of us have reasons to remain alone.

I don't know how to answer Laoth's question, so I change the subject to something more urgent. "We're going to face Chassak interference from Earth. They may not have had a chance to board this particular ship, but as we've discovered, the Chassaks have been kidnapping human females for a long time, selling them on the black market. I've no doubt that they have discovered our alliance with Earth and our plans for a testing center."

"You think they will kill off staff and begin to impersonate them," Laoth states.

"It's what they do. Everyone at the testing center has already been isolated with no new personnel added, and security has not been breached, but we have to interrogate new arrivals. It is especially vital we work in pairs. The last of the team will arrive within a week, I believe. A head geneticist and her subordinates. They have also been vetted carefully, but we keep an eye on them regardless. We keep an eye on everyone."

"Hand signals, perhaps? We give a hand signal to each other to prove we have not been compromised?" Bodeth asks.

"Not a bad idea," I muse. "We'll talk it over with personnel once we arrive."

"Until then, we just hurry up and wait," Dywrr says, rubbing his hands together. "I don't know about you warriors, but I'm anxious to discuss the sexual anatomy of the females we're about to plunder."

The rest of us groan in unison.

"Leave it to you to think female genitalia an appropriate discussion during dinner," Laoth says.

"There's no food yet." Dywrr points at the empty table. "We've all had to get up to speed on the human female body. I'm fascinated with the area known as the clitoris. Did you guys know the clitoris has 8,000 nerve endings and its only purpose is for pleasure? It's literally designed for a female's pleasure. It's just there to be stroked, and licked, and sucked—"

"Really?" Bodeth asks, sounding intrigued.

"Annnnnnd we've lost Bodeth." Laoth smirks at me.

The thought of sucking on any female's clit is enough to get my horns burning at an uncomfortable level. By the time we arrive, we'll be mad with lust. I make a note to encourage everyone to spend extra time on the combat deck.

"We've got a long way to fly, boys. Maybe we should spend the first night getting blackout drunk," I say, jumping to my feet and heading to a chilling unit to take out four bottles of sweet drink.

"Now, that's an offer I can't refuse." Dywrr is never one to miss out on a celebration.

And soon dinner arrives, a meal of *Okega,* a tender, juicy meat and various leafy greens. We eat with a ravenous hunger that can't be sated by normal food and drink. Each one of us will go to bed tonight alone and frustrated.

And each one of us will wake up wondering if our arrival on Earth will lead us to the one female in this Universe meant to be our mate.

The thought terrifies me.

I make good on my intention to get blackout drunk.

~

"THIS IS THE T-1 STARLIGHT. EARTH CONTROL, DO YOU READ us?" My voice cracks between words, preparing to breach this new planet's orbit.

"T-1 Starlight, this is Earth Control. We read you loud and clear," comes the reply through my comm's system. Bodeth turns, giving me a gleaming smile. I take note of his fangs and realize how intimidating our incisors must look to a species with harmless, blunt teeth.

"We are preparing to enter Earth's orbit and make our descent. Are we clear?"

"You're clear for entry, T-1 Starlight."

This process feels tedious. There's an obvious necessity for prep time on their side while we enter the orbit and prepare to land, but the series of instructions for communication, getting a yes, and then following through feels like extra steps where none are needed. Why not just let us go where we have to go and land where we have to land?

"Thank you, Earth Control, we are entering orbit in three, two, one..." The T-1 shakes and rattles for a few seconds as we break into Earth's gravitational pull, but it stabilizes without much fuss.

"You're cleared for landing, T-1 Starlight. Do you know where to go?"

"We're heading in the direction of Rock Creek where we'll land

and meet with your representatives. Preparing to touch down in give or take five Earth minutes."

"Okay, T-1 Starlight. You're clear, over and out."

I pull back and rub at the burning sensation at the base of my horns. "Is it just me, or was that like moving through *achrem* mud?" I ask, turning to Bodeth.

"They might value their privacy, and making sure no one comes or goes without consent isn't always a terrible idea, but they don't have the technology we do," he responds, flicking dials and buttons on various machines. The rest of the crew are doing the same to ensure a safe landing.

"It's archaic," I reply.

Thinking about it further, this is only the second time Earth has welcomed guests to their planet, and now they know a different alien race has been stealing their females. It has to be unnerving for them. They also seem a bit terrified to face the unknown void that is space. Well, a few of their representatives do, anyway.

As tedious as it is, I can't fault their need for communication.

Time passes as we descend. It's time we don't have, but we can't exactly teleport to our destination. Once we breach the cloud bank, there is a collective inhale from the crew. Earth is a planet filled with color, lush with vegetation.

It's unlike anything we've encountered before.

"I think I already like it here," Bodeth says.

"Don't get too attached." I study the computer readings and focus on possible threats as we descend. "We don't have any idea how long we'll be here."

After what seems like hours, we approach our destination. I'm definitely ready to be away from my crew for a moment. The combination of tension, anxiety, excitement, and male lust is a distracting mix. Several males with horns burning in one location? Things can become territorial quickly.

"Are we ready for this?" I ask, looking at the giant monitor before the captain's chair, inspecting the ground we're moments away from landing on. The second we touch down, there's no going back. Not that we have much choice to do so.

"Ready as we'll ever be," comes the reply.

All eyes are fixed on the screen displaying the scene before us. There are several human vehicles spread out in a wide semi-circle surrounding our landing spot. I see tiny humans standing at attention before those vehicles as they await our landing. My heart races in my chest at the sight of them. On Elysius, it's easy to stand before the Council and command their respect since I spent years earning my place. I'm a known entity on my planet with acclaim carried forward in my name alone.

Here, I'm just a big green alien, and they're the norm.

I suck in a few deep breaths, get up from my chair, and head to the back of the craft. Dywrr, Bodeth, and Laoth join a few steps behind. The engine of the T-1 starts revving low before finally ending in a soft rumble as it touches down on the ground.

The ramp descends before me, and for the first time since leaving Elysius, I feel confident in myself. I am in control, no matter how much I fought the idea of coming here. My readiness, though lacking up to this point, feels enhanced.

Standing here, with the ramp near the terrain and the Earth's yellow sun heating up the air around us, I'm filled with a sense of renewed purpose. We are pioneers for our people, extending into a new dawn that might be the final saving grace to continue our bloodlines.

"Are *you* ready for this?" Bodeth asks, knowing my question not moments ago was a coping mechanism.

Down on the ground, standing in the middle of various military personnel, is Mark Jameson, the President of the United States.

"Ready as I'll ever be," I reply, adjusting my long coat, cracking my neck from side to side, and taking the first step to formally greet the Earthlings.

I hear Mark's voice from a distance as he makes his way toward us with a smile. Brown skin.

Not green.

Everyone on Elysius has varying shades of green skin. I'm enthralled with the many colors and shades the human species possesses.

I reach my hand out and shake it as is customary among humans. It is odd to not grasp higher up the arm, but the sentiment is the same.

"Welcome, Ambassador Tarian. I can't tell you how momentous this is for us. We're thrilled to have you here and dedicated to helping you throughout this process."

I'm taken aback by the lack of posturing on his part. His smile and expression are open and easy. I don't detect a hint of deception in his gaze. I'm relieved that my initial impressions of him through our previous conversations are intact. I truly believe that this human wishes to help our species and is grateful for our protection and assistance as well.

I give him a half smile so as not to appear aggressive were my fangs revealed.

"President Jameson, my brother and Dr. Ada Charles are truly happy together. The idea that we can bring this happiness to other Elysiums and save our species brings us untold joy. We are thrilled to be working together to save and preserve both our species."

"Wonderful," the President says. "You'll forgive me if I step on any cultural pleasantries you may have, but we like to get down to business in this part of the world, and recent attacks make it necessary to bring you to our testing center and its secured facilities immediately."

I drop all diplomacy and go into an entirely different mode.

"Attacks? By the Chassaks?"

"Human factions this time. We have hate groups on this planet who are firmly against the idea of interspecies relationships of any kind. Radicals and terrorists. Our head geneticist was attacked two days ago and barely met up with our extraction crew."

This is alarming. From what I understand, the head geneticist is a key player in this process, working in conjunction with our scientists to understand human DNA and how it interacts with our own biology.

"Was he injured?" I ask as my crew and I are led to black, boxy vehicles.

"*She* is just fine. Dr. Bree Adams made it out alive with the help of her lab partner, Dr. Micah Scott, and the extraction crew we sent in. She and Micah are set to meet us there within the hour."

"A female is taking on this role?" I ask, feeling alarmed. "This is far too dangerous."

President Jameson chuckles as we get into the vehicles and take off. Bodeth, Laoth, and Dywrr remain blessedly silent.

"I'm not sure what role females once played in your society, Ambassador Tarian, but our women have fought hard for equality and rights to education. I'd keep any negative remarks to yourself if you find it hard to work with females in the field."

"You mistake my meaning, President. After meeting Ada, I'm aware of the role of women in many countries on your Earth, and I am filled with admiration. My main concern centers on Dr. Adam's safety. We fiercely protect any and all females. Elysium warriors are instinctively hardwired to do so. To place a female in a position that endangers her goes against our very nature."

President Jameson slaps his leg and smiles. "And that's how I knew this was going to work out. You can always tell exactly who you're getting into bed with by the way a country treats their women, or in this case by the way an alien species is inclined to treat their females. You'll find Dr. Adams completely up to the challenge, but if any of you feel protective of her, don't hold back."

"Don't hold back?"

The President locks me with a steely gaze. "Dr. Bree Adams is by far the most important piece of this elaborate puzzle. She's brilliant, she's determined, and she gets shit done. She will go above and beyond what the job demands, even to the point of putting herself at risk. So if you feel the urge to give in to those protective instincts, then do so. That woman has no sense of self-preservation, and the lack of it is alarming on a good day."

I nod, having felt protective of her the moment her name was mentioned and not liking those instincts in the least. "I'll assign myself to her personal security detail."

"Excellent. I can't wait to see her reaction."

"She is headstrong?"

All I get in response is a shit-eating grin from the leader of the USA.

Great. As if I don't have enough responsibilities. I'll be on watch making sure this female takes care of herself.

I'm not happy about it, and from the sound of Dywrr's soft chuckle in the backseat, he and the rest of the crew find it all hilarious.

FOUR

Bree

"Y ou have no new messages. If you would like to hear previously recorded messages, press one."

I don't know why I do this to myself. Maybe I'm a sucker for the pain, but hearing his voice is worth it sometimes. It keeps me motivated, strong, always striving to be the best me I can be. Not that he wanted that of me. If it had been up to him, I'd have been some doctor's perfect bride, raising the kids while my husband was off having all the fun, sleeping with his secretary.

I'd heard it all my life. That I wasn't good enough to take on a role of power. That my mom and I were exactly the same, and being at home was the best place for us.

I look around my new quarters at the testing facility and find the room surprisingly pleasant. I had expected sterility. Instead, I'm offered a beautiful view of the Sonoran desert…out in the middle of nowhere.

Secret location means literally out of touch with civilization, but I do feel much safer being on a military base built for this very purpose. I stare at the beauty of the Arizona sunrise, pinks and purples meeting a colossal explosion of reds and oranges.

And then I think about my parents and what their reaction to my current career path would be.

My mom had a doctorate, but Dad brought her down at her peak and never let her use it. I was bound and determined to not only get mine but make it count. Still, I never should have let things get that out of hand. You only get one dad, and where I dedicated my whole life to standing up for myself and fighting him on every point imaginable, getting back those years without him is impossible.

Most days, I know it's not right to blame myself. But when anything tragic happens, like a near-death experience, a person goes looking for meaning and gets stuck in an endless cycle of "what if?"

And near the end, he had finally started to change his views. Not soon enough for my tastes, but it was satisfying to finally hear him verbalize his regret at the way he had so brutally undercut my mother.

I feel a single tear running down my cheek as I press 1 on the Numpad and wait for the recorded message to play.

"Hey Bree-bear, it's dad. I know you're out there being a big girl and all, but I'd love to see you again. I know things haven't always been the best between us, and since your mom passed, you've been on a personal vendetta to prove me wrong, but I miss you, Bree. Come over for lunch, please? Okay. Take care, and I love you."

By the time the message is finished, I'm weeping, nearing a fetal position on my bed, and thinking about the good times we had together. That message came through four years ago, and I've never had the heart to delete it. My shrink, at least the first one, told me that getting rid of it was a way to heal, while holding onto it only invited more heartache. I guess I understand that, but it's the last thing I have from my parents—that and money.

And no matter what people think or how they act because of it, money definitely doesn't buy you happiness. I spent most of my adult years alone, doing everything in my power to show my dad that I was worth more than any of the men on his team. Money never factored into true worth for me.

He died three days after that voicemail, and I've never been able to forgive myself.

After my pity party, I compose myself enough to take a shower. Today is a monumental day for me and for the human species as a whole. I've spent the last few months reeling from the proof that we are not alone, and the world as a whole has known for a mere three weeks.

We need female volunteers after all.

This scenario is unlike anything the human race has experienced before. Hell, if you'd asked me about aliens a year ago, I'd have considered the possibility and left it at that. Now? It's become the norm for me. The topic on everyone's lips. I always find it amazing how adaptive the human race is. One day we preach it's the end of the world, and then after a while the same news is mundane because it doesn't fit someone's agenda.

I get out of the shower and quickly towel myself dry.

The sound of my cell ringing breaks my concentration. It's a welcome relief from thoughts of my dad and the general fickle nature of humanity.

"Bree Adams speaking."

"Are you ready for today?" Micah asks. There's a rustling in the speaker, no doubt a tie being tightened.

"I'm assuming your question is rhetorical," I reply, pulling on a long, black pencil skirt.

Micah has been a part of my team since day one, and I'm damn lucky to have him. He's a genius in nearly every subject he studies, from our little bubble of science to music and more. And he is nearly the only damn friend I've got. Most people are surprised to find I have Micah and Remy in my life since I'm nothing but reclusive.

I have too much work to do to make friends anyway.

And certainly no time for dating.

Which is another reason I feel so comfortable around him. He will never be interested in me, and that is a relief considering the attention and disrespect I'm used to getting from men.

I'm a blonde bombshell, and I say that with no ego. It's annoying as hell to try and get anyone to take me seriously when a person's initial physical impression of me is that of Marilyn Monroe. Any time an idiot newbie in the lab asks me, "Do you know who you remind me of?" I cut them off before they attempt to answer their own question and end up on my shit list for life.

In a male dominated industry, I'm fighting to be taken seriously, but when you add my appearance to the mix, there is a level of unconscious bias that I combat nearly every week because no male assumes I have half a brain between my ears.

Constantly being compared to a movie actress might seem great, but the lack of respect I get when I tell people I'm a scientist is downright insulting. Apparently, big boobs must get in the way of my own intelligence.

I'm convinced a male's dick always gets in the way of his.

"Clearly, you're ready," says Micah. "But I'm wondering if you can keep a level head considering your unease where Elysium intentions are concerned."

Right. My reservations, of which there are many. Today, Earth introduces itself to aliens. I just hope we know what the fuck we're doing.

"If you're wondering whether I will lose my cool and run my mouth if one of the Elysium scientists pisses me off, you already know the answer to that question."

I hear a familiar sigh of long suffering. Micah knows me so well.

"Consider Remy before you create an awkward scenario. She can't handle the confrontation or the anxiety that goes with it."

I concede the point. Remy is about as fierce as a fluffy bunny and triggers all of my protective motherly instincts even though she is a mother of one and an incredible peer.

"Fine, fine. For Remy's sake, I shall behave."

"Well, I'll be heading out in about twenty minutes. You want Remy and I to swing by your room? We're supposed to get a grand tour of our new digs before we greet the little green men."

"How about I meet you there?"

There is a pause on the other line before Micah says, "I know it's the anniversary of your dad's death. You gonna be okay?"

"I'll be fine," I insist, but his concern warms my heart.

"Okay. See you soon."

~

"YOU THINK THESE THINGS ARE GOING TO WORK?" MICAH ASKS, rubbing the back of his ear.

He's talking about the chip they implanted in all personnel on base. Something I was blessedly unconscious for. I was told it felt like a tiny robot was rooting around in your eardrum.

How unpleasant.

"I'm sure. It was sent with the first crew of Elysiums, right? I don't see why Elysium scientists would give us faulty tech," I reply, typing away at the computer in my new office.

Micah shrugs his shoulders, shaking his head in an *I don't know* fashion.

Remy walks through the door, positively vibrating with excitement. "My ear is sore. Is your ear sore? I'm half afraid we've been implanted with tech that's currently eating through our ear passages and will soon find its way to our brain matter and feast on every scrap of tissue that it can find, thus taking away all our memories, will power, and ability to make choices. Then the Elysiums will use us as mindless slaves to do their bidding."

Micah and I stare at her for a moment.

"Remy," I say, "did you get your hands on some coffee?" I'm praying the answer to that is no. Remy's poor frame can't handle the enhanced power to her adrenal functions. It's like watching the equivalent of the Energizer Bunny on crack.

She smiles wide and lifts a decidedly jittery hand to her ear, tucking a strand of long auburn hair behind it. "Oh no. I just had that yummy protein stuff from the mess hall."

That does not sound promising.

"What yummy protein stuff from the mess—oh, dear Lord." I tilt my head, giving Remy an exasperated look. "Do you mean the Ka'Chava meal replacement shake?"

"Yes. So yummy. My favorite is chocolate."

Micah's groan echoes my own.

"Remy, did you check the label to see which one you grabbed?

Because one has zero coffee added and the other has two shots of espresso."

Micah's question is unnecessary. Just looking at Remy, you can tell she's a live wire ready to detonate.

Her eyes are wide as saucers. "I did not read the labels."

Micah bursts into laughter. "You couldn't pay me to miss this first meeting with the Elysiums. Ten minutes in Remy's presence, and they may reconsider their alliance."

"But I already volunteered for the program," Remy says, missing the joke entirely.

"What?"

"I volunteered my DNA to see if I was a match."

"Remy, why the hell would you do something like that? What if you actually *are* a match?" I say, getting to my feet and rounding the desk.

Remy's hands shake, so I pull them into mine and start rubbing them to calm her. I need to watch my tongue. Worrying her won't make this scenario better. She has a sweet little six-year-old she's raising on her own, although her mother is taking care of him right now.

But Remy's life has been hard, and I can understand why it would be nice to have some support in the form of a strong Elysium warrior, but only if they turn out to be as great as they seem on paper. Single momming it has not been a cake walk for Remy.

"I just wanted to try. You know?" Her blue eyes are bright, filled with unfounded hope. Something she always has. So much unfounded hope.

I envy her for it and worry for her because of it.

"Okay, Rem, no big deal. It's going to be fine." I look at Micah, his expression filled with concern. "Can you grab us some water? Preferably a jug? We gotta get her jitters under control and get her hydrated."

Micah exits quickly and makes record time, bringing back some ice cold water and a large cup followed by some fruit and whole wheat toast. We get the first cup of water into her, a few slices of apple and a bite of toast. Anything to disperse and soak up the caffeine in her system.

I have her take a seat at my desk and watch as her shaky smile brightens. "Look, I know you guys worry about me, but you don't have to. I really have a good feeling about these Elysiums. If I have a mate out there somewhere, then I want to go for it. You know? If you want something, you have to try."

If I didn't love her so much, I'd shake her. But her positivity is damn endearing, and I know it isn't fake. She's an annoying optimist with a can-do attitude that has pulled Micah and I through some hellish times.

"Drink more water, Rem. We gotta get your shakes under control." I hand her another full glass and then I get down to business. "So, here are my thoughts on the meeting. The government has been rather hush-hush about today's agenda. I'd like to skip the inane introductions, pomp and ceremony, and start working with the three Elysium scientists, but diplomacy is in order, especially since I'll be working quite a bit with their ambassador as well."

"Playing nice with others?" Micah asks. "They really should have consulted with me first."

"Har, har, you jerk." I take a slice of apple and chew for a moment, contemplating my next words. "I want to think the best of this scenario here, but we keep our eyes peeled and our ears open. If one alien race is all about conquest, it stands to reason others would be as well."

"Or maybe they are who they say they are," Remy says. She takes another bite of her toast.

"I'd like to believe that. It would make this entire scenario less complicated on an ethical and moral level, but we just see how it goes, and if we have cause to believe that the Elysiums' intentions are not at all what they say they are, then we reassess."

"You know about Ada Charles, Bree. She's a doctor herself," Remy points her toast at me. "You've watched the recordings of her being interviewed by our president. You've had endless chats with the woman."

"She could have been under duress."

"She looked blissfully happy," she counters.

"Or drugged."

Remy sighs in defeat.

"She was not drugged. She was able to give detailed information about the Nadir Trench and warn us to avoid it until we can get a handle on how the hell it became a wormhole."

"I actually wish we were the kind of scientists who studied phenomena like that. Can you imagine trying to figure out how a wormhole got there?" Micah's eyes alight with that same curiosity that always tends to get us in trouble.

We are a group of scientists that like to go a bit rogue when given enough leash.

"Remy's right. You can see that Dr. Charles and her mate are happy and well."

"Fair point, but I don't know what is happening behind the scenes, and we have no way of knowing if all Elysiums are as great as her mate, Kyllell, seems to be. So we reserve judgement until we have more information."

"Sounds good to me," Micah says. Remy nods her agreement and drinks the rest of her water down.

I'm not sure how fast that will get her shakes under control, but at least she has some good food in her stomach.

Ka'Chava.

For fuck's sake.

I'll need to advise the cook in the mess hall to hide any hint of coffee from Remy. She's a damn menace with that substance in her system.

I listen to the goings on of personnel beyond the door of my office, the low murmurs of staff in the adjacent lab. The vibrant hum of electronic whizzing from servers and machines breaking the silence. It fuels me with my own adrenal boost.

The research facility is enormous, and when working at maximum capacity, has nearly sixty people darting back and forth, feeding information down the necessary channels. Or up the channel.

"It was probably always there. We just didn't know it until it ripped open."

I blink at Micah, having no idea what he's talking about.

"What was always there?"

"The wormhole in that trench. It's probably been there for thousands of years. We've just never had the technology to find it until now."

"But how many are there, and what the hell do we do about it? Our planet is falling apart here."

Yeah. Endless storms. Nature's way of saying we had really fucked up. But it wasn't my field of study, and not my current problem to solve.

"Bree, Dr. Charles is just fine," Remy says, circling back to what she knows has really been bothering me.

"Yeah, yeah. I know. She has a wealth of information at her disposal, and she's been great to work with on this project so far."

I know she isn't under duress, but I'm always looking for someone's angle. Trust is not my strong suit.

But a wormhole in an ocean trench?

Now that is a hell of a thing. And to chat with renowned scientist Dr. Ada Charles was another.

Years ago, I had managed to meet up with her and discuss her work on tectonic shifts, global warming, and mass pollution. She was a genius in my eyes and everything I strived to be moving forward in my career.

"You know what they say about ignorance, right?" Micah says, checking his watch.

"Yes, it's bliss."

"No, it makes an ass out of you and me," Micah feigns his own *ignorance* for a second and shrugs it off. "Wait a minute, that's what they say about assuming." His look is pointed.

"Same difference, right?" I ball up a napkin he brought in and throw it, hitting him in the face.

"Hey, that's workplace harassment. I'll have your badge for that, officer."

I chuckle at his antics and collect my things from the desk, tossing my phone into my purse.

"You ready to move, Rem?" I ask.

She takes her last bite of toast as she stands. "I'll just keep quiet during the meeting."

"I think that would be wise." I can't hide the smile as I think about the effect caffeine has on Remy's verbal patterns. She'll run her mouth for as long as you'll let her, bouncing from one subject to the next.

My team follows me out of my office and through the research lab, heading to the main conference room a few doors down. I note the security guards stationed at intervals, the most heavily concentrated of them near the lab itself.

For the past few weeks, the facility has been collecting female DNA samples from willing women. I've got no clue as to how many women have actually volunteered for this project, but I'll soon find out. None of those samples can be damaged or jeopardized, but the sample I'm most interested in is the one from Ada and her mate, Chancellor Kyllell, son of Koath.

I want to understand what made them biologically compatible for anything and everything. So that lab, above any other space on this base, needs to be protected at all costs. I'm just concerned as to how much protection that lab might actually need.

WE ARRIVE AT THE CONFERENCE ROOM AT THE PREDETERMINED time to await the arrival of the Elysium crew and the President of the United States with all the security staff that will entail.

I like Jameson. Never voted for him, but my interactions with him over the last few months have been favorable.

Before entering, I surreptitiously glance through the door's window and study the other scientists in the room, trying not to gawk too much, but honestly, they are the very image of massive, muscular demons.

Devils with those stunning, curved horns.

The three other human scientists on our team are seated across the table from them. I've already gone over everyone's files, specialties, and roles each will play, but I'm eager to speak with the head scientist from Elysius. I note the female scientist, Dr. Fae Sandoval, is looking a little flushed, keeping a firm grip on the arm of her chair, her knuckles white. She stares at one of the Elysium scientists like a deer caught in some massive headlights, and I realize what is happening.

That alien dude is using his pull on her, something Ada Charles explained in great detail during one of her sessions with me. I'm not sure if I'm amused, intrigued, or furious, but I figure I'll let Dr. Sandoval's response guide my actions.

"We going in any time soon?" Micah asks.

"Yep, prepare for a confrontation."

"Ah hell," he mutters as he and Remy follow me in.

The moment we enter, the Elysium drops his attention from Dr. Sandoval and all eyes are on me. Dr. Sandoval's relief is palpable as she slouches forward in her chair, I realize my assumption is correct, and then I'm hit with several overwhelming desires at once.

All three of these bastards are using their pull on me. I make eye contact with the one who was staring at Sandoval and give him a sweet smile.

"You're Dr. Jaran? Head scientist for your people?" I mentally bat down the energy he sends my way as I continue to punch and swipe at the other energies thrown at me.

Fascinating. I really want to study this phenomenon since I can feel myself getting wet due to their sexual pull, but I get hold of myself and hone in on my own steely resolve.

Dr. Jaran is all strength and muscle beneath his white lab coat. He tilts his head to the side and scrutinizes me with his yellow, slitted eyes, clearly attempting to unravel my odd reaction, or rather, non-reaction to what he and his staff are doing.

"I am," he says in a gruff voice, a hint of a smile in his tone, and in that moment I see the playfulness in his gaze, and for some reason it puts me at ease.

Rather than berating him as originally planned, I opt for humorous diplomacy.

"Your pull is extremely potent, Dr. Jaran. If you and your colleagues continue to use it on me and the other female scientists in this room, we're not going to get a damn thing done in this place. You'll have a full blown orgy on your hands. Not that I mind." I give him a wink.

His eyes widen in surprise and then everyone bursts out laughing. I feel their energetic pulls retreat at the same time. Dr. Jaran spares a sheepish glance at Dr. Sandoval. She doesn't seem to be worse for wear, her little smirk giving me some reassurance.

"You'll forgive us, Dr. Adams. It's been a long time since we've had the pleasure of such beautiful female company and our instincts to pull you toward us are hard to turn off at times. The fact that human females offer up such a challenge makes it even more difficult to refrain from doing it."

"Perhaps you could avoid using your pull during office hours. I'd hate to drop a beaker."

Dr. Jaran chuckles as he stands, pushing his chair back, and walks over to me offering an outstretched hand. I place my tiny one atop his and watch in fascination as his claws gently curl around it. He shakes it with a grin. "It's nice to see that other females on this planet are just as feisty as Ada."

"Thank you. I'm a fan of hers, so any comparison to her is greatly welcome. Can I meet your other scientists?"

My request has him beaming as he guides me over to the other two males with a hand at the small of my back.

It feels protective and safe.

A woman could get used to that.

"This is Dr. Rask," he points to the one on the left, "and Dr. Korsk. They will be closely working with your team to identify bond mate markers within the DNA."

"Wonderful to meet you guys." My smile is wide in response to theirs, and I note the way they gently shake my hand as if I might break altogether.

Very interesting. Ada mentioned they were protective, but I still hadn't been willing to believe she wasn't coerced by the pull on a regular basis.

These green aliens are damn charming.

Micah, as usual, takes everything in with his easy calm, even giving me a grateful look for not opting for abrasive confrontation as I introduce him and Remy to the males.

I take special note of the way the males behave around Remy. If anything, they are even more gentle with her than they were with me. Dr. Korsk looks as if he is trying to sink into himself a bit to minimize his daunting frame and appear less intimidating.

He needn't worry. Remy's shyness in this moment is completely overcome by her curiosity. Before she opens her mouth to ask a question, I hurriedly suggest we all take our seats and get to know each other better.

This whole event makes Roswell feel like a day at the races. Not that I was there, but I imagine it was nothing like this.

We're all well acquainted by the time the president, his entourage, and the Elysium Ambassador and his crew arrive. I'm at the very end of the table next to Dr. Jaran, who pulls out my chair for me as we stand for the President. The chivalry is unnecessary, but I appreciate the respect he offers.

Our fierce leader is a small man with big energy. I can't help but smile as he enters the room with childlike joy emanating from every part of him. It reminds me of Remy. All that unfounded hope again.

Immediately on his heels are four Elysium males looking just as fierce as the others in the room.

"What the hell do you guys eat?" I whisper under my breath. From the slight twitch of Dr. Jaran's lips, I can tell he's heard me.

I study these newcomers with interest. On their heads are the usual coiled horns, a bit discolored for reasons I'm unaware. I've never seen consistent coloring among their horns and I wonder what makes them change shades. Tufts of hair surround the horns at the base where the darkest discoloration sits, hiding an extra smaller pair of ears.

At their waists are guns that are clearly alien tech, with weapons strapped across their chests and backs. All four look ready for combat.

Interesting.

"Dr. Adams, how are you?" the President asks as he comes to my side.

"Healthy and happy, Mr. President. You?" He takes my proffered hand and shakes it.

"I understand that nearly wasn't the case. Seems someone tried to kill you before you could reach the base."

I'm about to respond when low growls emanate from the Elysium scientists in the room.

"Dr. Adams was under attack?" Dr. Jaran asks. "Unacceptable. She should have a full detail wherever she goes."

"And she will," says the alien dressed in a more vibrant color of gray combat gear. "Aside from overseeing this entire project, my crew and I will be taking over the security detail for Dr. Adams."

I'm about to protest when my eyes lock with the alien who just spoke, and I feel as if I'm falling down a rabbit hole.

I watch as his eyes widen in surprise and his coiled horns unfurl, radiating a luminescent black. He stares at me with a mixture of terror and desire in his expression, looking as if ravaging me or running away from me are two options he is deeply considering.

My body feels flushed and aroused on a level I've never experienced before.

What the hell is going on?

President Jameson and the rest of those assembled stare in surprise, their glances going to the alien, then to me, then back to the alien with the ebony horns.

"By the Great Goddess," says Dr. Jaran. "Already Elysarah blesses us."

I'm missing something here that only the Elysiums seem to understand. The only thing I *am* overwhelmingly aware of is the physical reaction I'm having toward this particular Elysium.

President Jameson turns to me with what I can only describe is a shit-eating grin. "Dr. Adams, may I introduce you to Tarian, son of Koath, Ambassador for the Elysium race and...apparently...your bond mate."

FIVE

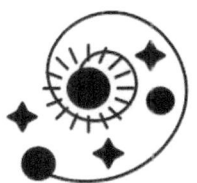

Tarian

S taking your claim a little early, aren't we, Tarian?" Dywrr mutters when the rest of the room explodes into conversation. I notice one male human standing next to Dr. Adams with a hand on her shoulder, looking as if he might explode. My instincts demand action.

No one touches Bree Adams but me.

I'm by her side in an instant, lifting her in my arms and stepping back from the puny human who thought he had the right to touch her.

"Tarian," Bodeth warns as everyone stops shouting and stares at me like I've lost my mind.

"He was touching my mate," I snarl.

I notice an armed guard near the entrance inch toward me. I follow my snarl up with a low warning growl that rumbles deep from my chest.

"He meant her no harm," Dywrr says, slowly stepping toward me, talking to me as if he is talking to a mere *vernex*. His words are lost on me, while my attention remains fixated on the human standing before me, staring at my mate with concern on his face.

As if she ever has anything to be afraid of when it comes to me.

"Micah, you need to back down," says a sensual voice.

I look at my female in my arms and am struck again by her fragile frame. Everything about this woman is tiny. Curvy, but tiny. She can't work at this facility with a target on her back. She could easily be wounded or killed if the facility is attacked.

Then I would lose her.

There are too many males in the room. Too many challengers for my Bree. My mind is slowly beginning to unravel as instinct takes over. My next move is to fight my way out of here, take my mate to a safe location, and—

"Everybody sit your asses down, now," she yells, startling me and the rest of the room's participants, although I notice President Jameson simply appears smug. "You, asshole," she nods to the guard, "put your gun away and back out of the room. You're triggering his protective instincts, and the rest of the males in here are too close to me. Everybody either sit down or back the fuck up."

I stare at her in surprise as her arms wrap around my neck as if to comfort me, and then I glance around the room as the occupants, including President Jameson, file to the back and line up against the wall. It would be comical if I had the presence of mind to laugh. Everything is tinged with a purple hue and the need to battle my way through the lineup.

"Dr. Adams," President Jameson says once the room is silent. "What's our next move?"

"Ambassador Tarian and I will sit at the head of the conference table while everyone else sits at the far end until his protective instincts are no longer triggered."

I stare at her in disbelief as she calmly discusses my outrageous behavior as if it doesn't bother her at all even though in the back of my mind I'm fully aware that my actions could have been seen as an act of war. That she could so effectively assess the situation and offer up a resolution—while a scary alien crossed personal boundaries to grab her in an aggressive way—is astounding to me.

"The males in the room are considered challengers, and Tarian is no doubt an Alpha. Until he acclimates, the males in the room need to sit at the far end and the women need to be near the front."

She turns her full gaze on me, and I feel a sense of calm wash over me.

"Ambassador, I'm in no danger here, and these males have no interest in me beyond professional." She places a hand on my cheek and the contact further eases the tension, clearing the battle rage that interferes with my logic and reasoning. "Shall we sit down at the head of the table and start the meeting?"

Her gaze is strong and steady, as if she isn't confused or afraid of what has happened let alone the revelation that she is my bond mate. It's as if she has accepted it.

She is nothing like Ada in this respect.

"Yes." I clear my throat to get rid of the growl and steady my breathing. "That would be fine." I address the rest of the group. "I apologize for my behavior. I have never experienced that before."

"No shit," Dywrr says with a happy smile on his face.

I will take great joy in beating his ass later.

"Can you set me down?" she asks.

"Not yet."

"Well, how about you sit down at the table and keep me on your lap?"

"I think I can manage that."

Dywrr is fighting back his chuckle, but Bodeth hits him over the head, looking completely flummoxed by this turn of events. Laoth doesn't show any emotion whatsoever, but he'll have thoughts once we reconvene.

I take my seat with my mate in my arms and do all I can to hide the evidence of my arousal, but I'm certain Dr. Adams can feel it, especially since her plump ass on my lap is the sweetest form of torture I have ever experienced. For her part, she appears completely unruffled as she motions the group to sit.

Everyone slowly makes their way to the table with the females near the front, but I note the puny male human from before, glaring daggers at me.

I'll take great joy in fucking him up as well.

"Remy, go ahead and sit here, next to us."

The female smiles brightly, her shiny auburn hair flowing to her waist and swishing back and forth as she takes a seat to our right. She is pale and fragile looking. It's at odds with her steady gaze as she smiles at me, in no way terrified by my behavior or appearance. I note my mate reaching for Remy's hand, patting it for reassurance and realize this is a female who is special to my mate. This Remy is now special to me and will be treated as family from now on.

The male she instructs to sit near the back, this Micah, most certainly will not.

"Are you ready to speak?" President Jameson asks, interrupting my thoughts.

"Sorry, yes," I reply, turning to face him. If I don't look at her, don't focus on her, maybe the sensation of finding my mate will be alleviated for a while.

How wrong I am, with my attention continually darting back to this goddess on my lap.

"I am Tarian, son of Koath, brother of Kyllell who is chancellor of Elysius." It is the first time I've ever used my full title since my brother became chancellor. "My crew and I are here to oversee the success of this project and to assist in any way we can. We are not scientists, so we trust in your intelligence and your capabilities to solve this problem and bring together two races that have the power to save one another. It's an enormous undertaking, but I've been assured time and again that the brightest and the best are here to make it happen. My crew and I will do all we can to protect you in the process."

The room erupts into appreciative applause as Dr. Adams rests a supportive hand on my shoulder. The burning in my horns begs relief from this female, and I know she's the only one who can make me whole again. I do my best to focus since she seems to be able to as she takes over with the ease of a practiced diplomat.

"As we all know, over the last few months, communications have gone out between Earth and Elysius in preparation for Ambassador Koath and his crew's arrival."

My mate continues to speak about what we're doing here. That our arrival is to set up interplanetary relations, and to those willing and interested, become mated to Elysium warriors.

The longer she speaks, the harder it is for me to hold myself back. This isn't the place for it. Not after my previous abhorrent behavior. She continues to lay out the schedule for the coming weeks. An intricate discussion concerning genetic research and DNA testing ensues with scientists listing problems and issues and answering each other's questions about Elysium and human differences and similarities in our blood and genetic coding.

It's beyond my understanding, but I'm too focused on not taking Bree right here and now as she commands the attention of the entire room. She sits on my lap as if she always directs meetings on the laps of males.

Remarkable female.

A genius, if I'm not mistaken.

I must find a way to remove her from this facility.

Bree

FUCK WITH THIS STRANGE FEELING. IT'S TOO DISTRACTING.

It's like a magnetic force between Tarian and I, and I'm fairly certain that the no-nonsense approach I took to diffuse the situation is about to wear off if we don't end this meeting soon. Because if anyone thinks I'm okay with being an Elysium's bond mate, or sitting on an Elysium warrior's lap, they are absolutely nuts.

I don't do relationships. I work.

I work hard. I have a career. I'm not making babies and staying home to raise them. Reduced to "the one and only thing a woman is capable of" as my father so often said to me. I've fought too hard to get where I am, and I'm not allowing a ridiculously good looking alien to come in here and ruin everything I've built for myself.

End of discussion.

But if I'm going to have this conversation with Ambassador Koath, it has to be in private where he doesn't feel threatened.

God, how did this happen?

I should have read the signs better. I know what black horns mean for fuck's sake. I just never imagined an Elysium male's response when finding his mate would be similar to the protective instincts of a lion.

Even now, the tight grip of his hands on my waist are evidence of his unease. He isn't totally relaxed, but it's far better than what I saw in his eyes before logic and reason set in. He was about to go fucking crazy on everyone and crack skulls. My heart flutters as he squeezes my waist, causing massive butterflies to flitter through my stomach.

He has a hard-on the size of Texas, and it is positioned right at the apex of my ass. I'd try to wiggle away from it, but I know that would just get us both more aroused, and from the possessive behavior he displayed earlier, it's obvious we need clear heads to navigate this scenario.

"Mr. President," I say, as if sitting on a male with a hard-on is exactly how I lead a meeting, "did you have anything else to add before we end this discussion and get started on the day's tasks?"

"Two things, if I may. I'll remind everyone that the storms in the area are nothing to be trifled with." He takes his time to look everyone in the eye as he speaks. "There are subterranean levels built here at the base to handle any weather conditions due to their increase in frequency. Within these levels we have barracks that you must retreat to the moment the storm alarm sounds. Make sure you follow the safety protocols and security checks you previously trained on before entering the base. Take no risks, not even to save equipment."

The increase in natural disasters over the years is just one more problem needing to be solved. One that Dr. Ada Charles and many other scientists are working on. I have to wonder if she is still attempting to work on the problem all the way from Elysius. A conversation for another day.

For now, I'm focused on an entirely different problem to neutralize an entirely different threat. If it isn't the Earth trying to get rid of humans, it's Chassaks trying to steal all the females.

One problem at a time.

"We'll be sure to follow all procedures and protocols laid out by the Ambassador's security team," I say. "And the second item?"

"I'd like to answer that one," says one of the Ambassador's crew. I note Remy's eyes swiveling to the imposing warrior as she takes in a deep inhalation. She's clearly interested, but he doesn't exhibit any mate bond symptoms, something I can see Remy note immediately, trying to hide her disappointment.

I know her way too well.

That and Remy's poker face is nonexistent.

"Before any of you leave this room, you will learn a series of specific hand signals that we will use to identify you. Chassaks are adroit infiltrators due to their shifting capabilities. We will do everything in our power to protect you, but we must make sure that throughout the project, we periodically check your identities to make sure you are still you. It's basic and rudimentary, but effective."

"What will that be?" Remy asks.

His attention moves to her where he pauses for a moment, seeming distracted before composing himself. "The President suggested that the easiest way of identifying ourselves is simply by using American Sign Language to spell out our names. Elysiums and humans will become familiar with the ASL alphabet and learn this quickly before the end of the day."

"Thank you," I say. "Anything else, Mr. President?"

For God's sake, let's be done with this.

He considers me for a moment. "Not a thing, other than to congratulate you on finding your bond mate. It thrills me to no end that we're already ensuring the survival of both our races. And should you need anything, I'll be at the White House bossing people around and pretending I don't know what I'm doing."

His sly grin makes me want to punch him.

Yep. I want to deck the President of the United States. He knows that not only did I have my reservations about this entire operation, I refused to give a blood sample to be tested. I didn't want to find a damn mate, despite his insistent urging that I participate.

He is no doubt having a field day with this one.

"Excellent, Mr. President. Thank you for attending our first meeting."

He rises and we all stand—*thank God*—watching as the president is escorted from the room. Fortunately, Ambassador Koath seems to have himself under control and doesn't make another grab for my waist as he towers behind me.

"I'll meet the rest of you in the lab in twenty minutes and we'll get started," I say, looking pointedly at Micah as he gives me a worried glance. Remy just nods in jubilant satisfaction, probably so excited that I "finally have someone to be with so I'm not so lonely anymore." Her past commentary on my lack of a love life. Not mine.

I need to clear this room out and clear the air with this alien.

Sexy Ambassador.

Dammit to hell.

He places a hand on my back as people file out. The Elysium males lower their eyes in deference and don't look at me even once as they leave.

Definitely interesting behavior. Not even Dr. Jaran offers me any eye contact.

The moment the door closes behind everyone, I shoot away from him like a ball out of a cannon, unable to handle his proximity any further. He moves to follow, but I sense it, turning to hold up a hand and warn him off.

"I need some space." I take in a deep breath, my face feeling flushed. I press my hands to my cheeks, but they're too damn hot to be of any help. He looks worried, but to his credit, he keeps his distance. "That entire…thing…overloaded me on multiple levels, and I need a clear head, which means I don't want you touching me." I see him flinch at my words, and I wish I had delivered them with more tact. "Sorry. I'm just a little thrown by what has happened."

"Thank the Goddess," he says in amusement, although his intense gaze never wavers. "You seemed so calm about the whole thing. I couldn't get a read on what you were thinking."

"Oh, I'll tell you what I'm thinking." I scratch the back of my neck trying hard not to look at him.

"Did my behavior frighten you?" he asks in concern.

"No. I didn't feel threatened by you." I meet his eyes with my own. "Not sure I can say the same for the rest of the group."

The ambassador chuckles and touches his horns, horns that have failed to coil back but shoot straight up from his head.

"So, the...your horns." I break the silence and point to them "Why won't they stop peacocking?"

"Peacocking?" he asks in amusement.

"Yeah, well, I guess you don't have them on Elysius. Peacocks are birds that display brightly colored feathers to attract potential mates," I say, and before the sentence leaves my lips entirely, he bursts into laughter.

The sound of it floods my senses and makes my neck and shoulders relax. I take note of it and file it away for future reflection.

"We're much like your peacocks then," Tarian says, a hand raising to the right horn and tugging on it.

Does that give it relief? A momentary thought of him tugging on something else flashes across my mind. I can't help but blush, knowing how unprofessional that is. Of course, I've just spent the last hour sitting on his lap with his very noticeable erection, so I think we're beyond standard etiquette at this point.

Don't lose your head. This is important.

The gripping sensation that has me drawn to Tarian gets worse. "Are you using your pull on me right now?"

"Yes," he says with a smirk.

Bastard.

"Why?"

"Because you've distanced yourself from me, and my instincts drive me to pull you back."

"You need to stop that."

"Okay."

I wait, but the pull only diminishes a tiny margin.

"Seriously, stop that. I need to focus."

His grin goes wide and smug. "I did stop. What you're experiencing is your natural need for me. You sense the potential bond we will make, and your body yearns for consummation."

I snort, rubbing the back of my neck. God, if only I had known how badly I needed to get laid.

Hindsight.

59

"Well, I'm going to stop you right there. Look, I don't want to be rude here, but I didn't donate my DNA for a reason. I'm not looking for a mate. I'm not a test subject or a volunteer. I'm the head scientist, and I'm not interested in a bond mate, or a family, or anything that will derail my career."

His jaw drops as if I've upended his entire belief system. "You're saying you won't be my mate?"

I tread carefully, unsure what his reaction to rejection will be. "I hope you aren't offended, but this...it's just too much for me."

"Offended doesn't factor into this. You really think you can resist fate, resist biology...resist me?" His expression turns predatory as he walks toward me, a glint in his eye at my fierce denial of what lies between us.

As he invades my personal space, I place a hand against his very muscular chest—God, those muscles—before he decides he might actually be in charge of this conversation.

I realize my mistake when he enfolds my hand in his enormous, clawed one and lifts it to his lips, gently kissing it before pulling me closer, holding my hand against his chest.

"I didn't want a bond mate, either. I'd rather not be faced with the constant risk of losing you, but I won't deny what the Goddess has offered me. I accept you as my mate and will take you from this base where you can be held under guard until the genetic markers can be found."

"Excuse me?" I couldn't have possibly heard him right.

"You are not safe here. You're the top geneticist in your field, which means you are going to be the main target for anyone and everyone against the alliance between our races. You were already attacked once before getting here. I'm sending you back to Elysius where my brother can protect you until my return."

"You're serious?"

"Of course."

I rip my hand from his grasp and give him a glare that has never failed me over the years I've clawed my way up the career ladder.

"As you stated, I'm the top geneticist in my field, which is why the president asked me to head this first testing center, and I will not allow you or anyone else to place me in a corner, put me in a cage, and sit me on the sidelines. I am not a breeder, baby maker, or a compliant little housewife. So that's not happening."

He grabs my arm as I try to walk past him.

"It's for your own safety, Bree. I'm not trying to cage you. I'm trying to protect you."

I'm seeing red, his every word triggering old issues with my father.

I grab his large, clawed hand and throw it off my arm. He doesn't fight me, but the victory feels hollow.

"My name is Dr. Adams. You will address me as Dr. Adams. I went through a hell of a lot to earn that title, so show me a little respect, Ambassador. Furthermore, I am not leaving this facility, and if you think you're too inept to protect me, then I suggest you get someone else to do it."

His eyes flash and my heart leaps in my chest as he pulls me into his arms. "You think I can't protect you? No one can protect you better than me."

I hear the hurt in his words. I've no doubt emasculated him on an issue these males take a lot of pride in. Protecting your mate seems to be everything to them. Comforting to know, since I really wasn't so sure about Ada's many claims.

I slowly slide my hand against his chest and then move it higher. I lower my voice and lift onto my tiptoes. His hands automatically move to encompass my waist. And God help me, it feels amazing.

"Prove it," I say, appealing to the alpha in him, challenging him on a level I know he can't resist. I've successfully backed him into a corner of which there is no escape. "Protect me here while I help save your species. Unless you think you're not fit for the job."

Then I disengage from him, not even bothering to give him a backward glance as I open the door and sail out of the conference room.

My triumph is somewhat less awesome when the urge to go back to him nearly has me doubling over. What a shitty move, using his pull on me as I walk away.

This is gonna be a real problem.

SIX

Bree

"This is trippy, right? I'm not the only one who thinks so?" Micah asks.

"It is. It's absolutely insane." I tuck a strand of hair behind my ear, never breaking my gaze with Tarian. At the same time, it looks like he can't take his eyes off me as he stands in the hallway just outside the lab, looking through the windows at me as if he'd like to ravish me...or throttle me.

Can't say I hate either one of those options.

God, this is not good.

"I think it's romantic," Remy says, as she furiously types on her keyboard. Our computers are located within a larger cubicle that separates us from other cubicles on the east side of the lab.

"You would," Micah says, disgusted. "What is this, Bree?" He nods toward the warrior.

Tarian's stance instantly changes, puffing his chest out, ready to rush over here and start a fight with Micah. I can't help but chuckle.

"Seriously, I get the bonded mate thing, but you and I understand this is a biological response. There could be any number of women who would be genetically compatible." The idea of that hurts my heart a little, not that I'd ever admit it.

"Not according to these Elysiums. One bond mate. For life. Fate or something." Remy takes a sip of her water and gets back to her work.

I grimace at the lack of science behind that statement. There is an explanation for it, as DNA testing will no doubt reveal.

"I don't know what it is, but the ambassador has decided you are his, Bree. Dammit I was afraid of this happening." Micah's muscular arm is flexed as he grips the edge of the chair in front of him, never taking his eyes off Ambassador Koath.

"Hey," I say, snaring his attention. "I'm not leaving you and Remy. Ever. We're family and in this for life. I'm not leaving this planet to go make babies on another one. I can promise you that. Besides, he is head of security and overseeing the project on an upper management level. I won't have that much interaction with him."

I turn away, taking a step outside the cubicle and watching the other six scientists setting up their supplies. Dr. Sandoval was one of my top picks, but the other two guys were suggested by the president.

A scientist from Germany by the name of Dr. Meyer and another from India by the name of Dr. Devi.

I've done my research and know these two are top in their fields, but we'll need to establish a solid working rhythm with these guys since Remy, Micah, and I have always worked better on our own.

Time to learn how to expand the team a bit.

While we may have had one meeting already, this new one will be within the sealed walls of the lab. We're simply waiting for an all clear from Tarian and his crew before my team of scientists and the Elysium scientists get down to comparing notes and workshopping the issues.

They're all chatting and laughing happily with the rest of my staff. So this might actually work out really well.

"What if he tries to kidnap you and force you to be with him?"

"That would never happen," Dr. Jaran says as he approaches us. "Forgive me for eavesdropping, but I feel it necessary to interrupt. Elysium males, once bonded, are hardwired to protect and provide, but their sole interest is in the happiness of their female. The only thing that could possibly cause an Elysium male to do something contrary to their mate's wishes is if their mate is in danger..."

I give him a pointed look, and he swallows hard. "Oh, I see. Yes, I'm afraid if the ambassador feels that it is impossible to keep you safe in this area, he will insist on removing you."

"Dammit to hell," Micah mutters.

"Dr. Jaran, I suggest we gather the scientists together so we'll be ready to discuss first steps here," I say pointedly.

His wry smile is filled with good humor as he gives Micah a sympathetic look. "A wise idea."

As the scientists take their seats at the table in the center of the lab, Ambassador Koath and his crew finally enter. I turn to him with a raised brow, a silent question in my gaze.

His curt nod is all I need to know the area is secure.

I head to the table and take a seat giving everyone a pleasant smile.

"I think the first place to start is in understanding the reaction in Elysium males when they are in the presence of their bond mate," I say. "Dr. Jaran, what can you tell me about this phenomenon?"

He clears his throat. "Most of what we know about bond mates comes from our own religious beliefs of fate and mating. What I can tell you is bond mates have never been studied as a science on our planet because it is widely known to be what your kind would refer to as supernatural in nature."

I try not to show my astonishment, but I'm pretty sure my eyebrows are at my hairline. I take a moment to get my thoughts in order before something snarky leaves my lips.

"Do you mean to tell me that even as a scientist you believe the bond mates are determined by fate and not by biological factors?"

"That's what I'm saying, Dr. Adams. There is only one individual capable of opening their aura up and bonding with another aura."

"Auras." I pause again, realizing I should have spent a lot more time studying their religious beliefs. "Dr. Jaran, please don't be offended, but auras have nothing to do with genetic compatibility."

His smile is broad as he says, "Well, I suspect you're about to find out they do. Everything has matter of some form or another. Auras are forms of spiritual energy filled with matter completely invisible to the naked eye. It's nothing we've ever truly studied because it is simply something that has always existed in our species. We never considered looking at it as what you refer to as genetics because the only species we thought we were compatible with was our own."

"So we're starting from square one," Micah says.

"Not necessarily." Dr. Jaran picks up a laser-pointer, aims it at the whiteboard across from us and projects the skeletal and internal organs of an Elysium male. "Interestingly enough, our genetic make-up is remarkably similar—99.9% similar, in fact. Similar chromosomal structures, base pairs, and so forth. I suspect DNA sequencing for both races would be a good place to start."

"I think it would be a good idea to not only do some gene sequencing on Dr. Ada Charles and her mate's blood samples, but it wouldn't hurt to get samples from myself and Ambassador Koath for sequencing and comparison," I say.

"Agreed," Micah says, albeit reluctantly. "The more mate samples we have to work with, the more we can assess possible mutations within the genes themselves. Anomalies. We may even be dealing with minuscule parts of a dormant gene somehow being activated for reasons unknown and playing a role in this."

It's a good theory, and definitely something I've taken into consideration.

"First steps, then. Blood samples and sequencing. It's going to take anywhere from a week to two weeks to get mine and Dr. Charles' results. I'm unclear as to how long it will take to sequence an Elysium genome. I'm not even clear as to how it is structured or if the compounds and proteins are similar although they must be in some way due to compatibility. We have a lot of work ahead of us. Let's get on this immediately."

The words are met with a flurry of activity. I stand, but before I have time to approach Tarian, he's already next to me, his hand at my lower back.

"I'm happy to give you any fluids you may need," he says in a low voice.

How the hell did he turn that into an innuendo?

I narrow my gaze at him. His innocent smile isn't fooling anyone.

"Follow me," I say. "I'll have Micah take our blood."

"Not him," Tarian says tersely. I note his nostrils flaring as his horns do something weird, fluctuating agitatedly.

"Forgive me, Ambassador, but I don't have time for diplomacy at the moment, and honestly, I'm beyond pissed at you." I move away from him and head to my desk. I can hear his crew chuckling from the sidelines, but I ignore them. "Micah is my family and my best friend, so he is taking my blood, and I will take yours."

"That human is not laying a hand on you," he growls, drawing attention from the rest of the occupants in the lab.

I grab his arm and pull him aside. "Look, you need to get this possessive shit under control. I understand it, but it can't interfere with my job or your concentration. Micah has been a part of my life for years, and I trust him with my life, so you will stand there and watch as he draws blood from my arm, and you will do it without attacking him."

He takes a step forward and glares down at me. "You do realize I'm the one overseeing this project, and I'm not accustomed to taking orders from anyone."

I don't back down. "You may oversee this, but you don't get to micromanage it. This is my job. Let me do it. If you can't control yourself, then maybe one of your crew members should relieve you of your post."

I give Dywrr a smile, noting his broad grin. It's obvious the ambassador and I are offering up some wonderful entertainment for the crew.

He growls low in his throat, making me very aware of his disapproval.

"And I think we better be clear on another issue," I say. "I'm very much accustomed to throwing orders around, and I won't hesitate to boss the hell out of you if you need it. Sure you still want me as your bond mate?"

His slow smirk does something completely criminal to my insides. "More than ever. Do you have any idea how much your defiance turns me on? I think I want you even more than I did in the other room."

"Ambassador—"

"Tarian. You call me Tarian from now on, and I'll be a good little warrior and watch as another male draws blood from my bond mate."

I sigh and glare daggers at him. "A little melodramatic, but I'll take it."

"And what do I get to call you?"

"Dr. Adams," I say.

Soft chuckles from Tarian's crew follow me as I head toward Micah who already has his supplies ready. He smiles at me before shooting Tarian a glower.

As Tarian follows, he gets his own digs in.

"I think it best we get along, Dr. Adams, especially since I've been assigned to be your personal bodyguard."

I spin around on that one, nearly getting jabbed by Micah's ready needle.

"Excuse me? Aren't you the one who makes those assignments?"

"That is correct."

"Then change it. Any one of your crew members can be my bodyguard on base."

The thought of having Tarian as my personal bodyguard all day long is my worst nightmare. How the hell will I concentrate?

How the hell will I avoid him long enough to clear my head and think straight?

"Unfortunately, as you stated before, you are our top geneticist, and that means you need our top warrior for the job."

"And you've dubbed yourself top warrior, I presume?"

His grin is infuriating. "I have."

"How very male of you."

I turn to face Micah who looks about as amused as I feel.

God, this is going to be a long day.

Tarian

GODDESS, BUT THIS HAS BEEN A LONG DAY. ONE OF THE WORST days of my existence. I stare at Bodeth as he goes over a few more security plans, detailed evacuation strategies, and anything else we might need should this place come under attack.

And all I can focus on is Dr. Bree Adams and her sexy defiance. Did I think she wasn't like Ada when it came to the mate bond?

She's far worse.

I swipe at my horns, now curled into place thanks to the lack of Bree's presence, but they burn and ache with the pent up pressure of no release. If I don't take my mate soon, I'm going to lose my mind.

Was it like this for Kyllell?

How did he stand it?

I'm suddenly feeling some heavy remorse for the pain and suffering I must have caused him when I stole Ada out from under him and took her back to Elysius...with a crew of three other very sex deprived, aggressive males.

I'm amazed my brother didn't kill me outright.

"He's not listening," Bodeth says, smacking me across the face.

I snarl in response before coming back to myself.

"Of course I'm listening. I've heard every mind-numbing plan you three have presented."

Bodeth sends me a smirk as he leans back in his chair.

"Oh yeah? Then why did you just agree to Dywrr being in charge of leading Dr. Adams to the helipad in case of a fire, intruder breach, or explosion?"

I sigh in defeat, knowing I never would have agreed to that if I had been paying attention.

The smaller security room we sit in is halved with security detail sitting in front of monitors, screening personnel coming and going within the base as well as without. I find the systems primitive, and we've put forth plans to improve the technology over the next few days, but my more primal instincts are demanding that I return to Bree's side and watch her every move.

She's already been attacked once. What if it happens again?

I feel that old panic rise within my chest and tamp it down as Dywrr goes over a third option for safely evacuating the scientists from the base.

"I'm calling it a night," I interrupt.

"Thank the Goddess," Bodeth mutters. "You're awful to be around right now. Go find your female and mate with her as soon as possible."

As if it were that simple. "Bodeth, these human females are not like our females once were—or other species of female. They are stubborn, willful, and strong enough to fight off our pull."

This would never have been a problem with a Varlock female.

So easy to entice.

Now the very thought of touching another female is repugnant.

"She's your bond mate," he says, placing a hand on my shoulder. His sympathetic expression is one I'm not used to. I find it unnerving. "And that Micah guy keeps sniffing around her."

"I will challenge him when the time is right." Something about him is off. When he speaks, I smell a lie. Something he isn't saying. Something he withholds from Bree.

"He certainly smells funny." Dywrr wrinkles his snout.

"You noticed it too? I can't pinpoint it, other than it's similar to the pheromones given off when one is dishonest."

Dywrr smiles, showing a mouth full of sharp, intimidating teeth. "We'll have to find out what he's lying about."

"My mate's life depends on it."

I'm sure of it.

I sense Laoth and Bodeth's eyes on me. "What?"

They nod at Dywrr, encouraging him to speak. Dywrr grunts, appearing agitated, but he turns his attention back to me. I don't like it.

"I know you wanted to avoid this because of what you lost when—"

"Enough," I hiss, preventing any other expressions of sympathy. "Have you three had your blood taken for testing yet?"

The subject change does exactly what I want it to. It leaves them on the defensive, quickly latching on to something other than my flailing insecurities where Bree is concerned.

"Dr. Jaran took care of that," Bodezh says. "For better or worse, we're part of this experiment now."

"Great. I think we all need to get some sleep. We'll meet back here tomorrow morning to firm up our security detail."

"You'll be a constant bodyguard to Dr. Adams?" Dywrr asks.

"Of course."

"Does she know that?"

"She knows."

"How did that go over?" Dywrr already knows the answer to that question.

"Exactly as expected."

I could do without their knowing smiles. When did my crew become so insufferable?

"Then I suggest you go check on her now. You know. Under the pretense of going through her room and *securing* the area."

My lips twitch at his brilliant plan.

It lacks subtlety, but that's Dywrr for you. And something tells me Bree will see right through me either way.

SEVEN

Bree

I groan, feeling a migraine coming on and knowing if I don't hit the lights and get prone in a few minutes, I'm going to have to take my meds, and I really need to be alert for tomorrow.

While the sequencing is well on its way, I spent a great deal of time with Dr. Jaran, learning more of his species' biology and mating processes. All the while, Tarian had stared at me from the sidelines, occasionally increasing the gigawatts of his pull on me, as if waiting for a chink in my defenses.

What exactly is he expecting me to do should he succeed?

Like I'm going to fling myself into his arms in front of the other scientists. What bothers me is that there were many times I nearly did just that.

I'm in my pajamas, ready to crawl into bed for the night, when I hear a knock at the door.

Shit.

I just want to sleep.

I need to sleep.

Migraine on the way.

I rush to the door, hoping to deal with whoever is behind it as quickly as I possibly can.

Flinging it open, I see Micah standing in front of me, a mug of something that smells suspiciously of cider in one hand and a plate of donuts in the other.

"Room service." His wide smile disappears as he gets one good look at me. "Shit, Bree, why the hell haven't you taken your meds?"

He pushes past me and sets his offering on my night stand.

"You know, Micah, you have been swearing an awful lot lately. Are you okay?"

He stares at me like I've lost my ability to code.

"Bree, we were nearly killed two days ago, you've been labeled as a bond mate to an alien ambassador, and we're on a private base guarded by the military, hoping to solve the DNA question of the century and match up bond mates between Elysiums and humans. Are you seriously asking me why my language has become more colorful?"

"Are you going to eat that donut?" I ask, pointing to the chocolate one covered in sprinkles.

"It's all yours. Now where the hell is your medicine?"

I point to the duffel bag on the floor next to my bed as I reach the night stand and snatch up my treat.

"How do you always ... know ..." I swallow my bite so I can get my question out.

"When you're moments away from a bad one?" Micah grabs my meds from the bag and screws them open, dumping a pill into my hand and giving me the thermos. "Your eyes get a little funny and you start to talk slowly. Like you're pulling words out of thin air with no ability to determine if they even fit into the sentence. You also squint like crazy."

"Hmm. I guess I never really thought about it." I quickly swallow the pill even though I know it will make me sluggish tomorrow. I sit on my bed as Micah flips the lamp on and turns off the light.

Then he does something completely weird. He stands in front of me and starts massaging my temples.

Not that I mind. It feels hellah good, almost keeping the pounding at bay, but Micah usually just hands me the meds and makes sure I land in one of the overnight beds at our lab. He's never done *this* before.

While his hands are nice and cool, I can't help but think about a certain ambassador whose touch I've been longing for all day.

Entirely against my will.

And as if thoughts of him have summoned his very presence, I hear a low growl before Micah yelps and is shoved against the wall.

Tarian stalks toward him, his fists raised.

Surprisingly, Micah doesn't back down, a snarl of his own in place.

"Hey," I say, jumping off the bed and grabbing Tarian's arm, tugging as hard as I can. "Tarian, you gotta stop."

But it's like he can't hear me, and I realize he's gone into that weird mate mode he was in during our initial meeting. Since they protect their mates, I decide to get in the line of fire and insert myself in front of Micah just as Tarian throws a punch.

His fist stops a mere inch from mine and he jerks back abruptly.

"What in the name of Elysarah are you doing?" he yells. "I could have killed you." The look of horror on his face is funny. It's all just so damn funny.

"I'm trying to get you to snap out of whatever this is," I say, waving at him. "You can't attack Micah."

"He was molesting you."

"He was helping me."

"He was touching what doesn't belong to him," he snarls.

"She doesn't belong to you, either." Micah growls as he steps up behind me, but I lean back, pushing him away.

"That is enough," I yell. The noise and the stress are not helping me. A sharp pain lances through my skull, the migraine gaining ground due to my elevated heart rate and adrenaline.

I grab my head and wince as my peripheral vision darkens.

"Shit, Bree, did we not get on top of it in time?" Micah asks, grabbing my arm to steady me.

"No," I say.

I feel Tarian's hand on my other arm. "What is happening? Didn't do what in time?"

They both help me to the bed as Micah explains my condition.

"Bree gets migraines when she is sleep-deprived or stressed out of her damned mind, and I'm thinking the events of the last few days have played a role in that."

"And what were you doing to help this?" Tarian asks.

"Rubbing her temples. Trying to push on different pressure points so the migraine doesn't get worse."

Tarian's voice rumbles low with pent up fury. "You should not be touching her."

"Not this again," I say in distress, feeling the urge to vomit. "If you're going to throw your dicks around, do it outside my quarters. Your voices hurt my head."

"Your meds aren't going to be enough, Bree. I'm getting the good stuff."

"Micah, don't you dare. I'll be out for a day if you do."

But he's already gone. "Shithead."

Tarian kneels before me and takes my head in his hands, giving me a worried look. "You are in pain. What do I do?"

"There's nothing you *can* do. Micah is going to get my emergency meds to help me sleep, and then I will just have to sleep through it." I take a deep breath to hold back my nausea. "Did you come here for a reason, Tarian?"

He looks a little uncomfortable before saying, "I wanted to check to make sure your room is secure."

"Thanks. I think I'm covered. There are guards at both ends of the hallway. Have a nice night."

The spikes of pain are now a constant, and the pounding in my brain feels heavier and more painful with each moment that passes. Breathing hurts. Everything hurts.

"I'm not leaving you. It is physically impossible for me to do so when you are in pain."

I let out a groan and slump onto the bed, but the nausea doesn't abate. After a few moments, I feel Tarian's thick fingers press against my temples, but his claws aren't there. Retracted? Do they retract?

His cool touch as he rubs soft circles along my temples begins to have an effect on my nausea. The scratchy, leathery feel of his skin is actually soothing, slowly getting the pain under control. His fingers slide to the base of my skull before pushing on different points, unknotting areas that I hadn't been aware were tight and further alleviating the pain in my head.

Within moments my migraine has subsided and my nausea is gone. My eyes flutter open only to see his face inches from mine.

"Better?" he asks, his voice still laced with concern.

"How did you do that?"

"My brother used to get tension headaches all the time. I'm well-versed in massaging them away."

I blink a few times in disbelief. "Yes, but migraines are a different story. They aren't tension headaches. They are huge problems for me, and I've never had anyone capable of simply massaging them away. I have to take awful medications to get them under control."

"Well, you don't have to anymore. Now that I'm here."

"Now that you're here," I repeat stupidly.

I stare into his eyes, filled with kindness, admiration even, not taking advantage of my obvious weakness or even taking the opportunity to hint that I might not be up for the job. Tarian just saw one of the things I've hated most about myself for a while now, a chink in my armor, and thought nothing of it.

Instead, he just labeled it a tension headache, easily fixed now that he was here to help me.

I'm so floored by this, I don't know how to respond. How to process. In a world where Micah is the only man to not take advantage of my weaknesses, I'm not sure what to do about this.

"Thank you for getting rid of my migraine," I say.

He scoots me over and sits next to me, placing a hand on my shoulder. His gaze is deadly serious when he says, "It's my honor to help you, especially if helping you can also get rid of your pain."

I nod, suddenly feeling a little choked up. His eyes ensnare mine, and that damn pull of his feels more potent than normal. Just when I think I'll spontaneously combust if I don't follow my instincts, Micah comes running back in with meds in hand.

He stops abruptly when I turn to look at him. His eyes go from me to Tarian and back again. Then they widen in disbelief. "It's gone. Your symptoms are all gone, aren't they?"

I nod, slowly sitting up. Tarian gives me space, but not much considering he is now sitting next to me on my bed.

"Tarian seems to have some weird powers when it comes to getting rid of migraines. I don't think I'll be needing those meds after all."

Micah sags in relief. Then he looks at Tarian. "Look, I don't like you one bit. You're a pretentious ass who thinks he can order my best friend around and destroy her career."

"Micah—"

Tarian cuts me off with a snarl, but Micah raises his hand in a placating gesture.

"However, if you can protect our girl here and also get rid of her pain, then I'll try to hate you a little less. Drunk and high Bree is hilarious, but she ain't getting shit done in that condition, and I don't like her hurting."

Tarian nods. "Well, that makes two of us."

Micah and Tarian size each other up for another moment while I try to figure out what the hell kind of weird male conversation is silently passing between them. Then my best friend smiles and says, "Okay, I'll give you two some privacy. See you in the morning, Bree."

Then he walks out like it isn't a big deal that a big Elysium male is in my room.

In my bed.

"Well, that was interesting," I say. "You guys somehow become buddies during that silent communication?"

"I wouldn't go that far." He turns to me. His horns have calmed a bit, although they are just as black as they have ever been since the moment he laid eyes on me. It must be pretty uncomfortable.

"Does it hurt? Your horns?" I lift my hand to touch one. Tarian wraps his clawed fingers around my wrist before I succeed in satisfying my curiosity. His touch is warm and sends an electrical jolt down my arm.

"Our horns are very sensitive, especially when we've found our bond mate. If you touch me there, I won't be responsible for what happens next."

I'm spellbound as I stare into his eyes. His thumb rubs the inside of my wrist. I swallow hard before asking, "What *would* happen next?"

He suddenly releases my wrist and pulls me in, securing his arms around me, forcing me closer until my lips are inches from his. This is an unfortunate position I've found myself in. Resisting his pull in front of a group of scientists was no picnic. Resisting him here, with zero space between us and no audience?

My thoughts take on pinpoint precision, which is weird for me. I'm generally the type to have a million thoughts racing through my head. Checklists, plans, analysis, not to mention my incessant future tripping about things I can't control. It's like the noise in my head can't find an outlet or an antidote, so it resorts to migraines to cope.

I know scientifically that isn't the real cause, but I've always felt like it is. Yet in Tarian's presence, there's no pain and no noise. There's just him. One thought.

Him.

Tarian.

"You want to know what *would* happen next?" He slowly leans in and then stops just before his lips touch mine.

His smell is something I can't describe, but whatever the hell it is, it's definitely got pheromones that are uniquely him, and they've completely immobilized me.

I know I should put a stop to this, but after the week I've had, not to mention the constant battle of wills with this alien, I'm not really up for any kind of battle of wills. I am quite literally putty in this warrior's hands.

And he knows it.

"Bree?"

God, the way he says my name.

"Yes," I say, feeling his breath on my lips. "I want to know what would happen next."

"Thank the Goddess," he whispers. Then he closes the distance between us and takes my lips in his with a fervor that curls my toes, leaves my arms and legs limp, and completely pulverizes that solid wall around my heart.

And I don't even care. Not when his kiss is something I recognize as an absolute necessity in my life. As essential as oxygen and water. A flood of warmth rushes through me as I kiss him back, wrapping my arms around his broad shoulders, but not quite managing the breadth of them.

He deepens the kiss, letting out a possessive growl as his tongue deftly explores mine, dipping and dancing in a hypnotic way. Then he plunges his tongue deep, and I imagine his cock exploring me in the exact same way. The thought draws out a low moan from me, and he tightens his hold, giving me one last mouthwatering stroke before abruptly pulling back and letting out an unhappy growl.

We're both breathing heavily. My thoughts are fuzzy and my mouth just wants to explore his, but I manage to ask, "Why…did you…stop?"

"Bree, if I keep going, I will mate you. I won't be able to hold back, and I don't know that you're ready for it."

I swallow hard, taking that in. "And our auras would…?"

"Join. Connect. I don't know how to describe it properly since it has never happened to me, but my brother says it is indescribable either way. Beyond anything he could have ever hoped for with Ada."

I smile, thinking about the logistics of shared auras, my brain whirring again with the possibilities and scientific implications. Another mystery for another day. I'm not ready for that level of commitment. I'm not ready for a lot of things. But I'm also not ready for him to leave.

"You're right. That's not something I want to pursue. I know the importance of a bond mate, but I didn't bargain for this, Tarian. I'm truly sorry about that."

"I'm not deterred in any way."

"Why?"

"I don't plan on leaving you alone. I'll wear you down, eventually." He gives me a smirk that I find adorable.

"You've given your plan away, and now I know how to fight it. I can outlast the best of them."

He leans in closer. "Not me, Bree. You'll never outlast me."

That promise is more than loaded, and now I'm back to lusty thoughts and feelings when I've already voiced several times over why a relationship with him is not happening.

It just can't happen.

But that doesn't mean I'm not immune to his presence or feeling damn weak at the moment. I heave an internal sigh. Why not enjoy his company for the night? Just for the night?

"Will you hold me while I sleep?" I ask, surprising myself.

I must surprise him, too, because he's speechless for a few seconds. Then he quickly flashes me a cocky smile. "My kiss was that good, huh? Just can't get enough of me."

"Or maybe," I say, leaning closer until our lips are almost touching, "I know you'll just stand outside my door to keep watch over me, which means you'll get zero sleep tonight. What good is a bodyguard if he isn't sleeping?"

"Elysium males can go a long time without sleep," he says, but he's back to staring at my lips again. He rests his forehead against mine and blows out a frustrated breath. It smells like cinnamon. Or maybe he just smells so good because I'm biologically predispositioned to be drawn to everything about him. "I'm not used to this. This driving need to possess someone completely. It's distracting."

I feel somewhat vindicated that he's been just as tormented as I have all week.

"I would love to hold you in my arms while you sleep, Bree."

"Okay."

I slide under the covers as Tarian spoons me from behind. The moment his arms encircle me, my eyes get heavy.

"Sleep, Bree," he says, placing a kiss on my temple. "You're going to need your rest. I've got a feeling the next few days and weeks are going to be challenging for us."

Not even that warning helps me fight the pull of sleep. Not when I'm in Tarian's arms.

Which means I am in big trouble here.

Finishing my general morning routine, which is usually pretty limited—I am not much of a primper—I check my cell. Staying off the phone in the earlier mornings is important to me. Making sure that I've got everything sorted before the crazy starts is essential for my sanity, but my thoughts still whizz around Tarian, so my phone's screen isn't something I can really focus on.

He wasn't next to me when I woke up this morning, and I can't tell if I'm relieved or annoyed. Would facing him right after that night of vulnerability have been too much for me? Was he trying to spare me the awkwardness of it all?

I get the feeling he left because he knows me that well, and I find it disconcerting.

"Are you going to think about him all day, or are you going to go out there and get your shit done?" I mutter to myself.

A part of me wants to stay in bed with a tub of ice cream and just hide from reality. A reality I keep compartmentalizing and placing in a box labeled denial. I've never fawned over men. Every inch of ground I've walked, I've walked alone. No help from my father and his old-world values, so why change that now? Especially over someone who has traveled the stars and probably has some kind of space herpes.

I snort at my idiocy.

"Stop lying to yourself," I say as I stare at the small round mirror against the wall. My concerns about Tarian center around his need to protect and dominate. It doesn't pair well with my need to maintain my independence. My need to choose. My express wish to pave my own way. I don't like this irrational mate-bond scenario that gives couples zero choice in the matter.

And I hate how much I enjoyed kissing him last night.

There's nothing more terrifying in this universe than need because that driving need for something or someone can get the best of you, overrun all logical thought, and leave you open to actions and reactions completely foreign.

Completely out of control.

"What are you even doing?" I fall onto my bed, holding the phone in my hands.

A small light in the top right corner blinks green, indicating I have a message.

"So, your migraine was just gone," Micah says without preamble.

I chuckle, listening to his voice. He never wastes his words. It's not his style.

"I think we'll need to study that phenomenon in the near future," his message continues, a hint of amusement lacing his words. "It would be interesting to note if this mate bond is capable of healing ailments other than migraines. What's causing that? Magnetic fields? Energetic properties? Because I've never seen anything other than meds fix your migraines."

The message pauses for a moment, and I can picture Micah wrinkling his brows, deep in thought. "We'll figure it out, but it's good to know, either way."

The message ends. Weirdly enough, I get the sense that Micah is disappointed, and I wonder if he thinks I'm leaving him for planet Elysius when this is all said and done. When our job here is "complete."

The answer to that?

Not a chance.

Tarian will probably see it differently. A challenge for another week. As I open my door, I set boundaries for the day. No looking at Tarian for more than five seconds at a time. No conversing with Tarian unless absolutely necessary.

No kissing Tarian.

Because that left me loopy. I need to focus, dammit.

My mental pep talk is interrupted by a large Elysium's rock hard chest as I inadvertently walk right into it.

"Sorry, Dr. Adams," Dywrr says, righting me with a chuckle.

"No problem." I peer around his broad shoulders and notice Laoth is in the hallway as well. An interesting guy. He never says much. Not that I've had much time to observe him. "What are you two doing here?"

"Tarian asked that we watch over you and then accompany you to the lab."

"Ah," I say, hating the monitoring but recognizing that it has more to do with my own issues. "I thought Tarian had assigned himself as my personal bodyguard. Gave up on me already, did he?"

Dywrr gives me a knowing smile. "You sound disappointed, Doctor. Do you miss your mate's presence?"

The comment rankles when it shouldn't...because he's spot on, and I'm irritated as hell by that. I try brushing that comment aside, but I'm more concerned that it bothered me in the first place or that Dywrr is actually right.

I miss Tarian.

How inconvenient.

"I'll survive the separation." I give him my resting bitch face. Micah says it's scary. Doesn't seem to have much effect on Dywrr since his grin takes over all the real estate on his dark-green face.

Smug bastard.

I honestly hate having a bodyguard of any kind. It just reminds me of a prison. Being placed in a gilded cage very similar to the one my father placed my mother in. The one he wanted to place me in.

Logically, I know I need protection. I haven't forgotten the chaotic way in which Micah and I fled. My thoughts jump to the helicopter ride, a blurry haze surrounding those memories. Something about those last few moments before the drugs kicked in pick at me. An issue that needs to be analyzed.

I do this whenever something eludes me. Some discovery, some answer, a massive revelation at play, but I know myself. If I think about it too much, try to dredge up the answers, or force the epiphany then I'll get nothing.

"You okay?" Dywrr asks.

I stare into his bright golden eyes, a slightly different color from Tarian's, although I've noticed that all Elysium males have some variation of yellow, orange, and gold. Different shades of sunsets and sunrises. His slitted pupils narrow in on me with concern, and I realize I've been staring and thinking like a moron, something my therapist describes as hyperfocus. It's a pain in the ass when I do this since social cues are not my strong suit sometimes.

"Fine, Dywrr," I say, deciding to shoot for honesty. "I was just comparing your eye color to Tarian's and wondering about Elysium male traits. Does anyone on your planet have eye color similar to humans?"

His scaled brow raises in amusement, then his expression becomes troubled. "Our females," he said. "Our females had variations of blue and purple eye color.'

My brain zeroes in on his gender specific comment. "That's fascinating. Eye color is strictly tied to gender-based genes? How is that possible?"

"You're the genetic scientist, Doctor. I'll leave those discoveries up to you."

I shake my head and walk past him and Laoth. I sense them behind me as I navigate the twists and turns of the facility. Today's task involves transferring all pertinent data from Tarian's ship, including multiple samples of Elysium males as well as samples from his brother and Dr. Ada Charles.

As we round the corner and approach the lab, Dywrr reaches my side.

"A word of advice, Dr. Adams."

"Yes?" I stop walking and face him, giving him my full attention.

"He's been alone for a while."

I try to figure out what he's talking about when I realize he's referring to Tarian.

"I don't understand—"

"He wasn't expecting you, and he's been alone for some time. He will be fiercely protective and act like a stubborn *gorgrineck*. There will be moments of unreason. Just try to be patient with him."

I have no idea what a *gorgrineck* is, but I gather from context we're not talking about a gnat here.

"Moments of unreason meaning he's going to be confrontational, overbearing, and an overall pain in my ass?"

Dywrr smiles. "Among other things.'

"Just fabulous."

I head for the lab again as I hear Laoth and Dywrr laughing behind me.

Tarian is not the only pain in my ass.

I go over the goals again, locking them in, bigger picture included, trying to snuff out the image of Tarian's full lips from my mind. But I can't seem to do it.

Sure, it was nice to sleep with someone by my side.

Sure, it had been a bit of a relief to let Tarian take charge and care for me in those few moments. Not bad at all, really.

So maybe there is something to be said for having someone in your life who you can depend on.

Of course, I have Micah, and there's no need to complicate things with romance. The minute you take it to that level? That's when a guy thinks he owns you.

But maybe things would be different with Tarian.

I ignore that traitorous voice in my head telling me I ought to let down my guard and give someone a try. That voice isn't taking into consideration Elysium culture, their protective natures, their possessiveness, their domineering behavior toward their mates.

That voice isn't remembering Tarian's initial decision to take me off the project and away from the base.

That voice is stupid.

Focus, Bree.

Uncovering the science behind the mate bond between Ada and Kyllell—the only officially mated interspecies couple that we know of—is all I can think about. Fine, it's all I *should* think about. The sooner we find the key to that, the sooner I can get away from Tarian. We find the key to that, we make the whole of Elysius our allies and receive permanent protection against the Chassaks.

I think about Tarian and admit that having two samples of "officially mated" couples would be a bigger, better pool to study from, but I'm not about to share auras or interrupt magnetic fields or whatever the hell it is that happens when a mate bond is created. I'm confident that my abilities as a scientist will make short work of this mysterious genetic compatibility that determines one specific human female meant for one specific Elysium male.

Although, it wouldn't surprise me if I discover their little soulmate scenario is bogus, and the only reason they believe in it to begin with is because not a single couple on Elysius ever continued to date anyone else after a male's horns burned black.

What if multiple Elysium males had black horns for one female?

Fascinating thought.

I can't help the small smile that tugs at my lips. I might just turn their entire belief system on its head and cause an intergalactic mind fuck.

The thought absolutely delights me.

EIGHT

Tarian

T arian," Dywrr says, stepping into my quarters.

I've just ended a transmission with Ada, and as I feared, my brother is being about as subtle as a *rurkshas* when dealing with the Council. It's cause for irritation. Now I'm watching a human transmission.

Primitive.

"What do you make of this, Dywrr?" I ask, pointing to the flat screen along the wall. He stands next to me and observes the humans on the screen as a human narrator discusses the current events occurring at a place called The White House.

The house is indeed white, but if this is their headquarters, why not pick a more ferocious name?

Human protesters with large signs bearing inscrutable scribblings repeat the same words over and over again.

"God smites the devil. The devil will be destroyed. God smites the devil. The devil will be destroyed."

They stand in large groups chanting things over and over again, spitting at security detail as if their saliva is as poisonous as the serpents on *Tarigua*.

The leader of the group stands on a podium, holding something that amplifies his voice.

"Get the hell out of here," he shouts. "There's no place for your kind here. Leave our women alone."

Dywrr chuckles under his breath. "Looks like human males are a bit intimidated by our impressive...physique. Afraid they won't make the cut. We do have bigger cocks."

I grunt in agreement. "We have bigger everything, but the intimidation factor aside, these protestors think we're actually demons. Devils or unholy creatures. Evil. Ada explained the religious structures, myths, and odd belief systems within this world. Apparently, we look like something that would drag their souls to hell."

"I don't even know what that means. What is hell?"

"A place of eternal burning where you are tormented and punished for your sins. Or maybe it's a place of outer darkness. Their religious beliefs differ."

"Outer darkness?" Dywrr considers this for a moment. "That actually sounds nice. A total break from sensory overload."

Watching the antics of these humans further reminds me of how fragile my own human is.

I must protect her.

Not just from the Chassaks, but from any human intent on stopping her from accomplishing what I know she is fully capable of accomplishing.

I wish she wasn't.

I want her off this project. Off this base. Safely deposited on my ship where no one can touch her. I'd build an entire fortress around my mate if I thought it would keep her safe. Somehow, I must find a way to do that.

"Where is Bree?" I ask, unhappy that my warrior isn't by her side.

"Safely deposited in her lab with the rest of the team, including our battle-hardened scientists. She's safe, Tarian. You don't need to worry about her."

I laugh in disbelief. Until his horns burn black for his future mate, he'll never know the fallacy in that statement. I will forever worry about Bree.

I'm hardwired to do so, and past history with other females has shown me how quickly those in my care can be ripped from me.

"This is nothing like *her*," Dywrr says, sensing my thoughts. "You know this is different."

"The stakes certainly are."

If I lose Bree, I lose everything because nothing in my life will hold meaning without her, and this absolute certainty of my desperate need for her is nothing short of terrifying.

Not that it was going to stop me from pursuing her further.

While I didn't seek this out and certainly didn't want to find a bond mate this early on, I'm more upset that my female doesn't come to me willingly.

She fights my pull as if it's nothing. She's capable of actually walking away from me when I'm in her presence, with seemingly zero strain.

Which is unbelievable and bruises my admittedly enormous ego.

That it took an episode of severe pain for her to allow me access when she'd originally turned to Micah?

As Ada would say, fucking unacceptable.

As is her dependence on this Micah character.

"What do you think about Dr. Micah Scott?" I ask.

Dywrr's knowing expression causes a purple haze of battle lust to sweep my vision. I take two deep breaths and shove it away.

Barely.

"I think he's fiercely loyal to Bree. Dr. Scott has worked with your mate for several years. As far as I can tell, they've been...let's see...what's the term I heard Ada use when referring to you...? Ah, yes. Besties."

I narrow my brows, annoyed by the ridiculous term of endearment assigned to Micah when Ada's using it has never bothered me.

"I want a detailed security check. Full background. Birth. Who are his parents? Where did he attend school? How did he and Bree meet?"

"We already have that information from–"

"The United States government," I say. "No. We're doing *our own* check. I want to know absolutely everything about this male. His associates. His connections. What was he doing and where was he living before he met Bree? And why does he always smell like deceit?"

There is definitely something off about Micah, although I can't pinpoint what it is that has my internal alarm triggering on repeat.

But if I can prove that he's a security breach, then maybe I can get clearance to take Bree somewhere safe.

Not that I need clearance. At the end of the day, if my mate is in danger, I will not be catering to the US government's need for protection from the Chassaks.

I protect my own.

"You really think Dr. Scott is a danger to your mate?" Dywrr studies me, no doubt wondering about my mental state. "Or is this a personal vendetta due to their shared history?"

"I want Bree off this project. If Micah proves to be a risk, then I have leverage."

Dywrr lets out a low whistle, his brow ridges raised. "I haven't spent much time in your mate's presence, but she's headstrong, independent, determined, and capable. She is no weeping female. She is not going to appreciate your interference. Not in her work and not in her personal relationships."

"Too bad."

"Careful, Tarian. You walk a fine line here when you mistake control for protection."

I think about that but immediately dismiss his words. I can't lose any more females in my life. I won't.

"Besides," he says, "what if Dr. Scott is another layer of protection for her?"

"I think he loves her." The words taste like the worst kind of strong drink as they leave my lips. "And if I were him, I'd go to whatever lengths possible to keep her from me."

"And that makes him dangerous?"

"In my mind? Very."

Bree

MY SCIENTISTS—HUMAN AND ALIEN—ARE SEATED AROUND A large table within a room surrounded by windows, the lab just adjacent to us for easy access. My staff and I are getting a crash course in Elysium DNA, and I'm both excited and worried. If we didn't have so much riding on insta-answers while right-wing extremists tried to thwart us, I'd enjoy taking my time studying their genetics. Complications, combined with pressure and a deadline, are not my favorite work conditions.

But I'm comfortably sandwiched between my favorite team members, and I know Remy and Micah are going to be key in moving our progress forward.

My excitement doesn't permeate the room. Everyone else, including the aliens, are nursing coffee mugs and rubbing their faces in an attempt to wake the hell up. Micah has always said my morning perkiness is in no way normal.

Even Remy is looking worse for wear. Her expression shows signs of strain. I lean over and touch her arm during a lull in the conversation. She jerks from her thoughts, startled.

"Remy, what's going on?"

She bites her lip, her face paling for a moment. "It's my boy. We got the latest results from his oncologist."

"Shit," I say, realizing the results weren't good. "We'll talk to Tarian about it. The Elysiums have advanced medicine, Remy. I'm sure they could help."

Her expression lightens for a moment. "You think?"

"Why don't you speak with Tarian after our meeting? I'm sure he could offer assistance."

She blinks back the moisture in her eyes. "You're right."

I want to offer her more reassurance but we've got to get moving on our agenda. My heart hurts, though. Her son's cancer was in remission. And getting him to that point had been a hellish battle no parent should ever go through.

"I've found it fascinating that humans share 99.9 percent of their DNA base sequence. Elysium DNA shares the same percentage between gene variation," Dr. Jaran says. "However, the difference in DNA base sequencing between humans and Elysiums is 2.6 percent, and I'm sure you realize how astounding it is that we would find mate compatibility among us considering those numbers."

I nod, feeling a sense of purpose, an adrenaline rush that comes with any new scientific venture. My mind is also jumping about with implications of DNA similarities and the idea that eons ago Elysiums and humans came from the same ancestry. So how did we get here, and how did they get there?

I clear my throat, my coffee more bitter than I expected. "Since we're looking at finding the answer to this process of mate selection among your males, I think we need to focus our hunt on a genetic compatibility test between Dr. Ada Charles and Chancellor Kyllell Koath."

"We already know they're compatible," says Remy.

"But we don't know how or why. We don't know if this compatibility has to do with reproduction, immune system functions, neurocompatibility, or a host of other things."

"You think this most likely has to do with reproduction, though," Micah says, already reading my mind.

I nod. "Survival of the fittest via mate selection."

"That makes sense to some extent, but this biological imperative to mate with the strongest partner doesn't explain the mate bond or that it can only occur with one partner," Dr. Jaran says.

"Do we know that for sure?" I ask.

If I thought the room was quiet and a bit subdued before, that leading question leaves a black hole in its wake.

"Dr. Adams, what are you implying?" Jaran asks quietly.

I know I need to tread lightly here, but every single avenue has to be explored.

"Is it possible that you could have more than one mate? Is it possible that once you are mated to a compatible female, then the drive to find another simply subsides due to the bond being...uh... consummated? Have any of your males or females ever resisted a mate bond to determine if you respond in the same way to more than one potential partner?"

"Why would anyone ever resist a mate bond? It's madness. Elysium males mate for life." His eyebrow ridges dip in confusion.

I'm working with an advanced species possessing technology that far surpasses our own, yet these folks have never bothered to pursue this line of questioning?

"I believe that. I believe you. But if no one has ever continued searching after finding one compatible mate, how do you know there aren't others out there?"

Dead silence meets the room once again as the Elysium scientists stare at me in horror. I'm not only suggesting we reexamine their mating selection process, I'm asking them to reexamine an entire belief system, culture, even religion if this aura connection or spirit connection plays as big a role in the bond as I suspect it does.

I love critical thinking. It's always such an eye-opener.

"Are you suggesting you could be one of many potential mates for the ambassador?" Micah asks.

Before I can answer in the affirmative—something that would simplify my future considerably—I'm interrupted by a low growl that manages to sound threatening and overtly sexual. I blink in surprise when I see Tarian standing just within the doorway.

That sensation of missing him abates and a whole new set of feelings emerge.

"Is that what you're suggesting, Bree?"

"Dr. Adams." Micah corrects him with a smirk which gets him a menacing smile in return.

Dr. Jaran chuckles and gives me a look that communicates how very sorry he feels for me right now.

Bastard.

"As a scientist, I have to consider all the possibilities. If we want to zero in on genetic markers, we need to assume more than one woman has specific compatibility for more than one male and vice versa."

Tarian moves from the doorway. The light from the interior adds a hypnotic luster to his black horns. Or maybe I'm losing my mind as

I sense his pull burrow into my soul and give it a good tug while the males in the room watch the exchange like they're attending a live tennis match.

I'm surrounded by bastards.

"It doesn't work that way. It isn't about reproductive abilities or survival of the fittest as you so crudely put it." I let that comment slide since I've questioned his way of life. "It's about the connection between souls."

"I don't believe I can measure that with genetics," I say.

He shrugs, the movement sexy and masculine. "Then find a way to measure it with something else. Everything has substance and form, even spiritual matter."

I shake my head and smile, loving the challenge. "I don't believe I was tasked to study auras."

He enters the room more fully, making it seem a million times smaller. "You've been tasked to identify mates for Elysium males. Which means you'll need to follow up on every possibility, as you just stated."

I see heads swivel back and forth, taking in our game of verbal ping pong. All eyes turn to me.

"That's exactly what I'm doing, Ambassador, and in the spirit of following up—"

"Tread lightly," Micah mutters, nudging me with his foot.

"What happens when an Elysium's mate dies? Are they left alone without a partner for the rest of their lives? Is there any documentation of a second mate bond after the loss of a previous mate?"

"Shit, Bree, I said tread lightly."

The room is silent, the human scientists turn to Tarian, waiting for the answer while the Elysiums in the room look like their skin is draining of color.

Tarian takes a few deep breaths before getting his emotions under control. I've got a funny feeling I've really stepped in it.

"There is no documentation of this."

"Because it's never happened?"

"When we lose our mates, we lose our lives."

My eyes widen in surprise. "Your biological systems fail or—"

"Our minds fail. We lose the will to live, and then the rest of our functions fail."

"All of you do this?" I ask. "Not a single Elysium has managed to live after the loss of a mate?"

"God, Bree, let it go for now." Micah's nudging foot only annoys me.

"Why was this not in our records?" I press. "Do you have any idea of the implications? I thought I made it clear that we needed to know everything about the mate bond before we started our research."

"Every single mated male died when the Chassaks succeeded in murdering our females. Do you have any idea how that impacted our military forces, our numbers, and our species as a whole?" Tarian's words come out slow and steady, but the guy is fuming. "It's a weakness and it's tactically dangerous to surrender this information to anyone, especially to a race we know nothing about."

That gets me on my feet. I place my hands on the table and lean forward. "A race that is, at the moment, the only thing standing between your species and extinction."

"Bree, diplomacy. You promised," Micah warns.

"Fuck diplomacy! It needs to be said," I insist, staring at my best friend, daring him to challenge me again. He lets out a sigh, but I can see the underlying smirk. The jerk is loving this. And Remy knows me far too well to interrupt me at this point. I turn back to Tarian. "Your people have a hell of a lot of nerve expecting our females to give up their families, their lives, their livelihoods, and even their own planet without offering up every damn piece of information concerning the mate bond. Because it's not just the males, am I right?"

Tarian's jaw tightens, a mulish expression setting in. But his eyes show a hint of remorse, and I know I'm right.

"Shit," I say on a breathy exhale. I feel the enormity of this revelation hit with the force of a two-by-four. "Shit!"

"What? I'm not following," Remy says.

"Dr. Charles?" I ask, knowing how this will affect her. "Is she aware?"

Tarian's face is stormy when he bites out, "She is now."

I rub my face, feeling all the perkiness of the morning drain from my body. I look at Remy, knowing she and a few of the other scientists are still confused.

"What Ambassador Koath has just confirmed is that the mate bond creates a type of biological symbiosis humans don't normally experience with other humans. I'd label it parasitic in nature, but the symbiosis is beneficial to both parties."

"Until it isn't," Micah whispers.

I nod. "Until it isn't. In other words, the joining of auras, of electromagnetic fields—and I'm still trying to wrap my brain around that—is possibly the cause of the physical shutdown of the partner left behind." When no one corrects this assumption, I level my gaze at Tarian, knowing he wouldn't have told me this, knowing he would have pushed me to mate with him long before telling me this. "If your brother dies, Ada dies. If someone assassinates him tomorrow, she's gone too."

Tarian swallows hard.

"How long? Within a week?"

He pauses for so long, Dr. Jaran has to answer. "Within a day."

My thoughts race, spiraling out of control. Goddammit. How the hell do we encourage anyone to mate with these males on those terms? How do I expose our women to these risks? How...do I fix it?

Now my thoughts are going in an altogether different direction. I'm a geneticist. Surely I can figure out why it happens and then figure out how to prevent it from happening.

"Oh, no. She's got that look," Micah says with a chuckle.

"What look?" Tarian's anger is palpable, but I don't have time for him or his feelings. I need logic and reason...and science now.

I shake my head, biting my lip, worrying it between my teeth as I come up with a game plan. "It's not just gene compatibility we're looking at. It's the whole of the individual. We'll find parts of the answer within the DNA, but there is more to consider and possibly reverse."

"Reverse?" Dr. Jaran asks.

"Do you really think I'm going to allow mate bonds to kill off our females should any of you kick the bucket?" I ignore Micah's low moan. "I'll help you find the various answers for identifying mates, but I'm also going to figure out how to save lives here." I point my finger at Tarian. "With the understanding that every human mate identified is given all the information necessary to make the best, most correct choice for herself. Our women have a right to know, and they have a right to choose."

Because if Remy is identified as a potential mate, I'll never accept that she's just doomed herself to something that shortens her life exponentially.

Tarian stares at me for a moment, no doubt knowing his agreement solidifies my ability to get out of a mate bond when the time comes.

"Agreed," he says.

I take a deep breath and head over to the whiteboard. "Great. Then let's get started. We'll be focusing on reproductive compatibility between Dr. Charles and her mate today. Here are your assignments."

I can feel Tarian's eyes on my back as I work, burning me with their intensity. He may have agreed to my terms, but I don't expect him to play fair. He's going to do everything he can to convince me that a mate bond with him is the best choice I'll ever make.

And he'll be in for a rude awakening.

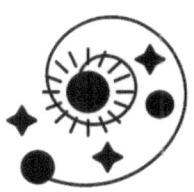

NINE

Tarian

*I*f *my mate thinks she has a choice in this matter, she's in for a rude awakening.*

As if I would ever give up on Bree after finding her. I study her movements as she directs the research team's duties for the day and makes quick work of the first stages in their game plan. Terms like genomes, base patterns, chromosomes, and gene testing have little significance for me. It's not my specialty, but Bree is certainly in her element.

She's utterly magnificent, brilliant in so many ways. Whether she has any idea of what she just showcased is irrelevant. Bree most likely assumes her behavior is not in alignment with an Elysium male's expectations due to male human's rather backward history of oppressive patriarchy—I did my own research.

But we revere strength and spirit as she just demonstrated. We revere feminine power as she has just wielded. We're impressed with intelligence, logic, and reason, and Bree, despite her lack of tact in the matter, demonstrated all of these traits by asking the hard questions and forcing the issue, no matter how badly I wish she hadn't. I didn't want to keep that information from the potential mates, but revealing this revealed our diminished numbers.

And whether she realizes it or not, it gives humans an advantage should they attempt to get rid of us. Instead of attacking an adult Elysium, go after the male's weakness.

His mate.

Not only would his love for and connection to his mate cause his own judgement to be impaired, he would absolutely die should she die.

Yet Bree is right in a different way. Every female identified as a possible mate has a right to the knowledge of the risks. They also have a right to the knowledge of the benefits, of which there are many.

Not a battle I was ready to fight. Not with an audience in the room and a fiery Bree setting off all my possessive mating instincts. As it is, I'm barely keeping my more primal urges at bay. And once again, my pull seems to have little sway over her.

It's a damn challenge I can hardly turn down.

I swivel around and exit, despite my body's need to remain in the same room with her. I'll merely distract her, and she's absolutely a distraction for me. I have security to oversee and a massive erection to control.

"Dr. Adams doesn't pull any punches," Dywrr says, walking next to me as we head to the main security station overseeing the base.

"No, she does not."

He lets out a low laugh that I find irritating.

"She'll figure this out, Tarian. She'll identify the mates and do much more while she's at it. But I have to wonder if you realize what you're up against."

I stop short and turn to face him. "What does *that* mean?"

"Have you checked her background? Looked at the particulars of her upbringing and who her parents were?"

I'm stunned to realize I haven't. Of course, I've seen the brief the United States government handed over, but we have our own ways of seeking out information, and I haven't once considered running such an extensive check on her yet. I was too focused on Micah.

"What did you find?" I ask, barreling down the hall and taking a right. I note the security cameras and guard detail, identifying holes in their patterns and making mental notes to tighten a few things once we reach the main security hub.

"I think you better read it yourself when you have the time. Knowledge is power, my friend."

"Knowing more about Bree makes me powerful?" I joke.

"It makes you less likely to fuck this up."

I give him a punishing blow to the arm without missing a stride, but he bounces back quickly, laughing at my response. He's not wrong. Bree has voiced some serious reservations concerning her own feelings on the subject of identifying mates. My guess is she's torn, even more so now that she feels she is risking human females' lives by unearthing their identities.

She's also voiced many concerns over being a mate herself, and I know several of those concerns stem from past experiences rather than present risks. I have to wonder where her personal demons come from and how to help her heal from them without making everything worse.

~

Bree

I THINK ABOUT MY ILLUMINA NOVASEC GENE SEQUENCING machine back at my old lab and realize how truly lucky we are to benefit from Elysium scientists' superior technology. To be fair, the sequencing by synthesis process wasn't completely accurate and took a little time, but it did the job.

Now as I listen to the slight hum of the alien equipment at my desk and stare at the data filling my computer screen, I feel as if the world has handed me the keys to the genealogical universe, and all I need to do is turn that key and unlock answers.

"Are you seeing this, Bree?" Micah says, twisting in his chair and turning his screen slightly.

"You blasted the Sanger sequence already?"

"What am I, an amateur?"

I chuckle as I lean forward and stare at the long line of

nucleotides spread across his screen. I check Dr. Ada's base alignment with that of the human genome specific to fertility.

"What have you found?"

Tarian's voice makes me clamp the arm of my work chair to prevent myself from reacting. I keep my eyes on the computer screen even though I'm no longer seeing or making sense of the endless lines of As, Ts, Gs, and Cs or the results from the software.

"We're still looking," I say.

"What does that involve? Nothing on that screen makes sense."

I lean back in my chair and finally have the grit to meet his eyes even though I have to crane my neck a bit. He frowns for a moment and then bends down to my level, kneeling next to me as if doing so is no big deal.

It's sweet.

It's also effective in getting in between me and Micah. I suspect that was his plan. I take in a deep breath and get a nose full of Tarian's alluring smell. It short circuits my brain for a moment before I'm able to respond.

"Micah and I can make sense of what we're looking at."

"What *are* we looking at?"

"A dead end," I say. "We were sequencing and comparing Dr. Charles DNA to see if she had any genetic mutations that might cause fertility issues. There are several we can look at, but what we have here is the Nlrp gene. Specifically Nlrp2 and Nlrp7."

"Why would you be looking at that?"

"Because it has been linked to the impairment of embryo development. If Dr. Charles has a mutation, it doesn't necessarily mean this will happen, but it could. She could also pass that gene down to any kids she and your brother might have."

"How does knowing whether or not she has it help you determine anything?" He stares at the computer screen, making a face at what I'm sure he sees as gibberish.

"We need to know if gene mutation that causes fertility issues in a mate or possible fertility issues in future children has any bearing on the mate bond," I say.

His eyes flit to mine, holding my gaze for a moment, considering what I have to say. I've become used to the way his horns stick up, burning an angry charcoal.

"I take it you didn't find anything?"

"Nope," I say. "We've searched several possible gene mutations and found no mutations relating to fertility issues. Which either means reproduction has nothing to do with mate selection, or there is a gene mutation linked to fertility that we have yet to identify in the human genome."

"But you said she *doesn't* carry any gene mutations linked to infertility. Doesn't that mean fertility does have something to do with mate selection? She was a good candidate because fertility was not an issue. Kyllell's mate bond sensed no problems."

"No. We have my genetic code to compare hers to, and even though she doesn't have problems that we can detect, I most certainly do. And yet, your horns burn black for me."

Now I've really got Tarian's attention.

"What do you mean, you have fertility issues? You've tried getting pregnant?"

I laugh at the horrified look on his face, the way his horns roll up and down in agitation.

"No, I've never tried to get pregnant. I had my own gene sequencing done a long time ago because I wanted to know if I had any gene mutations that could explain things like the migraines I get or if I inherited something from my parents." Specifically, I wanted to know if I had the same genetic disorder my mother had and if I would die early as well. But I wasn't about to get into that with Micah and Tarian. "Lots of couples do gene compatibility testing to make sure they aren't saddling any of their kids with identical mutations. If you get the same bad gene from both parents, you're screwed. In the process of having my own genes analyzed, I found a mutation relating to fertility issues. And that's all I'm gonna say on that."

"You'll not have trouble bearing young for me, Bree."

I hear Micah make a choking sound but ignore it.

"Wow." I roll my eyes. "I'm bothered by your assumption that I would choose to have children with you, but I'm intrigued by the confidence. Why would you think this wouldn't be an issue?"

"Because there have never been documented cases of any of our females failing to bear young in our records."

I stare at him for a moment, not sure I've heard him correctly. Then I slowly peer around him to stare at Micah who also appears amazed by that revelation.

"That can't be right," Micah says. "DNA mutates over time. It's inevitable. Humans alone carry at least one or two recessive disorders that they could pass down to their children. And either the kids are carriers or they have the disease. Are you saying there is no incidence of a recessive genetic disorder linked to fertility among the Elysiums?"

"I have no idea what you mean by any of that. I'm just saying our females did not have problems getting pregnant."

I stare at Micah in amazement. "Dr. Jaran has several samples of female Elysium and male Elysium DNA. Go grab them. I want to compare it to the Elysium gene sequence and see if we can locate mutations."

"We're not gonna know what it means, Bree. Different types of genes determine different things from species to species."

"Dr. Jaran can explain what we're looking at."

I watch Micah jump up and move across the lab to where Dr. Jaran is staring at a particularly nasty looking formula on the plasma screen that extends from wall to wall. Elysium tech is a bitch. Their language even bitchier. I can't make heads or tails of what he's doing.

I sense Tarian's eyes on me, challenging me. I force myself to meet his gaze again, feeling the full power of that damned pull of his. How the hell does that work? Pheromones? Brain waves? Is he emitting frequencies that attract females on a magnetic level?

It definitely gives new meaning to the phrase animal magnetism.

"I promise, you'll be able to have children, Bree."

I swallow down a mix of emotions, hating that he senses it's a sore spot for me.

"I've got a few health issues, Tarian. My mother had even more, which is why she died so young. It's also why I jumped into the field of genetic research. When we can identify the causes of disease at the base level, we can work on gene therapies to replace mutations with perfectly formed genes."

He grabs my hand and lightly grazes the point of one claw along my palm. My nerves fire off one by one, creating a heat that burns my core. I don't pull away, though. It would cause a scene and make him think he's won some kind of victory. I can see the playful gleam in his eye, but I can also see the concern at the mention of my mother.

"I know what that's like, Bree." He retracts his claws and begins to massage my hand as he speaks. "I didn't lose my mother as soon as you did, but the loss of a parent is always devastating. To sit there and watch them pass with no way of helping them is even worse. Especially when they are suffering."

I take a moment to really consider what Tarian has lost. His mother and sister. His father. He had to watch it all, and he had absolutely no ability to determine the cause or the solution. For a male very used to solving problems and getting answers, that must have been the most helpless, hopeless feeling imaginable. I suspect he will forever punish himself for it. All Elysium males will.

"Her quality of life certainly suffered." I let out a shaky breath at the memory of my mother dealing with depression and anxiety. At the memory of her struggling to form words, that brilliant mind of hers slowly being attacked by something modern medicine couldn't reverse. At Tarian's questioning look, I continue. "She had Huntington's Disease. It's a brain disorder. Neurons in the brain begin to die. Eventually, cognitive function, motor function…well, everything is affected, really. A slow deterioration that you can attempt to manage with drugs, but so far we don't have a cure."

"And you watched her decline in that way. For how long?"

I swallow hard. "Long enough."

"It's why you work so hard. Why you seek out answers. Ask the tough questions." He looks at me as if he can really see me. As if every particle of my being is visible. My wants, my needs, my motivations, and even my secret desires that not even I am willing to acknowledge. "You're trying to save *your* mother by saving someone else's mother."

The air whooshes out of me with that last statement. It takes me a moment to gather my thoughts. Because he's exactly right.

"I think the answers are in the DNA. We just need to keep looking." And I mean that for everything. For my mother. For others who have debilitating diseases with no hope of a cure.

"But at what cost to you, Bree? Do you ever take time for yourself? Do you ever do anything for yourself? Do you ever let anyone do anything for you?"

I blink in surprise at the rapid-fire questions. All easy to answer since they all have the same one.

No. I don't.

He nods, my silence saying it all. "It's okay to eventually be able to say yes. It's important that someday you say yes. If not for your own health then at least for your own happiness."

"I *am* happy." Funny how those words sound a bit hollow.

"Are you, Bree?"

I can tell, he genuinely wants to know. And if I'm not, there's no doubt in my mind he'll move heaven and earth to make me happy.

It fills me with euphoria.

And fear.

"I lived with the burden of that disease for some time. There was a fifty percent chance I had it. I made a promise to myself that if I didn't, if I somehow managed to avoid inheriting HD, then I would do everything in my power to find answers. To find a cure. I may have other problems, but I don't have HD."

Tarian reaches a hand up and smooths back a lock of hair from my forehead. It fills me with so much peace, I nearly lean into him.

"And that's why you became a geneticist. Saving humanity one mutated gene at a time?"

My smile is a bit teary. "Something like that."

He squeezes my hand, looking as if he'd like to hold me, and I'm worried that I would let him if not for all the scientists in the lab. It's such an unwelcome need, the need for touch, for companionship, that I reverse direction as quickly as possible. I lean back in my chair and pull away from him.

"I never plan to have children, Tarian. I think that's something you should come to accept."

His brow ridges narrow in consternation, looking a bit disoriented at my quick change of subject. Not to mention my quick withdrawal. "Isn't that something we should decide as a couple?"

This I can handle. This side of Tarian making demands and acting as if we are already together. Give me this Tarian any day. Not the Tarian that makes me think I might have it all wrong when it comes to romantic relationships.

"No. We aren't a couple, and even if we were, I'm the one who would have to carry the child. I'm the one facing the health risks involved. I'm the one handling the changes and the challenges to my body and hormones, and I'm the one who has to recover from the pregnancy, labor, and delivery. Did you know it takes our females up to a year to recover physically and emotionally from a full-term pregnancy? It takes up to two years for our abdominals to recover and only if we don't get pregnant again. Two years and beyond we're still working on pelvic floor issues and possible abdominal separation, not to mention body issues, self-esteem issues, and weight issues, but males think nothing of impregnating us."

Tarian stares at me for a moment and swallows. "I was unaware."

"Yeah. A common refrain from the opposite sex. And here's the thing, there are a lot of women in our world who want to get pregnant. They want to take on that burden and that recovery because any children they have will be worth it to them. It's their most fervent desire to have children. And that's their choice. Many have infertility issues, and I'm here to make sure they can have what they want. Which means my career is my focus for so many reasons, infertility being one of them. Children, for me, do not factor into the equation, but I can work towards making it possible for any other woman who wants a child to have a child. And at the end of the day, having that child is their choice."

"You'll change your mind." He says it with so much assurance, I'm reminded of all the conversations I had with my father.

Anger flares hot and steady within my chest, but I hold it back and temper it with all my experience in handling males who think they know better than me.

"Fortunately for me, I don't have to."

Before he has a chance to set me off with another rebuttal, Micah and Dr. Jaran approach with a silver device the size of a ballpoint pen. Tarian gets to his feet in one fluid movement. He's like a sleek cat, every move measured and precise.

"Am I to understand that you want to analyze the gene mutations of some of our females?" he asks.

"Your boy here says Elysium females never had fertility issues." Micah flips a thumb in Tarian's direction.

"That is correct."

"How is that possible? There were never any gene mutations linked to infertility?" I ask.

"There was no infertility for gene mutations to be linked to. If there is no problem, there is no reason to go searching for the source of a non-existent problem." He shrugs his shoulders. It looks less sexy and more adorable on him.

My lips quirk despite the news.

I'm having yet another conversation where something has never been considered simply because it has never happened.

"Will you identify the genes that contribute to reproduction and fertility and help us compare your samples? It's not that I don't believe you. I just don't think we should walk away from this with zero verification."

Dr. Jaran happily takes the silver pen and inserts it into the ebony machine on my desk.

Hmmm. Like a USB drive.

In all honesty, it's foreign to me, but it clicks into the side of my alien sequencer and uploads data before I can blink. Within minutes we're looking at different genes specific to our needs. Then comes a process I'm positive will take a while. Comparison and analysis of over 10,000 samples of Elysium female DNA, all needing to be translated into a language we can understand.

Knowing we're in it for the long haul, I look at Micah to see if he's finished his coffee yet.

"I will see to your needs, Bree." Tarian looks to be fuming, but his touch is gentle when he places his hand on my shoulder and gives it a slight squeeze. He leaves the lab quickly, no doubt heading toward the mess hall for some life-saving liquid.

A pang of regret tugs at me, making it difficult to breathe. I could have handled that conversation better. My complicated relationship with my father, the slow decline and death of my mother, and all the triggers that go with it need addressing.

Tarian's culture is one of absolute devotion to family where children are their most valued and protected beings. And that's as it should be. Humans could learn a lot from an Elysium's way of life.

And instead of airing out my conflicted feelings of wanting children, fearing what my children might inherit from me, wanting a career, and desperately needing control over everything, I struck where it hurt him most. A female mate refusing to have children. Talk about emasculating the guy.

I'm right and I'm wrong. My body. My choice. But children, if you can have them, and care for them, and love them...I blink back tears, thinking about a future baby in my arms.

The bleeping noise of my computer brings me out of my thoughts.

Micah stares at me, a knowingness in his expression.

I clear my throat. "Not a word."

"Wouldn't dream of it."

Tarian

MICAH MUST BE DESTROYED.

Removing my mate's best friend and long-time coworker might be frowned upon in what is referred to by humans as polite society, but it's only natural that an Elysium warrior would call out and confront any male that has the audacity to be as familiar with his mate as Micah is with Bree.

I am perfectly within my rights to challenge him, beat him within an inch of his life, and uphold my mate's honor while simultaneously proving my strength and ability to protect her.

But in this instance she doesn't need protecting, and I doubt that she would look upon any violence toward Micah in a favorable light.

And he is human. The male would never survive a normal Elysium challenge. I'd probably kill him while trying to teach him a lesson.

The thought is not a bad one.

I consider what I've learned from Bree. The things she revealed, and the things she didn't realize she revealed. She let me touch her and didn't pull away—at first. An enormous win in my mind. She's clearly driven by a goal that is both understandable yet possibly dangerous long-term. Mainly because I suspect Bree is willing to sacrifice her health, her life and her happiness in pursuit of a cure for the disease that killed her mother. But one cure won't be enough for Bree. Her work isn't just about finding answers for herself. It's about finding answers for others. It's her life, with deeply emotional and significant attachments at play.

Any threat to that life pursuit will not be met favorably.

But Bree is not a machine even though she might wish it. She craves touch. She craves companionship.

And she craves me, whether she knows it or not. Whether she likes it or not. I just need to get her to recognize what she truly needs and show her that she can still accomplish what she wants to accomplish even in the face of happiness. Her own happiness.

She'll come around. I just need more time with her.

I'm upset with Micah all over again, knowing that at the end of the day, due to the very nature of their work, he will always be with her more than I will.

The pain in my hand brings me up short. I stop on my way to the mess hall and stare at the damage I've done.

"How many times have I told you to retract those claws before making a fist? What in the name of the Goddess has your battle rage on high alert?" Bodeth asks.

He approaches from the direction of the mess hall, hot steaming cup in hand. The aroma of coffee is pleasant. The drink is now an addiction more for its taste than anything else. We seem to thrive on its bitter tang.

I make the necessary hand signs to confirm I'm talking to Boden and not a Chassak interloper. He offers his signs and we move on.

"Has Dywrr finished with his background check on Micah? I'd like to review his and Dr. Adam's history as soon as possible," I say.

I despise the understanding that fills his expression. My lack of emotional control, not to mention my difficulty to focus is cause enough to set off insecurities I didn't know I had. For a male in constant control, my emotional instability is a sore point.

To break the skin of my palm is an infant's mistake. We learn at a very young age how to retract our claws without thought. What I've just done is a clear sign of turmoil, something unacceptable in my position as Ambassador.

Instead of giving me a hard time about it, he uncharacteristically answers the question and avoids the real issue.

"The reports are ready. You can review them in your quarters whenever you wish."

"Security problems were tightened?"

Boden nods. "We've replaced their pitiful security system with our more sophisticated tech. This facility may be the safest place on planet Earth, but you know the saying."

I know it well. Nothing is completely impenetrable. If anyone, human or Chassak, wants to find a way in, eventually they will. Which is why I need to get myself under control

My instability is a danger to Bree in many ways, mainly in my ability to be as alert and aware of external factors that may be at play. I'm very good at reading individuals. I sense betrayal long before a traitor is able to act. My team and I are not convinced that everyone at the facility is here for the right reasons. Someone tried to have Bree removed from this project. Someone had access to their government's highly classified intel, and I'm concerned that this individual has enough information to breach these walls or is already within them.

"And the reports on the rest of the staff and the lab members?" I ask.

"It's all done. I need to ask, though, why did you have all the Elysium scientists checked out? You don't trust them?"

"I want to, but we have traitors on our own planet. We tried to keep the scientists we chose sequestered until they arrived on Earth, but I have no way of knowing if they are all trustworthy."

"I'm surprised you would allow Dr. Adams to work with them."

"No one allows Bree to do or not do anything." Bodeth chuckles as I shake my head. "But I don't believe they would hurt her. I'm more inclined to believe that they would simply sabotage data to prevent us from achieving our goals. No matter the amount of underlying dissent among some of our people in aligning with human females, we still value female life. No Elysium would ever harm a female."

"No, but a Chassak would."

"Then we make certain no one among us is a Chassak infiltrator."

Bodeth grins, aching for a fight. My crew is probably anxious at the lack of action here at the facility. Security detail is never exciting unless something is going wrong.

And absolutely nothing can go wrong.

"You headed to look at those reports right now?" he asks.

"I'm on my way to grab a coffee for my mate." The moment I say it, I regret it.

Bodeth's laughter echoes down the hall. "I won't give you a hard time about your domesticated state. Even though you've clearly been tamed."

"Ridiculous."

"Lost your malehood."

"My more than adequate balls are still intact."

"Not according to Dr. Adams." Bodeth ducks as I take a swing at him and then deftly maneuvers around me without spilling his drink. "If I were to go looking for your balls, I'd find them firmly clenched in Bree's fists."

I refrain from pursuing him down the hallway. He continues his retreat, laughing. A small smile tugs at the corner of my mouth. In truth, there's nothing more I'd want in this universe than to have Bree's hands securely fastened around my balls, not to mention my cock.

My horns unfurl at the thought as my cock responds in kind. I visualize Bree on her knees, that small smirk framing her lips just before she takes me into her mouth and sucks.

Hard.

I shake my head and hurry down the hall, adjusting myself as I go.

TEN

Bree

"This is nuts," I say.

Micah and I stand behind a seated Dr. Jaran, staring at the data on my computer as he struggles to come to terms with the information he's just shared. Surrounding us are the rest of the scientists, everyone throwing out possible theories as to what this data means.

"I have no way of knowing how these mutations would have presented themselves," Dr. Jaran says after identifying several gene mutations related to fertility and reproduction among his samples. "There is not one record of a mated couple failing to have children. This idea of infertility does not exist on Elysius. I do not...I simply..."

The poor guy is clearly flummoxed. I'd feel bad for him, but I can't understand how they missed something like this.

"When studying these samples, previously, why wouldn't you look for gene mutations like this? Even if you weren't looking for infertility specifically, surely you would have noticed these abnormalities when identifying other genetic diseases and attempting to treat them."

"We don't have genetic diseases," he says.

"Beg your pardon?" I'm sure I didn't hear him correctly. No way I heard him right.

Dr. Jaran turns in his chair to look at the rest of us. "We don't suffer from disease or illness. Our species is a dominant force in the Universe due to low mortality rates and high birth rates. Or we were, anyway."

"That isn't possible. These genetic mutations are right here. Clear as day. No doubt there are many others with different genes affecting different parts of the body. You're telling me that over the course of Elysium history, none of you dealt with diseases that could be linked back to recessive gene disorders? No one died from long-term illness?"

"Death came in the form of war or external causes for illness such as viruses or bacteria, anything contagious, all of which we were able to fix as medicine on our planet improved. Chronic issues, genetic disorders, and diseases were not things that we as scientists or even medical doctors needed to study or research."

"Then how do you explain these mutations? Why did they not present in these females?"

Dr. Jaran shakes his head. "I just don't know. I…we never went looking for mutations when we gathered this data."

"Why did you gather it in the first place?"

Dr. Jaran swallows hard, looking visibly upset. "We gathered these DNA samples from the dead and the dying. It was unpleasant, but our goal in doing so was to give birth to new females and clone the living females before they died."

Shit.

"So this information was gathered only recently. After your females were murdered by the Chassaks."

He nods, looking heartbroken, and now I'm feeling hellah guilty for having to put him and the rest of the Elysium scientists through this. The silence in the room is thick. I stare at the two other Elysium scientists, their eyes burning, shoulders held back, proud yet resigned. These males have experienced some absolutely horrible shit.

And I'm the bull in the china shop that has to press forward no matter how badly it might hurt them to discuss this topic.

"That must have been an awful burden for you and your medical workers to bear. Collecting all those samples. I assume you have far more than the ten thousand here?"

He nods, rubbing his face and appearing completely wrung out.

"I take it you weren't successful in cloning females."

Obviously, Bree. Why do you think we're here?

"We attempted several things, including retrieving the eggs from the females, it's the equivalent of human ovaries, just housed a bit differently."

It was some seriously good thinking. I'm reminded of an Israeli case I recently read about where a seventeen-year-old girl died in a car accident. Her parents petitioned the courts to save and freeze her eggs so they could eventually be fertilized in the future. That petition was granted, but the second petition to fertilize the eggs was dropped by the family due to the media circus that followed. It made sense, though. A frozen embryo, or fertilized egg, had a better chance of survival.

It was the heart-wrenching attempt of a family trying to preserve their daughter by eventually bringing forth a child from their daughter's genetic material.

Grief will cause you to do all sorts of crazy things, but was it wrong? Was it ethically and morally wrong to give life to a dead teen's eggs if that teen had not given permission for children to be created from her genetic material? Some said yes. Others said no.

Still, it was possible to do it, so why hadn't the Elysium scientists followed through?

"We wanted to freeze them and begin with mated female material first," Dr. Jaran continued.

"Why mated females?"

"You must understand, our females didn't all die at once. Some of them lasted several weeks as the Chassak bio-weapon slowly destroyed them from the inside out. Once these females were lost, their males died within a day of losing them. We didn't just extract DNA and eggs from the corpses of our mated females. We took it from those who were still managing to fight the toxin, hoping we could find a way to reverse the illness in time and also hoping we could possibly fertilize their eggs. We were going to lose these females no matter what. I knew it. We really didn't have time to find a cure, but I had hopes that we could genetically engineer female children from their fertilized eggs."

I saw where this idea had been going. "So you wanted to preserve children from a mated couple to ensure that line continued, and you wanted to clone the female's genetic material as an embryo hoping that if a clone of the female existed, even in embryo form, it would somehow prevent the male in the relationship from dying."

"Correct. Something about a specific female creates a symbiosis that allows the male to carry on. If her clone is alive, then the male can't perish. Or so we thought. We hoped the mate bond would still be intact within the cloned DNA."

I let out a heavy breath. "That is some elite guesswork with millions of holes to fill. So much testing and research to consider. There's no way you had time to achieve this."

"What we achieved was a dead end." He's silent for a few moments, letting that sink in. I study the rest of my team as they listen to Dr. Jaran. His story is upsetting, and I can see it in their faces. Remy appears especially distraught by Dr. Jaran's story, and I consider how lucky I am to have been able to find scientists who care about these issues as much as I do.

"The males died anyway," he continues after a few more moments. "The majority of the embryos never lasted longer than a day. No matter what we did to preserve them. They never made it. Nor did the embryos meant to bring forth their children. We couldn't explain why other than the material was somehow corrupted by the Chassak bioweapon."

"But you were able to save some?" I ask.

"We froze them." Dr. Jaran swallows hard. "It was the only way to prevent the corruption from spreading and destroying them altogether, but we have no way of reversing the damage."

"And these gene mutations we see in these women could have come from the bio weapon?" I ask, although I find it hard to believe.

Would gene mutations occur that quickly? Within a matter of weeks?

"It's possible," Dr. Jaran says.

"This data is from mated females only?" I ask.

"No, this is a mix of mated and unmated females."

I don't say anything, letting it all sink in.

Some of this is unmated female DNA.

"What are you thinking, Bree?" Micah asks.

"I want a comparison of genetic mutations of females who are mated and women who are unmated. Did the bio weapon affect these females differently? I know that whether mated or unmated they still passed away, but I want to know if matehood created any variables."

I study the screen, trying to form into words something that's itching at my subconscious. "Out of the females who lasted the longest, how many of them were mated?"

Dr. Jaran stares at me in surprise. "I...we never looked at those numbers."

"We need to. I've got a theory about this mate bond, and if I'm right, it might give us a better sense of the genetic markers we need to be looking at within our own females. Let's get to work."

Everyone scatters in various directions with renewed purpose and a new target to pursue. I stare at the coffee mug Tarian dropped off at my table several hours ago before I sit down and begin my share of the workload. It's completely empty, the ceramic of the mug cool to the touch now.

Still, as I wrap my hand around it and feel its smooth texture, I swear a hint of warmth transfers beneath my skin. I have this odd sensation that a bit of Tarian's essence has bled into me.

I hate that the thought makes me feel less lonely.

"Bree, I think we've done about as much as we possibly can tonight." Micah rubs his face and then pushes away from his desk.

I blink bleary eyes and look up from my screen, not at all surprised to see that we're the last ones in the lab. We've burned the midnight oil for the past three nights, insisting the rest of the team get their sleep. It's always this way. I work until I'm ready to fall over, and Micah is the calm voice of reason, making sure I stop working long enough to get some food and sleep.

"Remy?"

"She left a little early, saying she needed to discuss something with Tarian. I'm guessing it's about her boy."

I'm relieved to hear it. I turn back to my computer, knowing I need the sleep, knowing Micah and I are about to argue.

But this time there is too much at stake and too little time to seek out answers. And I'm determined to explore this idea of multiple mates since I can't help but think that this is my way out of my mate scenario with Tarian. I've studied records, courtesy of Dr. Charles, on Elysium mate bonds, the cultural norms, the patterns, the histories of mates chosen, and not a single individual on record has ever just waited it out to see if their horns might burn black for someone else.

I figure if I wait it out with Tarian, I'll be able to prove my hypothesis and find him an entirely different mate to woo. And it would make identifying mates a hell of a lot easier. Instead of there being just one human for one Elysium, we have a plethora of potential mates for a male. Win-win in my book.

"You go hit the hay, Micah." I point to my screen. "I've got a few more samples to look over."

By the shift in his stance, I'm not gonna get my way without a fight. He's about to open his mouth to argue when Tarian speaks from the doorway.

"You'll not be able to convince her. I'll stay with Bree while you get some sleep, Doctor."

Tarian again. Always lurking. Okay, he's actually quite busy keeping the facility safe, but it's uncanny the way he shows up when he's least wanted, especially when he's walking me to and from my room, or the mess hall, or any other damn place I need to visit. I can't seem to go anywhere in this facility without him by my side.

I expect Micah to get grumpy and object, but he does something worse. He completely backs off. That slow smirk he's been giving me as of late is really starting to rankle.

"Ambassador, the stubborn female is all yours." He sweeps his hand forward with a "be my guest" flourish. "Make good choices," he singsongs as he walks past Tarian and exits the lab.

What an ass.

I stare at Tarian for a moment, assessing his mood. Tightness around the eyes and jaw. A wary readiness in his stance. A tension within his shoulders that either speaks to the warrior in him or hints at issues buried just below the surface.

Overall assessment? The dude needs a professional massage and a day off. He's also pissed about something, and I really don't have the time to investigate. I turn back to my screen and continue my work, fully expecting him to take on Micah's role and cajole me into calling it a night.

I'm surprised when he sits in Micah's seat and says nothing. I continue working while Tarian's quiet presence gives me a level of focus I hadn't been expecting. Eventually, I look at the time stamp at the bottom of my screen and note that two hours have passed in companionable silence.

Realizing he's not going anywhere, and that I really do need to get some sleep, I save my files and retrieve the alien tech, making sure we have multiple copies to work with as well as the original files on hand.

I lean back in my chair and finally turn to look at him. His eyes connect with mine as awareness of a different sort shoots straight to my core and a few other areas that I try not to focus on.

"You let me keep working," I say.

"No one lets you do anything, Bree. Do I think you need sleep? Of course, but I also respect your process and your work. I'm not interested in controlling you or your process. You deserve far more respect than that."

Damn this alien. And here I was getting ready for a fight. But if I'm being honest, he's just said the words I always longed to hear from my own father. They're words I always feared I would never hear from an actual partner.

And my mate just gave me exactly what I've always wanted with a few simple words.

My mate.

Shit. I'm actually beginning to think of him as mine.

"You're upset with me, though. And it has nothing to do with the way I get reckless with my own health."

Tarian nods and leans back in his seat, his eyes never leaving mine. "We can talk about your penchant for self-destruction a little later since I know it's motivated by a truly admirable savior complex rather than a desire to actually hurt yourself."

I bark out a laugh, so surprised that he's read me as well as he has. A savior complex. I'm not at all insulted by the observation. Micah has admonished me time and again when it comes to my need to fix things and save people…one mutated gene at a time.

"This is about the questions I'm asking. The avenues I'm pursuing to get the answers I need. Am I right?"

His look is one of complete and total exasperation, and I realize I've somehow missed a beat.

"Bree, this is about you and me. I'm aware there is some fault to be found with our council for not addressing the risks to your females, but it's clear you're asking certain questions to get yourself off the hook."

"What do you mean?" *You know exactly what he means, you coward.*

"If there's a possibility that the mate bond can be established with more than one mate then you're interested in pursuing that line of reasoning, not only because it's applicable in identifying potential mates but because it gives you a reason to ignore the possibility of us. If more than one female can mate with me, then you don't have to."

I debate the merits of denial, but I have far too much respect for this guy to go that route.

"You're right. I did not sign up for this research project to find a husband. I didn't go into this thinking I would be compatible or that my very presence would kickstart your symptoms."

"Symptoms." Tarian shakes his head, but his eyes suffuse with amusement. "How very clinical. In my culture, black horns that burn for their mate are the epitome of what humans would categorize as romance. It's symbolic of a deeper connection. Something to be celebrated. Something sacred. It's the most meaningful outward sign of belonging one can exhibit."

He moves his rolling chair forward until his legs are positioned on either side of mine. He slowly reaches for my hands and turns them over, palms up. I barely contain the shiver this contact with him causes. He rubs a knuckle against my palm, slowly. Then he does it again.

"Do you feel that?" he asks.

I let out a shaky breath before responding. "I feel it." The dance of a million jolts of electricity sing their way from my palm to my shoulder and back again while the synapses in my brain fire off, a tingling symphony of energy and arousal.

"I suppose we could break this down scientifically. We could talk about molecules and atoms, chemical responses, and biological compatibility when it comes to what attracts an individual to another. We could look at this mate bond between us as the give and take of biological and chemical signals because that wouldn't frighten you. That might actually make sense to you."

"I'm not frightened," I manage to squeak out. I swallow back a moan as his claw lightly traces the lines along my palm and follows the zinging path up my arm until he's lifted my chin and cupped my face.

"You're frightened," he says in a gentle tone. "I'm frightened. Because there are feelings and emotions and connections with individuals in this life that defy science and go beyond the scope of what can be measured, explained, and even understood."

He leans in and lightly grazes my lips with his. He may as well have lit my entire world on fire. The sensations running through me are unearthly. Nothing I can explain and certainly nothing I want to give up.

But can I give in?

"I can measure it," I say faintly. "There's always an explanation as to why we do what we do, think what we think, or feel what we feel."

He pulls back slightly and gives me a kind smile. "Maybe. Or maybe fate, destiny, and the one individual in this universe meant for you isn't a scientific phenomenon not yet understood. Maybe it's one of the most basic laws of nature that's meant to do nothing more than make us as happy and content as we need or want to be."

My smile spreads slowly without my consent. He's too charming for his own good, and far too charming for mine. "You think a soulmate could be a basic law of nature meant to make an individual happy? As if nature or even the universe is concerned with the individual?"

His lips are firm this time when they meet mine, but the pressure is gentle as he works his magic on me. Then he slowly pulls back.

"Why not?" he says.

His lips take mine fully this time. I'm unclear as to how I've gone from the safety of my computer chair to the euphoria of being held in his arms, but I'm in no position to fight it. My legs straddle him and my hands trace the path of muscle along his chest. He deepens the kiss, tightening his arms around me.

In this moment, a sense of rightness settles within my chest, a sense of knowing that not even I can ignore no matter how badly I want to. This new idea builds within me. A kernel of truth that I've never been willing to explore.

What if I can have Tarian? What if I can still be a geneticist? What if I can still be a mother? What if I can have it all?

And I realize that maybe I could. With him.

Suddenly, Tarian tenses and pulls back, cocking his head to the side.

"Tarian, what—"

He pulls me to the floor and covers my body just as an explosion rocks the work station behind me. I'm stunned, my ears ringing, clinging to the protective breadth of Tarian. Computer debris showers over us while another explosion destroys more equipment. The fire alarm lets out a piercing shriek, and blaring lights and intercom warnings create a cacophony of confusion, sending sharp pain slicing through my head. I'm so disoriented by the ringing in my ears and the black smoke surrounding us, I barely register Tarian pulling me under the desk.

"Don't move," he says before disappearing from sight.

Don't move? Stay here?

It's like he doesn't even know me.

I scoot to the edge of the weakened shelter, wrinkling my nose at the smell of melted plastic and charred flooring. A hand grips my wrist before I'm able to duck out. I nearly scream, but I make out Tarian looming before me.

"Someone is loose in the building. We've got my men combing the area, but I want you in a safe location."

I nod, not really understanding what happened, but knowing I'm not any help when it comes to security and open combat. He covers me in a lab jacket and assists me in making my way out the lab doors, smoke billowing behind us. Though my eyes are red and burning and my throat is a bit sore from smoke inhalation, I can clearly see the hallway we're moving through. An intercom warning continues to encourage people to take shelter in their rooms while guards and security teams branch out and attempt damage control.

"What happened?" I shout, trying to be heard over the noise of the blaring alarm.

"Thermal laser tech and then some," Tarian says. "He shot up yours and Micah's computer equipment."

"Why would the intruder do that?" I ask as we round a corner and head toward the mess hall.

"I'm sure it was to destroy all the data you were working on."

That makes no sense to me. Sensitive data like this is encrypted and backed up to several devices and the cloud, not to mention the copy I have on Dr. Jaran's alien USB. It's an awful risk to blow up inconsequential computer equipment when the data has been backed up and saved in multiple locations.

Unless the goal wasn't really to corrupt data. Maybe it was simply to cause confusion. A distraction.

But why?

As we head past the mess hall, I expect us to turn right, heading to my quarters, but we go left.

"Tarian, where are we headed?"

"My quarters."

Alarm bells go off, and I'm not talking about the ones around us. I know where Tarian's quarters are, and they can't be reached from this direction. For the first time since he grabbed me, I realize I don't know if I'm actually with my mate.

My mate. Why the hell do I keep thinking that?

"Tarian," I say, pulling my arm from his grip and taking a step back. "I need a moment. I don't think I can keep going."

"Why?" he asks. His voice is hard, the possessive tone that usually tinges his words when he speaks to me is no longer present. And his eyes. Cold and disinterested.

"Too much smoke inhalation." I'm not lying, either. The pain in my chest as well as the pain in my head are building. I bend over for a moment, gripping my temples.

"What's going on?" he asks. "We need to keep moving. You're only safe within my quarters."

I test him with my next words. "I sometimes get migraines."

"You do? Well, how do we stop it? Because we need to keep moving."

Tarian would have known. He stopped it last time, and he wouldn't be surprised by my having another one. The male before me may look like Tarian, but he isn't.

I think through my next words carefully.

"We need to go to my room first. If this gets any worse, you'll have to carry me to your quarters. I won't make it without my medication."

"There's no time, and the threat could be in that direction."

I don't respond. I simply turn and make a break for it. Fake Tarian lets out a shout in a language I don't understand, but I'm more alarmed by the thrum of a thermo-weapon powering up. I dive through an open doorway of the mess hall just as a blast of energy singes my shoulder. The wall ahead of me explodes in an orange and bluish flame, creating a large hole in the process. If I don't find some cover, I will be completely obliterated.

I weave my way around various tables, using the flashing red lights of the security alarms for a bit of visual guidance. But if I have some visibility, a Chassak is going to have more. I duck underneath a circular table, feeling something sticky under my hands. It has a coppery tang to it that makes me want to vomit. I scoot to the middle and curl into a ball, trying to take up as little space as possible. I just can't get my breathing under control. The sound of it, along with the pulsing in my head is like a thundering beacon calling the Chassak right to me.

I let out a scream when the table is thrown back and Fake Tarian growls at me, pointing his weapon right at my face.

My hands raise slowly as I try to buy myself some time. "Why are you doing this?" I ask. "We're just trying to help people."

"Help the Elysiums, you mean. I'm afraid we can't allow that."

"Who the hell is 'we?'"

The thrum of his weapon powers up again, and I stare him down. If this is how I die, then this bastard is gonna look me in the eye when he fires. I slowly get to my feet, facing him, but he doesn't take the shot. He hesitates, indecision marring his features. Tarian's features. I hate that he chose Tarian's face.

"Just come with me," he says. "You don't have to die. I can give you safe passage off this planet, a safe place where no one can find you, so long as you agree to walk away from this project."

My eyes narrow in disbelief. He doesn't want to kill me? That's interesting.

"I can't do that. It's my job to help people."

He lets out what I can only assume is an expletive before closing his eyes in defeat as if my answer has pained him.

"I have the utmost respect for you, Dr. Adams. Please know this."

I'm surprised by the familiarity in his tone, as if he's worked with me. As if he knows me.

He firms his stance as his eyes harden, focused and determined.

And all I can do is look him in the eye. Because I'll be damned if I leave this world cowering before my murderer.

I'm shocked when a blast of light hits him on his side, sending him flying across the room, taking out round tables and chairs in his wake before crashing into the soda dispenser on the other side of the mess hall.

My head swivels to see Tarian, the real Tarian, chest heaving, eyes ready to commit murder...and I guess he has. My eyes snap back to what is left of Fake Tarian, feeling a strange sense of loss even though it's a relief that my attacker is dead. An adult version of some kind of humanoid porcupine is crumpled up against the wall.

I mean, there's really no other way to describe it. Not that the Chassak looks like a porcupine exactly, but its spikes are definitely... uh...everywhere.

There's also an enormous amount of torso missing. That gun tore him apart.

I take an unsteady step toward him, studying his alien form, trying to assess how those quills work and what their poison might have done to me if the Chassak had attempted to use them first. I mean, a thermal weapon? Wouldn't his instinct have been to shoot his quills and then his gun?

I finally notice Tarian at my side, holding my waist to support my weight and shouting things to others who have managed to make their way into the mess hall. He says something to me, but the alarms are still blaring, smoke circles the area and further disorients me, and I'm still hyperfocused on those quills, a tiny fragment of an idea itching away at my thoughts.

"Bree? Goddess, please answer me." Tarian tilts my chin to look at him, breaking me from my thoughts. His expression is nothing but anguish as he searches my eyes for a sign of...something. Maybe that I haven't lost my mind?

I should reassure him, so he knows I'm okay.

"Hi Tarian," I say. "Do you think Dr. Jaran kept any samples of the remaining frozen embryos at the base? Or is that material safely stored on Elysius?"

His look of alarm suggests I have failed.

"Bree," he says, very slowly, like I'm five, "your shoulder is bleeding. Did that intruder hurt you anywhere else?"

"My shoulder's bleeding?" I try to look at my left shoulder but Tarian keeps my chin tilted toward him.

"Let the medic do his work. I think it best if you don't see the damage until he's fixed it."

I can't feel anything. I'm pretty sure that's a bad thing. A shock thing? Or maybe my ability to compartmentalize pain has increased. None of that sounds good.

I reach up and rub at the crease between Tarian's brow ridge, smoothing it out as he looks at me with worry. The alarms finally go off, and the remaining ringing in my ears seems louder for it. I realize I'm sitting in one of the few chairs that hasn't been tipped over or damaged, and Tarian is on one knee by my side, his arm firmly held around my waist.

"I'll be fine. Whatever damage was done to my shoulder, I can't even feel it. I can't feel my migraine anymore, either."

"You had a migraine?" he asks, his voice raised in alarm.

"Yep." I'm starting to feel really drowsy now. "I had this crazy pain shoot through my head. Then a burn on my shoulder. Then bam. You're here. No pain. I feel good. When are we kissing again?"

I hear a familiar snort at my side, but my eyes are glued to Tarian who just stares at me, clearly alarmed.

Tarian looks at the medic by my side and sighs. "What the hell kind of meds did you give my mate?"

"The kind that could tranque an elephant."

I turn to look at the medic, only to see Micah standing next to the guy fixing my shoulder. "Hey, it's you."

"It's me." He's wearing a smile, but there is tension around his eyes.

I know Micah. He's every level of angry right now.

"I thought the famed warriors of Elysius were invincible," he says, glaring at Tarian.

I sense Tarian's shoulders tightening. God, I can't handle a pissing contest right now, especially with a fuzzy brain and knees that do not cooperate when I try to get to my feet. "What did you have the medic give me, Micah? I feel like my head is no longer connected to my body."

Micah's lips quirk in amusement. "The same thing I gave you for the helicopter ride."

"You son of a bitch."

Micah's laughter is contagious, but I can't join in because I'm starting to fade. There's no way I'm making it to my room on my own, but there's no way Tarian would let me. He's already gathered me in his arms, carrying me from the mess hall.

"I almost lost you." His voice is tight. An emotion I can't identify tinges his words. I wish to hell Micah hadn't given me those meds. Tarian is not okay, and I'm too drugged up to focus on anything.

"You can't lose me. I'm like...an annoying...cockroach that won't...quit."

He pulls me closer and gently kisses my forehead. "I have no idea what a cockroach is, but I can assure, Bree, this will never happen again."

His words are pure steel, and there is an undercurrent of meaning that I can't grasp hold of, but I'm barely hanging on here, and I figure the sooner I let sleep take me the sooner I can wake up and get back to work.

ELEVEN

Tarian

"What do we know?" I ask.

Bodeth and Dywrr sit at the table in the security room, and the anger radiating off them is nothing compared to the rage I feel after seeing my mate's shoulder. After knowing how close I came to losing her.

Losing her on my watch. Never in my life have I ever felt so incompetent. So utterly helpless.

Not true. There was one other time…

I let that thought slip away because I don't want to face it, and even then, it wasn't quite like this. When it's your mate.

I'm finally coming to terms with what our males went through when they watched their females die, following them within hours. Hard enough to watch my mother and sister. But a mate?

Unbearable. Thank the Goddess those males passed as soon as their mates did. Living with that torment would be impossible.

"Not nearly enough," Dywrr says. "Nothing was breached. No security alarms went off. Nothing shows on the data feed, and no hacking has been identified, and you know we would find any trace of a breach with the tech we have. The Chassak was inside. Before we got here. Biding his time."

"Which means the likelihood of there being another is high. Chassaks rarely operate alone." Dread threads its way through my nerves, my emotions, an insidious sentient presence teasing me with what I know could still happen. "Bree has been the target from the beginning. I want to know why."

"I think that's pretty obvious," Bodeth says. "She's the head geneticist for this project. She's even outmaneuvering *our* scientists, thinking about possibilities that our culture and belief systems never allowed. She is going to figure this out."

"She is clearly the only one who can," Dywrr says. "It makes her a massive liability to the Chassaks' end game."

"We need answers. Background checks are not going to cut it. Not when any number of staff were most likely murdered and replaced with a Chassak infiltrator. Find out who among our staff is missing. We'll then know which human the Chassak killed and impersonated to breach the facility. But we need to find his partner. And even then, there may be more."

"We might have a lead in the case of Micah," Dywrr says.

My eyes shoot to him fast, my focus sharp and cutting. "You're referring to the first ten years of his life?" I think back on the information Dywrr was able to discover. Reading the reports on Bree and Micah gave me insights into Bree's hang-ups. It was certainly something I had thought long and hard about last night before relieving Micah of his duties and staying with Bree while she worked. Not that I had ever been gone. I'd simply been standing guard outside the lab, waiting for my chance to be alone with her.

But Micah's missing childhood had raised some red flags. I wasn't sure what it meant, though.

"No one knows anything about those early years," Dywrr says. "He was raised in foster care after being found abandoned on the side of what humans call a highway when he was ten. He was then passed around to different homes within this notoriously ineffective system. He could be an issue."

I think long and hard about it. "How? You think the Chassaks might have gotten to him at a young age? That doesn't make much sense."

"At this point, anything is possible. I'd like to know what he remembers of his first ten years because he's shared nothing of his past. Nothing on record."

I stare at the computer monitors, seeing personnel come and go. Any one of them could be another Chassak impostor. It takes all of my control and then some to respect Bree's wishes and allow her to remain here where the danger to her is the greatest. But an Elysium male can only handle so much when it comes to threats against his mate's safety. And I'm already putting a plan into motion that will ensure my mate is safe, even if she hates me for it.

I struggle with guilt and an uncomfortable sense of disloyalty. As if my planning and plotting is a betrayal against my mate. "I'll talk to Bree first. She's known him for what seems like a very long time."

"Her answers may be biased. She won't see him as a threat when he's been the closest thing she's had to family for quite some time now," Bodeth says.

"A valid point, but the threat is internal. With no evidence of a security breach, we have to consider this an inside job, and we have to suspect anyone who hasn't been cleared. Who was this recently deceased Chassak impersonating?"

"A security guard. One assigned to the lab," Laoth says, striding into the room. "We've just confirmed all personnel. He's the only one missing." He looks ready to rip heads from shoulders. My crew will take any threat to my mate's safety as a personal attack on them. This has provoked their ire in ways which can only help.

"The lab." I feel my blood heat at how often this Chassak was close to Bree. Watching her. Biding his time. Most likely interacting with her if he was stationed at the lab door often enough. "How convenient. Very strategic."

"Do you want us to interrogate the rest of the guards? One at a time?" Dywrr asks.

"No. These filthy *churtnas* would not have diverted all their forces to one department. The next best place to look would be among the actual team of scientists."

"Ours or theirs?"

"Both."

My team doesn't seem the least bit surprised that I suspect our own males. We have to at this point. I'm aware that precautions were taken. Every Elysium scientist had their own way of identifying themselves—a way that a Chassak should not have uncovered, but if I know anything about our enemy it's that they are resourceful.

"I want added security on my mate."

Dywrr grins. "She's not going to like that."

"She has no choice."

That knowing look never leaves his face. "Can I be present when you use that as your compelling argument?"

My soldiers chuckle, knowing Bree to be fiercely independent. She's proven it time and again. But I'm stubborn, and nothing will dissuade me from ensuring my mate's safety. Not even my mate.

Bree

Achieving a state of consciousness after being drugged by Micah's all powerful knockout juice is next to impossible.

But I'm an overachiever. I'm slowly working my way into an upright position when a swooshing noise indicates someone entering. Since I vaguely remember Tarian carrying me to his quarters, I don't freak out.

He, however, does.

"What in the name of the Goddess are you doing?" he says, rushing to my side and lowering me to the pillow.

I'm not really able to fight back, and his verbiage gets me sidetracked.

"You guys are consistently using the name of some mysterious Goddess. What is that all about?" I ask, feeling the pull of the drugs and the softness of the bed lull me back into a state of grogginess.

"The Goddess Elysarah," he says, giving me a soft smile as he sits on the edge of the bed. "In Elysium lore, she is a divine cosmic energy that is represented as feminine energy."

"Feminine energy. I have a hard time envisioning Elysium warriors worshipping a female deity."

"I think that has more to do with your culture and patriarchal history than mine."

I give him a smile, knowing he's probably right.

"In Elysium culture we revere feminine energy because creation happens within the female. A female gives all of herself to create life. We also revere masculine energy as feminine's equal, which is why the consummation of the mate bond is so important." He reaches out and softly caresses my cheek. "Our energy, the feminine and the masculine, join together and quite literally bond. It creates a balance and a sense of harmony that is symbolic of unity, a sense of oneness. It's a give and take of your very essence all happening within the auras. And we believe that Elysarah created us in this way to offer balance within couplings."

"So only males and females can be mated?" I ask.

"Feminine energy is not strictly found within females," he says. "And masculine energy is not always found within males. It isn't tied to gender. It's tied to your very essence."

"That's actually quite beautiful," I say, feeling my eyes grow heavy as Tarian continues to softly caress my cheek.

Wait. Wasn't I trying to do something?

My eyes blink open as I fight to regain consciousness. The bed is very comfy, but I have a shitload of work to do. I try to sit up and hear a warning sound vibrate from the burly chest of the alien next to me.

I let out a laugh. "Did you seriously just growl at me?"

"You need to rest."

"Tarian, before you go into protective mode, I'm going to circumvent this argument by stating the facts." I'm finally in a sitting position, and I count that as progress, but now I'm staring at an expansive, muscled chest, and I feel the sudden onslaught of desire blossom in a particular area of my body that has consistently betrayed me from the moment I first saw this damn devil.

"My shoulder will be good as new...eventually."

"Your shoulder has a hole in it. And you don't exactly regenerate the way my species does."

That sets me back a moment. "You have regenerative abilities? Like if an arm gets sliced off you grow it back? How long does—"

"Bree. Focus. While our tech can do a lot of things to help you heal, you still need some rest and a full day to recover." He sits next to me and presses down my good shoulder when I try to sit up again.

"I can recover while sitting in a lab chair staring at data. It's not exactly grueling."

"To quote your good friend Micah: *The hell it isn't.* Do you have any idea what tech can do to an individual's electromagnetic field?" His eyes blaze with a protective fire that turns me on in ways wholly unwelcome.

And now he's asked me yet another thought-provoking question I'm eager to explore. "Are Elysiums' electromagnetic fields stronger than a human's—"

"Goddess, your brain never stops spinning, does it?"

I'd take offense, but his expression hints that he finds this somewhat adorable. I have no idea how to feel about that.

"Look, I've found some interesting information that I need to report to the team, and it can't wait a day just because I have a hole in my shoulder."

"Did you hear what you just said?" He rubs his face. His black horns rolling up and down in agitation. "Hole. In. Your. Shoulder. I have to protect you, Bree. I can't do that if you are a threat to yourself. Working under duress—"

"Necessary."

He stares me down for a moment. "Migraines."

"Par for the course."

"Hole in the shoulder."

I pause. "Okay, that's not usual working conditions for a geneticist."

He lets out a low growl and inches closer, resting his forehead against mine and breathing me in for a moment. The way it steadies me is incredible. My own focus returns as I do the same. The grogginess of Micah's meds begins to alleviate.

"It's cauterized, cleaned, and wrapped in gauze. Not to mention sealed, or whatever the hell it's doing because of your advanced medicine. I'm good to go, and this news can wait a night but not a week. My computer may be damaged but I was able to save everything before we called it a night."

"You mean before I kissed you?" He pulls back to look at me, assessing my response. And damn the male, I can feel a slow blush flooding my cheeks. Always so transparent.

His low chuckle does strange things to my insides.

"That was a one-time thing."

"Oh, no. We're beyond one-time kisses when there have been two instances of our mouths joining in the most intimate of ways." He leans forward, his weight pushing me further into the mattress of the bed, careful not to touch my bad shoulder.

He runs his lips along mine, softly kissing the top and then the bottom. He gives me a playful nip at the corner of my lips, causing me to let out an involuntary moan. He stills for a moment, looking at me, his eyes flashing heat and want. Then he takes my lips fully, claiming them as his, sliding his warm tongue deep and offering languid strokes that mimic an altogether different kind of joining.

Heat floods my insides, traveling to my core, stimulating it in ways I've tried to ignore for far too long. One arm circles my waist as his other hand slowly travels the length of my side, drawing languid circles along my skin. It's only then that I realize I'm no longer in my lab uniform.

From what I can tell, Tarian stripped me down to my bra and panties, and instead of feeling outraged by it I feel nothing but desire.

He cups my breast and lightly squeezes, drawing out another low moan from me. His tongue dances with mine as he slowly runs a clawed finger under my bra and softly strokes it along the outline of my nipple. Slow and maddening stimulation. When he reaches the peak, he applies light pressure, just a scratch that sends a jolt of fire straight to my core. I moan into his mouth and he devours it, devours me, while he administers more strokes of his claw and his tongue.

His clawed finger slowly leaves as he draws it along my ribs, down my legs, and circles just above my pubic bone. He runs it softly along my panties, painting a slow path to my pussy as my legs open for him. Then he runs it along my folds, above my panties. A rush of arousal hits me and soaks them. Tarian growls low and pulls back. He retracts his claws and slides his finger under my panties and finds my wet core. Running the tip along my seem, gently stroking my labia and circling. He works his way slowly upward, stroking me as he goes.

Bending down he snares my mouth in his at the exact moment the tip of his finger reaches my clit and applies pressure.

My cry escapes me, but Tarian takes it with his mouth as his finger lightly dances over my clit in slow, smooth circles. The constant stimulation is almost too much, but then he slowly draws his finger down, and in one swift move he plunges it deep within my folds.

I arch my back, pleasure traveling along my spine, building as it goes. Every fiber of my being feels like it's vibrating on a frequency I've never achieved before. Then Tarian moves back and takes my nipple in his mouth, sucking hard as he slides his finger deep within me.

My orgasm crests and breaks with the power of a tsunami. Washing over me, through me, lighting up every cell that I own and setting it all on fire. My cry is long and drawn out as the waves wash over me again and again, as he suckles my nipple hard and taught, continuing to thrust his thick finger into my core.

As I come down from my euphoria, he slows his movements, softening his attention to my nipple. Soon he wraps me in both of his arms, kissing me as if I might disappear on him. As if he might lose me at any moment.

And perhaps, last night, he almost did.

I'm completely undone here. I was not expecting anything like that from him, and I'm unprepared for the flood of emotion it's unlocked as a result. He pulls back to look at me, a possessive fire lights his eyes, but I note his concern. He lets out a heavy breath.

"I'm telling you that you can't work today due to your injury, and then I proceed to have my way with you. Did I hurt you, Bree?"

I let out a surprised laugh. "Hurting me is the very last thing you've done. I feel amazing." I smile up at him, giving him a wicked grin. "And since it's safe to assume I've been cleared for all bedroom activities, I think that means I'm in tip top shape to sit at a computer for the next few hours and share my findings with the team."

Tarian lets out what I can only assume are a few expletives. He chuckles and gives me a rueful look. "You've got two hours to share your findings and give out instructions. There are plenty of scientists on the team who can work on this once you do."

"I think that's fair, so long as Micah is in charge of the data. He's the only one I trust to keep everything safe."

I note Tarian's complete shift in mood and I roll my eyes. "Are we back to the pissing contest again? You do realize Micah and I are friends and nothing more. Right?"

"Does he know that?" Tarian counters.

"Of course he does. And it's not like you own me."

"I'm going to dodge that very obvious bait and simply reiterate that we are mates and that's how I will look at this relationship from now on. There will be no other female for me."

I open my mouth to protest, ready to bring up my theory about more than one mate– though after what I just shared with Tarian, even I can acknowledge it's a dick move–when Tarian interrupts.

"It's not just about your relationship with him. His background check has a few issues that need to be addressed."

That gets my attention. I shift out from under him and get into a sitting position.

"What are you talking about?"

He looks at my peaked nipples longingly, but he manages to focus. "You're aware that there is no record of Micah's existence before the age of ten?"

I nod, wondering where he's going with this. "Micah was found abandoned on the I-10 near downtown Tucson. He was in and out of foster homes until he graduated from high school and began his studies in science."

"It's those ten previous years I'm most concerned about. You don't know anything about that? He's never shared anything with you?"

I bite my lip, knowing my response is not going to make him happy.

"He shared plenty with me, but that's Micah's story to tell. I'm not going to discuss what his home life was like before he ran away or what he went through afterward. It wouldn't be right."

Tarian's expression is thunderous. "This is for safety and security."

"His life as a child has nothing to do with security."

"He doesn't have a birth certificate within the United States, Bree. And no known record of birth anywhere else."

"I'm aware."

He stares at me like I've grown two heads. "Genetics may be your field of expertise, but assessing threats and identifying red flags is mine."

"If you want to know about Micah's life before he came to the United States then you'll need to ask him. It's his choice to give you that information."

Tarian's shoulders lower just a bit as if he's resigned himself to my level of stubbornness. Smart male. He leans over to give me a light kiss and then stands.

"We'll circle back to this later. Right now, let's get you ready for the day."

"I can do that myself. I'm sure you have plenty to do at the moment."

"It's nothing my crew can't handle, and I'm not leaving you alone for the rest of the day, especially with the type of injury you sustained."

"Tarian—"

"I ask that you humor me. You have no idea how an Elysium male gets when his mate is injured. It has not been easy to keep myself in check when what I really want to do is take you from here and never allow you to come back. Taking care of you isn't just a sense of wanting, Bree. I *need* to take care of you, especially when I failed to keep you safe."

I stare at him, surprised at the misery I see in his expression. "You think it's your fault I was shot."

"You were almost killed, Bree. For an Elysium warrior there is no excuse in the universe for failing to protect his mate."

I maneuver my legs off the bed. My toes curl as they touch the hard floor. "Tarian, there are things that not even a warrior like yourself can account for. You can't possibly see all the variables and outcomes and prepare for them."

"I can and I should."

I puff air through my lips and laugh. "Okay. You're as hard on yourself as I am. Good to know we have that in common. But keep in mind you're the reason I'm not dead. Just saying."

He barely nods, refusing to take on any kind of praise. "Be aware that I will remove you from this facility if things get worse. If I don't believe I can keep you safe in this location, I won't allow you to stay."

My spine stiffens. It's not an ultimatum I'm willing to accept, and I'd think that by now he would know better. "Fortunately for me, you have no authority as far as my staying and leaving are concerned."

His eyes are two blazing bursts of fire when he says, "I have the backing of your president, and even *he* agrees that you may need to be removed from the program since you seem to be the target."

A whoosh of air leaves my lungs. It takes me a moment to process his words. "This is not just my career, Tarian, this is my calling."

"It's also your life."

"A life that would not be given this type of ultimatum or consideration if I were male and NOT your mate." I stand, feeling the pinch in my shoulder, but I don't allow the pain to register on my face. "You have no idea what it has been like to get where I am as a woman in this field with the kind of father I had."

"Bree–"

"No! I have had to work harder and longer and prove myself more fully than any man I've worked with because I'm a woman. This is all I've ever worked for. To help people in a way science never could for my mother before she passed."

"You're not thinking clearly," he says. "If you die, I die. I won't be able to go on without you."

"Don't you dare place that on me. We're not officially mated, so you'll be just fine."

"I mean I won't want to go on!" he shouts.

I shake my head, frustrated beyond words, but I manage to find them anyway. "My God, no matter the species, males are so damn emotionally weak. Females go on no matter what. We have to. We always do. Because we have shit to do, dammit. You think suffering from heartbreak and loss is something you can use as an excuse to give up? To not move forward? Women on my planet have to soldier on and raise families, and work several jobs, and DO the thing no matter what. They do not have the luxury of dying on their sword in the name of heartbreak, abandonment, or loss."

"This is the Elysium way. Our love and devotion to our mates are everything."

"I understand that, but our scenario is different. If being mated to you means I give up helping people, if it means it puts you in jeopardy, and if it means I can't continue my work, then we will never be mated because your death will not be placed on my shoulders. You do not get to play that card here."

"You don't know what you're saying, Bree," he says, pain bleeding through his words.

It hurts me. It hurts me to hurt him.

"This project, what we are doing, is not about us. There are more people to consider, and making decisions based on what is wanted rather than what is needed isn't acceptable to me, and as a male used to making tough choices for the greater good, you know that. You know it, Tarian." I take a moment to breathe because I'm not sure I've been able to since he threatened me with being fired. "You will not interfere with my position here because if you do, so help me, Tarian, I will never speak to you again."

He swallows hard, not liking *my* ultimatum.

Not liking to be told how things will be and what I fully intend to do.

Tough shit. This is not about us.

144

"Fine," he grinds out. "I will respect your wishes. Now let's get you into the shower."

"I can handle myself just fine. Thank you."

He lets out a low growl and heads for the door. As it opens, he says, "This conversation is not over," getting the last word in before the door closes behind him.

My eyebrows narrow.

"Come at me again, Tarian. I dare you," I mutter.

TWELVE

Bree

───────────

W hat have you discovered?" Dr. Jaran asks as we finally get everyone situated in the lab. I note the extra security within and without, but I don't see Tarian anywhere, and my guess is he's watching everything from the security room. He's probably making himself sick monitoring everything from there.

Whether I like it or not, he's definitely that dog with a bone. He won't be deterred from his target, or any of his asinine ideas concerning my leaving the base.

I pull up a graph of data on the projection screen. I indicate the red bar on the right.

"These numbers represent all of the samples your team collected from females who were unmated." I motion to the red bar on the left. "These samples come from the females who were mated. And this," I reveal another graph that shows the results of how many unmated and mated females had mutated genes. "This shows all the females who carried a gene mutation."

Dr. Jaran asks, "Why is the entire graph in red?"

"Because the only females who had gene mutations were unmated females." I watch as realization sets in. It's truly the most incredible thing I've ever seen, and I'm not sure how to think or feel about it simply because I'm having trouble believing it.

"You're saying not a single mated female carried a gene mutation?"

"Correct. Which means one of two things: either we had a one in a million group of samplings, or the actual consummation of the mate bond healed the females…and I suspect the males as well. Something about the mate bond eradicates genetic mutations. Which means gene compatibility is completely irrelevant if I'm right. If the actual act of mating and fusing auras together completely heals the couple at the genetic, possibly molecular level, then this idea of survival of the fittest is off the table."

Tarian had been right. That lore of his was spot on. The mate bond created a balance between the masculine and feminine energies. Because that's what we all were in the long run. Beautiful, complicated, intricate beings of energy.

"And we're back to square one," Remy says, looking absolutely delighted.

I get it. This discovery is incredible. Especially when applied to gene therapy and its advancements. A disease like HD would be gone the moment a human female mated with an Elysium warrior. The very idea of it makes me weak in the knees. It's something I want to begin research on as quickly as possible, but I have to focus on the current agenda, not my personal one.

This latest discovery also means we get to ditch one hypothesis and pursue another.

"That's why you never had failed pregnancies or infertility issues, not to mention disease or chronic issues. The mate bond essentially heals gene deficiencies."

"I'd say that would be an amazing trade off for any female dealing with things like cancer, heart disease, or any other chronic issues," Micah says. "It might be the bargaining chip we need in the face of the very scary reality that if their mate dies then they die."

I nod, my brain whirring at a thousand MPH.

"What now, Dr. Adams," Dr. Jaran asks.

"Now we focus on genetic similarities. And by that, I mean, what did Ada and Kyllell's samples look like before they were mated, and what do they look like now that they are mated? I want to go over all of it, no matter how long it takes. I'll need Ada's medical records pulled so we can assess her DNA, pre-mate bond."

I can tell Micah, Remy, and I are the only ones excited by this prospect, but that's nothing new. We always did like to tackle the obscure and the challenging. It makes victory all the more satisfying in the long run.

"Let's get to work, people," Micah says.

I give him a grateful nod and swiftly walk toward my office. While I enjoy being out there and available to my team, I need some quiet in the space of my own assigned private area. I also have some bureaucratic paperwork to fill out after last night's debacle, and as much as I hate to admit it, Tarian was right. I'm exhausted, and my arm is a bit sore.

Alas, my solitude is but a pipe dream in this place. The moment I sit at my sterile desk, Tarian storms through the room and slams the door behind him, his expression stoney.

"That doesn't have to be closed." I point to the door.

"On Elysium, a closed door means important conversations are being held," he bites out. "Is that also something different about human customs that you would like to educate me on?"

Yeah. I've trampled on a million nerves here by meeting his ultimatum with my own.

"No, but I don't have anything to hide from the rest of my team or yours. We're all in this together, so we stick to an open-door policy," I say.

"I'm not opening the door just so you can avoid this conversation."

I sigh, feeling another migraine coming on, but I'll be damned if I let Tarian know. "And what conversation would that be?"

Tarian slams a folder down and waits for me to open it. I do, knowing what's inside.

"You went above me and had the president sign an order stating that under no circumstances were you to be taken off the project?" he asks, his tone disturbingly calm.

I'm not sure what he expects me to say or feel, but it's clear to him that this is an absolute betrayal.

Instead of defending myself, when I know I shouldn't have to, I go for a more indirect route. "Tarian, how long have we known each other?"

He blinks in surprise. "Less than two of your Earth's week."

"Right. And in less than two weeks, you've told me that you are my mate even though we know very little about each other, and neither one of us has had time to put in the effort to know each other or even trust each other. Within less than two week, you've let me know in no uncertain terms that I'm yours and to hell with the life I had, the life I planned, the career I've worked so hard for, or the choices I've made to get to where I am."

"When you find your mate nothing else matters."

"And here's where our cultures clash. Because it very much matters. You matter as an individual. I matter as an individual. We could matter as a team, but not at the expense of individual needs. Losing ourselves in each other like that. Not healthy. A scientific phenomenon such as a mate bond does not trump knowing each other, liking each other, or loving each other. That level of affection takes time and trust."

"And you don't trust me?" He looks like I've gutted him, but it's like he's purposely being obtuse.

"With my life? Yes. With my happiness? No."

He starts to argue, but I raise a hand to cut him off. "Before you tell me that my happiness matters, please review the argument we had this morning. Because that is not a conversation I want to repeat."

I hand him his orders. He takes them with steel in his eyes.

"I have to protect you, Bree," he says.

"I know you do. And I trust you to be able to do that here... where I'm needed most."

Tarian turns and begrudgingly opens the door, stopping a moment at the sight of Micah approaching with coffees on a tray. Tarian mutters something under his breath and barely manages to get past Micah without knocking him over.

Micah's eyes widen as they track Tarian's exit. Then he looks at me and mouths "wow" before coming in and shutting the door.

He hands me my coffee and pulls out the chair facing my desk.

"What the hell was that all about?" he asks.

"I don't want to get into it. Let's just say these males are overprotective and leave it at that."

Micah nods, staring at me in his assessing manner. "You all right? Your shoulder? Everything?"

"My shoulder is fine."

"But Tarian wants to take you off the project."

"How—"

"It's not a huge leap to make, Bree. And if I'm being honest, I think it's a good idea."

He could have slapped me in the face for the way he's shocked me just now.

He holds up his hands in a placating gesture. "Bree, hear me out. I'm not saying 'off the project' as in not working on it. I'm saying off base. There has to be a safer place where you, me, and Remy can work, where no one can find it and no one can breach it. If we worked with Tarian to find that place, then we could do this remotely with the team here and still get just as much done."

I take in a deep breath, rubbing my neck and shoulder to alleviate the beginnings of my migraine.

"Look, just consider it. You're still aces in my book, Bree, but you need to be alive if you're gonna save the world."

I stare at my desk and smile. Micah definitely has a way of breaking things down so I can reason without emotion obscuring things.

"I'll think about it," I say. "Let's just get through this initial day of research. I really think we might be able to pinpoint some differences in Dr. Charles' DNA now that we know the mate bond changes things. What did it change for her? And is that important?"

"I also came to tell you that Tarian's crew finished setting up the hybrid tech promised us. It's been running for a few hours now."

My heart rate quickens. "That's going to speed things up. I just wish we actually had the answers for the machine to utilize. We need some kind of marker, physical anomaly, anything within the cells, DNA, genes, something we can identify that determines how mate bond selection works."

Micah stares at me for a moment, contemplating his words carefully. Like always. "And what if there isn't anything specific that we can identify? What if mate bonds are determined by fate? Destiny? By an individual's soul plan?"

"You believe in that?" I ask, my smirk displaying skepticism.

His soulful eyes grip mine for a moment, and I swear I see something within them shift. He blinks at me, his smile sad. "I sure as hell wish I could."

I stand up and round the desk. I pull him to his feet, giving him a huge bear hug.

"Just because we haven't been able to find your real family, doesn't mean they aren't out there, Micah. Besides, you still got me. I'm still your family."

He pulls back to look at me like I've given him little consolation. "You call that making me feel better? Your graphic tees are a menace to society. At no point in this friendship have I ever been proud to be seen with you in public."

I scoff at that. "You're just jealous because I grabbed the last Storm Trooper tee from Boxed Lunch."

I give his shoulder a jab and head for the door.

"Where are we going?" Micah asks, following me out.

"We need to take a look at that alien tech. I want to see how it works."

Tarian

I KNOW SPYING ON MY MATE HAS TO BE THE LOWEST OF LOWS AT this point, but I'm able to justify my behavior by shelving it under security sanctioned activities. After all, there is no doubt in my mind that my mate was the target of last night's unsuccessful assassination attempt.

Unsuccessful, yes, but far too close for comfort. A restlessness stirs within me as I stare at the recording of Bree and Micah on my monitor. Every cell in my body urges me to take Bree and place her in a cage. To protect her.

I'll lose her the moment I take that step, but it might be necessary. I'll have to shoulder those consequences.

And I could. Orders or no orders, I could absolutely say to hell with this project, order my crew back to our ship, and drag Bree kicking and screaming onto it.

But she made some significant points that I'm begrudgingly willing to admit were reasonable. Our cultures are different. In mine, a mate bond trumps absolutely everything. Any previous plans. Any questions concerning what the future will hold.

But she's wrong about individual needs. Her needs are at the forefront of my every waking thought. It's the Elysium warrior way. I'm simply having to adjust my own expectations since Bree's needs are so different from what I'm used to in a female.

And I can tell she is not without reason. She is infuriatingly reasonable most of the time. She was clearly considering Micah's suggestion concerning an off base site in which to work. It's a brilliant idea. One that I wish I had thought of, but I'm convinced that relocating her will only buy us time. It won't stop the assassination attempts on her life. Not unless she is completely off the project.

And possibly off this planet.

But I showed my hand too soon. And I knew better. After everything I read in her file. Her troubling history with her father. His very controlling and domineering views on a woman's place and their responsibilities.

Threatening Bree's position on this project was not the way to handle things. It triggered old memories for her. It brought back old wounds that I never should have unearthed. But I'm operating on instinct, and instinct is rarely easy to control when dealing with one's mate.

It's maddening to witness how well Micah and Bree know each

other, but it further proves her point. I do not know my mate as I wish to, and she does not know me as I long for her to.

I will work on this.

I'm not surprised by Micah's suggestion, either. He is clearly in love with her and will no doubt do whatever it takes to protect her. He simply approached the subject far better than I. And I despise him for it.

"Staring at Micah as if you wish to bash his skull in will only further your bloodlust, my friend." Bodeth walks in carrying another cup of coffee. The drink has become an addiction I do not believe my crew will ever wish to give up.

"He's in love with her, and now he knows he will never be able to have her. Not with me around."

Bodeth appears puzzled. "Annnnnd?"

"He didn't organize that attack last night. He loves Bree. He would never target her. The target that makes the most sense for him to pursue is me. He isn't a risk to her or this project."

"He could still be working for the Chassaks in some form or another." Bodeth reaches my side and sips his coffee. I give him the side-eye until he offers me his cup.

I have also succumbed to the addiction.

"Perhaps," I say, "but I'm more inclined to think that Bree's safety, for him, will always be his priority. It's the only reason I haven't challenged him."

"Well, that and the fact that any challenge would kill him. I doubt Bree would respond favorably to that scenario. He's her bestie." Bodeth is all smiles as he says the ridiculous words.

"Must you remind me?"

We stand in silence for a moment, listening to Micah and Bree discuss their plans for the tech that has just arrived. I memorize every expression, every micro-expression on my mate's beautiful face, aching for a connection I know she isn't ready to pursue.

"This is not like Lynnak," Bodeth says quietly. "And Lynnak was in no way your fault, Tarian."

"Wasn't it? Didn't I tell her we had no future? Didn't I send her away?"

"That was the right thing to do, and you know it. You could never have known how she would be targeted."

"I sent her away because she *was* a target. She was my only weakness as I sat with council members, plotting in my head how I would make everything right, how I would get my brother back, and how I would root out the traitors and the Chassak scum."

"It wasn't safe for her on our planet. You were right to send her back to hers. She was of a different species and one of the few females on the planet at the time. There was no protecting her on Elysius."

I drain the coffee down, wishing it was something a bit stronger.

"Yes, well, it's a shame she never lived long enough to make it there."

"Again. Not your fault."

"It doesn't matter. I pushed her away believing it would protect her. I'll not do that here. With Bree. I will do better. I must."

Bodeth lets out a weary sigh and changes the subject. "Are we going to meet Bree and Micah sublevel? We'll need to explain how the technology works."

"I'm sure Dr. Jaran is already meeting them at the elevators, but yes, it would be best if I remain a constant, annoying presence in my mate's life."

"And the fact that you're the only one who has access to that level." Bodeth chuckles and heads for the door.

I follow him out. As we stride down the hall, side-by-side, I feel his eyes upon me.

"She wants you there, Tarian, even if she thinks she doesn't."

We will see.

Bree

THE WHIRRING OF THE ELEVATOR AS IT TAKES US SEVERAL FLOORS down—floors I didn't realize existed—is the only thing breaking the awkward silence within the cramped space. Dr. Jaran and Tarian are big enough on their own. To have Micah and I join the party leaves little oxygen.

Not enough space.

But I know I'm thinking that on a more emotional level. Am I furious that Tarian attempted to hijack my project? Sure. Do I understand his reasoning? I absolutely do. And at the end of the day, Micah made an excellent point. I'm not exactly effective if I'm dead.

Tarian is also right, and I've allowed old grievances to get the best of me. I understand what he means to do, and keeping me safe should be both our priorities. I'm having a hard time deciphering the difference between protectiveness on Tarian's part, due to concern, and possessiveness and control, like the kind meted out by my father.

They're different emotions with different intentions, and I keep mistaking Tarian's protectiveness for a grab for control. A desire to take away my choices and my own way of life. But it's not his intent, and I can see that in the way he looks at me. In the way he sat there the other night and just watched me work. If he were truly controlling, he would have picked a fight rather than respecting my workspace.

Why the hell is life so complicated?

My eyes slide to Tarian, but if I thought he'd be ignoring me after our argument, I'm dead wrong, and if I'm being honest, a bit relieved. He stares at me. Not to challenge me, but as if he's longing to hold me and won't be whole until he can. The space between us crackles with energy. I clear my throat just as the elevator doors open.

Micah's soft chuckle nearly earns him an elbow to the ribs.

We file out and head down a hallway made entirely of cinderblocks. The fluorescent lighting is not my favorite.

As we approach the sublevel lab, I hear a light thrumming. Upon entering, the lab opens up into one, spacious area with complex machinery that appear similar to supercomputers, but they're not nearly as bulky.

Tarian directs us to the center where something like a gaming console sits upon a steel table. He gingerly picks up the metal-like box. The shift in position makes it shimmer beneath the light. Almost pearlescent in color. A mix of human and Elysium tech, the computers will process data and extrapolate while this box receives and delivers data that will identify Elysium mates.

Screens blink and flash, processing DNA from female volunteers. It won't do us any good until we know what we're looking for, but at least we're getting this part of the work done. I want all of the volunteers' data processed and ready for analysis by the time we figure out exactly what it is we're supposed to identify within their DNA.

"How many female volunteers have we had?" I ask.

"Well over a million and counting. It's a bit staggering," Tarian says. "Considering the number of people who have taken to protesting against mixed species couplings, I've been surprised by the amount of females interested in seeing if they have a mate amongst our males."

"I'm not surprised," Micah says. He smirks as he paraphrases something one of our congressmen stated as a plug for the program. "They're promised a better life where they will be loved and treasured by fiercely protective spouses. A lot of women would appreciate that and find it beneficial. Especially single moms."

I am not amused. "Micah, you're an ass."

He shrugs. "Hey, there are a lot of deadbeat dads out there, and a lot of women who can't provide for their kids by themselves."

Tarian stares at Micah in alarm. "Are you suggesting that human males leave their females? They leave their children? They do not provide for nor take care of their own families?"

"Look, Tarian, we don't have mate bonds here, and there are many cultures on Earth where men do not respect women. And then there are just men who don't want to take on the responsibilities that they should. Many women are like that too, but that's a conversation for another day." I stare at the console, wondering how safe it is down here. "Micah is saying the numbers aren't surprising due to the incentives."

Although, most of these females will be sent back to Elysius. So therein lies the trade off, among other trade offs. Considering the amount of women and the possibility that thousands could be potential mates, I'm beginning to wonder how that will affect population, potential spouses for human males, and so on. Issues that have also been brought up by different factions pushing to stop the program.

Considering the state of our planet, I can almost understand why some women might not mind leaving.

Nothing I can solve right now, but it does make our jobs even more dangerous. It also means we have a lot of enemies. Not just the Chassaks.

"How quickly are the computers able to process the DNA data coming in from all these volunteers?" I ask Tarian.

"Genomic analysis of an individual takes up to thirty of your Earth minutes." Tarian states, but he stares at the tech as if he's a bit worried.

"What is it?"

"The influx of data is overwhelming. There are still hundreds of thousands of volunteers to process. It's only been running a few hours." He rubs his face, looking tired. "I think my main concern is not the overload of data, but the time it will take to process everything. If we didn't have several enemies, not to mention possible traitors within the base, I wouldn't be so worried. But I believe we need to get this done as soon as possible. Before another bomb is thrown."

"You think the Chassaks know about this machine?" Dr. Jaran asks.

"I have no proof, but the attack on Dr. Adams was coordinated from within our ranks. I think it better to err on the side of caution. It is not enough that only I have access to the sublevels. Someone will eventually find a way to get down here. There have been too many leaks within your government and mine to think or believe otherwise. And my people did not build this facility or install its security. I have no way of knowing who had access to what before we arrived. There's only so much we can control when we did not start out with it."

Valid points. For all we know there is an air vent missing on the schematics of this base. One that someone could crawl through.

"So what you're saying is there are really two targets here. Bree and this mix of human and alien tech," Micah says.

"Correct."

I feel immense pressure at this point. We have limited time before someone strikes again, whether human or Chassak. Dammit, I have got to unlock the key to this mate bond selection so all this DNA gathering and analysis can actually be utilized.

"Right," I say, blowing out a breath. "Then let's get back to work."

THIRTEEN

Bree

The pounding in my cranium is my punishment for waiting things out instead of listening to my body. I'm too distracted by the pain to notice Tarian following me into my room and closing the door.

"We have an open-door policy," I say weakly, almost jokingly. It's my bedroom, and my heart is not in the argument either way.

He takes my hand as I reach my purse for my meds and wraps me in his arms. A rush of heat starts at my toes and slowly works its way up, loosening my muscles at my legs and moving its way up my body until I feel like I'm floating in a warm cocoon of soothing energy.

"What are you doing?" I mumble as the heat travels to my shoulders and neck and unfurls beneath the base of my head.

"Holding you. You're in pain. You've been in pain since our argument. Just let me make it better. You can get mad later."

I chuckle as my body goes limp in his arms. For as much as I rail against it, there is definitely something to this mate bond thing. For his presence, his touch, to have this effect on me? I want to study it, but I'm too relaxed to pursue the thought. Tarian begins kneading my back muscles, causing me to let out a low moan.

He stills for a moment, his arms tighten around me, and he lowers his forehead to rest against mine as he breathes me in.

"If you keep making those needy, moaning sounds I'll lose sight of what I came here to do." Tarian's voice is low and gruff.

I'm not sure what possesses me, maybe his earthy rich scent or the feel of his skin against mine, but I graze my lips along his jawline and press a soft kiss there. "What did you come here to do?"

"Take away the pain." His voice comes out labored. His breathing is heavy. His arms tense and tighten, flexing and unflexing as if he isn't sure of what he wants to do.

"You already have." I allow my hands to wander, tracing the outline of the muscles on his chest.

"Bree, you have to stop."

I peer up at him, noting the tightness in his jaw, the way his horns are black and ramrod straight. "Does it hurt?" I ask, slowly reaching up and running the tip of my finger along the base of one of his horns.

He shudders in response and his arms tighten even further. He buries his face in my neck and breathes deep.

"They ache with need," he rasps. "For you. I ache for you."

"Does it ever let up?" I whisper. I close my eyes as his lips deliver soft kisses along my neck and shoulder.

"Not since the moment I laid eyes on you."

A warmth grows at the base of my spine, my body tingling as his soft kisses become more intense. His hand glides along my side with purpose, brushing against my torso and the side of my breast, swollen and heavy with need. He brings his lips to the base of my neck and administers light kisses as I cling to him, holding on for dear life, sensations slamming into me and interfering with all the reasons why this entire scenario and anything that follows is a bad idea.

He circles his knuckle against the side of my breast, moving ever closer to my nipple, already aching and erect, eagerly waiting for any attention it can get. His lips glide along mine until he takes them soft and slow just as that knuckle of his lightly traces the outline of my nipple. So close yet so teasing. I let out a soft moan of protest, but he swallows it with his kiss and growls low in the back of his throat. Then he gives me exactly what I want and lightly pinches my nipple between his knuckles. To be brought to near orgasm with these light ministrations is something I'll never believe, but Tarian doesn't have to do much to get me seeing stars.

With one arm holding me against him, his mouth eagerly exploring mine, he uses his free hand to slowly unbutton my blouse, gaining access to that same nipple and administering light stimulation with skin to skin. Arousal soaks my panties, and Tarian no doubt scents this since he immediately drops to his knees and unzips the back of my black pencil skirt, sucking in a deep breath when white, lacy panties are revealed.

He runs his tongue along the outline of the fabric where lace meets thigh. His finger grazes the area of fabric covering my clit and applies pressure. I moan with need and run my hands lightly over his horns, only adding fuel to this burning torment. Tarian pulls my panties down, revealing my pussy, ready and aching for his attention.

He places my right leg over his shoulder for better access and I hold onto his horns for dear life as he kisses and licks my folds and clit, once…twice.

"Oh god, Tarian," I cry as he buries his tongue deep and circles my clit with his thumb.

His satisfied growl vibrates against my already sensitive skin. A pressure builds at my core, growing stronger with each thrust of his tongue, and then he sucks me hard, bringing me to the brink before pulling back and lightly licking my clit, circling his tongue there and softly running his finger along my slit.

I whimper with need, wanting more, feeling the pressure, that burning need present yet unfulfilled.

"I'm going to make you come, Bree, but not yet. I want to be buried deep inside you when you do."

I can hardly think straight as Tarian unbuttons the rest of my blouse and slowly slides it off my shoulders. My bra is gone within seconds, and all I can do is watch as Tarian takes his own clothes off, revealing a cock that makes my pussy clench with need. I've studied Elysium male anatomy. I know everything there is to know about their physiology, their *skeema*, their ability to bear young by extending it and burying it deep within their mate to spread their seed. But seeing it in the flesh, literally, is something else.

I reach my hand out and lightly run my fingers along the smooth texture of his cock. His breath hitches but he keeps his hands at his side, allowing me to explore him. I cup the two sacks that house cum meant to stimulate the female from the inside out. Ada mentioned that Elysium cum was its own aphrodisiac, extending a female's orgasm and driving her damn near crazy.

My hand moves to the middle sack, a flaming red, meant to be released via his skeema when Tarian is ready for children. He sucks in a deep breath as I lightly handle his sack. Then he moans when my fingers slide along the ridges circling the base of his cock up to the tip of his skeema. That perfect point that will hit my clit very soon.

I grab his cock and softly explore its length, watching Tarian as he fights for self-control. But it doesn't last long. He grabs my hips and pulls me flush against him.

"I'm going to take you slow, Bree. Savor you with every thrust of my cock. And we are not stopping until you've come as many times as I see fit."

He picks me up and gently lays me on the bed, covering me with his body and taking my lips with his. Within the circle of his arms, his hard body flush against mine, and his lips taking my own, I don't think I've ever felt more safe or more cherished…or more aroused.

He nudges my legs a little wider with his knee and dips his head down to kiss my breasts, circling his tongue around one nipple and then another before trailing kisses along my chest and then down toward my pelvic bone. He wraps his arms around my thighs, holding them apart and spreading me wide.

His eyes greedily take me in as he licks his lips. Then he leans in and gives my pussy a long, hard stroke with his tongue. It's wet and rough to the touch, causing delicious friction to ignite within my core. A rush of wetness floods my pussy and Tarian drinks it down, licking and suckling in long slow strokes that gradually build tension within my core, rippling outward but never quite peaking. I'm teetering on the edge, but Tarian senses it and runs his tongue along the outline of my seem. Offering little touches and licks that tease and torment.

"Tarian," I say, fisting the sheets and lifting my hips to meet his gentle suckling. He holds my hips in place, letting out a warning growl that vibrates along my pussy and causes my inner walls to tighten. Hot arousal floods my folds, and Tarian catches it with a long, hard lick before plunging that wicked tongue of his deep.

It's the most tantalizing game of cat and mouse, as he builds my pleasure, stoking the flames, bringing me to the brink but never allowing me to completely fall over. I'm so wet and needy for him, I'm not thinking anything coherent by the time he kisses his way up my body and moves to his knees. He runs his thumb along my soaked folds, making me groan.

"You're ready for me, Bree?"

"God, Tarian, yes," I say, nearly choking on my words.

He gives me a wolfish grin before pressing the tip of his cock against my opening. I feel my lips widen, welcoming him in as he slowly buries his cock between my soaked folds. I'm so turned on, the slight pinch I feel as his cock fills me only enhances the pleasure. He pulls back a little, helping me adjust and then he pushes forward even further, his eyes never leaving mine as he watches every expression on my face.

I gasp as he buries the last inch of himself within my channel and hits a spot I didn't even know I possessed. We both moan at the same time as he seats himself fully and begins circling his hips. Thrusting and circling in slow, rhythmic movements, building upon what he's already prepared. Stoking those flames a little higher.

He grabs my hands and pins them to the bed, thrusting a little faster, a little harder, kissing me with each tantalizing pulse of his cock. My moans and whimpers are caught up in his kisses, his tongue plunging into my mouth and circling my tongue as his cock hits me in just the right spot again and again. His skeema rubs against my clit, stimulating me to the point where the building pleasure takes hold of my entire body.

"Tarian," I gasp, "I'm…"

He circles his cock and grinds against me before pulling back a little and then plunging in hard and rough. I explode, falling over the edge, my entire body vibrating with the nuclear force of it.

My walls clench with my orgasm and Tarian lets out a feral roar, thrusting hard, pistoning in and out as we both ride our pleasure out together. He thrusts one last time and collapses on top of me without crushing me with his weight. He buries his face in my neck as I wrap my arms around him and just hold him close to me.

Dear God. That was…I'm…

I fight for some level of coherency, knowing the pleasure will abate, knowing that once the euphoria is gone, an altogether different emotion will sabotage whatever happiness I might have grasped in this moment. I wait for that sense of panic to set in, the feeling I always get when emotions are raw and exposed, but all I sense is a level of fulfillment and peace that defies all the preconceived notions I've ever had when it comes to romantic relationships or anything even close to resembling one.

Then I feel another sensation take hold. Erotic tingles sweep along my core as Tarian's cum works its magic on my sensitive skin.

Tarian is still rock hard, seated so perfectly within me that when he shifts to look at me, the slight friction of his movements coupled with his cum makes me feel as if I'm being softly licked and stroked from the inside out.

I make a pleading noise I swear I've never made before, and Tarian's horns slowly stand at attention as he zeroes in on my mouth.

He traces his lips along the outline of mine as he slowly withdraws his cock barely an inch and then pumps his hips forward again.

We both moan into each other's mouths, and I reach for his shorn, silver hair, running my fingers through it and circling at the base of his horns. He pumps faster, taking me harder as I gasp and beg for more. The intensity of his gaze is too much for me, and I close my eyes, overwhelmed by the truth of what I see there, by the sensations building and growing, a connection I can't begin to explain with logic, reason, or even science.

Tarian has never minced words when it comes to what he wants, but the level of adoration and tenderness in his gaze is enough to make me believe that his feelings for me don't purely stem from some biological imperative.

"Bree, open your eyes and look at me," he says, his tone a throaty command.

I can't help but comply as he leans back on his knees and pulls me on top of him, cupping my chin in one hand and wrapping his other arm around my waist to hold me firmly against him as he rocks into me hard and deep.

My legs are wrapped tightly around his waist, my hands gripping his shoulders, nails digging in as he pumps in and out, building that delicious pressure up until I feel as if every single atom I possess will burst into a blazing inferno of raw pleasure, but it isn't the pleasure I'm sure will be my undoing. It's the level of connection that goes with it. I can't not feel for this alien, and I'm terrified by that truth.

"No hiding...from me...my mate." He kisses me, a deep and savage taking of my mouth as he stakes his claim on the rest of me. He breaks the kiss to trail his lips along my jaw and down my neck until he reaches my shoulder and bites down hard.

I gasp and then cry out as my body explodes over the precipice and takes flight. A golden shimmer of light flares around me, reaching for something of its own volition, knowing exactly what it wants, what it needs. Determined to fill that void and become whole as it never has been or ever could be.

"Goddess, Bree, I've...never seen anything...more beautiful." He buries himself within me one more time, prolonging my pleasure as he roars with the force of his own.

Tarian's voice only fuels the light further, my orgasm rocks my body as it convulses with the power of this light. Tarian cups my chin and fixes his gaze with mine as we ride out this endless euphoria.

The light surrounding me begins to dim, slowly returning to my body, never truly finding what it was seeking, and although I feel more in that moment than I ever have in my life, I'm puzzled by the sense of loss that soon follows.

Tarian and I breathe hard, neither one of us speaking for a moment. He holds me close, resting his forehead against mine.

Whispering soft words to me in a language I don't understand, but there's really no need for translation. I can imagine what he's saying is exactly what I'm feeling.

And that damned peaceful feeling remains, shocking me with how right everything is, everything except that light. That sensation of failing to complete…something.

"Tarian," I finally say, "what was that? The light? Did you see it?"

Tarian

I SAW IT. BREE'S AURA. AND IT'S MORE BEAUTIFUL THAN I COULD have possibly imagined. It's also something I never should have been able to see without her permission.

But I bit her and opened those channels.

I have no regrets doing so since I didn't bite her a second time and consummate the mate bond. I know she is not ready for this, but the very fact that I lost control and bit her even once is unacceptable. Kyllell unknowingly bonded Ada to him against her will because he thought she understood what was happening, and Ada simply did what her heart and instincts dictated even if she didn't know how the mate bond actually occurred.

It caused them a bit of confusion, although things worked out in the long run. Fortunately for me, I'm a little more astute at reading females and knowing what they want, and Bree does not want this. Not yet, anyway.

Although her aura certainly knew exactly what it wanted. Whether Bree is willing to accept it or not, she is mine on a deeper level than she could ever imagine.

And I am hers.

Her aura never would have received me like that, beckoning me to her, seeking mine with so much determination I barely had the willpower to resist it. I had to refuse her, and it hurt more than I can ever put into words.

I regret my actions.

Well, that's not entirely true. I run my hands up and down her arms, circling my finger against the bite mark on her shoulder, a sense of primal satisfaction filling me at my claim on her. She shivers at my touch and stares at me with wonder, a question in her eyes.

"Your aura, Bree. Your aura sought out mine, wishing to bond with me."

Her eyes widen in shock. "Did we…"

"No," I say, pulling her closer when I feel her stiffen. I've made so much progress here. I must tread carefully. I nestle her head under my chin and embrace her, relieved when her body relaxes against mine and she finally returns my embrace, her delicate arms encircling my waist.

"What do you know about the consummation process, Bree?"

"Not much," she says. She pulls back to look at me. "But we didn't consummate the bond?"

"No, we did not." I watch her, fearing the look of relief I know is soon to follow. I'm surprised when she appears disappointed. As if she's lost something and can't figure out how to get it back. In that moment, I realize I can win her over. She just needs more time.

"You've made it very clear where you stand, Bree. You're not yet ready, and I would never force something like that upon you. I want all of you because you have given me all of you. I will not take you. Not like that."

She nods, looking at me thoughtfully. "Does that always happen? Did your females' auras reach out first? Then the male takes the next step to bond them together? Or do I simply not have any self-control." She laughs, appearing a bit flustered and self-conscious.

It's adorable. But she must know my mistake if we are ever to build the right kind of trust between us.

"No, my mate. I'm afraid that was my fault. My instinct will always be to bring you as close to me as possible, and in this case, consummating a mate bond is going to be my number one priority. I've never felt the urge to bite someone until you. I was not prepared to fight it."

I run a finger up and down her spine, feeling her shiver beneath my touch. The tingling from my serum is a bit distracting, but this is an important conversation. I slowly slide my cock from her sweet folds, groaning as I do so since I'm nowhere near done with this delectable female, yet knowing we must resist at this point or I will bond her against her will.

Her breath hitches at the shift in position, but she bites her lip before letting out a moan that surely would be my undoing and break all of my power to resist her. I seat her on the bed and hold her hands, staring into her eyes as she gazes into mine, appearing so trusting, I'm afraid to ruin it by my confession.

"So biting is what triggers the consummation?" she asks, appearing more intrigued than angry.

I nearly chuckle. I forget who I am dealing with. Bree's curiosity, her natural inclination as a scientist to uncover knowledge and understand how things work might be the only thing that saves me here.

"When an Elysium couple are ready to consummate their bond, the male will bite his female on the shoulder. His incisors inject a liquid compound into her veins that activates her aura."

"Activates?" Bree's eyes are alight with wonder.

I cup her chin and give her a quick kiss, unable to help myself when she looks at me like that.

"It opens her aura to the male. It gives him access. I don't actually know how or why, but there is simply something within our...our..."

"Venom?" she asks, playfully.

I grin. "Only you could make it sound like a poison."

She laughs, and it's like nothing I've ever heard, sending waves of warmth through my being and filling me with a sense of fulfillment I've been searching for all my life.

"Why can't we call it an elixir?" I ask. "Something that benefits both parties."

"More like a love potion." She grins and then her expression turns curious again. "What is the technical term for it in your language?"

"*Kaimree.* In your language it's meaning could be directly

translated to completion. Making what is only part of a half a complete whole."

Bree considers this for a moment. "That's beautiful. Completion. To make whole."

"You mentioned before, Bree, that within a relationship there is the couple, but there is also the individual. I have not forgotten that. I don't want you to assume that *Kaimree* somehow infers that you cannot be whole on your own."

"No, I understand what it means. I understand the symbolism behind it." She traces the outline of my shoulder as I breathe in her scent.

She smells of me. Her very essence mixed with mine. Her skin will forever smell, for lack of a better word, claimed. My scent will be there as a warning to any male able to notice regardless of the lack of consummation. I decide it best to not mention this to her.

"So there is something within *Kaimree*, some kind of property, that opens a female's aura?"

"Yes. More specifically there is something in my *Kaimree* that can access your aura and yours alone, something that only your aura will respond to."

"I would really love to study that."

I grin. "I'm not at all surprised."

"What prevented us from bonding fully then?" she asks. "I felt myself reach out to you. I couldn't contain it or control it. So how did it stop?"

"It requires a second marking. I bite you again, injecting a second dose. When I do this, your aura opens further, allowing me to plant my spiritual essence, my cord deep within your aura's center. If your aura accepts this then we are bound. Forever."

I swallow hard, remembering the way in which her aura went searching, not fully open but nearly leaping from her body, seeking me out with a level of focus and persistence that I nearly failed to resist. I ache with the loss of it. But I ache on a consistent basis now that I have Bree in my life.

"And you didn't bite me again."

"No. I knew you would not appreciate being bound against your will, no matter what your aura claimed to want from me."

A slow smile steals its way across her beautiful lips. "Thank you for giving me that choice."

"You're welcome."

We stare at each other a moment longer before I decide it best to leave things as they are. I don't wish to ruin this moment nor the progress I've made here.

I kiss her gently and pull back, cupping her chin. "I must check in with my crew. If we're going to protect you and that alien tech, then I need to make sure the subterranean level can't be breached."

I make a move to stand, but she grabs my hand.

"Tarian, I've been thinking about what you said, about moving me off the project."

It takes me everything I have to remain quiet, hoping she has finally seen reason.

"Micah mentioned another solution that might make us both happy. Micah and I could move off base to a secret location of your choosing. We take the alien tech and any other supplies we need, and you and your crew keep us protected until we figure this out."

It's not exactly what I want to hear, and it angers me that she is considering Micah's plan rather than simply considering her safety, but I'm not about to give her my feelings on the subject. Not when I already know what the outcome would be. This is her way of compromising.

I must learn to do the same.

"I'll begin the necessary preparations and find the right location," I say. "But you tell no one of our decision. Not even Micah. It's best if he only knows once it is happening."

"What about the president?"

"The more contained this is the better. I'll let you know when we're ready to leave. It might take a few days. Until then, just continue working as usual, and make sure you're doing the hand signals you're supposed to. Do not lag in this."

"Okay."

I hesitate before adding one more thing. "You'll no longer sleep alone, Bree. This isn't just about my desire to be with you in every way I can. It simply isn't safe."

I wait, gauging her response, gearing up for an argument that I don't wish to have. She considers me for a moment and then nods.

"As long as you don't look at it as a sign of moving in together," she says.

I'm puzzled by the phrasing, but she isn't arguing, so I'll take my wins where I can get them.

I lean forward and kiss her one last time before getting to my feet and dressing for the evening. I scent her arousal as she watches me, her eyes taking the whole of me in.

Leaving my mate naked and aroused in that bed is the worst form of torture. I do it anyway. Her safety is my main priority. No matter what I have to do to achieve it.

FOURTEEN

Bree

The moment Tarian leaves, I have to pinch myself a bit to make sure I'm fully conscious. That entire…uh…event had not been on the agenda. The enormity of what I felt and what I shared with him just now? Also not part of the plan. My brain is scrambled. Obviously.

Did I really agree to him staying with me from now on? Just like that? With that weak caveat that he couldn't consider it moving in together?

Not only did that not make any sense in this scenario, but it certainly wasn't going to make sense to a male who already considers this a done deal and wouldn't understand the concept of "moving in together" or the significance behind it.

From what I gather, once you find your mate, you find your home. There is no such thing as a trial period where you test the situation out. It's a done deal.

I bite the edge of my fingernail and try to sit with my emotions for a minute, but I'm really not bothered by this development.

And that bothers me!

I should be freaking out, angry at the possible distractions this could cause, the inevitable struggle over career and relationship, the ramifications when this is all over and I'm still not interested in hopping a spaceship to Elysius with Tarian.

But are you okay with watching him hop on that ship without you?

Maybe not. And maybe Tarian's ability to set aside his needs and consider mine is starting to win me over a bit. He could have easily taken advantage of my lack of understanding concerning consummation of the mate bond because that information was definitely not in any of our files.

Rather than taking away my choices, he opened my eyes to possibilities and stepped back so I could see how I felt about it. When I think about my aura and the way it went seeking his, not to mention the sense of loss I felt when I never connected with it, I'm thinking Tarian played that whole scenario like a pro.

Not to manipulate, but to prove that I could trust him.

And I'm definitely starting to do just that.

I'm seriously contemplating the idea that I might be able to be me and be someone's significant other at the same time.

Across the room, my halo screen beeps a notification. The AI security feed says, "Incoming call from Dr. Ada Charles. Do you accept?"

Not wanting her to see me like this, I quickly jump off the bed and find my discarded blouse. I fight to get my arms through the sleeves and then button the damn thing. So many buttons.

"Come on. We couldn't have a blouse with a zipper." I just have to look half decent from the waist up.

"Incoming call from Dr. Ada Charles. Do you accept?"

I sit back on the edge of the bed with the covers drawn over my lower half and say, "Accept."

Ada's smiling face appears on the holocomm. Then she's smirking at me as she gives me a once-over.

"Bree, it's so nice to see you. Taking a midday nap?"

"Just changing into something more suitable for the office."

"Well, you missed a button. Sex with a gorgeous alien who is completely devoted to you and your pleasure will mess with your motor skills every time."

I point a finger accusingly. "This is all your fault. Insisting I consider the possibilities. Breaking down my own defenses. I was completely helpless in the face of his–"

"Massive charms?"

I splutter for a moment. "This is all your fault."

"I gotta be honest, Bree, in the last few months that I've known you, I don't think I've seen you looking so well."

I glower, but she's immune to my bitch face.

"So how was it?"

I sniff, folding my arms across my misbuttoned blouse. "I'm pretty sure you already know, and I'm pretty sure you're benefiting from all the happy side effects that interactions with an Elysium mate has to offer."

"Side effects?" she asks, appearing intrigued. "Do tell."

"As much as I hate to admit it, my chronic headaches go away when Tarian and I are together. I feel more energized. I just feel whole."

Her expression sobers, all traces of her teasing set aside. "Wait, let's revisit your chronic headaches. You're telling me that Tarian's presence somehow heals them? That doesn't seem right."

Now I'm the one who is confused. "You've never noticed that illnesses or any other ailments seem to get better when Kyllell is around?"

"I don't think I've been sick since Kyllell and I consummated our bond. Although I did have a bad reaction to some pain medication when I was being used as a guinea pig, but I got better fast."

I have no idea what to make of this.

"Not sick in any way? At all?"

She shrugs. "I didn't get sick too often before I met Kyllell. My main battle in life was brain fog and chronic fatigue, but that's pretty common when you're always working and never sleeping. You work ten times harder than your male counterparts just to get ahead."

Yeah. So goes the career path of a woman of science.

"And before you and Kyllell consummated the bond?"

She considers my question before responding. "I recovered from Chassak poisoning. Three quills to the neck."

I nearly choke on that information. I thought she was only hit once. But three times? Tarian said she recovered remarkably well, but three times the amount of poison that would normally fell an Elysium should have done more. In my book it really should have killed her. Different physiology or not. How the hell did she survive that?

"How quickly did you heal from the poison?"

"I think it was just a day or two."

I pat around my bed and then my night stand, searching for a pad and pen. I open the drawer quickly and find what I need. My notes are messy, but at least I know how to read my own chicken scratch.

"What else," I ask once I finally finish.

She quirks her head to the side, trying to remember. "Well, I broke my leg trying to free Kyllell from a clam the size of Toronto, but that healed quickly with the leg brace he gave me."

"A leg brace healed a broken bone?" My tone is dubious.

"It was an alien leg brace. Better tech."

I narrow my brows, wondering if I can add that to the data but decide it's an incident that can't be completely relied on. I make a note of it anyway, intending to ask Tarian how long it would normally take a break to heal using those types of braces.

"What are you thinking, Bree?"

"I'm thinking I don't have enough data to work with here. Once I have more, I'll let you know. But you feel good? Everything is fine?"

"Physically, yes. Mentally, we're all stressed out and worried over here. Kyllell has become more diplomatic, but The Council is about as helpful and effective as Congress. Everyone is fighting to be right rather than simply working to *make* things right."

Yeah. That sounds familiar. "Just let me know if anything changes with your health."

"And you let me know if you need to talk about what you shared with Tarian. I know you have a lot of reservations about relationships, Bree, but you won't lose yourself in this one. Not in a negative way."

"I'll think about it." I'm not really ready to talk about it because I'm not sure I want Ada to know that my aura has a mind of its own.

But maybe she experienced the same thing since she didn't even realize what she was doing at the time.

"Before I let you go, I need to share with you the reason I called. Kyllell has contacted a source on Draioch, asking for information on when the trafficking market began on that planet."

Draioch. The planet Kyllell was exiled on. The one Ada was accidentally transported to via wormhole.

"It's been there for some time?"

Ada's expression is grim. "Over fifty of our Earth years. The earliest records identified by this source as to the types of females being trafficked shows that several of them were human, and the most recent records indicate brand new 'cargo' as they put it, being sold at auction within the last week."

"Which means either brand new cargo was stolen from Earth before we made an alliance with Elysius or..."

"Or the Chassaks are still able to access Earth and get women off our planet despite Elysium ships and defenses operating round the clock to protect Earth from any unidentified spacecraft."

"How? How are they doing this?"

She shakes her head, looking just as upset as I feel.

"Can you let Tarian know?"

I rub my neck, feeling the tightness and stress of the day getting to me. "I'll tell him. He'll need to let the president know."

It's a grim end to the conversation with more problems than solutions. I've barely had a moment to hypothesize how the Chassaks are still arriving on Earth when my cell phone rings. It's Micah. I don't bother with pleasantries, and neither does he.

"What's happening?" I ask.

"More data to sift through in the lab."

Good. I need to get my mind off Tarian, Ada, and all the other problems I face. Data is something I can wrap my brain around and analyze with zero bias and zero emotion.

Exactly how I like to operate.

I let him know I'm on my way, and then I go to the closet to grab some fresh clothes. When I lift my arm, I feel a slight ache. I go to the mirror to check out the mark Tarian made on my left shoulder.

There is mild raising of the skin where the puncture marks are prominent. A few drops of clear liquid can be seen around the mark. I carefully walk to my smaller kit on my desk and use my supplies to take a sample.

I wasn't kidding when I said I wanted to study this stuff. Maybe I'll be able to find some answers within Tarian's *Kaimree*.

I'm back in the lab within fifteen minutes, but I already see Micah at my desk, nursing a coffee and staring at the screen with tired eyes.

"Is it all looking like Greek to you?" I ask as I pull up a chair.

"More like Mandarin." He rubs a hand over his face and turns to smile at me. "Your headache go away?"

"Yep."

"Because of Tarian?"

I hesitate for a moment. Micah sounds a bit defeated when he says it, and I know the closer I get to Tarian the more likely it is that Micah thinks I'm leaving Earth forever. "He does seem to be the migraine whisperer."

"Hmmmm."

I wait for more from Micah, but he just sits there with a sad smile on his face.

"I'm not leaving you, Micah."

"I didn't say you were, but I do think we've got an addition to the crew now, don't you? On the plus side, he's handy to have around when one finds themselves in the middle of a coup."

I grab his hand and squeeze tight. He leans forward and reciprocates, but the resignation on his face bothers me. "Nothing is going to change. I'm still the same Bree."

"Everything has changed, Bree." That sad smile still lingers. "And I'm happy for you even though it means you're probably going to be off planet for some time after this."

I sigh, realizing Micah is just preparing himself for abandonment because he's that used to disappointment. But we're family, and I have no intention of leaving him behind. I have no intention of leaving, period.

"And what if Tarian disagrees?" he asks, and I realize I said that last part out loud.

"It doesn't matter. This is my home. It's where I belong. It's where I can do the most good, and it's where my family is." I look at him meaningfully so he knows that's exactly what he is to me.

He nods, not looking convinced. I'm not sure what else to say so I change the subject and drill down into the data with him. But in the back of my mind, I'm wondering how this is all going to pan out.

I look around the lab and notice Remy is missing.

"Where did my second in common go?" I joke.

"Remy got some news about her son. She said something about firming up the details for getting him treatment."

I let out a sigh of relief. "I knew Tarian would be able to help her."

Micha rubs his face, looking a bit sad. "I wish she would have told me Gabe's cancer was back. She's been so distracted lately. She could have come to me."

"You know Remy," I say. "She has a hard time asking for help."

"Sounds like someone else I know."

I ignore his smart ass comment as I spot Remy entering the lab. She looks like a wreck, her hair disheveled and massive bags under her eyes.

I stand and move toward her, pulling her into my office quickly.

"Is the news not good?" I ask, once the door is closed behind us.

"No, it's good. My mother called and said that she and Gabe have been moved to Phoenix Children's Hospital where he can receive advanced medical treatment. Tarian arranged it."

I rub her shoulders, trying to pull her out of this funk she's in and knowing she has every right to be this upset. She can't leave the base and be with him. She can't be by his side as he fights this.

"Remy, this is going to work out. I promise."

She clears her throat and gives me a smile that fails to reach her eyes.

"I'm sure you're right. Can we keep this just between you and me? Obviously Tarian knows, but please don't discuss this with him.

I just…I'm having a hard time with this. The well-meaning questions, the pity…it messes with me."

"Of course. I completely understand."

As we leave my office, I'm saddened to realize that Remy isn't holding out much hope this time around, and the thought is truly disturbing to me. She needs to be with her son, but it won't be safe for her to leave the base and be near him.

Rock meet hard place.

We've been running into a lot of those scenarios lately.

Tarian

I SIT IN THE SECURITY ROOM, STARING AT THE SCREEN, WATCHING Bree and Micah hold hands as she tells him she's never leaving him or this planet. It rips at my chest, like a fire consuming my nerve endings, burning them to a crisp.

I turn the transmission off and wonder why I do this to myself.

I can always rationalize this level of privacy breach as a security measure since my crew and I are recording and listening to every staff member's conversation–and everyone is aware of the necessity of this, including the staff–but I know this is a symptom of my jealousy. Not to mention my possessiveness.

This matter would be so easy to solve among my people on Elysius. Challenge issued. Challenge met. I win. My competitor leaves my mate alone.

But this dynamic…this idea that a male and female can be as close as Micah and Bree are with zero intimacy involved is something that does not exist in my culture. It worries me. Her level of devotion to him might be the one thing that holds her back from me. I can more than prove to her that she can still be Bree and still be a scientist and pursue her career even if she is mated with me. She won't lose herself in our love, in our connection. If anything, she will find more of herself than she could possibly imagine.

But if she won't take that leap due to obligation and familial duty to Micah, then I may lose her despite her feelings for me. Despite the strides we've taken in getting her to see me as a positive in her life rather than something pulling her down.

I think of her father. It is clear the man had much to account for based on certain conversations she had with her therapist. I cringe at the thought of her ever finding out that I accessed those records, but I needed to understand why she was so resistant to me.

I wonder how she feels about her father now that he's gone. So many things I wish to learn about my mate.

Yes, I'm worried. For all of those reasons. Certainly not because I think Bree has feelings for Micah.

I scoff aloud at the thought, causing Dywrr to give me a questioning look. When I say nothing he goes back to his work, shaking his head at the screen since he knows I'm just spying on Bree at this point.

"Someday you'll understand," I say.

"I'm not judging your actions. I'm judging your inaction. At what point do you kill the scientist?" The wide grin that spreads across my face earns me a chuckle from Dywrr. "So you have thought about it. I was worried you'd been touched by the Goddess for a moment."

"You know I can't kill Micah. I can't even give him a good ass kicking. He's too fragile."

"He's family to her, Tarian. You've poured over their files, and you know that Bree is never going to cut Micah out of her life. What are you going to do?"

I think for a moment, giving that question the consideration it deserves.

"Nothing."

"Nothing?" Dywrr's sour expression, his level of disappointment, is understandable. Doing nothing is akin to backing down and stepping aside. Forfeiting your own mate.

"We're not dealing with the same expectations here, Dywrr. The rules on Earth are different. Humans are different. Micah may have feelings for her, but I can't hurt him without hurting her, and I will not hurt my mate."

"If she won't leave him and go to Elysius, what are your options?"

It's a very good question.

And I don't have a workable solution yet…unless…I can follow through with her suggested plan, and make sure Micah is never part of it. She works off-base with me and my crew until she finds the answers we're all desperate to have. Then she's done with the program, and I get her to a safer location.

Without Micah.

Maybe I can use the excuse that it's for her own safety and security.

I've got a feeling that no explanation will be good enough for Bree, but I would rather risk her wrath than have her lose her life.

I'm not losing another female, my mate, to these Chassak scum.

"And it's not just Micah I have to worry about. Remy is also her family."

I notice Dywrr's ears perk up at the mention of this female. I sit back and decide to test the waters.

"She has a son, you know."

"His name is Gabe." Dywrr bites back whatever else he was going to say. He turns to see me wearing what Bree describes as a shit-eating grin. "Do not say it."

"You just seem to know a lot about her."

"I'm supposed to know a lot about everyone here. It's my job."

"Right."

Dywrr appears ready to throttle me, but Bodeth rushes in before he has the opportunity. He heads directly to one of the computers and pulls up some information on the screen. He is always intense, but it's clear this matter is urgent. He moves the information to the larger screen and steps back.

"Take a look at this," he says.

Dywrr and I stare at a number of monetary transactions that date back to over four solar orbits.

"What is this, Bodeth? What are we looking at?" I ask.

"This is a record of Dr. Jaran's financials."

He has my attention. My eyes focus on the amount of money

being transferred to Dr. Jaran. The number of times these transactions have occurred.

"Who was he receiving money from?"

"Derwag." Bodeth folds his arms over his chest, looking ready to kill Dr. Jaran.

I admit that this looks bad. Derwag, once a loyal friend to our family, had taken over the Council during the attack on our women and pushed my brother out. Later it was uncovered that Derwag had really been in league with the Chassaks, working with someone unknown to overthrow the government. To assassinate my father.

"How was this missed?" I ask. "We did extensive checks and rechecks of every scientist before they were sent to Earth."

"He created a dummy file of financials. I found this when you asked me to do more investigating into our own males."

Actively hiding these records is a clear sign of guilt. Not a chance Dr. Jaran was an oblivious pawn simply taking orders and getting paid for it.

"Do the dates of these transfers correlate with anything specific?" I ask.

"The latest payment occurred the night Ada was taken from your home and used as a test subject."

My fist clenches, remembering Kyllell's fear, his crazed search for her. Some of her eggs had been harvested and fertilized. Those operating on her were ordered to implant all of them in her womb to see if they would take. She very nearly died.

But Dr. Jaran wasn't a surgeon. He hadn't been anywhere near that facility the night Ada was taken. At least, that's what the records showed.

Was it possible that Dr. Jaran played a hand in those tests done on Ada? Was it possible he had done far more and was paid for it?

"You want to move on this?" Dywrr asks, looking ready for a single nod from me.

I do. If Dr. Jaran had a hand in Ada's suffering. If he's been in Derwag's treacherous pocket this entire time, then we have plenty to imprison him on. But we need to play this smart. I did not get Kyllell back on that council after years of exile by being impulsive. No. This is a game of strategy, after all, and we don't know enough about these transactions.

"I prefer we do more digging. I want to know the correlation dates of these payments. What major events occurred during those instances? What has Dr. Jaran's activities over the last four solar orbits looked like. Friends, family, acquaintances, business dealings. I want to know everything. We paint a bigger picture here, and then we will know our next move."

"Do you think he is really a Chassak infiltrator?" Bodeth asks.

"Anything is possible. Dr. Jaran could be dead. Might have been dead for some time now. He could be the partner that this other Chassak was working with. We don't have enough information, but we don't move until we do, and we make sure Bree is never left alone no matter what."

Bodeth and Dywrr get on their latest assignments while I leave them and head to my quarters as quickly as possible. My baser instincts tear at my restraint. This scenario is more maddening than I could have ever foreseen. I require a cool head. I always have a cool head when plotting and planning my foes' demise. I pride myself on remaining ten steps ahead of everyone, anticipating my opponents' moves before they are ever made.

With Bree's safety on the line, I find my ability to predict these variables, to see things coming before they arrive, nearly impossible. The smart move to make is to find out more about Dr. Jaran and then pull his strings until he has managed to entangle himself in his own death trap.

The warrior in me wants to barrel into the lab, grab Bree, throw her over my shoulder, and carry her kicking and screaming back to my ship where I know I can protect her. By doing so, I'll lose her trust and any progress we've made, and I'll tip my hand too soon.

I arrive at my quarters and wait impatiently as the door whooshes open. I immediately head toward my gear, searching for a compartment hidden within the casing of my photon guns. I flick it open and pull out a tiny communicator, something I gave the president for emergencies. It cannot be traced. It cannot be tracked. It cannot be hacked.

It's the only way I can be sure that what I share with him goes absolutely nowhere. I pull out a blocker, preventing any possible hearing devices from picking up this conversation. I leave a coded message on the communicator and wait for the president to respond. I have no way of knowing how quickly he will see the message and get back to me, but I know that Bree is in good hands with Laoth stationed at the lab. I have a few minutes at least.

My communicator beeps, surprising me with the president's speed. I click the communication button and clear my throat.

"Mr. President, I'm aware that you gave orders for Bree to remain on the project, but I need orders for her to remain on the project and be taken somewhere else entirely."

There's a soft chuckle on the other end before the president speaks. "You're not one for chit chat, are you, Ambassador?"

I have no idea what he means so I just wait for a response.

"Has the situation escalated further?"

"It has. We believe we have identified the other Chassak infiltrator, or at least someone of interest, but I want Bree out of here. She can find her answers at a place of my choosing with all the equipment she needs."

There's a moment of pause before he speaks again. "And once Dr. Adams has found those answers and we begin identifying compatible females?"

"She's ordered off the project for her own safety."

"Understood."

There's a moment of silence, but it's made heavy with the weight of my previous words.

"Ambassador, Dr. Adams will not take kindly to this. She will know you are directly responsible for this request. You'll lose her."

"Maybe, but at least she'll be alive."

"You don't think this is her choice? Her decision when it comes to her safety and how much risk she is willing to take on?"

I understand what he's saying, but my instincts cannot abide his reasoning. "I do think it is her choice, but I know what her choice will be, and I can't allow it. Not when I know it will lead to her death."

I hear the president let out a sigh on the other end of the communicator.

"You can protect her, Ambassador. Have a little more faith in your own abilities."

"My abilities are not in question, but the variables are. The longer she is here at this base, the longer she is a waiting target. She might as well be bait, at this point. A way in which to draw more traitors out, and I'll not allow that to happen."

More silence on his end. In all honesty, this is merely a formality, offering respect to this leader and making sure I do not burn down this alliance with any impulsive actions, but if he refuses, I will take Bree off this project myself, and we may never get the answers we all need.

I suspect he knows this.

"Do what you must, Ambassador. I'll not officially sign off on anything as we both know that nothing is secret or sacred over here at the White House. Find the appropriate location for Dr. Adams to finish her research, and when she has the answers, get her the hell off this planet."

"Thank you."

He chuckles. "If I were really doing you any favors, I'd try to talk you out of this. It won't end well for you or Bree as far as your relationship goes."

I'm aware. But I have to assume that at some point down the road, Bree will be able to forgive me for this.

FIFTEEN

Bree

I'm the last one in the lab again, with Dywrr hovering in my peripheral, silent sentinel, oozing menace and definite Clint Eastwood vibes. Like he's just dying for some action.

At this point, I prefer the silence of the lab and the solitude since I would be hard pressed to explain how I came by Tarian's *Kaimree*. Studying this substance is fascinating. I watch as a tiny bit of the sample visibly recoils from the sample of female DNA I placed alongside it, refusing to mix with it. I look at another dish where the substance is coiling around my own DNA.

I can't, for the life of me, explain it. I'm sure one day I'll get to the bottom of this, but every single DNA sample belonging to other human females I've introduced has been rejected by Tarian's *Kaimree*. Every sample but mine.

Testing a drop of it for its chemical properties is the damndest thing I've ever encountered. There are properties I can't identify simply because they don't exist on Earth, but then there is one property that has me a bit stumped.

Methyl-folate. A lot of it.

It's not something a human can make on their own, but it is a form of folic acid that humans need to form healthy cells. It would make sense that other life forms would need it too, but why the hell is it in their *Kaimree*? How are Elysiums producing it on their own?

All I've done here is give myself more questions to answer.

And I love it.

I'm about ready to create another control group when Tarian's voice echoes from the entryway, sending light shivers along my spine. I turn to see him sending Dywrr off, relieving him of his bodyguard duties for the night.

I watch him approach, so sure in his steps, in the way he carries himself. His eyes are laser focused on me, and that amount of attention from a male like this is enough to put any woman's brain on hiatus.

It's enough to make me wet even before he takes me in his arms and lowers his lips to mine. The fact that I don't pull away, panic, or even feel as if my professional and personal life are colliding at that moment speaks volumes. Then again, I haven't been able to draw that line between personal and professional since the moment I laid eyes on Tarian.

His kiss is gentle at first. Tender in its delivery. Then he deepens the kiss, causing my core to heat with anticipation, a rush of warmth ignites a far deeper desire, soaking through my panties and Tarian growls low in the back of his throat.

"I can smell your need, Bree. I think it's time for you and I to retire to our bed."

I smile, shaking my head, trying to clear it of this hypnotic stupor he always puts me in.

"I'm jealous of your heightened senses. Humans don't have all the advantages Elysium physiology has."

Tarian shrugs, a playful grin teasing the corners of his lips.

"I think that's especially true of human male physiology, Bree. I can think of one thing in particular that holds several advantages that you can benefit from."

I chuckle, gazing into his eyes, feeling a sense of empowerment at the way he looks at me, as if I'm the most important person in his life.

The mate bond dictates I should be, but among all the damn

worries I've dealt with when it comes to a life with Tarian, whether he truly cares for me is a big one. Nature dictates Elysium mating practices, but how does natural affection play into this?

"Were there couples that ever mated but never actually fell in love on Elysius?"

He assesses my words, studying my expression, no doubt wondering where that came from.

"I've learned to never take your questions at face value, Bree. What you're really asking me is if what we feel for each other is real. Do I care for you because of you and not because nature dictated I should."

"I think it's an important thing to look at."

He nods, clearly searching for the right way to express himself. It's what I love about Tarian. He isn't dismissive when it comes to my questions and concerns. He doesn't shy away from the hard conversations even though I know he doesn't like to have them.

"I've studied your fairy tales and your romantic comedies."

I blink, not expecting that response and having no idea how it's relevant, but my brain short-circuits as I visualize Tarian sitting down to watch something like *Miss Congeniality*.

"Okaaaay?"

"Humans have this prevalent ideal when it comes to what is known as a happily ever after. There are portents and signs, guiding individuals to their soul mate or their one true love."

"Which is why it's all make believe. It's not real."

He shrugs. "It may not seem likely that a guiding force within this universe could bring that level of fulfillment to couples, but the desire, the desperate need is still there. It's in your culture. So many people look for love and companionship with the right individual, and so many people experience heartache and disappointment because this process of human dating is so damn infuriating for you."

I laugh, realizing he's right. How many times have I heard Remy go on and on about her dating mishaps and the amount of assholes in the world?

"So what you're saying is Elysiums don't have to deal with the guesswork behind finding their soulmate."

His arms tighten around me as he places his lips against my neck. My hands tighten on his shoulders as my body responds. He leaves his lips there, hovering just above my skin.

"I'm saying that we do not fall in love because the mate bond dictates that we should. It isn't giving us zero choice in the matter. It simply guides us to the individual who will offer us the most joy, the most fulfillment, the most happiness, and by extension, as the relationship grows, the most love."

I pull back to look at him and don't bother to hide my skepticism. "I'm supposed to believe there's a force in this universe that knows better than me? Just helping people find their other half like its moving pieces on a chessboard?"

"I have no idea what a chessboard is, but of this I am certain. There will never be another female for me, Bree. I will never want any other female but you, and I don't need a scientific explanation for it."

I consider his response. I feel the weight of it as well as his sincerity. I'm not a fan of puzzles that can't be solved. Everything has an explanation. It has to. It's how I make sense of this world. This life. How I navigate every dynamic of it.

Even relationships.

But I have no answers for this pull. The desire I feel. The affection that has grown over the weeks we've spent time together. If my mother were here, she would absolutely laugh at me. She'd find this so entertaining. I can even hear her words right now. Something she would say to me all the time.

Not everything requires explanation, Bree. Sometimes what you feel is far more informative than what you know.

And what I feel with Tarian is safe, loved, cherished, and respected. I feel a whole host of other emotions as well. Particularly for him, but I'm not really ready to analyze those yet.

"My mother would like you," I say, surprising myself.

His eyes widen for a moment, but I can tell I've made him happy.

"I'm sure she was a wonderful female. She had to be if she raised someone like you."

I swallow down a lump of emotion, trying to get this conversation back on more firm footing or at least footing I know how to navigate.

"So you never felt affection for other females? It only happens when Elysium males are bonded?"

His eyes flicker, a burst of dark emotion shadowing his expression.

"Finding your mate can take some time, and Elysiums are not known for celibacy. We take many lovers, and we are completely capable of developing strong feelings for them."

Now I'm intrigued because his words have the ring of experience behind them.

"Who did you develop such strong feelings for, Tarian?"

I try not to let that thought bother me since we both had lives before we met one another. Of course he would have dated other females.

Her name was Lynnak. She wasn't an Elysium female. I had met her on one of my many runs with my crew before the Chassaks attacked our women."

"You found her on another planet?" I ask.

"She tried to steal from me." He laughs, although I can tell that talking about her is painful. I can also tell he needs to talk about it. "We were transporting some cargo between ports, and she managed to steal one of my prized daggers. I got it back, but I also made her join our crew and handle the cooking and cleaning in exchange for not going to the authorities."

I raise an eyebrow at that. "You made her cook and clean? Gender specific tasks, huh?"

Tarian rolls his eyes. Something I don't recall ever seeing him do before. It's so human and odd to see.

"I gave her those jobs because it was all her frail body could handle and it put her in close proximity to food, something she was clearly in need of."

Made sense. He gave her a home with his crew. Food and shelter. It just makes me like Tarian even more.

"You fell in love with her?" I ask, pressing for more details.

"Eventually, I did, but in the beginning, she was just some street urchin who needed a break in life. She needed someone to give her a chance. I didn't see her as anything other than a member of my crew until she accidentally cut her hand while cooking. It was a deep cut, but easily stitched. Easy to fix. But I was enraged by it. By her carelessness. That she accidentally hurt herself when I was doing everything I could to protect her. The anger was irrational. I couldn't figure it out until Dywrr set me straight."

"As he so often does." I cup his face and caress his cheek as he chuckles softly. He grabs my hand, guiding my palm to his lips and kissing it.

"He does know how to put a male in his place." He holds my palm against his cheek, breathing deep before continuing. "After that, she was mine and I was hers. It was natural. It made sense. Even though it wasn't a mate bond and completely impossible — as I thought at the time — due to our different species, I still wanted to be with her."

"And she never worried about you finding your mate?" That had to be the worst kind of expiration date, especially when you knew it might be coming but you had no idea when.

"Surprisingly she never worried. She would take me for as long as she could have me, and I found her approach to the entire scenario so brave. She understood risk, and she never shied away from it. To her, life was worth living to the fullest. Life was worth experiencing no matter the pitfalls."

She sounded fearless and brave. The type of brave I'd never been able to get a handle on.

I feel the tears gathering because I can tell this did not end well. It ended long before he met me. Dywrr said he'd been alone for some time.

"You broke up?" I ask, though I suspect the answer is much worse. Tarian is fiercely loyal. He wouldn't have ended things with her willingly.

"She died."

I knew it was coming, but it hits me hard either way. It's a blow to my insides, as if I can feel Tarian's pain, his anguish, and even worse, his self-loathing.

"It wasn't your fault." Because I know he's blamed himself for a long time. He would see her death as a sign of his weakness. Weakness that he was unable to protect her.

And suddenly, his overbearing attitude, his desire to get me off base and off this project, it makes a lot more sense now. He's not interested in losing someone else. He's already lost so much.

"It was. She was a target because she was with me."

"How did it happen?"

"It doesn't matter. Her death could have been prevented, but I didn't see my enemies' next moves. I wasn't ten steps ahead. Not in this."

I decide not to push this. Getting the details of how she died isn't important. I think he's discussed as much as he can, and my guess is it's more than he's been willing to discuss with his crew. He'll talk to me eventually. For now, it's time to let it go.

But not before I make one thing clear.

"You can't control everything, Tarian, and that's not a failing. It's simply a fact."

He grunts, unwilling to agree or possibly disagree. Smart Elysium. Not wanting to start a fight with me. I almost chuckle at how he navigates conversations with me, already knowing when to advance and when to retreat. A real strategist.

He leans in, resting his cheek against mine. Then he surreptitiously whispers in my ear. "I'm going to give you access to the sublevel. If everything goes wrong, I want you to be able to get to the only place that you and I have access to, but you must keep that a secret."

I pull back, studying his features, paying attention to the tick in his jaw. I nod my agreement.

His muscles are tense from the strain of our conversation. Reliving it was no cakewalk for him. I run my hands along his shoulders and begin massaging them until he lets out a soft sigh and folds me in his arms, burying his face in my neck.

"I won't lose you too, Bree. I won't."

I hold him close and bite my lip, wishing he hadn't said that. I've come to terms with my growing feelings for him, but I'm not leaving this planet. My home is here. My work is here. The thought of leaving fills me with a sense of wrong so fierce, I can't even begin to describe it. Which means Tarian will have to decide what he's going to do. His choices will determine how this plays out, and I'm not sure what they will be.

I just hope this tentative faith and trust I've finally begun to place in him is warranted. I hope he doesn't turn out to be like my father.

SIXTEEN

Tarian

I hold Bree in my arms as she sleeps, unwilling to allow her to be alone. Either I'm with her or one of my crew, but no one else protects Bree. Not after the attack where I nearly lost her. Not after my recent meeting with my crew where we discovered a few unsavory things concerning Dr. Jaran and his business dealings on Elysius.

We may not have consummated our bond, but the physical closeness and intimacy we've shared has revealed an entirely new Bree. A soft, vulnerable, and inviting side that I firmly believe wants love and companionship no matter how hard she fights it.

And if I understand defensive maneuvers when it comes to matters of the heart, I know they are almost always built upon past hurt and past fear. Bree is not singular in this issue. My guilt after losing Lynnak has made me even more overbearing and protective than normal. All based on fear. Fear of the past repeating itself. Fear of becoming just as mindless, desperate, and even hopeless as the males left to watch their females suffer and die without any recourse.

Not a single way to stop it.

Not a single answer, hope, or prayer in the world.

Discussing Lynnak with Bree has opened up a floodgate of

memories and emotions better left buried. I'm glad she knows, but I don't think the conversation was good for my own personal struggles and fears where Bree is concerned.

She is afraid of losing her identity and all that she has accomplished and might continue to accomplish in the future if she gives in to me. Sharing this level of knowing is no small thing, and she's finally letting her guard down and trusting me.

The stab of guilt I feel at the necessity of testing that trust annoys me. I've already put my plan into motion. My crew and I are preparing to relocate with the necessary equipment Bree will need. I have no intention of taking Micah with us.

Our tech, on the other hand…getting it moved from the sub-level will be a challenge, but we can't have the key to our success without the lock opening the doors to compatible mates. The tech goes with us too.

Our movement of materials has been a slow and steady thing over the last week. Due to the cloaking abilities of our ship, we've managed to maneuver it to the base near a sub-level exit. From there, my crew and I have methodically transferred materials onto the ship in the dead of night. The last item of equipment being the very thing that will take Bree's info and identify the females compatible for our males.

It is not without its risks, but as it stands, I do not believe our movements have been detected.

Bree shifts in my arms, and I relish the movement. The friction of her skin against mine as she sinks into my arms and relaxes further. I want to stay like this forever, cocooned in an impenetrable paradise of our own making where outside demands, responsibilities, and enemies can't reach us.

But there is too much to contemplate and so much that worries me. My brief moments of peace with Bree are just that.

I consider the possible threats surrounding my mate. Particularly Micah and Dr. Jaran, although Micah is a threat for an altogether different reason.

Bree will never leave him. Their bond is fierce, and it would pain her to let him go. While I hate this, I can't insist she come back to

Elysius with me. I won't ask her to make that sacrifice. Which leaves me with little choice.

Once all of this is over and I know it is safe for us, safe for Bree, I will remain here with her, and we will make a life here together. It's the only solution. It's also how I neutralize Micah as a threat. Well, a threat to me at least. She doesn't have to choose between us if there is no choice to be made.

Dr. Jaran on the other hand...

I've watched him this past week with even more interest. He does seem to be doing the work he is supposed to, and his behavior towards everyone on staff is normal. After learning of Bree's conversation with Ada, and receiving more intel from Kyllell's source, we've begun to fit the puzzle pieces together. Many of Dr. Jaran's monetary gifts from Derwag coincided during specific auction weeks.

Derwag and Dr. Jaran directly involved in trafficking, it would seem. And all of this happening after the attack on our females. It would be normal to seek out solutions to the future of Elysius, but for a government official to be involved in trafficking and even experimentation for possible mate bond compatibility in this manner? To hide what he was doing? There were better ways. We found a better way. We have volunteers. No need to kidnap unwilling females and test them.

It also begs the question, where are the human females Dr. Jaran and Derwag were using as essential lab rats? And was it just humans being experimented on for mate bond compatibility?

And how does that fit in with attempts to sabotage this particular program. It would seem counterintuitive since Dr. Jaran's goal is the same as ours even though he and Derwag went about it the wrong way.

Or if Dr. Jaran is actually dead and being played by a Chassak spy. The idea of a Chassak being anywhere close to Bree is enough to color my vision with battle rage on a consistent basis. More complications when it comes to seeing clearly and remaining several steps ahead of my enemies.

"Containment breach in room zero, one, nine. I repeat,

containment breach in room zero, one, nine." The intercom system connecting the lab is jarring, breaking that fragile peace I've relished with Bree.

Interrupted by more issues.

Bree stirs in my arms, her soft skin pressing against my stiff cock and bringing last night back to me in a rush.

"Did they say there's a breach?" she asks, her words soft and laden with sleep.

"Yes." I swing my legs over the edge of the bed and reach for my clothes. "It's an offshoot of the lab where we store sensitive data on the humans and Elysiums that we've collected."

She sits up quickly, the blanket falling to reveal her supple breasts. I have to tear my gaze away, knowing if I don't I'll lose all reason and take her again.

This time fast, rough, and hard. My already hardened cock responds to these pleasant thoughts as I visualize Bree on her hands and knees. Her wet folds taking all that I have to offer.

Her next question helps me focus on the here and now.

"Why would anyone breach that when we've got all of that information backed up? They can't corrupt or destroy it." She pulls herself across the bed and eyes me as I button my shirt. Seeing her naked and rumpled in that bed leaves me with a level of satisfaction I've not experienced in a very long time.

A shame I can't savor the moment.

"Get dressed," I say. "I need to investigate this issue, but I'll not leave you alone."

She nods quickly and jumps off the bed, wrapping her arms around me and giving me a quick kiss before walking to her drawer and pulling out some panties.

I could stare at this female's backside all day.

I shake myself, cursing at my inability to focus when someone has yet again attempted to derail the efforts of this program and those involved.

Now I just need to go figure out how much this latest move at sabotage might set us back.

~

THE DOOR TO THE SECURITY ROOM SLIDES OPEN, AND BODETH and Dywrr step through. After studying the security footage and noting the grim looks on their faces, I know we've had a casualty. I'm just surprised by it. I thought humans were more resilient to Chassak poisoning.

Micah follows behind them, an unwelcome presence. I'm not sure why he always feels the need to insinuate himself into every detail, but I'm irritated by it. I keep my thoughts to myself and focus on this latest breach to the base. Far too many have happened when it shouldn't have been possible.

Bree's presence at my side is a balm for my frustrations. In my mind she appears thoroughly claimed, or maybe that's simply my smug imagination since not a hair is out of place. She smells of me, but only my crew will notice. Humans have a terrible sense of smell. Most of their senses seem to be limited. Their continued survival would be a bit of a mystery if I didn't know just how determined and cunning they are.

"Ambassador, you've studied the footage?"

I nod as Dywrr walks to the security feed and manipulates the controls, taking our video back to the moment of the breach.

"The Chassaks aren't even bothering to shift," Bodeth says, staring at the feed in disgust.

"Do they usually?" Bree asks. She doesn't appear disturbed by the two Chassaks attacking the human security guards near the rear of the base.

But I know it bothers her even though she's excellent at hiding it. Her cool and steady head is one of the many things I admire about her. Between Bree and my new little sister, Ada, human females have shown incredible resilience and strength of mind.

"They hit a security guard by the name of Adam Kilpak. Shot quills out their backs. One got him in the neck." Bodeth shakes his head in disgust. "They always fall back on those damn quills. It will eventually be their undoing. Their weakness, if you ask me."

"How did they get on the base?" I ask.

"They were already on the base," Dywrr says. He approaches the feed and switches to a different camera view above the exit. It shows three different humans in fatigues, walking toward each other, meeting in the middle, turning toward the camera, and then quickly closing the distance between them and the other security guards. I recognize the humans right before they shift into their Chassak forms.

"Shit," Bree says, echoing everyone's sentiments. "It's the security guards that man the gates." She shakes her head. "How many? How many humans on the base are really Chassaks?"

"Don't forget, Bree. They could be posing as Elysiums as well. They can shift into any living form they wish as long as they've actually seen what that form is."

We watched the fight play out. Two humans are knocked unconscious while the other is shot in the neck. One Chassak enters the back exit while the two remaining keep watch. No alarms go off yet, but they should have.

They should have gone off much sooner than they did.

I assume this is when they breached room zero, one, nine. Within minutes they flee the base and disappear from camera view. I watch their retreat, something bothering me about the way one of them moves. I scrutinize the figures, but I can't place why my internal alarm is firing off.

"Can we track them as they move from the base?" I ask. "Any cameras with that vantage point?"

"Cloaking devices," Dywrr says. "They disappear the moment they pass through the gates."

"Gates that they were in charge of. Well, how incredibly convenient for them."

"Has the security guard been moved to the med center?" Bree asks.

Bodeth hesitates before responding. "He's dead. He didn't make it."

"He's dead?" She appears floored by this. It would be a normal outcome for an Elysium male if not treated quickly enough. A hit to the neck is not easy to come back from, but Ada took three and managed to survive.

"How is that possible?" Bree asks.

Bodeth points to the area of the neck where the security guard took the hit.

"Dear Lord," Bree says. "It went through his windpipe."

"It paralyzed the esophagus and enough poison drained into the lungs. He stopped breathing before Dr. Jaran could get to him."

"But Ada. How the hell did she survive three quills to the neck? That's too much poison for her system." Bree begins pacing while I analyze the video footage, taking note of the Chassak hierarchy evident in the length and pattern of their quills.

The Chassak who made the hit and killed the security guard is a general. The quills high up on the back have been allowed to grow longer. The poison held in reserve, making it stronger. More lethal.

Still, Ada was also shot by a high-ranking Chassak. Bree is right. If this human died then Ada most certainly should have expired within minutes as well.

"Hmmm," Bree says, standing next to me and staring at the images of the Chassaks attacking the three armed guards.

"What is it?" I ask.

"Something I need to test out in relation to the mate bond. Is it possible Kyllell's presence somehow helped her in the same way your presence helps me? With migraines?"

It's possible, but it would mean the mate bond has a slightly different effect on human females. One that's incredibly beneficial. Or maybe the bond has always done this, we simply never noticed due to how rare it was for our females to ever be ill.

"I'll discuss it with Kyllell," I say. "He might have more knowledge concerning this. Dr. Jaran would also be a good resource." She nods, looking as if she has more to say. "You've got something. What is it, Bree?"

Her lips quirk up in a rueful grimace. "I had a thought when that Chassak attacked me. Have you ever studied the properties of the poison in their quills?"

It takes me a moment to answer. The reference to the night I nearly lost her leaves my emotions spiraling. A purple haze descends, but this is neither the time nor the place for me to adhere to my instincts.

"Extensively. The poison is capable of paralysis, and where the quill strikes it is sometimes a cause of death. Struck in the leg, it is still debilitating, but if you can get away, then the Chassaks are unable to mete out a final death. When shot in the neck or heart, it can cause the paralysis of certain organs if not dealt with immediately, although Ada came through remarkably well, but we assumed human physiology handled the poison much differently than ours." I turn back to the screen, staring at the recording of the security guard, helpless and fighting for air.

It sickens me to see it.

"You've created antidotes?"

"Yes," I say, growing curious. "What are you getting at?"

"The bio weapon they used on your females. I'm just wondering if they genetically engineered the toxin from their quills. If it hurts your physiology that badly, did they target it specific to your females? Did they use it at all in that way?"

I stare at her in shock, having never considered that possibility, although I wonder if Dr. Jaran has.

"It's a puzzle for another day, Bree."

"Maybe." She stares at the screen, studying the Chassak aggressors as if they are a pinned insect on a board. "But what if they did use poison from their quills? What if we figured out how to reverse engineer the bio weapon they used?"

"How would that do us any good now?" Bodeth asks. "All our females are dead."

"But didn't Dr. Jaran say they preserved a few tainted embryos after their failed attempts at cloning and fertilization?"

My eyes widen in shock, the room going completely silent at her probing questions.

She always has them, and they are always quite revelatory.

"You're saying…"

"I'm saying if that toxin is analyzed along with some of the frozen embryos, Dr. Jaran might know just how to save them and birth new

Elysium females. Although, you would still need human females to continue repopulating, but it's worth mentioning to Dr. Jaran."

I swallow hard, glancing at Bodeth and giving him a nod. He quickly leaves the room, going to inform Dr. Jaran of just that.

"Now back to this unfortunate attack," she says, as if she hasn't just hypothesized the most mind-altering scenario that could quite literally change everything for the future of Elysius. "Why didn't they come after me? If I was the target, why were they in that lab room?"

"Because we leaked certain intel among staff that the volunteer DNA was backed up and located there," I say. "We wanted to draw our traitors out while diverting attention from the sub-level lab and tech."

"The better question is *why* did they bother?" Micah asks. "Why wouldn't they simply destroy the lab and the data? Why steal it?"

"It's so they can crack their own code for finding potential matches," I say.

"But it's just DNA data. It's just code. They have no answers, and neither do we. Not until we have that genetic key to cracking this."

"That's what they're waiting for,' Bree says. "They want to identify potential mates as well. They probably have their own geneticists working on it."

"Why would they do that? It's not as if those matches can work for their own species."

"No," I say, turning to Micah. "They aren't looking to match with human females, they're looking to identify and kill any female who matches with an Elysium male."

Micah sits down and removes his glasses from their haughty perch. "Well, shit. That throws a wrench in the works."

For once, we are in total agreement.

"Dr. Adams?"

I turn to see Remy standing just outside the entryway. She looks as if she hasn't slept in weeks. From the corner of my eye, I see Dywrr move toward her before stopping himself abruptly. Remy doesn't look well, and Dywrr exhibits all of the protective instincts of a male toward his mate, yet Remy isn't his mate. It has me baffled, and I'm sure it's confusing Dywrr on a number of levels, especially considering his past history with females.

"The comparison of data between Dr. Ada Charles pre and post matehood is ready for your analysis," Remy says, her eyes moving to Dywrr before snapping back to Bree. "We're just finishing up her mate's comparisons as well."

"Thank you. I'll come assess the results right now." Bree heads for the doorway, looking more determined than ever as Remy follows her out. Dywrr goes after them, anticipating my order to stay with Bree, although I'm sure he's just as anxious to keep his eye on Remy. And suddenly, I'm alone in the security room with Micah of all people.

"I understand you've had me checked and double checked," he says, leveling me with his frank gaze.

I respect that. Grudgingly.

"Can you blame me? You're working closest with Bree on this project. You've been in her life for several years. You're in love with her."

Micah doesn't seem fazed by my comments, especially the last one.

"I think I've loved Bree since the moment I began working with her. She's been my only family for a very long time, and I won't apologize for that. I won't apologize for knowing her on a level you don't, although I'm sure you will eventually. You're her mate, after all."

I assess his expression and realize it's one of resignation.

"You're not even going to try to fight for her," I say.

"It's a fight I won't win." He shakes his head and gives me a sad smile. "I see the way she looks at you. I also see the way you challenge her, forcing her to face her fear of connection on a level I never could. Because she doesn't love me. Because she really can't love me. Not the way she will eventually love you."

"You don't intend to challenge me?"

"You're capable of cleaving me in two with your sword. A smart human knows when he's outmatched. Besides, I still maintain best friend status." He stands and holds out his hand for me to shake. I do so, still thinking this custom to be a bit strange. "Just make her happy, and try not to fuck this up."

"Thanks for the pep talk."

He turns on his heel, laughing as he exits the room.

And for some reason, I sense the joke is on me.

SEVENTEEN

Bree

W hat have we got, Bree?" Micah asks as he leans over his workspace and looks at the monitor of my shiny new computer.

Remy sits at my other side, biting her lip and shaking her head in astonishment. She's gotta be as shocked as I am. I'm honestly blown away by the results, but I have no idea what to make of them.

"Both Kyllell and Ada had genetic mutations within their readings pre-matehood. Guess how many they had post-matehood?"

Micah quirks an eyebrow and leans back in his chair. "Well, if I were guessing based on the information we gathered from the mated females, I'd say zero."

"I would have said the same as you, but we would be wrong."

He stares at me for a moment, puzzled, then he leans forward to scrutinize the line of code I point to.

"One of the Chancellor's and Dr. Charles' gene mutations was not corrected. I've no clue what this gene marker is assigned to within an Elysium, but for humans the gene marker that did not heal is known as the MTHFR gene."

"Holy shit, Bree."

Yeah. Holy shit is correct because I'm starting to think Tarian's initial suggestions during one of our very first meetings holds some real merit.

"Let's gather our scientists together in the conference room," Remy says. "We need to brief everyone, have Dr. Jaran give us a rundown of that particular gene in Kyllell, and then test our hypothesis."

"No."

Remy and Micah look at me askance, their confusion palpable.

I lean back in my seat and rub my aching temples. "We take this information and go directly to Tarian. That's it. We don't reveal our findings to anyone else. The leak in this facility is still an unknown, and even though I don't have a full explanation, we're going to figure it out. But that means others will figure it out as well. So we pretend we've found nothing as far as our reports and communications with colleagues go. Okay?"

Remy nods. "Copy that. What's your plan?"

"Just keep analyzing the data and look like you guys are busy. Once I get the opportunity to speak with Tarian, I can let him know what we've found."

Micah smiles. "I excel at looking busy. You've tapped into my greatest superpower."

Remy snorts, suggesting his remark is not exactly a revelation. I'm happy to see a little more color in her face, but I still don't like the bags under her eyes.

"I'm going to save this information and erase all known copies. If anyone else asks what we've found just play dumb and say that we've found nothing."

I turn to stare at my computer screen, trying to keep my excitement from bubbling over. We're definitely one step closer to figuring this out. I just need to run more tests, but I can't do it with everyone in the lab. Looks like another late night for my team. I quickly back the info to my secured drive, a tiny little jump drive that I can easily hide if I need to.

"I almost forgot, Bree. Dr. Jaran asked about the results of Ada and Kyllell's comparisons." Remy bites her lip, looking nervous. "He's smarter than most. How do we stall him?"

I consider her question for a moment, but I know we need to stick to as much of the truth as possible. "I think our best bet is to say that we've found the same outcome. Once a couple is mated, any genetic mutations present are somehow corrected."

She nods. "I'll wait to chat with him about it. It might give us a bit more time."

"Good. I'm going to let Tarian know we have something. Micah, I'll need you with me to help figure out next steps. Just leave the lab a few moments later and then circle the mess hall before meeting up with me at Tarian's quarters. Remy, you man the fort until we get back."

Micah offers me a salute while Remy just dips her head and gives new meaning to the word focused.

I head out of the lab, texting Tarian to let him know I'm on to something without actually saying I'm on to something and asking to meet him in his quarters as soon as possible, even hinting at something that makes my face heat. It's for the benefit of anyone who might intercept our texts even though everything is supposed to be encrypted, but just the thought of his lips on my...I feel distracted and flustered all over again.

The look on Tarian's face when Micah and I show up together is priceless. He grunts as Micah and I walk in, but manages to hold in whatever snide remark he wants to make. And it's clear he wants to make it.

"What have you found?" he asks instead.

"Ada still has one gene mutation showing even after the mate bond," Micah says. "The MTHFR gene."

He waits for a moment, looking less than impressed and I have to remind myself that he has no clue what we're talking about.

"What is its significance?"

"In relation to the mate bond, I have no idea, but as far as what the gene is and what it does when it mutates, I can fill in those blanks," I say. "MTHFR is short for methyl-folate reductase. The gene produces an enzyme that changes folic acid into an active form the body can actually use. The number we use to specify the enzyme for a specific MTHFR is called a genetic marker, and that genetic marker for the MTHFR a1298c gene is Rs1801131. Humans get a copy of the MTHFR from each parent."

Tarian nods. "Why is the number so complicated and…never mind. What happens when the gene is mutated?"

"A number of things." I cycle through my knowledge of all the biological mishaps that can take place. "The folic acid needs to be converted into methyl-folate in the body. Without that conversion, different bodily functions are affected. The body can't repair DNA, it can't detox, it can't synthesize neurotransmitters related to sleep, cognition, mood, and memory, but what is most relevant to our scenario here is that this specific type of MTHFR gene mutation causes something we call Electromagnetic Hypersensitivity."

"Electro what?" Tarian asks.

"Auras," Micah says, almost to himself. "Those damn auras. He was absolutely right."

"Everything has an electromagnetic field. The cells in our bodies conduct electrical currents to communicate with each other and work in harmony so we can continue living. It's why our bodies need minerals. It needs ion charged nutrients to keep the electrical currents going and the functions of our systems to operate properly, but a human EMF is very small. Most tech surrounding us emits a much stronger EMF. Now when you have an electromagnetic sensitivity, your body begins to absorb radiation and energy from other electromagnetic fields on a level that is dangerous and destructive. Symptoms can range from fatigue, chronic fatigue, insomnia–"

"Migraines?" Tarian asks, pointedly.

I nod. "Mild to severe headaches. Yes. There are at least fifty MTHFR gene mutations, but I'm most concerned about the combination of two specific gene mutations. The MTHFR C677T and the A1298C. If you have a bad copy from one parent and a good copy from another parent, then you have a heterozygous A1298C mutation. If you inherit two bad genes from your parents, you have a homozygous C1298C. Neither one of these scenarios is stellar, but it's better than what Dr. Charles has."

"And that is?" Tarian asks.

"A compound heterozygous mutation," Micah says. "This happens when one parent passes down the 677 mutation and the other passes down the 1298 mutation."

"And why is this combination of gene mutations from both parents so bad?"

"While 677 prevents the conversion of folic acid into methyl-folate, 1298 affects the change of methyl-folate into tetrahydrobiopterin or BH4, directly messing with neurotransmitters. They transfer energy from cell to cell. In other words, electromagnetic hypersensitivity at its most sensitive."

"Your auras are drawn to the auras of weakened females," I say. "It's like the electromagnetic fields of certain women are completely compromised and open to invasion."

"But the mate bond isn't an invasion," Tarian says. "It's how we sustain each other on many levels."

"I'm not saying it's a negative trade off. I'm saying that this specific combo of gene mutation is quite possibly why Kyllell was drawn to Ada. Her EMF was compromised and his EMF was drawn to hers. Needing to complete it. But here's the funny thing. Once the mate bond was completed, her gene mutation remained the same. It didn't change."

"Which means?"

"No clue. I need more time to study this."

"Is this compound heter…uh…"

"Heterozygous," Micah supplies.

Tarian grimaces. "Right. Is this mutation common among humans?"

"I don't have exact numbers, but I'd say less than ten percent of the human population, and this will vary according to location, race, and environmental issues."

"And do you have this genetic mutation, Bree?"

I swallow hard. "I do."

"Was that the best choice of wording?" Micah asks in annoyance.

It takes me a moment to realize he's referring to what I said. Not what Tarian said.

I do.

I get it. Sounds like I've just agreed to marry my mate.

Shit, not my mate.

Just a genetic anomaly that draws him to me.

"There's more to this mate bond than your genes, Bree." Tarian reaches out and grabs my hand. "If all it took was a weakened EMF, why didn't the other males in the room respond to you the way I did?"

I'd like to avoid his gaze, but he has a point. There's only so much science can explain. At the end of the day, my gene mutation makes it possible for me to consummate a mate bond with an Elysium male but it doesn't explain why this particular male's horns burn black for me.

It occurs to me that the other half of the puzzle may never be uncovered simply because it isn't about natural selection or genes or anything even remotely scientifically identifiable. Maybe it's simply fate, destiny, a higher power, or the natural order of things.

And maybe I can live with that.

I shake myself, wondering where that asinine thought came from.

I need answers. Hard science. Facts.

I understand facts.

Emotions are far more convoluted. They aren't something I can measure. They aren't something I can predict or control.

I have an errant thought that therapy might do me a world of good.

I dismiss it. I can unpack this later.

"We need to take the human female data being processed and start identifying those with this particular gene mutation. We may not know which female can mate with which male, but we *will* identify the human volunteers who are compatible."

Micah shakes his head. "We can't do that. Not here. The moment we input this piece of the puzzle into that alien tech, our enemies will know about it, and remember, they now have all the volunteer DNA info that was collected right up until they stole it. There has to be a way we can process the information without anyone else in this facility finding out."

Tarian looks to be debating for a moment. "Continue on as if nothing has changed. I'll work on finding the leak in our security or a different solution. Until then, you know nothing. You just keep hypothesizing solutions."

I give him a quick nod before turning to leave.

"Bree, a word before you go."

I see Micah's shoulders tighten, but he plasters a smile on his face. "I'll meet you back at the lab. I'll be the scientist in the corner looking busy."

I chuckle as he heads out, leaving me alone with Tarian who stares at me for a moment before closing the distance between us and pulling me in for a heated kiss.

I practically melt within his embrace. It's criminal the way this male is able to short-circuit my brain. All thoughts of mate bonds, gene mutations, and the very real danger we're in just stutters to a stop as Tarian's hands cradle the small of my back and then travel to my ass.

He deftly unzips my skirt and lets it drop, all the while weaving a hypnotic spell around my thoughts. I barely register the sound of my panties ripping. Tarian cups my ass and lifts me, wrapping my legs around him and pushing my back against the wall. I feel the wide head of his cock teasing my entrance.

"Goddess, Bree, you're so wet for me already."

I can't even think of a single thing to say as sensation after sensation roll over me while Tarian squeezes my ass and gives me short, gentle thrusts with the tip of his cock, barely penetrating my slit, gently coaxing my opening to take him deep when he knows I will. He knows he can. He could take me right now, and I'd never consider stopping him, but it's the caring way he does it. The way he gives me the opportunity to accept or reject him. Always my choice.

He grips my thighs and spreads them just a little more, barely nudging himself further inside my channel. The extra stimulation and the promise of what's to come makes my legs shake with need. I let out a breathy moan, filled with desperation as he stokes the fire within me slow and steady. Titillating pulses and then slow circles, driving me mad with need.

He bends his head to taste one pink crest with his hot tongue as he continues his tender seeking between my thighs, my tight entrance gripping him, welcoming him in further, waiting for him to explore all I have to offer. I grip his horns, black and burning with his own desire. My touch elicits a low growl from him. He flicks his hips and pumps slightly harder between my lips, stimulating me even further. I cry out and clutch his shoulders tight, digging in my nails. His tongue traces the outline of my jaw to my ear lobe.

"You're mine, Bree. Every moan. Every sigh. Every single cry you make is mine. It's for me." The gruff, possessive tone unlocks my core, beckoning him deeper. "And I am for you." His musky scent heightens my need for him, imprinting this moment to memory and marking me forever.

A rush of liquid heat drips from my pussy, coating his head and marking him as well. He sucks in a breath and groans as the friction from this sweet torture continues. Short teasing thrusts with the promise of what's to come.

"Look at me Bree. I want to see everything you're feeling."

I focus on his golden eyes as he stares at me, deftly playing with my entrance and circling the head of his cock just beyond it. My walls pulse, clenching around his generous girth, wanting more, wanting it deeper. I gasp when his thumb softly circles the tender area of our joining, slippery and tight. He runs his thumb along my clit, and rubs back and forth to the same slow rhythm as his tiny pulses within me. The pleasure builds, tightening my core, just out of reach, and he keeps me on that edge. Soft slow circles, then a snap of his hips and shallow penetration that leaves me gasping, crying out with need.

"That's it, Bree. Everything you feel. I want to see it." I barely get out another moan as he nudges my channel open further. "I'll give you more. I'll give you all of me. Do you want that?"

"Yes. Please, Tarian," I say. His eyes heat at my desperate words, their golden hue almost glowing with pure possession.

He spreads my legs even wider and slowly slides his thick rod through my soaking channel. We moan at the same time as he seats himself, his skeema rubbing against my clit. He gently thrusts again and again, never pulling out completely, but circling and nudging as he did before, only this time he's buried so far within me, with every seeking pulse and greedy thrust, he rubs against the back of my channel, finding that hidden spot of pleasure and tapping into it, activating it again and again.

I'm boneless with need, want, and complete desperation, gripping Tarian's horns as his movements become less gentle, less measured and far more determined. He pulls back and thrusts hard, burying himself deep and unleashing a crescendo of pleasure that ripples through me as I close my eyes and scream his name.

He thrusts again and again. Hard and determined. His thick girth seeking out my core with wicked intent, not letting up for a single moment and building my pleasure even further until my walls clamp around him, milking his wide length, coaxing him to come with me. His fingers dig deeper into my skin as he moans my name. He pulls back all the way and drives into my core, slick against my channel until he hits that perfect spot again and pleasure ignites, rippling from my center until my entire being is awash with euphoria.

He thrusts again and again, only heightening my orgasm as he roars my name and gives me his rush of heat. It coats my walls and adds to my pleasure, stimulating me until my walls spasm with the force of my orgasm.

I can't think. I don't want to think. It's enough just being in his arms, being held and worshipped like this. Cocooned in this foggy haze of perfection and completely intoxicated.

I'm barley coming down when his cum activates more nerve endings. "Oh, God."

He chuckles, resting his forehead against mine. "I'm not done with you yet, Bree."

He cups my ass and seats himself more deeply. My legs clench around his waist as he moves us to the bed. I almost protest when his slick heat slides out and he sets me on my knees facing the wall. I spread my knees wide and feel him move behind me as he positions his legs between mine and has me lean my back against his chest. He crosses on arm in front and gently cups my breast, circling the peaked nipple as his other hand guides his cock between my wet folds, taking me from behind as I'm propped up against his chest. He slides in slow, and we both moan. My back arches as he gently pulls back and slides in again. One hand gripping my breast to steady me and the other hand working my clit, his fingers gently playing against that tiny nub as he fills me with his cock.

The stimulation is too much. The scent of musky sweat, sex and Tarian himself have me awash in sensations that completely overload my body, building until I'm on the edge again. He pistons faster and circles my clit, building that pressure again until I'm hovering on the precipice. I'm keening now. The soft moans and cries barely sounds I recognize as he thrusts harder, deeper. All that I am expands outward, seeking him, searching for more connection, begging for a level of fulfillment I don't understand.

Tarian's deep moan is riddled with longing and anguish. His lips find my shoulder, the scrape of his incisors nearly pushing me over the edge. And then he bites down hard and I explode, shaking in his arms, trembling with the force of my ecstasy as he pumps fast and hard. He releases my shoulder and pumps one more time before his own roar of pleasure explodes enhancing my own. We cling to each other as we ride that wave to its conclusion, his tongue circling the area where he marked me.

I go limp in his arms. My entire being completely undone by this experience. And yet that level of fulfillment I was seeking still remains elusive. As long as we avoid consummating this bond, I may never know what it means to feel completely whole.

And I have no idea what to do with that information.

Tarian gently withdraws and pulls me down to the bed, cradling me against his chest. We're silent for several moments, each of us processing what we shared, and what might have been if we had shared even more.

"You bit me," I finally say.

"Yes."

I grin, shifting to see his face. The male satisfaction there comes as no surprise.

"Is it difficult for you? To avoid consummating the bond with me?"

He doesn't reply right away as he traces his finger along my arm. "Is there something in the scientific world that can describe what it is like when two things are drawn to one another? Meant to connect? Meant to join rather than separate?"

"Well, I'm no physicist, but it sounds like Newton's Law of Universal Gravitation."

"Newton? Who is Newton? He is well-respected?"

I chuckle. "He's a well-respected dead guy who made several scientific breakthroughs that have helped us earthlings understand why a few things are the way they are." I lean forward and kiss his chest. He squeezes my arm in response.

"And what is this gravitational law?"

"All things in the universe are attracted to each other by the force of gravity. The closer the object to another, the stronger the pull, but there are some qualifiers."

"Meaning?"

"Not everything is meant to attract. Sometimes things are meant to repel. Magnetism is an important part of the equation."

He grins as I rest my chin on his chest. "Is this similar to electromagnetic fields?"

"Very. It's an opposites attract scenario. And the greater the mass of the two objects, the stronger the force of the gravity is between them. Electromagnetism is another force in this universe you have to consider. It's the force that exists between charged particles."

"So your charged particles are drawn to me, and mine are drawn to you."

I smile, taking in the fact that Tarian is trying to speak my language to describe consummation of the mate bond even though my expertise is really genetics. Pillow talk as only a scientist can have. It's charming. He's so damn charming.

"Yep. And the stronger the electric current, the stronger the magnetism."

He rubs his hand along the small of my back, his gaze tender. "So what you're saying is, your electromagnetic field is incapable of withstanding my electric current."

"Seems like you're having a hard time withstanding mine." My gaze softens as I take in his sad expression. "It's difficult for you. Not consummating the bond."

"It will be worth the wait."

"And what if I never agree to it?" I want to slap myself as soon as the words are out. I'm ruining the moment, but I need to know what he'll do.

He's quiet for a few seconds, but I can tell my words have hurt him. He takes in a deep breath and lets it out, a sense of resignation permeating the air.

"I want to be in your life for as long as you'll allow it. Bond or no bond, you're my mate, and I will never leave you. Even if it means staying on Earth."

I'm surprised by that statement. I thought it was Elysium or bust for him, and now he's thrown me a curve ball.

"You would give up your planet, your life, for me?"

"You *are* my life, Bree? Do you not see that?"

I hadn't. Or maybe I hadn't wanted to see it. Because it meant there was a very real possibility that he could be my life as well.

"What are you thinking, Bree?"

So many things.

I keep my eyes on his chest, trying to figure out how to verbalize the mess of emotions and thoughts swirling within me.

"There is safety in solitude," I say, feeling the tears come and not really understanding what the hell is wrong with me. "There is a comfortable kind of knowing when you shut the world out, limit the number of people you care about, and thereby limit the amount of negative impact those people can have on your life. Statistically speaking, you're better off alone than placing all of that power, all of that trust, in people who may not be reliable."

"You want to protect yourself."

"I want control. You can't control another person's choice or the impact it will have on your life. What my father did to my mother had this ripple effect. I know it doesn't make sense, but for years I blamed him for her disease."

"Why, Bree?"

I swallow hard, lost in thought, reliving the hell that my homelife had slowly become.

"Because he shut her down. He made her less than what she was and who she was. The moment she outshone him in the same field, the moment she proved her worth, he felt less than. Her success was something he felt diminished by when all my mother would have done was bring him into the light. This brilliant woman who asked questions, solved problems, and was a well-respected scientist. And he labeled her as nothing and shoved her into a corner. And then her disease took over." I shake my head, that well of anger bubbling to the forefront, buried so deep for so long it feels as if it's poisoned every molecule I possess.

"In my adolescent way of processing things, I watched as my father told her she couldn't think, couldn't discover, and couldn't be what she wanted to be. And she believed it. Her body believed it. Her cognitive abilities deteriorated along with all her fight, her curiosity, her wonder for life, and for the unexplained and unexplored. I thought he made her sick, and I hated him for it."

I stop speaking because the tears are there just like they've always been, waiting for some kind of acknowledgement. Just someone willing to listen.

"Safety in solitude," he says, rubbing my back and giving me comfort while acknowledging my pain. "I understand why you feel that way. And I agree."

"You do?" I blink tears away, looking up at him to gauge his expression.

"Do you have any idea how terrified I am to feel the way I feel about you? The pain I experienced after losing Lynnak will be nothing compared to what I will feel if I lose you." He reaches his other hand out and cups my chin. "I won't survive it, Bree, and I sometimes wish I had never met you because I was safe in my own solitude until I stumbled upon you."

He traces the outline of my top lip, staring at me with a look of wonder in his eye. "Then I remember that life can never be fully appreciated in all its goodness if all the bad is pushed to the side. How would I know what I have with you, if I hadn't already lost in so many other areas of my life? You can live your life in a bubble, Bree, but I think your mother would have wanted more for you."

He's right. He's absolutely right. And he's shown me a level of courage that I've certainly never been able to drum up. Not when it comes to relationships and connection to other individuals. My mother would have loved him.

"And you would stay here on Earth? With me?" I'm still not ready to believe it.

"I would."

"That's a very heavy promise to make, Tarian." I grip his hand, trying to believe his words, and battling old fears at the same time.

He shrugs. "The force of your gravity is something I will never break free of. It's a good thing I'll never want to."

His words dislodge the last few remnants of doubt and fear, along with something dense and stony, a calcified object wedged so firmly against my heart that its sudden removal shoots an electric jolt to the area. Shock waves ripple outward, followed by emotions I've never welcomed into my heart before.

I can't mask it either. I've never had a poker face, and this moment is no exception. Tarian's eyes gleam as he takes it in, the effect those words have on me. He kisses me, a gentle joining of our lips, pouring so much feeling into that simple show of affection.

I stay there in the circle of his embrace, shielded against the storm that's coming, knowing this peace I've found with him can't last forever, but this awakening within my heart is permanent, just like his mark upon it.

And like Tarian, I may never recover.

EIGHTEEN

Tarian

I stare at the security monitors, a sense of dread building within me.

After sharing that moment with Bree, finally feeling as if I've made a dent in those near impenetrable walls around her heart, I know she will feel this to be a betrayal. Taking her off planet. It's excessive. I know a different base, a different location, should be enough to keep her safe for a week, maybe two, but the enemy always knows what is going on. Five steps ahead of me at every turn, and I can't get my bearings. Not when her safety weighs so heavily upon my thoughts.

It can't be helped. The very moment those mates are identified, I'll carry her kicking and screaming to my ship.

I press the worry from my mind as I watch her and Micah in the lab, pretending to solve a problem that Bree has already solved. My mate. My life.

My thoughts replay our last moments together, the relief I experienced when my words finally registered. Her expression. I don't know that I'll ever forget it.

And I have to safeguard this progress, but first, I need to figure out why in the name of the Goddess I feel as if I've missed something important.

"Dywrr, I need you to run the footage of the Chassak attack again."

"You think we missed something?"

I shake my head, that dread returning, building to a crescendo. My subconscious knows something my conscious mind does not. Bringing it to the forefront can only be done by retracing my steps and reviewing the incident that kicked off this initial unease.

I shift position in my seat, the scrape of my gear on my hip irritating my nerves. "Can you play back the feed? Slower this time."

Dywrr and I watch as the attack plays out. I'm still disgusted by the brutality of it. They could have handled the human guards without killing them. They simply wanted to kill. As the three Chassaks flee the base, that gnawing feeling hits me again.

"Dywrr, zoom in on the Chassak to the right." He does as I ask, and just when I wonder if I'm losing my mind, I finally see it. "Those *charksis* scum. I can't believe I missed it."

"What?"

"The general. He isn't among the three."

"The what?"

"One of them was a general. The quills on his back weren't shaved down. High up and lengthy. Yet none of these infiltrators are high-born. They left their general behind."

"And he's still in the building."

"We're not waiting any longer." I turn to Dywrr and nod. "It's time to get her out of here."

"We've got everything ready to go, even the sublevel tech has been moved." He reaches for his com to signal the crew when an alarm goes off again, but this time, it isn't to warn us of a breach.

A storm.

A storm is coming in. I slam my hand against the controls, denting the frame. There's a Chassak general in the building, and he didn't stay behind for anything other than Bree. I know it.

I've got to get her out of here now, storm or no storm.

Bree

Looking as if I'm attempting to discover something I've already discovered is annoying the hell out of me. The sooner Micah, Remy, and I can get off this base and test out our theory, the better. For now, all progress is impeded by the fact that not a single individual here in the lab, aside from my two closest friends, can be trusted.

I enter my office, deciding I need to give the president an update without revealing anything that's actually of importance. When I move my hand to the secure line at my desk, the phone is already receiving an incoming call.

"Mr. President," I say by way of greeting, knowing he would be the only one to call this line.

"Dr. Adams. I'm anxious to hear absolutely anything that might give us some hope here, and I'm needing that hope soon."

"We're close, Mr. President. I think we'll have something to show for our efforts in another week or so."

There's a long pause on the other line before the president says, "You feel we can trust the ambassador and his crew? You're comfortable with his plans moving forward?"

I can only assume he's referring to moving us to an entirely different base. "Absolutely sir. I think it's for the best."

"He's told you everything then?"

His question raises a few alarm bells. Why wouldn't Tarian tell me everything? Unless the president knows something he thinks Tarian wouldn't tell me. I play along, not knowing what else to do.

"His plans and reasoning are solid."

I hear him let out a relieved sigh over the phone. "It will be safe for you once Tarian takes you off the project and gets you to Elysius. I'm glad you were both able to come to an agreement on that."

My thoughts go blank for a moment and then stutter to a stop. My vision tunnels, narrowing to a point as my hearing fades and muffles whatever else the president says.

Take me off the project? Go to Elysius? What in the world is…?

I think back on some of the conversations I've had with Tarian. The way in which he was so adamant from the start about taking me off the project so I wasn't in harm's way, but this? Taking me to his planet without consulting me on it first? Taking me off the project when we have an idea of what the marker is now? We still have to test out this theory. What the hell is he thinking? This is my career. My life. This…can't…

I don't remember ending the call. I don't even remember walking back to my work station. The only thing that's on my mind is crushing betrayal mixed with my own bit of self-hatred because I should have known better. I should have expected that any male coming into my life would eventually want to dictate the terms of my life and what I could and could not do moving forward.

I'll go to the new base and work on identifying mates, but my relationship with Tarian is absolutely over. And with that realization comes a burning pain that slowly unfurls before it detonates within my chest.

A bleeding heart. A *breaking* heart. Phrases that make sense to me now. My chest feels like it's being compressed internally. I can't reach in and remove the pressure building. I can't take medication to alleviate the hurt.

Emotions. Damn emotions. They aren't abstract to me. I know what's happening, and I'm pissed that my body responds just like any other woman's. Because I know this has to run its course.

Serotonin and oxytocin produce happiness, flooding the brain when forming attachments to people. Basically rewiring the brain as you create those connections. Increasing trust and bringing us stability. It's why so many women are upset with themselves for being duped—for feeling as if they can't trust themselves, for following their hearts. Their experiences are justified by their chemical responses. Until their significant other breaks that stability and trust. The wiring that cemented those attachments are short-circuited, and the brain is left with trauma.

I know my cortisol levels have just increased, my diaphragm muscles are tightening, and my breathing is heavy due to the shock.

Broken heart syndrome. I know it's a thing because I read a study on it. I found it both fascinating and validating, thinking of the way in which my mother deteriorated on so many levels.

But I just want this gone. I want it dead and buried.

At the very least I want it compartmentalized so I can do my damn job.

In a daze, I head over to the work table where I've been testing Tarian's *Kaimree* and my DNA when another alarm goes off.

But this time I recognize it for what it is.

"Incoming storm," says the system's AI. "Incoming storm. All military personnel and staff please head to your appropriate bunkers until further notice."

"Shit," I say, finding the timing of this more than a little suspicious.

Is there really a storm or has someone tampered with the security system?

The alarm has certainly helped me focus. I can compartmentalize far more easily when in crisis mode.

I grab my samples and place them in a container as quickly as I can. Even though the samples show me what I already know, I still don't want to leave them in an unsecured lab while everyone else is supposedly taking shelter in their assigned bunkers.

Not that it matters any longer. Studying my findings can give me more answers when evaluating the mate bond, but that's about it. Nothing in the mate bond seems to consider differing belief systems, personalities, or the probability that your mate is a complete and utter asshole.

Micah gives me a weighted look as our coworkers file out of the lab and head to their respective spots to weather the storm. I see Remy quickly following protocol, heading out of the room and to the bunkers without a backward glance. She's gone before I can signal her to stick with us since this latest alarm doesn't feel right.

"What do you think?" Micah asks.

"I say we find Remy and get down to the sublevel as quickly as possible. I don't like this one bit, and that alien tech is the most important item at this facility right now."

"So we find Tarian and get access?" he asks as we head to the exit, heads lowered so we can keep our voices subdued.

"I've got access. He wanted me to have that information just in case."

"If you're not where you're supposed to be, he's going to freak the fuck out, Bree."

At this point, I don't give a shit about what Tarian feels or thinks.

"Tarian has eyes and ears everywhere. He knows where I am. He'll know where to find us."

We make our way down the corridor, trying not to seem too obvious as far as the direction we're headed. I see no trace of Remy, but she should have been heading in this direction to get to the elevators that would take everyone to their respective bunkers. The red lights and consistent blaring of the alarm fills me with barely controlled anxiety. Not having Remy in my sights worries me. This whole thing does not feel safe.

We've just rounded a corner when the hum of a photon blaster gives us a moment of warning.

"Bree, down!" Micah yells, grabbing my arm and taking me to the floor.

My knee hits the hard tile at a bad angle, but the pain barely registers as adrenaline kicks in. The thermal heat from the blaster bleeds through the fabric of my lab coat. I'll probably find melted fibers on my clothes. Not that it's important. Not really something to be worried about but there's no accounting for random thoughts in the face of your imminent demise.

An explosion goes off behind us. I look back in horror to see the lab on fire. The open windows blackened and broken from the force of the detonation. I'm so shocked by it, my brain fritzes. We need to move, but I can't think at this point.

More explosions sound off in other areas of the building and screams echo down the corridors.

Micah keeps his shit together far better than me and snags a door handle to our left. He flings the door open and pulls me to my feet. Before I can protest, he shoves me into a supply closet.

"Climb these shelves to the top, Bree, and get into that ventilator shaft. Do not come out for any reason."

I look up, shocked to see the vent there and hellah concerned I won't be able to reach it let alone fit through it.

"What about you? You'll never be able to hide in there with me."

"I didn't plan on it. I'll draw them away from you."

"What? Absolutely not." My eyes widen as he steps back and slams the door. I race for it, trying the handle, but it won't budge.

That asshole has turned into some goddamned Rambo. He isn't even armed. I'm so furious that he's purposely put himself in harm's way that it takes me a moment to come to my senses and try the vent since, at this point, it's my only ticket out of here and back to Micah.

How the hell did he lock me in? He doesn't have a key to the supply closet.

I start climbing, grateful that the shelves have been secured to the wall and wondering if they'll buckle under my weight. I'm not exactly an expert athlete, and my knee is throbbing from that sudden jolt to the floor.

I sweep supplies off the shelves as I go, gaining purchase on the steel shelving and wishing I'd been going to the gym more often as my wimpy muscles strain against my own weight.

My focus is shot to hell as the screams of my colleagues are peppered with the sounds of photon blasters, explosions, and that incessant alarm. If the Chassaks intended to create mass chaos, they have succeeded. I just wish I knew how so many of them had managed to infiltrate this facility, the staff…ah hell, possibly even my own colleagues.

As I reach the top, I flick the latch on the vent's opening and ease the cover down. Reaching my hand into the dark maw, I feel my way forward and pull myself up a little more even though I don't have much to grab hold of. I take the shelves like a step ladder and get my upper half through the vent, pushing off with my legs and pressing my hands against the walls of the shaft to pull myself forward. I've barely cleared the opening with my feet, lying face down when I hear muttered curses and a slamming at the supply closet door.

Shit. If someone gets through, they'll see the vent cover splayed open and know exactly where I'm hiding. I don't have a way to turn and pull the vent cover closed which means I need to keep going. I army crawl my way through the shaft, trying not to make too much noise. My clumsy retreat is about as silent as a stampede of cows through a cornfield.

The banging at the supply closet door recedes as I navigate a bend in the shaft only after I manage to run head first into the wall. Sweat trails a slow path down my temples. Dust bunnies and a metallic tang sting my nose. My visibility at this point is shot to hell as I clear the bend and face who knows what. I'm hoping for another long tunnel.

Shit. I have no idea where I'm going. I haven't exactly paid attention to the schematics of the building, but I know Tarian did. He would know exactly where the vent is taking me.

Thoughts of him infuriate me, but I'm also worried about his safety.

And that angers me too.

Overall, I'm just fucking pissed.

I try not to worry. I know he and his crew are more than capable of taking care of themselves, but those quills will harm anyone, and their range and aim are a damn menace. Not to mention the inexhaustible supply of quills the Chassaks have. And it really only takes one to bring an Elysium down.

Micah doesn't stand a chance in a faceoff with a Chassak.

And that worries me even more. That idiot. I'm so angry with him for leaving me, thinking he needs to be all noble and offer up a distraction. If the Chassaks don't kill him by the time I find him, I will.

My stomach is already in knots when I finally pull myself forward into the darkened vent, and then it does several flips when I hear the sound of splintering wood echo down the shaft behind.

The Chassaks have broken down the door in the supply closet. I hear a scuffle, something being said in a completely foreign language, and then the sound of fighting. A blaster goes off, and then the fighting ceases. Low growls carry along the vent, tinny and warbled once they reach me. I have no idea what is going on or who has been shot now, but waiting around to try and understand the scenario is not happening. I can't breathe in this damn tube, and I have no intention of dying in it.

I army crawl my way as fast as I can, not caring that I can't see what is up ahead because the grunting sounds behind me are a real cause for concern.

A screech of metal and a loud snarl echo behind me, and then eerie silence follows. Not even the alarm is firing off any longer. Normally, silence would be music to my ears, but this silence is loaded with otherness. It seems like my enemies retreated after realizing the bulk of a Chassak wouldn't fit through the vent, but that thought doesn't give me peace. I crawl for several more feet and round another corner, clearing it a little easier this time even though my sweaty palms are slipping on the slick surface.

I pause for a moment, thinking I've heard something. A scuttling behind me. Too big for a spider. What the hell?

I see a pinprick of light ahead and begin moving toward it. That's when I hear a low growl, several paces back.

It doesn't make sense. These guys are too big to fit—

They're goddamn shapeshifters, Bree. Move your ass.

My breath comes out in short, panicked bursts as another surge of adrenaline kicks in, giving me superhuman speed as I slide my way along the tunnel, heading for the next vent opening, praying I get there before whatever stalks me manages to grab hold of my leg and tear it from my body.

Muted cries and the rapid, high-pitched release of gunfire accompanies my harried escape. I don't know what kind of hell is happening outside these vents, but my own personal nightmare is playing out in real time. Stalked in a small space by an alien hell-bent on murder.

This was not in the job description.

Whatever stalks me takes its sweet time catching up. Like it's simply playing with me, enjoying my panic and fear.

I reach the next vent opening and peer through it into the room. My stomach churns at the site of two security guards, their bodies riddled with quills. Their eyes bulge from their sockets, foam circling the outer edges of their mouths.

I take a deep breath, knowing the safest place to exit right now is in a room with dead bodies. That means the Chassaks have already searched this place. Hopefully, they won't come back right away, and I can deal with the threat following me.

I push the vent cover but it doesn't budge. A soft, creepy laugh pricks my ears. It pisses me off so much that I forget to be afraid. Instead, I bang my fist against the vent to dislodge the weak latch at the side. The vent swings open just as a low growl of warning draws closer. I kick my leg back, hitting something hard and earning a high-pitched squeal for my efforts.

I take that moment to dive head-first through the vent, not caring that I'm about to crash into an office chair and hard desk. It's either that or a hard floor for a landing.

But holy hell, the impact is worse than I thought it would be. My shoulder hits the desk first, popping it at a weird angle. The pain is a white heat that leaves me breathless. I hit the floor on my other side, right next to a dead security guard. Head spinning, feeling slightly nauseous, I look at the sightless guard and then I turn my gaze to the vent. Glowing eyes glint from the opening. A small animal about the size of a pug jumps from the vent and lands with grace onto the desk.

"What the hell are you?" I whisper.

The thing's fleshy green scales are riddled along its back. Quills run the length of its spine and puke-yellow saliva drips from its incisors. It stares at me, considering me for a moment before turning its attention to the exit as Tarian enters the room.

"Bree? Thank the Goddess." He sees me holding my injured arm and his gaze narrows. "We've got to get you out of here." He's so focused on me he doesn't see the alien pug. He rushes over just as the strange mutant jumps in front of me and lets out a low growl, warning Tarian off.

Tarian freezes, his eyes widening in shock.

"What in Elysarah's name…?"

The pug begins to shift, growing in height until a fully formed Chassak takes its place. Only this Chassak is enormous, bigger than I've ever seen.

Tarian's eyes glow a dangerous yellow. We're both screwed at this point. He's too close to the Chassak to avoid the quills.

Another Chassak enters the room, letting out a low growl. The one in front of me shifts his stance and says two words I never in a million years would have expected to hear.

"Tarian. Move!"

Tarian shifts quickly, diving toward my right just as the Chassak with its back to me shoots out so many damn quills I can't track what's happening.

Tarian has me in his arms and against the wall, his body protecting me. I can sense he wants to evaluate my injuries, but we have two enemies in the room attacking each other.

The Chassak that stalked me through the vent has managed to shoot quills into the neck and chest of the other alien. He takes two enormous steps forward, lifts a hand with curved claws the size of steak knives, and brings it across the Chassaks neck, completely severing the head from the body.

Blood spurts from the wound as the rest of the body goes down. Tarian continues to shield me, his gun aimed at the Chassak's back.

"I don't know why you just attacked one of your own, but you're not getting Bree."

The Chassak slowly turns around, and I freeze in disbelief. He isn't normal. Weird variations such as horns on his head, scales along his chest, and his slitted eyes tell me he isn't pure Chassak. He has genetic characteristics of an Elysium. It seems like the only things he did share with the Chassaks are his coloring and quills.

"What...what are you?" Tarian asks in astonishment.

The Chassak begins to shift again, growing smaller in size until he is no longer a Chassaks.

He's human.

"Micah?" I stare at him, mouth agape. The world tilts on its axis a bit before righting itself, but I know nothing will ever be quite right again.

Micah shrugs his shoulders, looking sheepish, vulnerable, and a bit nervous.

"Surprise," he says, lifting his hands in surrender. He looks at

Tarian and points at the weapon. "You don't need that. Bree is the only family I have. I would never hurt her."

I take a step to the side so I can see him better.

"Bree," Tarian mutters, shifting his weight to protect me, but I'm too distraught and pissed off to stand behind him.

And now that the current danger has passed, I'm reminding myself that Tarian is persona non grata.

I study my best friend, wondering how he could have kept this vital information from me for so damn long.

"Micah? What. The. FUCK?!"

NINETEEN

Tarian

Micah rubs the back of his neck, a defeated expression on his face. "I was gonna tell you Bree, but I didn't know when or how. I didn't even know what I was until we brokered that deal with Elysius and I got a good look at the Elysium and Chassak species. I'm a real mutt."

A likely story. I monitor his breathing, his smell, anything that would indicate he's lying, but I hear truth in his words, and his scent, although still not something I have ever been able to identify as human, doesn't have an acrid, bitter aroma to it. For once his scent makes sense to me. He isn't lying, but he still hid this truth from Bree all these years.

I'm not necessarily surprised that Micah is not what he originally appeared to be, but I never could have foreseen a twist like this.

"Those first ten years of your life not on record?" I ask him.

Micah's eyes darken. "I was on a slave trader ship. I'd worked on it from the time I was little. My mom was the ship's cook, working for an alien species I still don't know the name of. We crash-landed on Earth when I was young. I don't remember the how's or the whys of it. But I was the only survivor."

"Your mother was...?"

Micah grimaces. "A Chassak. I'm pretty sure my father was Elysium now. I didn't know that was what we were called until you guys showed up. She never talked about race, about my father, even though she kept a picture of them as a couple. Most of the time she shifted into human form. She taught me how to do it."

"Why human form?" Bree asks.

I'm relieved she's talking. I worried the shock of Micah's betrayal might be too much for her. I don't like the distance she's put between us, but I don't think Micah is a threat at the moment. Still, the distance is aggravating my possessive instincts. I grab her by the waist and pull her closer to my side. My internal alarms go off when she stiffens in my embrace. My gaze on her sharpens, but my attention is pulled to Micah again when he speaks.

"She was bait. They used her to steal human women from Earth. I never knew why she did it or why we didn't leave. I was too young to understand much of what went on. Then we crashed, I was the only survivor, and I had to figure things out. But I knew better than to shift into my true form in front of humans. I'd seen their reactions on the ship."

Micah is the threat I always believed him to be, but on a much grander scale. Surely now Bree will cut ties with him. We will take him back to Elysius to question him further and–

"The mix of genes you inherited is fucking awesome, Micah. Have you ever run your gene sequence?" Bree steps forward, but I pull her back, holding her in place. She hardly notices, so intent on studying Micah.

Has she lost her mind?

Micah's eyes light up at her question. "My god, Bree, it's the gnarliest stuff you have ever seen. I was never able to figure out what the shit was going on with me until we had access to Elysium DNA, and–"

"Bree, you've just discovered that your best friend is an Elysium hybrid with Chassak ancestry and instead of labeling him a traitor, you're asking him about his DNA?" My eyes flit between the two of them, feeling as if they've both missed the enormous gravity of Micah's revelation.

He is a Chassak traitor.

And Bree is quizzing him on his genetic composition.

"He might be the only one of his kind considering how much your species hate each other. It's so damn cool."

I rub my forehead, the blood rushing to my brain, my intense worry for my mate, that she came so close to death, again, all of it... spending years with a Chassak! For the first time, I understand the pain of a migraine because my head is a ball of fiery pressure ready to explode.

"Micah, what are your dealings with the Chassaks and its empire? How long have you been working with them?"

Micah appears confused. "I have no dealings with them. They're not my people or my family. I just told you I didn't even know what the hell I was until you guys showed up. Thanks for that, by the way. Cleared up a few mysteries for me."

More truth in his words, but I can't let this go. This enormous revelation. What Elysium male in his right mind would ever lay with a Chassak female? It was suicidal at best.

"And why didn't you report this once you knew? Why didn't you reveal your true identity?"

"Tarian," Bree says, sounding irked by my tone, but also infusing a lot of anger in that one word. "He's part Chassak, and we've been labeling Chassaks as enemy number one. He didn't have much incentive to out himself if the response was gonna be distrust, incarceration, and possibly death. Your reaction right now is proving my point."

Micah gives Bree a grateful smile. "What she said."

I'm ten seconds away from blasting that smile off his fake human face.

Dywrr runs into the room at that moment, saving Micah from further interrogation and his inevitable demise. "We have eight dead Chassaks and several human casualties. I know how the humans died, but our crew only took out three Chassaks and..." He glances at the headless Chassak on the floor and lets out a low whistle. "Your handiwork?" He motions to me, eyes wide with admiration.

Purple shades my vision as I grudgingly explain. "I'm afraid that credit goes to Micah."

Dywrr looks at Micah, surprise and respect marring his features. "How did you manage a beheading? There are two dead security guards in here, and you're still alive? You have a broadsword stashed somewhere?"

"He used his claws." Bree's tone is all unbridled enthusiasm.

My desire to kill Micah intensifies.

Dywrr looks between Micah and Bree. "I don't follow."

Micah looks a bit uneasy having to explain himself. "I killed two other Chassaks that were in the supply closet. They were trying to shift so they could go after Bree in the ventilator shaft."

He had protected my mate when I couldn't find her let alone get to her. I know I should be grateful, but all I feel is a jealous rage as if my place has been usurped by this abomination.

"You asshat," Bree says. "You scared the shit out of me when you followed me through the shaft."

Micah holds up his hands. "I was just trying to get you to move it. I didn't know if there were more of them and we needed to get to a safer space."

"You laughed when I tried to open the vent the first time."

"Your punch was wimpy. Face it, Bree, you punch like a girl."

She points a finger at him in warning even though her mouth twitches with amusement. It's infuriating. "I'm happy to practice my boxing on you."

She should be practicing on me. I feel my horns lengthening in rage. They are no doubt inflamed and a pulsating black, but nobody seems to notice how hard I'm trying to battle this rage building within me.

Dywrr is beyond confused now. "How did a human manage to kill three Chassaks and live through it? You don't look like you've suffered any injuries either."

"Apparently, our dear geneticist is an Elysium-Chassak hybrid who was abandoned here when he was a child." My tone has dropped an octave and comes out guttural, but the sarcasm bleeds through all the same. Which is somewhat gratifying.

I sense Bree's hand on my arm, running her fingers along my bicep. It mitigates my battle rage substantially, the purple haze of my vision shifting to something more manageable. She knows how to calm me, but she doesn't do anything more than that. Not nearly as affectionate with me as she has come to be.

There is something wrong, but I can't pinpoint it.

Dywrr takes a moment to process this before giving Micah a slap on the back and pulling him in for a rough arm hug. "So he's one of us."

Micah smiles big. I don't think Dywrr could have said anything more triggering. I make a move toward them, not sure who I plan on throttling first, but Bree's hand on my chest restrains me. Not that she has the strength to stop me, but I won't trample over her to get to them, and her touch clears away some of my muddied thoughts. I blink, trying to get myself under control and notice she's limping and wincing in pain.

"Bree? Where are you injured?"

"Just a shoulder and knee issue. I'm more bruised than anything."

"We can get her all healed up as soon as we get to our ship." Dywrr turns to Micah, handing him a blaster. "You know how to use this?"

This is too much. "You see him as a brother and not a threat?"

Dywrr looks at me pointedly, like I'm being a simple-minded *charksis*. "He protected your mate and killed three Chassaks. He has Elysium blood running through his veins. It's all I need to know, and it's not the craziest thing I've ever heard. Besides, we've needed a fifth crew member, and he's a scientist to boot. Do you have any idea how useful that will be in the future?"

"You're suggesting we add him...to the CREW?" My voice booms through the room.

Dywrr's expression sours. "Don't mind our grumpy overlord." He turns to Micah. "He's just upset that he doesn't have a good reason to kill you."

Laoth appears just then. Good timing since I've decided incinerating Dywrr will be just as satisfying as taking out Micah.

"We've secured the area as well as we can, but we have some clean-up to do, and then we need to get Bree on the ship and to a new location."

"The ship? But we can't leave without the equipment," she says. "We can't leave without Remy."

"It's already been taken care of, Bree, and we may not have time to find Remy."

"And we can't leave without Micah."

My voice flattens in response. "He's a security threat."

"He's my family. They're both family, and they are coming with us." She doesn't even look at me when she says this, and now I know something is wrong.

I stare at her for a moment, failing to understand how she can just accept this and move on like it's nothing. I try to ignore the gratitude and relief in Micah's eyes. He probably hoped for a reaction like this from Bree but never expected it.

Her jutting chin clashes with her pleading eyes. She is my greatest weakness and my most enduring strength. I don't know how to play this when Micah has done nothing but look out for my mate. Unless he's playing a very long game at the moment, and I don't believe he really is, Micah is the safest person aside from me and my crew for her to be with. He would be added protection rather than a liability so long as he is telling the truth and firmly on our side.

Still, I have to ask.

"What is your intention where Bree is concerned? You'll not be anywhere near my mate, my crew, or this project unless your answer satisfies me."

Micah steps forward, beginning to grow in size. His complete transformation takes less than five seconds, and Bree gasps, appearing fascinated rather than fearful.

Her sense of self-preservation is alarmingly lacking.

Laoth mutters a curse and takes a step forward, but Dywrr plants a hand against his chest and shakes his head.

My crew mates scrutinize Micah's true form with nothing but amazement. How they aren't ready to blow Micah's brains out is beyond me.

Micah's voice has changed with his transformation, coming out low and heated. "Dammit, Tarian, no matter what I am, it doesn't change how I feel. It doesn't change the life I've lived here as a human or the fact that Bree is the only family I have." Then he does something completely unexpected. He drops to one knee and beats his right fist against his chest. "My mother taught me one crucial thing that she learned from my father, whoever he may have been. An oath is sworn with words, bound by spirit, and—"

"Sealed with blood," I finish, shocked to hear him recite a secret Elysium rite of passage.

Micah slices his curved claw across his large palm, drawing black blood from the cut. "I swear on my mother's grave, I will never harm Bree. I swear on my mother's heart, I will never betray her trust. I swear on my mother's soul I am not a Chassak plant sent to kill Bree or sabotage the program, and I will take orders from no one but you."

He lifts his bloodied hand, although I'm not sure he understands the significance of what comes next. It's the intensity in his gaze and the sincerity in his tone that convinces me that trusting him is not only right but absolutely necessary for Bree's survival. And her survival trumps my jealousy and pride.

I slice my palm open and grab his bleeding one in mine, sealing his oath in blood and giving him something he hadn't bargained on.

I can see the shock in his eyes as my blood mingles with his, effectively binding us together as...well, brothers. A bright light enfolds our hands and travels up the length of our arms, hitting our chests and pulsing outward. Laoth and Dywrr's chests light up in response before dimming and then slowly fading back to their original color.

"Goddess," Laoth whispers.

Dywrr grins. "I knew this mission would be interesting."

"You're family now. My blood is your blood and yours is mine. You're bound to me and my crew. Don't fuck it up."

Micah blinks in surprise, and then a slow grin spreads across his face. I'm shocked to see tears in his eyes.

"Family," he says, swallowing down a ball of emotion. "That works for me."

I grunt, feeling conflicted by his response because I know he's telling the truth.

It would have been so much easier to kill him.

Bree

I'm shocked by the way Tarian shifts gears and makes Micah a member of his crew. I know Micah's revelation should leave me furious. It's a hell of a secret to keep for so long when he absolutely could have told me sooner. He knows me well. He had to have known how I would have reacted.

Then again, finding out your best friend is an alien. Maybe he felt the risk was just too great. There's not really a playbook for a scenario like this.

All those years…he must have felt so alone. Even when we had each other, he must have felt so…other. And now he's been accepted by Tarian and his crew. Family is all Micah has ever wanted. I see it in his eyes.

Leaving Micah was never an option, but now, he goes where Tarian and his crew goes, which means Tarian will be in my life one way or another. Micah and I have studied their customs enough to know that loyalty is of utmost importance. And that ceremonial exchange? It felt heavy. I don't recall ever finding any information on it before, but it's clear that Tarian understood its significance. It's the only thing that could have made him change his mind so swiftly. Which makes me ache to understand it better.

So much to learn.

And so much to discuss once I get a moment alone with my former would-be mate. Fortunately, my adrenaline makes it impossible to feel the previous pain in my chest. Buried emotions.

That I can work with that.

"While we search for Remy, we need to help any other wounded and get them to the med ward." Tarian hits his com device attached to his gear. "Bodeth, report."

"The storm system alarms were tripped. One guess as to who was responsible for that. We took out all the Chassaks that attacked, but there's absolutely no way for me to know if we got them all. We don't have any idea as to how many were already here impersonating humans, and from what I can see on the security feeds, none of the staff got to the bunkers. Many are dead."

I feel bile rise, worrying for Remy and the other scientists.

"We proceed with caution. An entire sweep of the base. Bodeth, I need you to contact the president and let him know what's happened." He turns to Dywrr and Micah. "Identify the dead and do a headcount. We need to know which humans are missing and may have been a Chassak."

"How will you figure that out?" I ask.

"When Chassaks die they revert to their original form. If we're missing humans, we can only assume they were really Chassaks."

"Shit," Micah says, appearing frustrated. "How the hell did so many infiltrate this place so quickly?"

"It's probably very similar to sleeper agents, Micah," I say. "They relocated here years earlier and assimilated into human society, getting into important fields like medicine, government, military, and who knows what else. My guess is we probably have Chassaks pulling strings in law enforcement, Congress...I mean. We know they've been stealing women from Earth for a very long time. They're playing the long game here."

"But how could they know that humans would be compatible with Elysiums?" Dywrr asks.

"I don't know that they did." I stare at the headless Chassak on the floor, trying to figure out what their long game actually is. "Do you guys remember that Chassak that tried to kidnap me?"

"You mean kill you, Bree?" Tarian's grip on my waist tightens. I try to ignore the warm fuzzies that produces.

"That's just it. He wasn't planning on killing me initially. He wanted to take me with him. He said he had the utmost respect for me."

Tarian mulls this over, but Laoth speaks first. "They've been looking for compatibility as well. This isn't just about female trafficking, although I'm sure there's a subgroup of Chassaks doing this. They're trying to figure out if humans are compatible with their species."

"Why?" Dywrr asks. "Especially when we've just seen evidence of Elysiums and Chassaks being compatible?"

"What if they're having a fertility issue as well? A population problem. You know I've never seen a female Chassak? I haven't even heard you guys refer to female Chassaks? Are they few and far between?" I look from Dywrr to Laoth, and then Tarian, realizing this has truly never occurred to them.

"But they had to have known our females were compatible at some point. Micah can't be the only hybrid. Why kill all of our females if they needed them to breed?" Dywrr asks.

"Maybe the bio-weapon wasn't meant to kill all your females. Maybe it was meant to kill your males." I wait as they consider that alarming idea. "Accidentally wiping out one source of their survival made them switch their focus to humans as viable options, although I'm sure we were originally meant for trafficking purposes. As far as biological advantages go, humans don't have them. Elysium females, however, do. We were not their first choice if this was, in fact, the plan." I shrug my shoulders. "I'm kind of spit-balling here, though."

"So they may not want to kill viable mates. They're just piggybacking off our research in the hopes that viable mates for Elysiums means viable mates for Chassaks." Micah shakes his head. "We don't know enough, but I don't think our theories are too off base."

"But do Chassaks have a mate bond? Is there some biological imperative to mate with a specific female?"

Tarian mutters something under his breath and Dywrr lets out an oath.

I look between them, confused. "What is it?"

"In ancient times, Chassaks revered matehood. The way in which they could identify a mate is different from ours, but it did exist."

"Did exist. So they just stopped finding their mates?"

"It stopped over a millennium ago. We aren't clear as to why. It isn't something they're very forthcoming about. But it didn't prevent them from breeding."

"Maybe it prevented them from achieving something else."

"We can figure this out later. We need to move now." Tarian grabs my hand and we follow the others, heading for the corridor. "Brace yourself, Bree. I'm afraid this won't be pretty."

Quills litter the long hallway with blood staining the walls. The further we move down the corridor, the more horrific the scene appears. On the ground, I spot a few guards, dead, or at least I hope so, and not suffering from whatever poison filled their veins. I feel sick, staring at the three security guards, eyes wide and mouths coated in foam.

I try to hide my limp and the pain in my shoulder, but I'm just not walking fast enough. Tarian has me in a cradle hold before I can protest. I don't say anything. My injured pride and wounded feelings can't make an appearance at the moment. I'm slowing things down when we just need to find Remy and get the hell out of here.

Down the long hall of doorways, a few to the left are open. On the right, a large glass window shows the natural world behind. Nature destroyed by mankind, with the military arriving at the entrance of the building.

Without another word, Tarian and Dywrr make their way down the hall while Laoth and Micah go in the other direction, looking for survivors of this horrific attack. Instead of taking the right turn that breaks off into the lobby and reception area, we continue onward toward the main offices.

The first thing I see when we reach the next hallway is Remy, sprawled out on the floor, blood pooling underneath her.

I squirm in Tarian's arms, trying to get to her. He holds me fast as Dywrr moves to assess her.

"Is she alive?" I ask.

"I don't see any quills, but there's charred marks along her clothing and a wound in her side." He studies her intently, worry etching his features and his horns rolling up and down in agitation.

She couldn't have been hit with a blast. Even to the side, it would have decimated her torso.

I can't even think at this point. Remy has been with me for years. I can't lose her like this.

"It looks like a stab wound," Dywrr says in surprise. "That's odd. Chassaks don't use weapons like that."

"Then what the hell happened?" I ask.

He shakes his head. "I'll carry her to med bay and get her fixed up. We can't wait until we get on the ship. I'm worried she'll bleed out."

I feel like this is just the calm before the real storm even though this attack could hardly be considered tame. I don't know what I'm expecting. Half of me wants to believe that we've managed to rid ourselves of the rest of the Chassaks at the base, the other half is looking for a fight. Grief has a funny way of screwing you over.

Dywrr quickly carries my friend down the hall, back the way we came.

"She's going to live."

"I shouldn't have encouraged her to sign up for this. It was a mistake. If I had truly understood the risks at the time…I just knew how badly she needed the extra money for her son's medical bills, and…"

"It's going to be okay, Bree. And this wasn't your fault. Blaming yourself does no good here."

He's right. I know he is, but I can't help the guilt gnawing at my insides or the dread I feel, knowing we've barely scratched the surface. We still don't know where all the scientists are or if they're even alive.

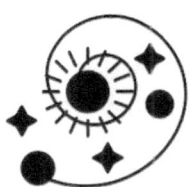

TWENTY

Tarian

W e slowly work our way through the base, searching for signs of survival, but the more we search, the more I wish I had insisted we evacuate to the ship and leave, survivors or no survivors. The carnage we've uncovered is something I can handle, but it's nothing my mate is prepared for. Despite the mass murders, we haven't located the rest of the scientists. I'm worried they may have been taken rather than killed, but I can't imagine the three Elysium scientists weren't neutralized. They would have been an enormous threat if left alive.

My mate's jaw is firm, her eyes bright with unshed tears, but she won't agree to leave until she knows if there is another survivor like Remy. Which means I may need to make that decision for her if things go from bad to worse.

But there's nothing. Not yet. Just narrow, empty corridors. Even most rooms are vacated and empty. The majority of the carnage took place within or near the lab and main offices since the Chassaks no doubt knew the protocols in place in the event of a storm alert.

I carry my mate to the mess hall, hoping we'll find more survivors, but I see nothing, and there isn't much that I can offer her when it comes to reassurances. Micah, Laoth, and Bodeth catch up to us with very little to report.

Bree will hardly look at me, and the sense that something is wrong between us increases. I don't have time to confront her on this right now, but I feel as if I've lost her in some way, and I don't understand it.

"Most of the chaos is near the bunkers. We didn't see a single scientist, though." Bodeth looks worried, which means he's found something he doesn't want to discuss until he has a better handle on it. "They may have been taken for the same reason the Chassaks tried to take Bree."

I'm finished with this. Any survivors will have to make do on their own. I have to get my mate and my crew out of here now.

"Dywrr," I say, after activating my comm. "Report. What is the doctor's status?"

My com erupts with static before his voice punches through. "I managed to find a few supplies that hadn't been destroyed by the explosions, and I did a temporary patch, but we're on the move now. I've got some unfriendlies closing in."

"Your location?"

"Near the mess hall. Headed to the rendezvous point. I'm coming in hot. I might need cover as I head down this last stretch of hallway."

"We're in the mess hall now. Forget the rendezvous point and just get here."

Bodeth and Laoth are already moving to cover the main entrance. Micah positions himself before the open double doors giving us a clear view of Dywrr as he comes careening around the corner, an unconscious Remy in his arms. A blast from a laser gun hits the wall, just missing Dywrr's head. Bodeth has already opened fire, hitting a Chassak in the forehead. The results are not pretty. A second Chassak skirts the corner and leaps over his fallen comrade, but he has nowhere to take cover once Bodeth takes aim and fires.

I'm momentarily distracted by movement from the corner of my eye and notice the swinging door to the kitchen is slightly ajar.

Dywrr manages to join us without a single scratch on him, but

Remy looks pale. From what I've studied, her coloring is not a good sign. I make eye contact with Dywrr, but his expression is unreadable. I don't think he found the medical equipment he needed to fix the internal damage, which makes it even more imperative that we get everyone to the ship.

But not before we take care of any last loose ends. I set my mate down on a chair as Dywrr spreads Remy out on the table. He hands Bree a healing wand from his pack.

"This isn't closing her wound like it should, but it's all we have. Keep it hovering over her body."

She nods and takes it as I stare at Dywrr, seeing the same concern on his face that Bodeth demonstrated. He stares at Remy as if he knows she's already a lost cause, but he can't reconcile himself to accept it. I recognize the look, but I don't understand how it's possible. His horns have not burned black for Remy. She isn't his mate, but he has the hollowed out expression of a male who is forced to watch his mate die.

I grab his shoulder to get his attention, and his expression closes off. I tilt my head as our eyes meet, asking with that one glance if he's okay? He nods and shakes it off. No time to press him, and not wanting to wait any longer, I decide it's time to get out of here, but we have to check something first.

Remembering the flicker of movement from the kitchen, I signal Bodeth to take up my flank, motioning Laoth to the other kitchen entrance on the left side of the mess hall.

They follow my signals without question. We've worked too long together to not understand what is needed.

Laoth quickly reaches the second swinging door and, on my mark, we rush through at the same time.

"Holy fuck." Bodeth's voice breaks the silence from the opposite side of the kitchen.

"What is it?" I call.

I'm faced with a line of refrigerators, cooking paraphernalia, and a steel table the length of a dining room. I move left toward Laoth with Bodeth taking up the rear. He stares straight ahead, his jaw slack with shock. Now I'm running. I make it to his side in seconds, but even *I'm* not prepared for the sight that meets me. The rest of the human scientists and two Elysiums lay dead, sprawled across the wide kitchen floor. Blood splatter paints a vivid scene across the steel appliances.

Chassak quills in their necks, mostly, though one Elysium in particular found the full force of a Chassak attack, with quills extending out of his arms, legs, back, and neck. Tortured, perhaps, to gain whatever information they could. About what, I don't have to imagine.

"They butchered everyone in here," Bodeth says, averting his eyes from the scene. "The Elysium males were a threat, but the humans weren't. Why were they brutalized like this? Bodies torn apart? This is unusual."

I agree. I can't explain it other than to identify the carnage as the result of hate and rage. There was nothing dispassionate or cold about these killings.

"What do you think they wanted here, and where the hell is Dr. Jaran?" Because he is the only Elysium scientist missing.

There's no question, really. They were here for the alien tech, possible answers to the mate marker, and they never found either. My crew has already moved the equipment to the ship without anyone the wiser, and Bree and Micah told no one else of their discovery.

The Chassaks most likely thought our scientists would have answers. My mind is a jumbled mess at the moment, considering how they knew this place was up and running, where everything was, the levels of treason involved. It couldn't have only been Chassaks. There were humans involved, too.

"Dr. Jaran was working with them this entire time," Bodeth says.

Yet that doesn't seem right either. Every monetary transaction was made between him and Derwag, and they were trying to find a solution to the mating issue. Illegally, yes, but his motivations were still the same, and this move right here, assisting Chassaks in this way. No. He was either taken for his knowledge or he is already dead.

We circle back and meet up with Dywrr and my mate who is still tending to Remy.

"We have to get her to your ship," Bree says the minute she sees me. "Did you find anything? Anyone else we can help?"

"No." I don't bother revealing more. Bree worked closely with every one of those individuals. If I tell her what is back there she won't be able to function, and I can't do that to her right now. I need her safe first.

Bodeth takes the lead and we follow him through the double doors, keeping an eye out for any other unpleasant surprises. We navigate a few more corridors, heading to the elevators that will take us to the sublevel and the tunnel leading to the ship. We make another right, and at the end of the long hall, right before the elevators, a Chassak stands before us, barring our escape. I recognize the lengthy quills high upon his back.

We've located the missing general far too late to make a difference. My feeling of failure is acute.

Bree lets out a choked sound of dismay. He has a female guard who looks *absolutely* terrified, standing just before him. The *charksis* scum uses her as a shield. To his right is Dr. Jaran, a blaster held to his head. A quill embedded in either arm, effectively neutralizes the scientist's ability to fight back. No doubt the female hostage motivated Dr. Jaran to cooperate.

From the way Dr. Jaran sways on his feet, the paralysis is most likely spreading. It's a cowardly, dirty move to make, and so typical of this species.

"The Emperor wants to thank you personally, Tarian," the Chassak says, never removing the blaster from Dr. Jaran's head.

"Why?" I ask.

"Single-handedly delivering us the names of every mate matching with an Elysium warrior. We'll deal with them swiftly. Possibly take some of them for ourselves. You don't have to worry about that," the Chassak hisses.

"You may have the names of the volunteers, but that is all. None of them have been verified as possible matches."

"Haven't they?"

I don't like where this is going. The male seems sure of himself and whatever information he possesses. But Bree and Micah are the only ones who identified the marker. No one else knew.

Unless...

"Dr. Jaran." Bree has already figured it out. She and Micah warned me that the other scientists had access to the same information. It was only a matter of time before one of them found out. "Please tell me you didn't give them the marker. Tell me you didn't hand that information over."

Dr. Jaran doesn't respond, but I see him wilting under her gaze. The male is a coward. He's put thousands of female's lives in jeopardy to save his own skin.

"You may know which marker to utilize, but you came here for a very specific purpose, too. You need the marker, and you need the machine. You don't have the tech necessary to identify them yourselves. And you don't have the right geneticist to help you." I look the female over a few times, trying to determine if I'm making a fatal error as I study her facial expressions.

"You'll tell me where that tech is, and then you'll hand Dr. Adams over," he says, pressing the gun more firmly against Dr. Jaran's head.

I push the battle rage aside, knowing it can't help me in this instance. I need clarity. Not rage.

"You'll not be getting either. I suggest you lower your weapon now."

"We can always create our own technology for matching the markers and the female volunteers' data. It shouldn't take us long."

"Then you really should have fled once you realized what you were after would be impossible to obtain."

The Chassak's eyes grow dark, his quills standing on end, ready to release. "The way I see it, I hold all the cards." He laughs, preparing to pull that trigger, but I take the gamble either way.

I raise my blaster, firing one shot through the female and into the Chassak soldier. He hits the elevators and goes down hard while Bree screams, grabbing my arm, but it's too late. The female drops to her knees, eyes wide as she stares at me in shock, looking up at me for a moment before her form shifts and contorts from human to Chassak. She collapses to the ground beside the enforcer.

Bree's voice is shaky. "How did you know she was Chassak?"

Bodeth is already at Dr. Jaran's side, offering him what we have left of our antidote for the poison. It's nice that we actually have time to use it when we've only ever come across the end results of being too late.

"The gun was pointed at Dr. Jaran's head even though he was no longer a threat. And it would have been more effective to train the gun on a female, but he didn't."

We move forward quickly and I activate the elevator while Micah and Laoth stand guard. Bodeth struggles with Dr. Jaran, eventually dragging him into the elevator since the male is still having trouble with his motor functions.

"Dr. Jaran," Bree says once we're all safely in the elevator. "How could you give them the marker?"

He shakes his head, able to lift his hands now that the toxin is wearing off.

"I gave them the wrong marker. It doesn't even exist in humans, but that's not something that low-life Charksis would recognize. He simply relayed the information to his superiors. My guess is it will take them a bit to realize they have faulty data."

Stunned silence greets his explanation, then Dywrr and Bodeth erupt with laughter. It takes a moment for the rest of us to catch up, but pretty soon we're all releasing a bit of our own anxiety and tension in the form of relieved chuckles.

Bree

DR. JARAN MAY HAVE COME THROUGH FOR US, BUT WE STILL NEED to get to the ship and get my mate's best friend some medical assistance. I look at Dywrr, but his eyes are fixed firmly on Remy. We need to move fast.

Let's get to our ship as quickly as possible," Tarian says. "We'll plan our next move from there."

"We aren't headed to the new base the president provided?" I ask even though I'm perfectly aware of the answer.

"We're going to head to space and orbit from there. I don't trust that we will find a single place on this planet where we can hide and continue our work. Our ship is our new base until further notice."

Smooth response. Not a lie since it makes sense for us to do this, all things considered.

How easy will it be for Tarian to simply take us all back to Elysius once we test out our theory? How easy will it be for him to effectively bench me once we're there?

Just another female with no purpose other than serving him and popping out babies. I won't let it happen, but I bury those thoughts and the burning emotions, focusing on the tasks at hand as the elevator doors open and we exit quickly. We've got to get Remy some help. That's all that matters right now.

Moving down the corridors and through a different side hallway leads to a dead end. I'm about to ask them what's going on when Bodeth places a hand on a patch of wall that glows under his touch. A door swiftly slides open, revealing a dark tunnel. We move through it at a rapid pace.

I may not be able to see anything, but the Elysiums' sharp sense allows them to move through the tunnel without any problems. Dry heat hits my face as a door slides open. A blue glow blankets the interior of Tarian's ship, giving contour and texture to sleek walls and what appears to be a small loading deck.

We enter in a hurry, the sound of the door closing behind me makes me feel as if I've lost a crucial advantage. I may be safe, but I've also just entered a potential cage. A gilded cage, similar to my mother's.

Too tired to feel anything other than resignation, I rest my head against Tarian's shoulder as he moves forward, carrying me in his arms. It adds insult to the injury. Depending on him so thoroughly when I know I can't really depend on him in the future. I know we had to leave the base. I know we're safer on this ship than anywhere else at the moment. I just need to take this one step at a time and focus on testing the markers even though this ship is likely to take me kicking and screaming back to Elysius with him.

Dywrr immediately hurries off with Remy to get her the medical help she needs. Tarian turns to the other members of his crew.

"You guys get the ship started and set a direct path for orbit. Cloaking engaged. We aren't taking any chances." He takes us toward one of the hallways when Micah interrupts his progress.

"What about me? What can I do?"

"Once we are orbiting, everyone needs a rest. Bree can't work on anything until we get her knee and shoulder looked at."

"In all honesty, neither feel as sore as they did. I think I can walk now." And I'm not lying either. Whatever power this mate bond has over healing properties, I'm finding that migraines aren't the only thing it can alleviate.

"You need some food, water, and rest."

"I need to make sure Remy is okay first. Then I can rest."

He growls low as I stare him down, ready for an all-out war if he tests me on this.

"Bree, I'll follow Dywrr and make sure Remy comes out of this okay. She's lost a lot of blood, but Dywrr seems pretty intent on getting her the help she needs," Micah says. "You know I won't let anything happen to our girl. She's gonna be okay."

I relent, knowing Micah is right. Tarian leaves him to find his own way around as I internally sputter in frustration. I'm losing ground here, but I'm just too fucking tired, and in all honesty, too fucking demoralized by what the president told me to even press the issue. Not when I know I've got this looming confrontation to deal with.

One that breaks my damn heart and makes me wish to god I'd never met this infuriating male.

Tarian carries me down a low-lit hallway, sleek in its construction. I don't see the normal seams for panels in this steel can. It's as if the ship just came to be without any attachment of parts. While I'd like to analyze that in the way I analyze so many things, I realize I'm just trying to distract myself here.

He's sensed the distance I've placed between us. No way he could have ignored it, and he's not about to let me off the hook here even though I'm not the one who needs to do any explaining.

We run into a few members of the skeleton crew as they greet Tarian and hurry to prepare for our ascent.

"Throdel," he says as a large, hulking Elysium rounds the corner.

"Ambassador." Throdel hits a fist to his chest. "My guess is you're all going to need some food once we're in orbit."

"Among other things. I'd take the time to introduce you to my mate, but at the moment she's in need of rest as well as a poultice for her shoulder and knee."

Throdel gives me a warm smile and a short bow. "I'll get right on that. Very nice to finally meet you, Dr. Adams."

"Likewise," I say, feeling awkward to meet a new member of Tarian's crew while being carried like this.

He seems to note my discomfort and just offers me a conspiratorial wink as if he understands. It's such a human gesture and so reassuring I almost forget the talk I'm in for with Tarian.

Upon entering what I can only assume are Tarian's quarters, I'm surprised by how bare everything is. Not in the sense of furniture. It's set up much like a studio apartment with a large bed in one corner, a seating area for guests, and a small kitchenette with hardware I don't recognize.

But there aren't any personal touches to the room. Nothing that identifies it as his.

"You spend much time in here?" I ask as he sets me down on the bed and drops to his knees to take a look at my shoulder.

His touch on my skin as he pulls back my loose work shirt stings with heat. I turn my head to get a look at the damage. All I see is some light bruising that will no doubt be better by tomorrow.

He smooths back my slacks to take a look at my knee, but I don't see any bruising at all.

"You were favoring your knee and your shoulder, Bree. Now it looks as if this has been healing for quite some time." He shakes his head, rubbing his tired face before resting his forehead against my stomach.

I place my hands on his shoulders, tensing, getting ready to push him away, but I find I just can't. No matter how angry I am after learning about what he has planned, I can't seem to put that necessary physical distance between us.

"Are you going to tell me what's wrong?" he asks.

"Are you going to tell me when exactly you planned on discussing your arrangement with the president concerning my continued presence on this program…and on Earth?"

Tarian's gaze shoots to me, his eyes lit with fury.

"He was not supposed to discuss that with you."

"I agree. *You* were. Discuss being the appropriate word. Instead, you made decisions *for* me. You went behind my back and got the president to agree to take me off the project once we begin finding mates. And then leave Earth?"

Tatian sits back on his heels, looking exasperated. "It's to protect you and keep you safe."

My insides feel hollow, as if someone took an enormous knife and cut out the most important parts of me. I'm surprised at how my anger has turned to hurt, to this bone-weary sadness that won't release its hold. How deeply disappointed I am that I believed in him. That I believed in the possibility of us. I didn't realize how hard I'd fallen for this alien until right now. Until sensing this level of loss, knowing it will never work out.

"Once we finish identifying the mates and I'm taken off the program, I'm going back to my home and my previous job."

Tarian's eyes search mine, desperately seeking something and clearly not finding it. He grabs my hands, clinging to them as if he can somehow keep me tethered to what could have been.

"Bree, I know that you see this as a betrayal. I was going to discuss it with you once we made it back to my ship. It's simply not safe. Your continued work on this project means you'll forever be a target. I can guarantee your safety so long as you're no longer a threat to the Chassaks and so long as you are with me."

"With you. On your planet. Living the life you want me to live. Giving up my job, my career, my dreams, my purpose."

"No. I would never ask that you give those things up."

"You just did."

"I won't interfere with your career, Bree." He appears desperate, his pleading gaze holding mine. "I want you to continue your genetic research for gene therapy. I also want to keep you safe. We can achieve both goals here. And I meant what I said. I will remain on Earth with you, but only after it is safe. You're less of a target on my planet."

"Tarian, I will always be a target! No matter where I go or who I'm with, I am now on everyone's radar. I won't be safe anywhere. Not now. Not ever. So we just have to live our lives the best way we can without this constant fear derailing us and fucking with our choices." My tears are coming, hot and punishing, but I can't seem to stop the damn waterworks at this point. "You can't dictate the terms of our relationship. We're supposed to work as a team. We have to make those decisions together. All you've managed to do is prove to me that you're exactly like my father."

He recoils as if I've struck him. It hurts me to say it, but if I can't trust him to work things out with me, then there is nothing left to say.

So why do I feel like my very atoms are being ripped apart?

Tarian stills, his eyes sharp and focused. "Don't do this. Please."

The words get caught in my throat, refusing to be released. My own body wars with my thoughts and emotions. I bring the image of my mother to the forefront. Her broken figure, her diminished spirit, her brilliant mind an utter wasteland of decay.

I bring forth that one fatal memory. The very day my father came home from work after a meeting with Naztech investors, after submitting my mother's genetic research proposal. As if it were his own.

"How could you?" my mother asked. *"We were supposed to present this together. We were meant to do this together."*

"Your responsibility is to our daughter and this home. I'll present the material and work on the project."

The fight that followed is something I'll never forget. I've often wondered why she didn't leave him. Why she stayed when he insisted on diminishing her on so many levels. But when I bring up that memory and recall with perfect clarity how she functioned like a zombie from that day forward, I have my answer.

My father broke her. In that goddamned patriarchal system she had been fighting for most of her life, if her own spouse couldn't believe in her, sustain her, and fight for her then no one would.

I steel myself against the pain my next words will cause me. Because I can't be broken. I can't be weak. I can't be my mother.

"This will never work. *We* will never work. When I'm taken off the project, I will walk away from you and never look back."

It's as if all the air in the room is suctioned out. The very essence of life ripped from me. Tarian feels it too. His haunted eyes staring past me, unfocused.

His eyes snap back to mine a few seconds later, his horns extending, battling emotions I can only assume are just as horrific as my own. Then he stands and walks to the door. With his back to me, he pauses for a moment.

"I'm not going anywhere." His voice is a hoarse whisper, filled with pain. "I won't push for a relationship, but I will make it my mission in life to keep you safe, even if it means living on your doorstep just to ensure that happens."

Then he's gone, leaving me to wonder if I've achieved something my mother never had or if I've just made the biggest mistake of my life.

I'm restless as I pace my room, wishing I could figure out how to repair this aching pain and frustrated that I'm even in this predicament when I know better than to love or trust like this.

A light knocking on the door interrupts my emotional spiral.

"Who is it?"

"Micah, your best friend who is actually an alien hybrid and thinks we might need to have a conversation about that."

I chuckle, feeling better now that we're are going to clear the air here. At least one conversation might actually go right.

I open the door and let him in. He hugs me before I'm able to close it, clinging to me with a fierceness I wasn't expecting. When he pulls back I can see the tears in his eyes.

"My God, Micah, you really thought I wasn't going to accept you, am I right? All these years?"

"I really worried you wouldn't be able to understand. I wanted to tell you, Bree, but I didn't even know what I was. It's part of the reason I was so interested in genetics. It's why I gravitated toward your mission and your goals. I thought I'd be able to figure things out, and I always meant to tell you. It just never seemed like the right time."

I pull him into the room, closing the door closed behind me. I know I should be upset by this massive secret he kept from me, but I can put myself in Micah's shoes, and I don't know that I would have behaved differently. He had far too much to lose if the wrong person had ever found out.

"How did you get through it?" I ask. "Landing on a planet that isn't yours? Living in that broken foster care system? Missing your mother?"

"I didn't make it until you, Bree. I was coasting, so isolated, and then there was you."

The way he says it makes me realize a few things. For someone meant to be a fairly astute individual, I have been denser than mud.

"Micah, I'm sorry. I'm so sorry."

He shakes his head, smiling even though I see more tears forming. "I always knew you wouldn't be mine. I knew it, but it never stopped me from longing for it." He pauses for a moment, looking like it pains him to say his next words. "You have some things to work out with Tarian, and I really encourage you to do it."

I open my mouth to protest but he cuts me off. "Bree, aside from me and Rem, you don't trust. You don't connect. You don't allow anyone in. But Tarian got in. He got in fast, and that was how I knew you two would work out. I didn't like it, but I knew it was right. Whatever struggles and misunderstandings you two have, it will be worth it because that male is absolutely right for you."

I shake my head. "He went behind my back to take me off the project."

"Not to bench you. To protect you."

"It's just like what my father did to my mother."

"This is actually nothing like that, Bree. Your dad had some antiquated ideas about a woman's place being in the home, and he was a glory hog. Tarian just wants to keep you safe. That doesn't mean he wants you to give up your career."

I grudgingly admit that Micah is right. Dammit. Nothing feels so justified than righteous anger. But nothing about my anger in this moment is truly justified or even righteous.

I need to decide if being right is more important than being truly happy, and when looked at it through that lens, the answer seems fairly obvious. But at the end of the day, will Tarian be able to avoid making that same mistake again?

I think I fear that the most.

"Get some sleep, Bree." Micah says, offering me a warm smile. "Everything is always a little clearer after some rest, especially the aftermath of an argument."

"When did you get so mature?"

"That hurts, Bree," he deadpans.

I chuckle, watching as he exits the room, giving me one last reassuring smile before he disappears around the corner.

I take in a deep breath, thinking about Tarian and wondering if I can actually have another conversation about this without seeing red. I exit the room in search of my mate.

My mate. Shit.

TWENTY-ONE

Tarian

I t's quiet in the control room now that we're in orbit, and even though it isn't my shift, I've given Bodeth leave for the night since I can't sleep after what happened with Bree.

I've lost her. I've broken something so fundamental within our relationship that I have to wonder how I could have made such a serious mistake when all I had to do was go to her with my proposal and find a way to compromise. Taking her off the project, taking her away from Earth, and keeping her caged is all for the sake of my peace of mind even though I know it will keep her alive.

But it wasn't my choice to make. She was right, and yet, she is also wrong.

"How is she also wrong?" says a familiar voice behind me.

I spin in my chair, cursing myself for being so distracted I failed to hear Dywrr coming into the control room.

"Talking to yourself again?" he asks. He pulls up the seat next to me and drops into it with a heavy groan. "I hear humans have medicine for that kind of ailment."

I give him a wan smile. "I doubt humans have a cure for what ails me now."

Dywrr studies me for a moment, leaning back in his chair. I've always appreciated his ability to gain the measure of an individual. To assess a scenario with lightning speed and make judgement calls that have quite literally saved my life and the lives of my crew.

At the moment, though, I don't like being on the receiving end of his intuitive genius.

"Why is Bree wrong?" he asks, gently prodding me.

I take a moment to consider my response, not sure exactly how to form everything I feel—everything I've observed about my mate—into words that are sufficient.

"She feels things deeply. She internalizes the pain of others within the scientific world she operates. With that level of empathy comes an unfortunate lack of judgement for her own safety and survival. She will die for this mission if I let her. And I won't let her. Not even if it earns me her eternal hatred."

Dywrr lets out a low whistle. "I take it you made a snap decision regarding her future and failed to discuss it with her."

I grunt, frustrated at the way he says it. As if it's a bad thing to be so worried about keeping her alive.

"I'm not saying you're wrong." Dywrr stares at the controls for a moment, contemplating his next words. "But I want you to think back on Lynnak. Whose idea was it for her to return to her planet?"

"Mine," I grunt, feeling the pain of that decision like a festering wound refusing to heal.

"And at what point did you discuss that decision with her?"

"You're an asshole." I close my eyes, realizing he is right. "I didn't. I put her on a ship back to her planet without her consent. I was so focused on her safety, I didn't take into account her feelings."

I open my eyes and look at Dywrr. He nods, sadness in his gaze.

"You and I know that her death was not your fault. Whether she had left then or later, she would have been a target, and she would have been shot down either way. But you've held onto that memory of her crying as you forced her onto that ship while she pleaded with you to let her stay by your side." Dywrr shakes his head. "We all have that memory. It was fucking painful to watch, especially since she meant so much to all of us. She was part of the crew."

It was one of the worst moments of my life. A close second to what just happened with Bree. I bury the memories as I always have. Not because I refuse to face the truth, but because the pain it causes won't help me right now.

Yet Dywrr is right. Bree's safety is my number one priority, but only if we agree on how we keep her safe.

"A prison, no matter how fancy it may look, is still a room with absolutely no way out." He waits for a moment to make sure I've received the message. Then he stands and slaps me on the back. "Get some sleep, Tarian. You can figure out how to win Bree back tomorrow. I can take over the watch for a while."

I reluctantly agree, only because I suddenly feel exhausted, the weight of his words and the truth in them zapping me of my energy.

I stand and grip his hand, my eyes thanking him for far more than just the advice he's given.

"When did you get to be so wise?"

He quirks his head, his horns curling tight with annoyance. "I've always been this way. It's not my fault the crew picks and chooses when to listen to my consistently sound advice."

I chuckle, knowing he isn't completely wrong about that. "How is our injured doctor?"

Dywrr sobers for a moment. "Her injury wasn't as bad as I thought. Her vital organs didn't suffer any damage." He shakes his head for a moment. "I just don't understand the stab wound. It's almost as if someone other than a Chassak attacked her. Like it was a random choice made amidst the chaos."

"Like someone was trying to get rid of her. Why?"

Dywrr shrugs, frustrated by the lack of answers. "We'll need to ask her once she recovers. See what she can remember."

"You care for this woman." I don't waste time asking.

"Maybe." His air is noncommittal. but I know Dywrr. This female has him frustrated on many levels, and I have to wonder why when they are not mates...and she volunteered for the program. She may be a candidate. She may have a mate on Elysius and Dywrr would have to accept that.

A noise at the entryway grabs my attention. I turn, expecting Bodeth or Laoth to approach, but no one is there. Shaking my head,

I wish Dywrr a good night and head out of the control room, making my way through the ship's twists and turns toward my quarters, anxious to see Bree.

I stop at Dr. Jaran's quarters, noticing his rounded door is open. I tap on it, figuring the time for this conversation may as well happen now.

Dr. Jaran pops his head around the corner and smiles, beckoning me in.

"What can I do for you, Ambassador?"

"I'd like to be honest with you, Dr. Jaran, although I might have played this differently if the base hadn't been attacked. I know you were working with Derwag on a solution to our mating problem long before we made our alliance with Earth's inhabitants."

Dr. Jaran's skin-tone goes about as pale as it can considering it's a hunter green. His horns roll in agitation as he takes a step back.

I hold up my hands in a placating gesture. "I have no intention of turning you over to the Council at the moment. But we do need to understand what you and Derwag were actually working on."

Dr. Jaran's shoulders slump and he lets out a defeated sigh. "Have a seat," he says, gesturing to the sparse furniture in the room.

I position myself in a chair closest to the entrance.

He sits across from me on the small sofa, worrying his lips with his pointed teeth.

"Where to begin?"

"Let's start with the bio-weapon. Bree has a possible theory that it was meant to kill off the males and not the females."

Dr. Jaran's eyes startle before his gaze sharpens in on me with keen interest, his previous hesitation gone.

"That female is a wonder. The things she considers...well, the only one who knew that with any kind of certainty was me, but I only discovered that recently."

"How?"

"When it was brought to my attention that Dr. Adams thought the bio-weapon had been made with Chassak poison. I tested a little of the material tainting one embryo and discovered that the chemical compound was identical, but engineered to attack and break down a specific gene. The very gene that is tied to our mate bond, or rather, the cord that finalizes the mate bond."

"So we were the targets and not our females. What happened?"

Dr. Jaran's eyes hold all the grief in the world as he collects himself. I know he's thinking about our females. How they suffered. "The mixture of other toxic compounds interrupted the bio-weapon directive. The genes for a female's receptive energies of that cord are so similar in their coding that the mixture of toxins managed to skew the programming."

"Meaning the females' *oricas* were compromised."

"And the rest of their genetic code soon followed. I don't think our females were the original targets, but I do think someone tampered with the bio-weapon to purposefully target the females in the long run. I don't see how a mistake like that could have been made. The coding is too precise for any other explanation than deliberate tampering."

"You're saying factions in the Chassak government—"

"Most likely purists—"

"Decided they would rather kill the females than be forced to mate with them."

"If that was, in fact, the goal, killing us off in the first place to get to our females, but it's clear the original target was us. The males. It's all there in the coding. And I never would have thought to look for it had it not been for Dr. Adams."

She's a genius in her field, and I wanted to take her from it all. Not forever, but benching her, a term I've heard Micah use, was something I was okay with. For the time being. But benching someone like Bree is unacceptable. There's too much good that she can accomplish in this universe.

"You experimented on Ada, didn't you?"

Dr. Jaran hesitates and then nods. "Derwag asked that I take one of her eggs and fertilize it, but the genetic material we took was destroyed when the hospital was raided." He sees my reaction and rushes to explain. "You have to understand, we were desperate."

"But Derwag is connected to the Chassaks on some level whether he knew it or not. Did it never occur to you that the work you did was being handed over to those in the Chassak government who were also looking for possible mating solutions?"

Dr. Jaran shakes his head. "We didn't even know. None of us could have guessed that Chassaks were trying to breed with other species for the survival of their own species. None of that was even considered until your mate started asking questions."

I realize that what this all boils down to is the survival of the Chassak and Elysium species and uncovering compatible breeding options. If humans are compatible with Chassaks and Elysiums then many within both governments will look at human females as potential property, resources to be fought over.

I can't allow it to happen.

"What was Derwag's involvement with our project?" I ask.

"Nothing. This alliance with Earth changed everything. I could continue my research legally."

"And what happened to the research subjects you studied before?"

Dr. Jaran shakes his head. "I was always blindfolded when taken to those locations where females were being held. Females of various species. I don't know what happened to them or how we could find them again."

Locating those research sites will need to be brought up with my brother, but I can't worry about it now. "I'll allow you to continue your work with Dr. Adams, but once mates have been identified I want you to return to Elysius."

Dr. Jaran doesn't argue the point. He knows he is lucky I don't call him out and challenge him. It would be a death sentence for him.

I stand, leaving the room without another word, trying to figure out how I'm going to explain all of this to Kyllell and prevent him from storming the Council and launching a rescue mission for all the females being held at these research locations.

I silently enter my quarters, relieved to see Bree is fast asleep. I know I won't be welcome in our bed, but I sit at the edge, staring at her peaceful expression, wishing I hadn't broken her trust so thoroughly and wondering how I can win her back.

TWENTY-TWO

Bree

I work next to Micah in the med ward where the alien tech has been relocated. We've turned the area into a makeshift lab of sorts. I look at Remy, gratified to see her color has improved. She seems a bit drained and fidgety, but I know it has everything to do with what she's been through. Not to mention what's happening with her son.

"How are you feeling, Rem?"

"Like I was stabbed and left to bleed out," she deadpans. Then she gives me a rueful smile. "I'm gonna be okay, Bree. I just need a rest after we finally get some answers."

"How is your son?"

Her smile fades. "The medicine is working, I just wish I could see him again. He shouldn't be going through this without me."

I reach out and wrap my arm around her. "We're gonna get some answers fast and then we're sending you back to your son. I promise."

"When it's safe," she says. "God, after all of this, we may be in some kind of government protection program. I doubt we'll ever be safe considering how many groups of people hate us for what we're doing."

She's made a valid point, something I've already said to Tarian, but hearing it from Remy reminds me that we have more threats to us on Earth than we would on Elysius. At the very least, the Elysium population is for this. We'd simply be dealing with Chassaks impersonating Elysiums. But here? We've got a host of hate groups plus the Chassaks. And who knows how far up the government hierarchy these people can be found?

It makes me second guess my own reasoning and logic where Tarian and I are concerned. Would it really be that bad to relocate to a place that is safer for the time being? I could still work. Tarian said as much.

I rub my tired eyes, wishing I had my mother here for those brief moments when she had so much clarity shining through her eyes.

"Dr. Jaran," I say as he enters the room, appearing well-rested despite the most recent events. "We plan on running the marker through the data to find anyone who possesses the same genetic mutation. Before we start, though, I wondered if you could shed some light on what we found. Why would mated Elysiums possess zero mutations, yet Ada and Kyllell each have one that wasn't corrected?"

"And if you could enlighten us as to what that gene is for in Elysiums, it would help us out too," Micah interjects.

Tarian walks into the room with the rest of his crew right behind him. My stomach takes a nosedive as my heart leaps and then sinks. We slept in separate quarters last night, and I already feel the loss. I'm grappling with what I should do considering the conversation I overheard between Tarian and Dywrr last night.

To some extent, it really does change things. I have to remember that he already lost a female he loved. It stands to reason that he would have heightened emotional responses to me, his own mate, being placed in danger. It's a scenario he would never want repeated, and in that sense, I can not only understand, but I can forgive him for the lengths he took to make sure he didn't lose me. Can he really come to me in the future, though? Will he be willing to treat me as an equal partner and decision maker in our relationship?

I just don't know if he can, and I don't know if I can give him another opportunity to prove otherwise. It would be too damn heartbreaking to go through this again. But I want to. I want to fix this somehow.

Tarian and his crew take up positions near the entryway and simply wait for Dr. Jaran to speak.

"I can only answer one of those questions. The gene mutation that wasn't corrected in Kyllell is an anomaly. I've run the DNA of males before they were mated, and I haven't found a single instance of this particular gene mutation coming up. None of them have this exact mutation. They have other gene mutations affecting this particular area before matehood, but not this one. It makes me wonder if biologically speaking, Kyllell and Ada were compatible due to the combination of her gene mutation and his."

"What is the mutation?" I ask.

"It's tied to Elysium auras, but only a tiny fraction of the aura. Our genetic material is a bit more complicated. We have thousands of genes that construct the development of auras that are tied to the process of mate-bond consummation, and since the male's aura has what we refer to as a *streeka*, an electromagnetic cord that buries itself within the females *orica* and finalizes the bond or tethers their auras together, the thousands of genes used for that particular purpose are wide and varied."

"So this mutation that didn't heal in Kyllell is one of the genes that is responsible for the development of your *streeka*? The cord that completes the bond?"

"That's correct. In other words, the type of gene mutation will be different for each Elysium male due to the complexity of each male's cord. Literally speaking, only a certain type of *streeka* will align with a certain type of human female's aura, and it appears that these gene mutations in Elysium males and human females don't heal once they are bonded. Only mated Elysiums healed completely."

"Why? And what does that mean?" Dr. Jaran looks just as clueless as I feel, so I move us along since it's one more thing out of the many things we'll need to research as we continue moving forward.

"Okay." Micah shifts in his seat. " So we have no way of knowing which *streeka* gene mutation will match with which human mutation, but at least we can use the machine to identify females who have the marker. From there it may be a case of getting those women to Elysius and in front of as many males as possible just to see whose horns burn for whom." He shrugs his shoulders. "Not terribly efficient."

"No, but we might be able to narrow it down by identifying all the Elysium males with a mutated *streeka* gene." I think about the substance injected when Tarian bit me and consider what we might do with that information once the mates are identified. It might help, but I'm not sure how.

"I think we can all agree that it's time to input the marker data into the machine so females can be identified," Tarian says. His voice tugs at me, screaming for me to fix what's broken between us. "From there, we will need to proceed with extreme caution as to how the females are contacted since the Chassaks are interested in getting their hands on these females as well." I face the sleek machine, looking at Micah to see if he wants to do the honors.

"It's all yours," he says, giving me a wide grin.

I move back to the machine with a grin, pressing an area near the front where a panel slides open. The keypad holds human and alien lettering. I input the gene data as quickly as possible and activate the sequence, holding my breath as the machine thrums to life. Occasional beeps are followed by information thrown up on the machine's black screen. Within moments a column of names fills the screen. I touch it, placing my finger on the first name in the column.

Remy Erickson

My eyes widen. I turn to Remy and see that she is just as shocked. I thought she would also be pleased since she was so happy to volunteer, but her skin tone pales substantially. Not wanting to point it out in front of the crew, I turn back to the screen and choose the second name in the column.

Corynne Matthews.

The file reveals her background information, date of birth, medical history, and absolutely anything else the government has access to.

"I think this is going to work," I say. "We found our first human mate, and it looks like she's located in Tucson, Arizona."

Micah and Dr. Jaran appear pleased, but I can't shake Remy's expression. She seems absolutely gutted by this. There is something seriously wrong here, but I can't cause a scene right now.

Tarian's crew appears relieved. The emotion I see there humbles me. The hope they feel just being given a name. Any one of these males would kill for a mate, die for one, and do anything to find and protect one. I don't feel too bad for keeping Remy's name a secret for now since no one on the crew has had a mate bond response to her.

I look at Tarian expecting to see anger or fear now that we're almost finished with the project.

Instead, he looks at me with love in his eyes. Pride even. My insides quake, knowing that leaving him is a mistake. Knowing we can still make this work if what he said to Dywrr is really how he feels.

But we need to get this job finished as quickly as possible. I can focus on personal matters after that. This work has to get done.

My team now consists of Micah, Dr. Jaran, and Remy. We have a lot of data to process, and I really want to see if we can find some information within the secretion sample I took from Tarian's bite.

"Grab some coffee if you've got it," I say to my team. "Wait," I turn to Dywrr, "do we have coffee on this ship?"

Dywrr scoffs, looking as if I've mortally wounded him. "What are we, amateurs?"

～

THE PERIODIC BEEP OF THE MACHINE AS IT CONTINUES TO identify females leaves me giddy. Still, I feel as if the job is half done since Micah is right. We know which females are now viable mates, but putting these women on a large ship and sending them to Elysius to be brought out to market isn't the best way to handle this.

"What are you working on?" Dr. Jaran asks. He reaches my side and stares at the samples I have.

"I'm testing Tarian's *Kaimree* and my blood. It's drawn to my DNA, but it refuses to bond with any other material I introduce."

Dr. Jaran's eyes widen at this and then he leans over, looking into my microscope and analyzing what I've found.

"You're testing this to help us create matches with the mates we've now identified, aren't you?"

I step back, biting my lip and thinking about the amount of work it would take.

"Once a female is covertly contacted, we would need her to provide a sample. It was one thing to break down the genetic sequence of each female, but we more blood samples and actual *Kaimree* samples to find a match."

"It's a good theory, but there is just one problem," he says. He looks at me sadly. "We only produce *Kaimree* when we're ready to consummate the bond. The substance will not come otherwise."

I sigh in defeat. "Well, there goes that idea."

Dr. Jaran lets out a loud laugh, startling me with its exuberance.

He shakes his head, wiping at his eyes. "My apologies, Dr. Adams, you just have so many ideas, all of them brilliant. There's no need to be upset that this one didn't hold the answers you were seeking."

My lips curl into a rueful smile. "I'll keep at it. Maybe we'll find something else that will work."

Dr. Jaran leans against the table and considers my comment. "Or maybe this is one mystery that science won't be able to solve."

"What do you mean?" I ask.

"I know that this goes against any scientific explanation that might be acceptable, but sometimes, Dr. Adams, the mate bond dances to the tune of fate."

I smirk, loving the idea of it, but knowing I can't measure it. I also find it charming that these Elysiums are so stuck on this idea of fate and destiny, but their religious beliefs have a lot to do with that. Sometimes culture and religion are their own respective sciences.

"I'm afraid I need a more solid hypothesis rather than an abstract concept."

Dr. Jaran's expression holds years of sage wisdom as he gazes at me with a level of respect I've only ever seen Tarian and Micah offer me. "If anyone can find a way to hypothesize and predict fate, I believe it would be you, Dr. Adams."

I blink, startled by the moisture blurring my vision. It's a damn nice thing to say.

"Well, we have to do something," Micah says. "It's inefficient to just put females in a room full of males and hope for burning horns."

Dr. Jaran's shoulders shake as he chuckles. "And yet, I'm afraid that might be exactly what we have to do."

"Terribly romantic," Remy says dryly, coming to stand by my side.

"I didn't peg you as the romantic type," I say. "You were wanting flowers and chocolates?"

She scrunches her nose in disdain.

I consider making a joke about her willingness to volunteer, but she still looks a bit ill, and even though Micah and Dr. Jaran have already seen her data on the drive, I get the feeling she still doesn't want to talk about this.

Maybe it's just nerves. The realization that your entire world has changed.

I've got to figure out who her mate is, though. She deserves all the love, help, and support she can get. I just hope the warrior lucky enough to be with her is worthy of her. Remy squeezes my arm and then heads to her desk to get back to work.

I rub my eyes, feeling the weight of the day, the enormous amount of material to process. It's been stressful, but satisfying at the same time. And we do have an alternative for Micah's issues. We really can test all the Elysiums for a genetic mutation within the *streeka*. At the very least, it's a starting point.

"I think we ought to get some rest," Dr. Jaran says, eyeing me for a moment. I'm about to protest, but he doesn't give me the chance. "The data isn't going anywhere, and we will be able to do much more tomorrow. Most of the crew has already turned in for the night." His eyes follow Remy as she sits slumped at her computer. "She's missing her son and could probably use some rest, Dr. Adams, but no one here is going to stop working until you do."

He has a good point. Micah and Remy are used to spending long hours with me in the lab, but the events of the last two weeks have been hard on everyone. The data is safe on this ship. There's no reason to process and encrypt everything as if we only have one day to do it.

"I think we call it night, you guys. We'll work on this a little more tomorrow."

I don't need to tell Dr. Jaran and Micah twice. They head out of the lab before I've had a chance to shut down my hardware.

I notice Remy lingering at her desk and approach her, sitting next to her and taking her hand in mine.

"Tell me what's going on, Rem. You haven't been yourself ever since we got assigned to this project, and you've been especially weird since we got on the ship."

Remy swallows hard, a haunted look in her eyes.

And the problem is I don't know why. Yes, her son is ill, but he's been making so much progress. Tarian gave her the help she needed. Yes, she's working hard to provide for her son and has to be away from him temporarily to do it, but this sense of hopelessness I feel from her just baffles me.

"Elysiums have advanced medical care, Remy. Your son is on the mend. Unless he isn't? Are you keeping that from me?"

Remy shakes her head, pasting a bright smile on her face. "No. He's much better. I'm just not sure how to process being a mate, you know? What if my mate doesn't like that I already have a child?"

That's not the real issue I'm sensing here, but I'll address this topic anyway. "I'm gonna stop you right there," I say. "You've seen how protective these guys are when it comes to their mates. A child will be no different whether it's theirs or not. I promise you, your mate will claim your son as his own."

Remy lets out a relieved sigh and slumps over, resting her head on my shoulder.

"You've always been my rock, Bree. Thank you for that."

I hug her, hoping that reassurances were all she really needed.

"I'm gonna go find my mate," I say, verbalizing the term for the first time. Remy's head lifts, her eyes sharpening to analyze me like she always does. Then a small smile curves her lips.

"Have we finally accepted the inevitable?" she asks.

"Maybe. I need to go find him and work out a few things, but I think this whole mate bond thing might work."

Her grin his wide even though I note some residual emotional pain in her expression.

"I'm happy for you, Bree. You deserve a slice of your own heaven for once."

I squeeze her hand and stand, deciding to leave so she has time to collect herself before she heads out of the lab. As I head down the corridor, I can't shake the feeling that something still isn't right. For her to be so upset, it would absolutely have to have something to do with her son or something even more serious with her viability as a mate.

Instead of heading to the control room to speak with Tarian, I circle back to our quarters, intending to use the holoscreen to pull up some data on her son. It would be just like Remy to need more help than she's letting on or to downplay her situation.

I enter the room quickly and call up the holoscreen. The HIPPA violations I'm about to commit are barely a blip on my radar. If her son is not getting better then she needs to ask for more medical assistance. Tarian would move heaven and earth for my people, knowing how important they are to me.

Unfortunately, I find nothing. Remy said he was relocated to the Phoenix Children's Hospital, but as I look at his records all I see are the details for his previous fight with cancer. Not his current fight.

My fingers fly across the holoscreen, searching for any medical history past that particular date, but there is nothing on Gabe.

I don't have any idea what this means, but it can't be good. I leave my quarters, feeling queasy, my trepidation rising as I work my way back to the lab. I notice a tiny light glowing from underneath the closed lab door and I slowly open it, trying not to make a noise.

Remy is on the other side of the room, staring at the machine's screen and entering data from the machine into a handheld tablet.

My heart drops. "Remy," I say. Her head swivels around, her eyes filled with guilt and shame. "Remy, what are you doing?"

She faces me now, shoulders shaking as tears track rivulets down her cheeks.

"I had no choice, Bree. They have my son."

My ears are ringing. Surely she doesn't mean…

"Chassaks? The Chassaks have your son?"

"They said they would kill him if I didn't help them."

I approach her slowly and reach for the tablet. She doesn't even fight me as I take it from her. Her stare is vacant as the tears continue. My eyes quickly scan the screen, noting the beginnings of a data transfer. I cancel it quickly, frustrated that some unencrypted data was already sent off, but I don't have time to figure out what that was.

"Remy, we'll take this to Tarian. We'll get your son back. It's going to be okay."

"No." She shakes her head in defeat. "It's too late for that. They're already here."

TWENTY-THREE

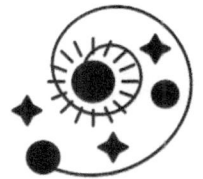

Tarian

Dywrr and I sit in the control room, analyzing some readings that don't make sense. An uneasiness has settled deep within me, making me feel as if we aren't as secure as I'd imagined.

"You feel it too?" Dywrr asks as he flips a few controls and then does another perimeter scan around the hull as well as a sonic ping outward into space.

"Is it possible our readings wouldn't pick up a cloaking device?" I ask.

"Anything is possible, but we have—"

An alarm activates near the rear of the ship.

Dywrr and I scramble to assess what we're dealing with. "Something has attached itself to hull." I grab my weapons as Dywrr curses and tries to get a visual on the object.

"It's jamming my signal. We need to get over to the lab now."

The lab. I know Bree is still there. I can't imagine she would have taken an early night considering the amount of work before her. With my heart in my throat, Dywrr and I race through the ship, every moment agonizingly slow. We burst through the lab doors to find Bree and Remy at the mercy of two Chassaks, their blasters resting against either female's head.

Before I have a chance to react, the Chassaks slap a small, circular device on Bree and Remy's necks.

I race forward, but they dematerialize before my eyes, transported directly from our ship to an entirely different one in an entirely different location. Not wanting to waste any time, Dywrr and I immediately circle back to the control room.

"Bodeth, I need you on radar. We've got to track a Chassak ship," I yell into my comm. "How in Elysarah's name did they get aircraft close enough to our ship to board without detection?" I direct this to Dywrr.

"My guess is those two Chassaks free-flew with limited cloaking which wouldn't have alerted our systems. Once they attached themselves to the hull and blocked our signal and our shields they could teleport in, grab the women, and teleport straight to their ship."

I'm crazed with worry. There's no way they had enough time to read my mate's biosignature before transporting her. Not to mention Remy. Without a proper read, the women could be floating in space at this very moment.

I try to push my fear aside and focus on exactly what we have to do now to track that transporter signal.

Once we reach the comm, all the males are present. Bodeth and Laoth are already working the controls.

"What the hell happened?" Micah asks.

"The Chassaks discovered our location. I'm not sure how they managed it, but Bree and Remy have been taken." I ignore Micah's stricken expression and Dr. Jaran's look of defeat. I'm aware of how unlikely it is that our females will survive this, but I can't focus on that right now or my mating frenzy and possessive instincts will absolutely render me useless.

"I'm getting something," Bodeth says. "It's faint, but I can make it out."

"Follow it. We need to get to that ship before they disappear on us."

"Why take the females?" Dr. Jaran asks. "They could have made off with the information they needed."

"They already have the volunteer DNA coding. What they need is the key, and even though Bree found matches, she was encrypting everything. My guess is they took our women to aid them in decoding. Once they get Bree to hand over the information, they'll have no use for her or Remy any longer."

"Then what?" Micah asks, looking as if he already knows.

"We'll get to them before that happens."

I say it over and over again in my head as Bodeth directs the ship toward that faint signal, feeling as if I'm reliving my worst nightmare and barely able to focus because of it.

Bree

I DROP TO MY KNEES AS NAUSEA AND LIGHTHEADEDNESS HITS ME. My vision is blurry, but I can make out Remy vomiting the contents of her dinner all over the shiny metal flooring.

I reach for her, but my arms are jerked upward at an awkward angle, irritating my sore shoulder muscle.

We're dragged along ill-lit corridors that wreak of ozone and body sweat, a sickening combination after traveling the way we just did. Remy and I are taken into a dim room filled with gadgets and glowing buttons that look as if they've been smashed into the ship's console haphazardly, or maybe that's just my blurry, watering eyes.

A large Chassak turns from the controls and eyes me with contempt. "Why would you bring them both? We only needed Dr. Adams."

"She seems to be motivated in the same way her friend here is," says the guard holding my arm in his unforgiving grip. "We'll need her to cooperate since the data transfer was interrupted. Did we get anything useful?"

"Just a few names," his superior says in anger. He approaches me, eyeing me for a moment before moving into my personal space. His fetid breath does not help the nausea. "We're going to need the marker you identified so we can do our own data processing."

"These females are compatible with Elysium males. Not Chassaks." *God, my head.* I inhale deeply, trying to ignore the pounding heat punishing my cranium. "Why would you need this information?" I'm fairly certain I know the answer to that, but I need confirmation. Their motives have been guessed at, but nothing concrete has ever been decided upon.

"We suspect the females may also be able to trigger the mate bond within our own males," he says.

I blink in surprise. Okay, it was one theory, but not the one I had thought most probable. "So, you don't want to kill them? You want to mate with them instead?"

"Well, that's a question loaded with complexity." His words sound raw and hollowed out. Despite our translators, his tonal quality isn't something the tech can fix. He considers me for a moment. "Our government is decidedly undecided on the mixing of species, but there is a large faction that believes true matings are the only way to restore balance among the Chassak population."

"Balance," I say, still trying to catch up.

"Females," he says, looking at me as if I'm the dumbest individual in space. "The birth rate of Chassak females has dwindled to the extent that we haven't had a female Chassak born for over a decade now. Males, yes? But no one is truly mated. We haven't had true mate couplings in over a millennium."

"And you think human females are the key to this? If they have the potential to be a mate for an Elysium then they might trigger this within a Chassak?"

He smiles, his teeth startlingly sharp. "Others would like this information to simply kill the women and prevent any other Elysiums from being born." Yeah. That theory had always tracked. He shrugs. "I'd like to think that the political party I'm engaged with is not so worried about trivial matters. The survival of our own species is now at stake."

"Whether you plan on killing them or mating with them, I'm not giving you any information as to which female volunteers are actual Elysium mates."

His grin widens even further. "I was hoping you would say that." He turns to his second in the room. "Bring in the boy."

On my right, a door slides open, and another large Chassak moves into the room, carrying an unconscious boy in his arms.

Gabe.

Remy lets out a choked sound and tries to rush forward, but the Chassak that holds her pulls her back against his chest, locking a hand around her throat, pinning her there.

Her eyes fill with tears as she stares at her boy.

I look at him, assessing his coloring. In all honesty, despite his unconscious state, he looks better than I've ever seen him. His cheeks are flushed a healthy pink, he's filled out a bit, and his hair has grown back.

"You did something for him."

The Chassak in charge grunts and nods his head at the one holding Gabe.

"You have him to thank for that."

The soldier lifts his gaze to his commanding officer. I'm startled by how fierce it is. "He had some underlying illness that wasn't completely taken care of. He was no good to us dead. If he had died on our ship, we would have lost our leverage.

The Chassak commander grunts. "And I'm using that leverage now." He pulls out a gun and aims it at Gabe. "We will kill him if you don't give us the information we seek, Dr. Adams."

I stare at Gabe's peaceful face, listening to Remy weep in despair, finally realizing that this is what she's been battling with for so long now. They probably took him the minute she signed on to the project. I doubt she ever talked to Tarian about his condition. Clearly his cancer hadn't been out of remission. And from the looks of it, Gabe will be just fine from now on. So long as he lives through this.

Remy had to do everything she could to save his life, and will no doubt have to pay for that if anyone finds out.

No way in hell I'll let that happen.

I look back at the Chassak general, gritting my teeth. "I'll need some equipment."

He chuckles, motioning for his guards. "Take the good scientists to their new lab so they can get to work."

My thoughts race as I consider one plan after another and immediately discard them. If it were simply me on the ship, I would refuse and just tell them to kill me, but Remy and Gabe make it impossible for me to be difficult with these assholes.

And they know it.

I'm certain Tarian is already coming for us, and if I can just do a little bit of stalling, then we'll make it back in one piece.

~

Tarian

"TARIAN, THESE CHASSAKS ARE DUMB AS FUCK." BODETH LOOKS disgusted.

"What do you mean?" I ask, taking a look at the readouts on the holoscreen.

"I wasn't sure of the exact signal we were following since its emission was barely giving off a read, but it's coming from the transport discs. Two of them. The Chassaks didn't deactivate the discs after using them on our females."

"Can you override the initial directive and change the transport coordinates to our location?"

Bodeth punches in information as the rest of us remain silent, our focus so intent on reaching them.

"I can't. The discs are a piece of shit. The technology isn't up to date. I'm surprised Bree and Remy made it there in one piece."

The "what ifs" sicken me, but I'm relieved the discs actually accomplished their task even if it did transport them within enemy territory.

"Our best bet is to transport onto their ship directly. But we'll only be able to do that if their shields are compromised."

"Then I suggest we compromise them. I'm not interested in stealth, Bodeth. We're still far enough away that they haven't detected us."

"What are you thinking?" Dywrr asks.

"We do a hyperjump, placing our ship next to theirs and we release as much fire power as we can. Enough to damage the shields and bring them down."

"We'll be open to attack as well."

I nod, knowing the timing will have to be just right.

"The moment those shields go down, you and I will transport onto their ship, while Bodeth hyperjumps the ship out of the Chassaks' line of sight. We find Bree and Remy and tag them so we can transport back, but the shields must be down on both ships. We won't be able to get back here if you can't outmaneuver the Chassaks and avoid taking on too much damage. Can you handle that, Bodeth?"

The look he gives me suggests I've insulted his malehood.

"I'm coming too," Micah says.

I shake my head. "I appreciate the offer, brother, but the less individuals we have in this equation the more likely we are to make it back in one piece."

"What's our plan B?" Laoth asks.

"You leave us there and get this information back to Kyllell. If Dywrr and I don't succeed in getting off that ship with Remy and Bree, the only thing that will matter after that is the results of the project. Get that info into the right hands."

Laoth hits his fist against his chest, acknowledging orders even though he doesn't like it. Neither do I. I have no intention of failing my mate. Even if I don't make it back, I will do everything in my power to make sure *she* does.

Our worlds need her. She has to continue her work. And if I ever get her back, I'll tell her just that. I'll fix everything I've destroyed, including her love and her trust in me.

"We need to do this now," Dywrr says, his horns red and agitated. "We have no way of knowing how injured the females will be. My guess is Bree and Remy won't cater to their demands."

I shake my head, knowing my mate. "They will. They'll play their game because the alternative is the death of the other. Those Chassaks will end Remy's life if Bree doesn't cooperate."

My words only enhance Dywrr's battle lust. But I don't view that as a bad thing. My vision is already tinged purple, and I welcome it with relief. It's the one time this level of aggression is not only acceptable but necessary. Dywrr and I will need all our senses enhanced and our reflexes heightened to pull this off.

"We're nearing the point where we'll be able to hyperjump," Bodeth says. "Are you two ready?"

I answer in the affirmative. "On my mark."

Laoth and Dr. Jaran take seats and strap themselves in while Dywrr and I brace ourselves against the back wall consoles. Micah, having never done a hyperjump appears perplexed but follows what everyone else does and takes a seat in my chair, strapping himself in. "Three. Two. One."

My ship, unlike many, doesn't need prep-time to pull off a jump like this. It's small enough and far more advanced due to the nature of our activities. I feel the familiar tug at my spinal cord followed by the rush of adrenaline racing through my body as it's pressed hard against the wall.

"Son of a bitch," Micah grits out. Normally, I would enjoy his discomfort, but I'm too focused on the timing of this maneuver.

The moment the Chassak ship comes into view Bodeth hits them with a barrage of firepower meant to inflict enough damage on their shields without actually destroying the ship. A tricky balance since shields can normally take on quite a bit of damage before being snuffed out entirely.

"Now!" he yells. "Do it now."

Dywrr and I activate our discs and transport just as the Chassak ship maneuvers to retaliate. As we materialize onto their deck, I activate my comm. "Get out of here, Bodeth."

"Copy that," he says.

Dywrr tackles me to the ground as fire from a blaster barely misses us and explodes against the steel wall behind us. I see the smoke against the wall and note the lack of damage. Looks like their ship isn't quite the piece of shit they normally fly around in.

Dywrr lets off a series of quick shots, hitting his mark as I roll to the side and take out another Chassak rushing the loading deck. We move forward carefully, reaching the exit and holding position for a moment.

"Do we split up?" Dywrr asks.

I shake my head. "They'll have the females together. Easier to control them."

I motion for him to take the rear as I move forward, not liking how open we are to attack as we advance.

I let that battle lust consume me as I listen for anything moving. These Chassaks won't live through this. I'll make certain of it.

~

Bree

I STARE AT CRUDE MACHINERY BEFORE ME, UNCERTAIN HOW THESE morons expect me to input anything into what looks like an upside down blender. The key panel has symbols utterly foreign to me. Turns out stalling won't be so difficult since I have no idea what they expect me to do with this. I don't even know if it's on.

"All the volunteer data you stole has been transferred to this machine?" I ask, daring to look the captain in the eye even though he's had his weapon trained on me since they brought us into their version of a med bay.

I hope it's a med bay, anyway, and not some lab for experimenting on other species. Happy thought.

"Just input the marker so we can get on with this." He looks like he doesn't have a care in the world, and it begs the question why.

"You do realize that the Elysiums will come for us, right? They won't sit on their asses hoping you'll return us."

"They can't track our ship. Our advanced cloaking is untraceable."

"That's how you're still managing to get to Earth, even though the Elysiums have been running interference around the planet?"

"It's certainly one of the ways we can still reach Earth and your females."

Cryptic. His superior attitude suggests we have several holes in our defenses.

"Uh, Captain," says the Chassak holding Remy. "Maybe we shouldn't say so much in front of the females."

"Who are they gonna tell?"

My eyes fly to Gabe as he makes a small chuffing noise in his sleep. The guard holding him adjusts his grip and Gabe settles. I notice the careful way in which he handles him, the concern on his face. I get the distinct impression that this particular Chassak is somehow fond of Gabe. He's probably been Gabe's main caretaker.

I'm wondering how I can use that to my advantage when the captain pushes the gun against my temple.

"Don't pretend you don't know how to do this."

I keep my eyes trained on the machine and study the keypad, scrutinizing the symbols. "I know how to input data so long as I'm using tech that I can understand. You'll have to tell me which buttons are which as I read off the marker numbers."

He grunts in annoyance but accepts my explanation. "Read it off then. I'll input the information."

He keeps his gun trained against my temple as I rattle off utter gibberish, a mix of my telephone number and home address since I'm fairly certain these guys won't have any idea what I'm talking about. I don't plan on giving him anything that remotely resembles a human marker. The machinery makes a slight humming noise, glowing beneath its base as it processes the non-existent marker.

A flash of red appears on the side of the apparatus followed by a stream of symbols I can't read. He tightens his hold on the weapon and presses it even harder against my head.

"Would you like to try that again?"

"I don't need to try it again. I know what the marker is and I gave you the exact information to put into your computer. Is it possible this machine isn't functioning properly?"

I'm dancing a fine line here. There's only so much I can do to stall, and once I read off the real marker, he'll know I was messing with him. I'm sure I'll be punished for that, but I have to give Tarian some time to find us.

"Enter it again," I say. "Pay special attention to what I say and how that translates to your numbers and lettering in your language." I try to sound helpful rather than patronizing, but I've got zero respect for these porcupines, and I'm not much of an actor.

We do it one more time with the same result and the crack of his weapon against my cheek is my reward for pissing him off. I hit the floor hard. Remy's screams sound far away as I do my best to shake off the pain and the darkness engulfing my vision.

"That was completely unnecessary." I look in the direction of the speaker and see that it's the Chassak holding Gabe. "Brute force on females is not the way we do things."

"Zerock, I believe you've been in this can and away from operations for far too long." The captain's voice sounds exasperated at this point. "I just blasted my way through an entire base filled with humans, some of them female. We do what must be done to find our human mates."

"And whose potential human mate did you kill on that base with your reckless behavior?" Zerock asks, sounding surprisingly mournful and irate.

"We don't even know if those females were potentials. What's wrong with you?"

"Zerock," says the other guard, still holding Remy, "we can't always operate the way your father wishes."

Zerock is incensed, appearing utterly shocked at his superior's behavior. It's good information to have, and I soak it all in, wondering how it might be of use to us in the future.

"But you answer to him," he continues. "How do you plan on explaining these casualties? When we present these females for testing, how do you think my father will react to seeing Dr. Adams abused in this way?"

My brain is awash in confusion. We've got a Chassak leader concerned about the safety of human females? It certainly isn't preventing him from kidnapping them and "testing" them apparently. Maybe we can contact Zerock's father if he actually reveres matehood and females in the way his son claims.

The captain is already blowing Zerock off. "We're wasting time with this. Dr. Adams thinks it's hilarious to give me the wrong information over and over again. Well, maybe this will motivate her."

He points his weapon at Remy, but I'm moving before he has a chance to get off a shot. I ram myself into her and her captor, feeling the heat of his weapon singe my ear before it blasts into the wall. These Chassaks are so fucking heavy I only manage to dislodge him a foot or two, but it's enough to prevent her death.

Not to mention the Chassak that was holding her. That blast would have punched through both of them, and it takes only a few seconds for the guard to realize that. He pushes Remy to the side, shoving her into the edge of the table where she cries out in pain before dropping to the floor. The Chassak attacks the captain just as an alarm on the ship goes off.

I reach for Remy and pull her to me, still feeling slightly dizzy but trying desperately to focus. She's wincing, favoring her side, but we have to get out of here. The ship shakes and buckles, causing Remy and I to lose our balance. It continues to shake for a moment, then it stops abruptly. I hear commotion beyond the make-shift lab. Chassaks shouting. Weapons firing off.

Tarian. I know he's here.

We crawl underneath the sterile table as another guard comes barreling into the room.

"Elysiums have teleported onto the ship," he yells. Before he can get anything else out his body jolts and shakes before dropping to the ground, a large barb embedded in his back.

Hope surges through me, but the captain is still fighting off the guard he nearly killed, and Zerock is looking around the lab in shock. His eyes flit from the bizarre fight happening in the room and the dead Chassak just outside the entrance.

He looks at Remy and I and quickly moves forward. He kneels next to her, placing Gabe in her eager arms and taking a moment to ruffle his hair. Screams and the sound of blaster shots continue outside the med bay while fighting ramps up within. Zerock reaches behind Remy and wrenches a vent door open, motioning us through.

"Take the boy. This will lead you to the docking area where you can all get into one of the emergency escape pods and jettison from the ship. I'm sure your Elysiums will find you after that."

I don't question his motives, I just push Remy through, trying to help her crawl in while dragging an unconscious Gabe.

"Is he going to remain this out of it?" I ask, worried that he hasn't woken up with all the commotion.

Remy finally gets her and Gabe through and motions for me to follow.

"The boy will be fine. I gave him a sedative so he wouldn't be awake for this. I didn't think it wise for him to see his mother held hostage."

I stare at him for a moment, taking in his haunted expression and finally coming to accept that not all Chassaks are the enemy.

"Thank you for your help," I say. "Perhaps, if your father and you have these views, we should be working together rather than fighting one another."

He nods. "I will find a way to contact you, Dr. Adams. For now, you need to get off this ship."

He motions me forward. I quickly crawl into the vent space, feeling an unfortunate sense of déjà vu. I hope nothing decides to chase me this time. I can hear Remy's labored breathing and halting progress as she tries her best to move her and Gabe as fast as she can, but it's slow going and we lose visibility the further we get from the vent's entrance. Echoes of weaponry and fighting surround us, a chaotic accompaniment to our terrified escape.

As we take a few corners and make our way through, I pray that Tarian can keep himself safe, that he isn't taking risks that will get himself killed. Because I still haven't had the chance to tell him I've been an idiot. I understand why he held on so tight. I understand why he did what he chose to do, and I can be patient with him if he'll be patient with me.

I have to apologize. I have to make things right.

Our past hurts and fears don't have to play into the present or the future. We can be different. We can do better. We just have to try.

But I can't tell him any of that if the reckless alien gets himself killed.

"I didn't want to do it, Bree," Remy says as we continue to make slow progress through the tunnel.

"Remy, I understand. I get it. They took Gabe right after you signed onto the project?"

"Yes," she says, choking on a sob. "I would never hurt anyone. I promise. But they had Gabe, and he wasn't getting his medication. I was so fucking terrified that he was already dead."

"Your mother?"

"She never even came to watch him. They showed up at my house and took him before I had a chance to actually make those arrangements with her. She doesn't even know what's going on."

Well, thank god for that. At least she wasn't killed.

"You gave them the information as to where data was being kept?" I ask.

"Yeah. I also gave them information about the military base. All of the updates. I told them about the marker you found. I had to. They had Chassaks watching my every move while we were there, and I didn't know who was who. I kept getting threats, little notes in my quarters. Pictures of Gabe taken on this ship with a Chassak behind him." She stops for a moment, breathing heavily. Her wheezing sounds terrible. "I had to give them our ship's location once we escaped the base. It's how they found us. They sent me proof of life. I knew Gabe was still alive, and all I could think about was getting to him. It was selfish. I know it was selfish. The lives of so many shouldn't be sacrificed for one kid."

"Remy," I say, placing a hand on her back as she pauses, her shoulders shaking. "You were put in an impossible situation and you did your absolute best to navigate it. The people who were killed? That isn't your fault. A mother does everything she can to save her kid. I understand."

Remy moves forward, slowly carrying Gabe's upper body as I try to lift his legs. "I doubt the families of those soldiers and scientists who died will feel the same way."

I can't argue with her on that, but at this point it's not the priority. Guilt won't help us get out of this mess. We finally near the end of the tunnel, finding the other end of the vent, but I grab Remy's arm, wanting her to wait. We have no idea if there are any guards within the area. I don't want to stumble upon more armed Chassaks and just be right back to where we started.

"You need to check for movement before we exit."

Remy nods and we gently set Gabe down as best we can, but this position with very little room has made our movements cumbersome and awkward. Remy and I remain silent for a moment, listening for noise on the deck but the majority of the disturbance is coming from whatever the hell Tarian is doing. Remy gently moves the vent, finding very little resistance. I can only assume that was on purpose since it really doesn't make sense for a vent lead directly to a dock filled with escape pods.

She moves forward, and for the first time I see her favoring her right side. I slide Gabe toward her slowly. She pulls him out, wincing as she does so.

"Remy, were you hit?"

"No. I landed hard on my side. I'm sure I just bruised something."

I don't believe her for one second, not by the way she's moving, but I don't have time to argue with her.

"Just rest here against the wall. I'm gonna get Gabe in the pod, then I'm coming back for you."

I know I'm right when Remy merely nods, stroking Gabe's hair before leaning back against the wall and cradling him to her chest. I notice a dark stain on her lower abdomen, and my stomach drops. I thought I got her out of harm's way. I scoot through the vent opening and give her an encouraging smile, reaching for him. She hesitates, not wanting to give him up, and I can't say I blame her, but she's in no condition to keep carrying him, and we have to get to the pod.

"We can do this, Remy. We get to those pods, and we're home free."

She nods, helping me as I pick him up, gritting her teeth with each movement. I hurriedly make my way to the pod, more concerned than ever about Remy's condition. Before I can get there, the entrance door is thrown open, and an enraged Elysium comes barreling through. He stops short when he sees me.

"Tarian?" I say. He has black blood spatter all over him. I can't tell if he's injured, but if he is it's hardly slowing him down.

He hits his comm. "I've found Bree and a small child, Dywrr. Still no sign of Remy."

"What do you mean?" I say, turning to where I left Remy. I'm shocked to see she isn't there. "Remy," I yell, desperate to find her. "She was right here, Tarian."

He approaches me and places a gray, sticky disc on me and Gabe. "I'm getting them out of here, Dywrr."

"No! She was right here. We have to–"

Tarian wraps his arms around us, holding us tight. My stomach muscles feel like they're being sucked to the back of my spine, the whole world spinning before righting itself after a few moments.

"Just breathe, Bree," Tarian says, still holding me while also helping me support Gabe. And it's a good thing. My arms are so shaky, I'm not really the one keeping Gabe from falling.

"We left Remy behind." My eyes water, my thoughts frantic as I try to figure out how she could have been gone.

Just gone.

I don't understand what happened.

"Dywrr will find her. But we need to get you checked out."

"No, I'm fine. It's Gabe I'm worried about. Remy's son."

Tarian really takes Gabe in for the first time, surprise marring his features. "This is Remy's son?" He touches Gabe's head, examining him for injuries.

"They've had him ever since she signed up for the project. They used him to get her to cooperate."

Tarian's jaw is hard as granite. "Using a child as leverage. How typical. It certainly explains a few things." He hits his comm again. "Dywrr, have you found her?"

I wait, wishing I could hear what Dywrr is saying.

"We have to get going," Micah says, striding into the room. The look of relief on his face is palpable. I can tell he wants to give me a hug, but he wisely refrains. Tarian's protective instincts are too keyed up for that to be a safe move. "The Chassak ship is going to get their shields up soon, and we don't want to be sitting ducks when they regroup."

Tarian ignores Micah, wholly engrossed in his conversation with Dywrr. "You have to get off that ship now, Dywrr. The damn thing is set to explode."

"You activated an incendiary device on the ship?" I ask, completely horrified.

"That was always the plan," Tarian says. "We can't afford to have them follow us."

"But Remy—"

"Dywrr is trying to find her. I don't know if he'll make it, though."

"He needs to check the vents. Check the—"

Dywrr materializes next to us, looking like death warmed over. He collapses to the floor, two quills buried in the side of his neck.

"Dr. Jaran," Tarian yells.

Micah kneels next to Dywrr, pulling the quills from his neck and then morphing into his true form before hefting Dywrr into his arms like it's nothing.

"I'll get him to med bay and get the antidote in him. Just look after Bree and get us the hell out of here."

"But what about Remy?"

Tarian's solemn expression says it all. We can't make it back to her. Not before the ship explodes. He hits his comm. "Bodeth, get us out of here. Now."

I stand there with Gabe in my arms, leaning against Tarian, feeling like a complete and utter failure for not keeping Remy with me the entire time.

And now she's gone.

TWENTY-FOUR

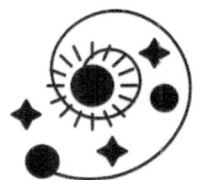

Tarian

I watch my mate as she hovers over our bed, smoothing out Gabe's hair and worrying over him as if he were her own. I suppose to some extent he is. She knew Remy long before Gabe was born.

She grips his hand as he sleeps on, no doubt dreading the moment when she has to tell him that his mother isn't coming home.

"Does he have any other family?" I ask.

She wipes away her tears. They've fallen endlessly, ever since we received confirmation from Bodeth that the Chassak ship was destroyed. I've never seen her so emotional, and I don't know how to fix this. I just know her pain is mine, and I wish I could carry it for her. I wish destroying that Chassak ship hadn't been necessary.

"Bree's mother, Cecilia. But Tarian, she isn't capable of taking care of him long term. She doesn't have the resources to do so, and Cecilia has her own health issues to deal with." She tucks the soft blanket under Gabe's chin, her maternal instincts warming my heart as I consider the type of mother she would be to our own young.

Amazing. That's exactly what she would be. Anyone who loves and sacrifices as much as Bree Adams does would be an incredible mother.

"And the father?" I prod.

She snorts. "That asshole left Remy the moment he found out she was pregnant. We haven't heard from him since, and believe me when I say we wouldn't want to. But it doesn't matter. Bree's most updated will makes me Gabe's sole guardian if anything happens to her. Gabe is mine now."

My heart stutters, stops, and picks up speed, considering the beautiful possibilities as I stare at this tiny child. He is Bree's child now, but he could be...

"Ours," I say. "He's ours now, Bree." I realize I've presumed too much. I still haven't made things right with her. I open my mouth to try and explain, apologize, beg even, but her expression when she looks at me is absolutely mesmerizing.

The love I see there is something I've wanted to see for so long it hurts.

"God," she says, "I was hoping you would say that."

Bree's words decimate all the restraint I've tried to exhibit. I reach for her, pulling her into my arms and taking her mouth with mine. I need her. I need all of her. I revel in her complete acceptance as she embraces me, her lips melding to mine.

I break the contact for a moment, knowing I need to make this right. "I'm sorry, Bree. I broke your trust and undermined your choices. I would never attempt to cripple your career or prevent you from doing the research that is so necessary for our two worlds."

She cups my face, running her thumb along my cheek, sending ripples of warmth and contentment through my being. I lean into it, kissing the palm of her hand.

"I owe you an apology." My eyes dart to hers, startled by her words. "While I didn't like your methods, I understand your motivation. I can't fault you for wanting me safe, and if the roles were reversed, I have to wonder the lengths I would go to just to keep you safe." She laughs, shaking her head as her tears come unrestrained. "I knew you would come for me, and I actually hoped you wouldn't. I wanted you safe. In that moment, I would have sabotaged your ship and grounded you for life if it meant you avoided Chassaks and stayed safe." She gently kisses my lips, soft and sweet, filled with a tenderness I've craved from her for so long.

"Putting myself in your shoes gave me a lot of clarity. Being taken from you offered me an even more crucial perspective."

Feeling as if I've been given an enormous gift and been let off the hook far too easy, I'm eager to explain my plan. The measures I've taken to make this right.

"Bree, you can still work on the project. I've already talked to the president. He's given me and my crew leave to find an appropriate place for you and Micah to continue your research without any government oversight. It will be so much safer. You'll be able to test Elysium males for genetic mutations and assist in matching the human females. You can do your research for genetic therapy. You…" I stop, breathless at the sight of her beaming smile, the happiness radiating from her.

"Thank you," she says. "It means everything to me."

I enfold her in my arms, feeling as if that last piece of my heart has finally been put right.

"So Gabe is ours?" I ask.

"Ours," she says. "You can't get rid of us now."

I smile, tilting her chin and kissing her soft lips. "It's such a very good thing that I would never want to."

Bree

THE SHIP'S CONFERENCE ROOM IS JUST BIG ENOUGH TO HOUSE Tarian, his crew, Dr. Jaran, and myself. On the whole, our party is slowly recovering from our harrowing confrontation with the Chassaks, but morale is low after losing Remy. I haven't been able to sleep much since the Chassak ship exploded, and sweet Gabe cries for his mother every night.

It's been heartbreaking for everyone.

But Dywrr…

I've never seen anyone take a loss as hard as he has. I recognize that grief, though. My father had that same look in his eyes when my mother passed. I hate remembering it because it demonstrated the depth of his love for her on some level no matter how often I painted him the villain in my world.

Dywrr has that hollowed out, lifeless look to him, and while I understand it to some extent, I keep puzzling over its severity. Remy was not his mate, and I rarely saw them together. I just can't understand it.

It's been three days since we recovered her son, stopped the Chassaks from getting the marker information, and prevented them from discovering who the potential mates were. Dywrr hasn't been the same since he woke up and found out Remy was gone.

"How many names did the Chassaks manage to unearth before Dr. Adams was able to stop the transmission?" Chancellor Koath asks.

I stare at the large holoscreen spanning the entire wall of the room. Kyllell and Ada are projected there, sitting side-by-side in what looks like a well-furnished, brightly colored living area.

"Based on the data we gathered from the aborted transmission, four names were decrypted and transferred over," I say. "I believe the Chassaks have first and last names for each female, but we can't be sure. I'm worried they gained access to more personal details such as their location."

Kyllell's expression is grave. "After hearing Dr. Adams' briefing, we know that some factions within the Chassak government want these females for potential mating purposes and others simply want them dead. Either way, we need to get to these four females as quickly as we can and place them under our protection until their Elysium mates are identified." Kyllell looks at me, gratitude in his eyes. "With Dr. Adams help, I think we'll be able to do that sooner rather than later."

I nod, giving him a silent thank you.

"We're going to get my crew on that," Tarian says. "Our goal is to divide and conquer at this point. The females are scattered across the globe. It will be necessary for us to find them and put them in protective custody within the next few days."

"I'd like to offer my services in that respect," Micah says, surprising me. "I can actually travel as a human while your crew will have a harder time. I'll draw less attention to myself. I also know the customs and the different ways of traveling. It's going to be better if I locate at least one female."

"Micah," I say, feeling anxious that he'll be putting himself in harm's way, "what about the work we're doing?"

Micah nods at Dr. Jaran. "It's a better idea for you to work with an Elysium scientist at this point since he can assist you in Elysium gene mutations surrounding auras. I can be more helpful posing as a human while we track down these other women and keep them safe."

He's right. I hate it, but I know it's going to make travel a hell of a lot easier for Tarian's crew if Micah is consulting on this particular operation and working with them.

"My crew will take the ship and locate the females," Tarian says, "while the rest of us relocate to a place on Earth where absolutely no one will think to look for us."

The Antarctic. Only Tarian, the president, and I know the specific location, and I'm more than ready to get to work on the other half of this process.

"We've also come to some troubling conclusions after learning that the Chassaks are still managing to make it to Earth," Ada says. "I have to wonder if the wormhole within that damn trench I was researching has anything to do with it."

I'm shocked by that. It had certainly never occurred to me that wormholes could factor into this.

"If one trench has a wormhole that can transport us between worlds, there is no reason to believe that there aren't other wormholes letting aliens in. There is so much seismic activity going on..." Ada shakes her head, thinking through her next words carefully. "We're going to need teams of scientists to start locating areas of unusual activity and discovering if more wormholes exist. If they do, how do we prevent other species from reaching Earth? How do we prevent people from accidentally being transported from Earth to other planets?"

Hearing the enormity of that undertaking, I'm relieved that my field of expertise is genetics. I can't imagine the manpower, the time, the resources, and the labor involved to locate other wormholes and resolve these problems.

"We have a lot of work to do," Kyllell says. "I know I can trust each and every one of you to do what is necessary to find these women and identify mates for our people. Keep each other safe. We'll work on some of the other problems on our end, specifically this wormhole issue."

The moment we end the call, Tarian's crew gets to work prepping for their various assignments. I give Tarian a quick kiss and head back to our quarters to check on Gabe.

When I step in, I find him in the middle of the room on the floor, playing with Throdel, flying tiny spaceships that Dywrr managed to build out of cargo materials on the ship.

"Hello, Dr. Adams," Throdel says, offering me a warm smile.

"How's it going? Have you guys discovered new planets and gone on some exciting adventures?"

Gabe smiles at me. He gets to his feet and runs over, wrapping his arms around my legs and resting his head against my stomach.

"Hi, Auntie Bree."

I give him a hug, holding him close as I look at Throdel for signs as to how Gabe did while I was gone. The cook's smile is a bit sad, so I know it took some time to coax my sweet little guy into playing a few games.

He's missing his mother, and he's been held hostage for weeks by an alien race that looked pretty terrifying. Then to meet another alien race on this spaceship and find out his mother is gone…

It's made for a lot of adjusting, and for the most part, Gabe has shut down, only speaking to me and barely engaging with what's happening around him. We've already made plans for his grandmother to join us on base, but that's going to take some doing since everything is classified, and contacting others outside of this operation leads to more risk and the possibility that our location and all our well-laid plans are unearthed.

I brush back his chestnut hair from his forehead, rubbing his back as he clings to me.

"I'm gonna get some dinner for the crew started," Throdel says, getting to his feet and heading toward the door.

I mouth a thank you and lead Gabe over to the bed, sitting next to him and holding him close.

"Your grandmother is going to join us at our new home pretty soon, Gabe. We'll be off this tin can in no time, and then we'll have endless snowball fights."

He looks up at me, giving me a tired smile and showing off those cute dimples. "Okay."

I wait for a moment, knowing he has more to say.

"Do you think mommy is really gone?" he asks.

I take a deep breath, knowing honesty is better than false hope and wanting to handle this the best way I can.

"I would love to think that she made it, Gabe, but that would mean she got off the ship somehow, and we don't have any proof that she did."

He nods, slumping against me. Without another word he bursts into tears. I just hold him. Knowing it's all I can do. Knowing this grieving process is going to take us all a really long time to pull through.

I just hope Tarian and I can give Gabe as much love as Remy always did, and that our love will somehow be enough to get him through this.

"How is he?" Tarian asks as I enter the bedroom adjacent to the one Gabe and I are sharing for now.

We both thought it best that Gabe not be forced to be in a room by himself considering the circumstances. Better to be snuggled up next to his Auntie Bree than miss his mother by himself.

"He's finally fallen asleep. It took some doing and lots of tears, but he exhausted himself enough that he's completely out now." I give Tarian a tired smile.

He crosses the room and enfolds me in a reassuring embrace,

giving me his strength and support as the tension from the last few days leaves my body.

"He'll mourn for some time. We'll need to help him as best we can," he says.

"Having Remy's mother on the base will help. Then he'll have two familiar faces. Two women he considers family."

Tarian leans back and places a soft kiss on my forehead. He brushes his lips against the tip of my nose and then plants kisses along my cheekbone and jawline.

"Are you trying to turn me on, Ambassador?"

"Is it working?" he says in a husky voice.

Like he needs to ask. With his heightened senses, I'm sure he can already smell my arousal. But I can't help it. It doesn't take much for me to go from zero to sixty in two seconds, but when you throw in a couple of days' worth of sleeping in separate beds and zero alone time, you've got a sexually deprived couple who need to get laid.

A couple who haven't yet consummated their mate bond. It's been on my mind ever since we finally resolved things, came to an understanding, and began planning our lives together, specifically the next few years.

There's no question it's been on Tarian's mind. Consummation of the mate bond is the driving force of an Elysium's instinct when he first encounters a mate, so I know this has been absolute torture for him.

"Do you think you can stay for a while?" Tarian asks. His gaze is hungry as he rubs his thumb against my bottom lip.

I catch it in my mouth, sucking and licking, running my tongue along the tip before kissing it softly. He lets out a soft growl, pulling me flush against him. I feel the pressing need of his erection as it rubs against the thin layer of my slacks.

"Gabe is asleep for now, no details need our attention at the moment, and it really is time for us to get some rest. If we're going to save the Elysium race then we absolutely need our sleep."

Tarian leans in and kisses me, slowly unbuttoning my blouse and lightly brushing his knuckles against the exposed skin above my silky bra. It sends light tingles that shoot straight to my nipples and zip along my nerve endings, delivering a delicious ache between my folds now slick with heat.

He bends down and traces the outline of my nipple with his tongue against the thin material of my bra. It peaks in response to his expert attention while my panties soak up the moisture dripping past my nether lips. He moves his attention to the other side as I grip his arms, trying to remember to breathe. I'm nearly fully clothed and yet I'm so needy with desire, I can barely think straight.

He slides the rest of my blouse off my shoulders and begins to unbutton my slacks. They drop to the floor and I'm left in my panties, my hard nipples wet and fully visible through the see-through bra.

Tarian stares at me, taking me in, his hard cock straining against his clothing. I reach out and cup him, gratified at the hiss he lets out, feeling the length of him as I trace my palm along the outline of his generous cock.

Precum seeps through the fabric of his pants, giving me a thrill as I work my hand up and down against the fabric, causing friction as he sucks in a breath and releases it slowly.

His horns burn black as ebony, pulsing at the base, standing erect and hard. I undo the buttons of his pants and his cock springs forward, long and hard, a dark hunter green and glistening at the tip.

I rub my thumb along those juices as he lets out a low growl in the back of his throat. I glide my fingers along his length, pumping once then twice, testing just how patient he'll be as I explore him, reveling in the softness of his skin. The sack in the middle is a fiery red, pulsing for release. I run my fingers along the underside of his arousal, wetting my hands with his leaking juices and circling the base before lightly palming his outer sacks.

His growling morphs into a loud groan and he finally pulls me forward, grabbing my waist and then running my hands along my ass. He tears my panties in two and lets the material flutter to the ground as he reaches forward and slices my bra off with one of his claws. I stand there completely naked, my arousal coating my labia and the inside of my thighs.

He runs a finger along my seem and reaches my clit, rubbing in circular motions as I push against his hand, needing more friction. I cup his outer sacks and then fist his cock in my hands, running them up and down his length.

"I need more, Bree." He grips my hips and lifts me. I wrap my legs around his waist as he carries me to the bed, feeling the teasing pressure of the head of his cock as it presses against my wet folds.

He sets me down, ripping off the rest of his clothing and covering me with his muscled body.

Our eyes connect as he runs the tip of his length along my seem until he finds my opening and hovers there, tracing its outline and further stimulating my pussy.

He gently pulses in and out of my opening and then slowly feeds his cock, inch by delicious inch, through my folds and deep into my channel. My walls clench around his girth as he fully seats himself, letting out a primal growl of satisfaction.

I hardly recognize the needy pants and moans I'm making as he pulls in and out with measured strokes, teasing me with the friction and keeping that slow, steady pace. It builds that bliss but keeps it from unfurling completely.

Then he thrusts in fast and hard, pumping his pelvis forward in tiny bursts that feel like fluttering vibrations, rocking my core.

"God, Tarian! I need—"

He circles his hips and plunges deep, both of us moaning our pleasure. "Look at me, my mate. Tell me what you need? What do you want?"

I stare into those steady eyes filled with so much adoration, and I know I'll never need anything more than this male and his unfailing love and faith in me.

"I need you. Always."

"Tell me you're mine, Bree. Tell me that you want this bond."

He pulses deep, his restraint as he does so walks a fine line between waiting and simply taking.

"I want this bond. With you."

His smile is filled with a lightness I don't think I've ever seen before. As he pistons his hips and thrusts deeper I tilt my head back, giving him access to everything he wants.

BREE SUBMITS TO ME, OFFERING HER NECK IN A SIGN OF acceptance. It's the most beautiful form of devotion she could have offered. A gesture of trust and a symbol of love. It's also the most alluring position I've ever seen Bree in as I thrust into her wet cunt, reveling in that tantalizing heat. I lean forward and nip at her ample breasts, teasing and licking until I've made my way to the soft area of her creamy neck. I swiftly plunge my incisors with perfect precision as I bury my cock between her folds. I stimulate he aura, using my pull to bring it to the surface. Her moans change to wanton pleading, begging me for more. My incisors fairly explode with their release, pumping her with my *Kaimree*, changing her scent and opening her further.

I piston my hips , building her pleasure as I pull back, looking down at her, at her aura, awash in the beautiful colors of her essence and seeking the very center of her soul. She arches her back, baring her neck again, as if she knows now is the time.

I lean forward and slide my fangs into the two puncture marks again, releasing my elixir and filling her veins for a second and final time. Her aura unfurls completely and her *orica* presents itself, its petals baring the very center of her being. I press my essence deep within hers, using my cord to seek out that tender bud so I can bury it there, sealing our connection.

Her aura pulls me forward, welcoming my cord of energy. Begging and pleading, radiating acceptance and a desire for completion. My cock throbs with the pent-up release I've kept from us both. Without hesitation, I thrust through her soaking folds, burying myself to the hilt as I plunge my cord into the center of her aura. The petals of her *orica* clamp around it, sealing off the connection.

Pleasure detonates along my spine, shooting straight to my pulsing rod as it seeks the depths of my mate's core. Bree's walls milk my cock, and she screams her pleasure as my sacks release. My cum flooding her channel, coating her velvety walls and filling her to the brink.

Her pussy clamps down harder, pulling more from me, vibrating with her orgasm. I take her lips with mine, her panting cries of pleasure now swallowed up as I lick and suck, plunging my tongue, my cock, my cord deep within her, giving her more of everything as we're both rocked with another euphoric wave.

After several more waves of pleasure, I nearly collapse on top of her, feeling more sated than I ever have and wanting nothing more than to remain as we are.

She clings to me, slick with sweat, shaking from the aftermath. I bury my face in her neck, breathing her in deeply. Her scent now aligned with mine. Our bond is final. Consummated. I can already feel her deep within my heart, my soul, even my thoughts.

"You are mine," I say, tilting her chin and looking into her expressive eyes.

"And you are mine." Her smile is warm. Those tempting lips are swollen and pink, making me think of other swollen and pink lips. My cock goes hard all over again, growing within her.

She lets out a soft moan, wrapping her legs around my waist and pulling me deeper.

"I'm not done with you yet." She runs her hands along my chest, and along my abdomen.

"You need more of me, my mate?" I flick my hips against her pelvis and revel in her soft cry as her eyes roll back in ecstasy.

She bites her bottom lip. "I need all of you. Always."

I gently kiss her, giving her all that she asks.

And Bree gives me everything.

Epilogue

TWO MONTHS LATER

Bree

I rush to the lab, unable to believe the message Tarian just sent me. My thoughts are reeling as I navigate the narrow corridor and make a quick right, nearly barreling into Throdel.

"I'm so sorry," I say, stopping to pick up a food item I've dislodged with my carelessness.

"It's fine, Dr. Adams." Throdel offers me a smile and gestures the way I've come. "I'm going to take Gabe off his grandmother's hands for a bit. She's been tired lately."

I chuckle, knowing Celeste has about had it with Gabe's antics. The underground base is a damn maze, and playing forced hide and seek with a six-year-old in a place like this is a lesson in patience as well as an exercise in futility.

"Good luck finding him. Celeste gave up about ten minutes ago and figures he'll show up in the kitchen by dinner time."

Throdel laughs. "I know all his hiding places."

I wish him well and move forward, finally reaching the lab. Tarian and Dr. Jaran stand before a holoscreen where Bodeth appears.

"You found her?" I ask, not bothering to greet anyone.

Tarian lifts his hands, a placating gesture. "Bodeth doesn't know for sure that it's her." He turns to his crew member and nods. "Why don't you explain what you've uncovered."

Bodeth takes a deep breath, his eyes tired and his frame a bit sunken in. The hunt for those four identified females has not been easy on the crew. Chase interlopers, government officials, and one particularly elusive female have made this one bitch of a mission for them.

"As you know, I've been searching for Corynne Matthews, finally coming to the conclusion that the Chassaks got to her first. There's been no sign that she was killed but rather kidnapped, so I've been reaching out to my contacts, trying to figure out if anyone with her description has been trafficked or traded within Chassak circles."

"And you found her?" I ask.

He shakes his head. "I think who I found was Remy."

My breath comes out shaky, the room feeling a bit off center. I sit for a moment as Tarian grabs me a glass of water, making me drink it before he lets Bodeth continue.

"There are rumors of a human being found in an escape pod that crashlanded on the planet *Tronoe*. It happened around the same time as the Chassak ship explosion."

Tarian and Dr. Jaran let out a few expletives that don't quite translate for me.

"My guess is this is not a great thing," I say.

Tarian is silent for a moment. "*Tronoe* is a beautiful planet with some of the most deadly flora and fauna you can imagine. The species that exists there are known for their slavery practices. It's not an ideal place for a human female to crashland."

"We need to get her back. We need to make sure it's her and get her the hell back," I say.

"Have you told Dywrr?" Tarian asks. I'm surprised by that comment since I've never mentioned my suspicions concerning Dywrr's feelings for Remy.

Bodeth hesitates. "I wasn't sure if it would be wise to send him or not. He hasn't been well since...uh...we thought she was gone."

"Send him," Tarian says. "He will be the most motivated of us all. Get it done."

Bodeth hits his fist to his chest and signs off.

"Do you think it's really her?" I ask.

Tarian pulls me to my feet and wraps me in his arms. "If it is her, Dywrr will find her and bring her back to us, Bree. I can promise you that."

I have no doubt he's right. I let the tension from the last few weeks slowly fade as I think of our progress and all we've been able to accomplish here. Elysium DNA has slowly been processing, and with the help of Dr. Jaran, we've been able to identify different aura mutations among the many samples and match them with female markers. We've already identified four mated pairings without needing to throw humans and Elysiums in a room and hope black, burning horns are the result.

We have a long way to go, and we need to speed up our process so it's more automatic, but the basic identifiers and programming has been accomplished now that our research is complete.

"We've been able to make this program a success. It's going to be the easiest thing in the world now to match Elysium and human female samples," I say. I blink back tears, barely daring to hope for a positive outcome. "It would be perfect if Remy were actually alive. If she could get back to her son and see what we've accomplished."

"We'll get her back," Dr. Jaran says. "From what I've seen of Dywrr, he won't rest until he's found out if she's alive. And if she is alive, he won't stop until he's brought her safely back home to us."

I nod, grateful for Dr. Jaran's encouragement.

Tarian tilts my chin and offers me a soft kiss, shoring up my courage and filling me with so much love.

It's exactly what I need to keep moving forward. With hope in my heart, and the kind of courage that I always admired in Remy.

Did I think there was safety in solitude? As I stare at my mate, I can't imagine a world in which that actually rings true. I've never felt more safe and whole than I do in this very moment.

Author's Note

The second book in this series was hard-fought folks. I was pursuing my Masters degree in publishing and single mumming it with four kids for the first time.

So life was exciting…and continues to be. I'm very blessed!

I appreciate the immediate outpouring of love and support from all my beta readers and those who wanted to review the book. If you found this read entertaining, then please feel free to leave me a review and let me know. I really enjoy the feedback.

Book 3 in the series is all about Remi and Dywrr. I'm excited for that one since I've played with some fun ideas as I've been writing it.

I'll have more updates as I go, but the best way to stay apprised of any and all announcements is to follow me on Amazon and Bookbub for now. You can do that at the links below.

Angelina's Amazon Page

Angelina's Bookbub Page

Until then, take care of yourselves, and keep reading so us authors can keep writing.

Plenty of love and a thousand hugs.

Angelina - xoxo

Also by Angelina Avery
Written Under C. J. Anaya

TEEN & YOUNG ADULT FANTASY ROMANCE

Paranormal Misfits Series

My Fair Assassin Book 1

My Fair Traitor: Book 2

My Fair Impostor: Book 3

My Fair Invader: Book 4

My Fair Princess: Book 5

My Fair Queen: Book 6

The Healer Series

The Healer: Book 1

The Black Blossom: Book 2

The Grass Cutter Sword: Book 3

The Prophecy: Book 4

Supernatural Treasure Hunters Series

Double Booked: Book 1